THE FISHERMAN'S DAUGHTER

ROBIN BAREFIELD

2019

For Betty,

Enjoy the adventure!

Robin

For Patti,

Enjoy the adventure!

Julie

An Alaska Wilderness Mystery Novel

The Fisherman's Daughter

Robin Barefield
Alaska Wilderness Mystery Author

Is a serial killer stalking women on Kodiak Island?

PO Box 221974 Anchorage, Alaska 99522-1974
books@publicationconsultants.com—www.publicationconsultants.com

ISBN 978-1-59433-747-5
eISBN: 978-1-59433-748-2
Library of Congress Catalog Card Number: 2017955315

Manufactured in the United States of America.

Prologue

Thursday, July 4th

"See you Saturday!"

Deanna turned and waved to her friend Jessica. "Okay, I'll be there if my parents let me take the skiff again."

The wind whipped the hood of her jacket into her face. She pulled the hood over her head and stared out at the ocean; it was getting windier by the minute. In this protected lagoon, only a ripple caressed the water, but Deanna feared once she pulled out into open water, she'd have to deal with choppy waves in addition to a swell. She knew she should have left an hour ago. Her mom had told her not to stay later than 5:00 p.m., but then Brad sat beside her at the campfire, and for a change, he seemed to notice her. He even touched her hand a few times, and she didn't think it was an accident.

Maybe he liked her and would ask her out on a date when they got back to town after the end of the summer fishing season. She shook off the thought. Once they got back to town, he'd have his pick of girls, including the cheerleaders and popular girls at school. She didn't stand a chance then. She had to spend more time with him out here in the bay this summer. Maybe if he got to know her better, he'd still want to hang out with her when they got back to town. Maybe he would take her to a movie at the Orpheum.

One of the Bender's crewmen gave Deanna a ride out to her skiff, which along with several other skiffs, was tied to a buoy in front of their fish site. She thanked him, grabbed her backpack and crawled over the high sides of his aluminum skiff into hers. He waved goodbye and headed back to shore, and Deanna donned her waterproof Mustang coveralls. She pushed the button to lower the outboard into the water and then turned the key to start the engine. The 75 hp outboard was less than a year old and usually purred to life on the first try. This time it coughed and died.

"Don't do this to me," Deanna muttered. She gave the key another turn, and the engine responded. Deanna hurried to the bow and untied from the buoy. She pulled her gloves from her backpack and returned to the stern, gripping the tiller and backing away from the buoy and the other boats. She cinched her hood tight around her face and rotated the throttle, slowly pulling out of the protected cove. As soon as she rounded the rocky point, she groaned. The sea was white with wind-whipped waves. Even this far in the bay, the waves were two-feet high, and she had to go 10 miles toward the open ocean to her family's fish site at Kuliuk. It would take her forever to plow through these waves. Luckily, it was light until midnight this time of year, but her mother would be a nervous wreck from worrying about her and would drive her father crazy by the time Deanna got home. She knew they wouldn't let her take the skiff again this summer.

Today was the first time she had ever taken a skiff so far by herself. Her parents and her younger brother and sister had followed her to the party in another skiff, but they had returned to their fish site at 3:00 p.m., telling Deanna she could stay at the set-netter's picnic two hours longer and then she needed to head home. Her mother reminded her at least five times there was a storm expected that night. The wind wasn't supposed to pick up until after midnight, though. Deanna thought she would beat it by several hours, but it looked as if it had arrived early.

The wind and waves would make her journey slow and unpleasant, but she wasn't afraid. She'd spent every summer since she was three years old at her family's fish site at the mouth of Uyak Bay. Her dad had taught her how to run a skiff when she was eight, and she became a permanent crew member when she was 12. She could pull salmon out of a gill net while the skiff bucked like a bronco in eight-foot seas. At first, she used to get seasick, but her dad told her to throw up and get back to work. She was tough, and she knew how to run a skiff in conditions much worse than what she was in right now. Her dad had also taught her how to change spark plugs, replace fuel filters, and troubleshoot engine problems, which was all well and good if she was running a two-stroke engine, but these four-stroke engines were another story. Mr. Dylan had explained in her outboard repair class that four-strokes were beautiful when they worked properly, but when they quit, they weren't easy to fix outside of an engine-repair shop. No sooner had this idea popped into Deanna's head when the engine coughed once and quit.

Deanna laughed. If she wanted to make it home, maybe she should stop thinking about engine problems. She quickly turned the key once, twice; it sputtered to life on the third try. She breathed deeply to calm her nerves. "Come on, baby. Get me home. Let's not do this now. You can act up all you want tomorrow when Dad's using you."

Deanna rotated the throttle too fast and plowed into a wave, taking a shower of spray over the bow. The cold salt water smacked her in the face, and she gasped for air. The engine quit again.

"No!" She slammed the clutch into neutral and twisted the key – nothing. She tried again, but no luck. She turned the key several more times in rapid succession. The boat turned sideways in the heavy seas, waves rocking it violently from side to side. Deanna's heart hammered in her chest.

"Calm down, calm down, calm down! You've got this, Deanna Kerr. You are 17 years old and not a little kid. Think!" She unhinged the hood from the outboard, her hands shaking so badly she could barely hang onto it. She set the hood on the deck and stared at the shiny metal cowling. Panic started to overtake her. She had no idea how to fix this type of engine.

"Think!" She commanded herself. *The engine isn't getting fuel. It must be a fuel filter problem.* A wave poured over the side of the boat, filling it with several inches of water. She fumbled for the bailer and started scooping water out of the boat, but then another wave hit and more water poured over the side. She had to get the engine started and get out of the trough of the waves; the boat would fill with water if she sat here very long. She realized for the first time that her father had forgotten to give her a handheld VHF radio to carry in the skiff. *How could he forget something like that, and why didn't I remember to ask for one?* If she had a radio, she could call for help.

Another wave crashed over the side of the skiff, and Deanna reached for the bulb on the gas line and pumped furiously. She turned the key. The engine coughed and died. "Please God, make it work!" She tried again but no luck. A wave struck her broadside and nearly knocked her out of the boat. She fell on her knees in the water in the bottom of the skiff. She looked for water in the fuel filter, but she didn't see any. *Maybe the filter is plugged by something.* She opened the tool box secured to the inside of the hull. Her hands shook as she grabbed the filter wrench and fought to loosen the filter from the fuel line. *Maybe I can bypass the filter.* She tried to think. *What would Dad do?* She wasn't sure how to bypass the filter. She pulled out the old filter and looked at it, but it looked fine. She had no time to think; she grabbed another filter and secured the housing. As she stood, another wave hit her and knocked her back into the bottom of the skiff. She chanced a glance at the angry ocean. Conditions were worsening at an alarming rate. Around her, whitecaps piled one on top another, but even more ominous was the black ocean toward the north, toward her home.

Deanna pumped the bulb on the fuel line again. She said a quick prayer and turned the key. Nothing. She heard herself sob before she even realized she was crying. She didn't know what else to do. There were oars in the skiff, but she would never be able to row against these waves. She would just have to hope the storm blew her back to shore before the skiff filled with water or capsized. She took several deep breaths and thought about home. When she got back to the fish site, her mother would make her change out of her wet clothes while she made Deanna a cup of hot chocolate. Then, Mom would wrap her in a quilt and stroke her head until she fell asleep. Of course, Dad would never let her take the skiff out alone again, but right now, Deanna didn't care about that. She would be happy never to get on another boat in her life.

Over the roaring wind and pounding waves, Deanna thought she heard an engine. She stood, but her legs were trembling so badly she sat again, and then she saw it, approaching from the north. She rubbed her eyes, hoping she wasn't hallucinating, but no, it was real, and it was coming straight for her. She was sure the driver of the other boat could see her, even with the swell and high waves, but just to be certain, she stood, waved her arms, and yelled at the top of her voice. She wiped her eyes and nose. Now that she was about to be rescued, she didn't want anyone to know she had been frightened and crying.

The other boat pulled alongside. "Are you okay?" the captain called.

"What are you doing here?" Deanna was thrilled to be rescued, *but why is he out here?*

"I'll toss you a line. Tie a bridle at the bow."

"Okay. I can do that." Deanna stood, but her legs were shaking so much she had to brace herself against the gunnel and pull herself to the bow of the boat. The skipper of the other boat tossed her a line, but with her trembling fingers, she couldn't hang onto it. His next toss was harder than the first, and the heavy line slapped her in the face. She grabbed the line and pulled it into the boat. She knew how to tie a bridle because her father had taught her. Her hands shook as she threaded the line through a hole on the port side of the skiff, across the bow, and through a hole on the starboard side of the skiff. She nearly dropped the line as she brought it back to the center of the boat, but she paused, took a deep breath, and focused on the line and what she was doing. *The rabbit comes out of the hole, around the tree, and back into the hole.* She pulled the line tight. She had it, a perfect bowline.

The skipper nodded and increased his speed. Deanna's boat swung into line behind the other boat. She slumped onto the forward seat, shut her eyes, and allowed herself to dream about a cup of hot chocolate and her mother's embrace.

Chapter One

Friday, July 5th

I struggled to maintain my grip on the 10-inch-thick slab of blubber while my colleague stripped it from the whale carcass. I cursed myself for the umpteenth time for not thinking quickly enough to get out of this project, but here I was, elbow deep in decaying whale blubber, and yes, the smell was worse than anything you can imagine. I had been offered my position on this necropsy team by marine mammal biologist Leslie Sinclair, and I'm sure she thought I should feel honored to be included on her team, but my scientific enthusiasm tended to wane when I was fighting the urge to vomit. As soon as I got home, I vowed to write a list of excuses for the next time Leslie tried to invite me to a necropsy.

It could have been worse. This whale had been dead for around two weeks, but it was only considered moderately decomposed. The tongue extended from the mouth of the bloated carcass, but the skin had not started to slough, and it was only slightly sunburned. Unfortunately, the external condition is not a good indicator of the internal condition of a dead whale because whales decompose from the inside out. Due to the large volume of tissue wrapped in insulating blubber, the inside cooks before the outside decays. I learned the necropsy team must be careful when making the first cut on the 50-ton carcass because it can explode if all those built-up gasses are expelled at once, and yes when the gasses do escape, the horrific smell just keeps getting worse. I wore a rubber rain suit, the legs duct taped to my boots and the arms duct taped to my gloves. This allowed me to wade into the project without getting biological fluid on my skin. A face shield protected my eyes, nose, and mouth, and I'd pulled back my hair and stuffed it under a rubber cap. A persistent drizzle rounded out the perfect day, but at least I was wearing rain gear.

It made sense for me to be part of this necropsy team since I was one of several biologists trying to discover why more than 50 whales had died near Kodiak Island during the past two years. The affected whales included fin whales, sei whales, humpbacks, and gray whales; all species that had baleen instead of teeth and fed on small fish and zooplankton. These huge animals feed at the bottom of the food chain, making them susceptible to pollutants, toxic algae, and changes in their food concentrations due to a variety of reasons, including warming ocean temperatures. Any one or a combination of these factors could be responsible for the whale deaths, or the cause could be something we hadn't suspected yet. The team was also considering underwater noise pollution from military sonar and other sources. Since I had been studying toxic algae at the Kodiak Braxton Marine Biology and Fisheries Research Center, Dr. Sinclair asked me to come at the problem from the toxic algae angle. Even though the alga I suspected might be the culprit in the deaths of the whales was a different species from what I had been studying, I was happy to do what I could to shed light on this disturbing problem. It seemed as if dead whales were being sighted nearly every week, but most were floating several miles from shore. This was one of the few carcasses that had conveniently washed up on shore where a necropsy could be performed. I wanted to do what I could to help, but I'd try to do my work from my lab in the future.

"Jane, can you hear me?"

"Sorry, Leslie. I was lost in thought."

"The smell is amazing, isn't it?"

"Oh yes."

"Since you're looking at toxic algae, why don't you be in charge of taking the stomach and intestinal samples as well as collecting feces, if you can find some."

Oh boy! My day just keeps getting better.

We had arrived at the whale carcass at 9:00 am that morning, and by 5:00 pm, we were stripping off foul-weather gear and loading coolers of samples into the De Havilland Beaver floatplane. It was Friday, the fifth of July, and I was supposed to meet friends at 7:00 pm for dinner and drinks at the Rendezvous Restaurant and Bar near Kodiak. We should be back to Kodiak by 6:00 pm, and I'd have the samples in the freezer at the lab by 6:45 pm. I could possibly make it to the Rendezvous on time if I didn't stop to shower, but no one would appreciate me skipping the shower, and I would probably be removed forcibly from the premises if I walked in smelling like a dead whale. I climbed into the rear seat of the plane. The thought of food made my stomach roil, but I could use a glass of wine and conversation about anything other than a decaying whale's intestines.

As we were taxiing in preparation for takeoff, an orange and white Coast Guard helicopter buzzed us. Our pilot, Dave, called the chopper on the emergency frequency and asked what was going on. Through my headphones, I heard the helicopter pilot reply that they were searching for an overdue skiff. He described it as a 19-foot aluminum skiff and said it might have had engine trouble. There was one person in the boat when it went missing. The searchers had seen no sign of the skiff up in Uyak Bay, so they were widening their search toward the mouth of the bay and into Shelikof Straight. Dave told the chopper pilot he would watch for the skiff on the way to town.

The flight took 15 minutes longer than expected due to the poor visibility from the drizzle and fog. The pilot had to pick his way along the outside shore of the island, and since he was forced to fly low, we all stared out the window, searching for a skiff adrift. We didn't spot a skiff, and the visibility was down to a few feet by the time the plane touched down in Trident Basin. I rushed the samples to the freezer in my lab and decided to avoid my office on the off chance one of my colleagues wanted to meet with me at 6:30 pm on the Friday after the fourth of July. You would think most of the staff would be at home enjoying the four-day holiday weekend, but I'd seen several cars in the parking lot when I'd pulled in, and the last thing I needed now was an overzealous colleague wanting to discuss a project with me.

I climbed the stairs from the basement labs, slid out the side door, and hurried to my SUV. I drove to the small house I'd recently bought on Lily Lake and sat in the driveway while I checked the messages on my cell phone. My friend, Sandy Miles, had called at 2:00 pm and had left a message, but that was it. I almost put off calling voice mail since I was already running late, but Sandy was one of the friends I was supposed to meet for dinner, so I decided I'd better listen to her message to see if our dinner plans had changed. By the sound of her voice, I knew the subject of her message was something much more serious.

"Jane, it's Sandy. I won't be able to make it to dinner tonight. My sister's daughter is missing. They're at their fish site in Uyak Bay, and Deanna didn't come back from a party she went to yesterday. She is only 17 and it was the first time she took the skiff that far by herself. They assume she's had engine trouble. The Coast Guard plus nearly every fisherman in the area is searching for her, and I'm flying out there to offer my sister moral support. She has two other, younger kids, so I know she'll need all the help she can get. I'll call when I get back."

That must have been the missing skiff we'd been watching for on our flight back to town. I felt terrible. I'd been so caught up in my own drama of spending the day with a dead whale and getting back to town in time to go to dinner with friends, I hadn't given the lone person in the missing skiff much thought. Of course, anyone missing would be bad, but the idea of a teenage girl alone and terrified while her skiff drifted out to sea, made me sick. I suddenly had no desire to go out to dinner with friends.

I called Dana Baynes, the friend I knew the best in the group and told her I'd just returned to town, smelled like a dead whale and didn't think I'd make it to dinner.

"Of course you will," she said. "We're all at the Rendezvous, and we have a chair reserved for you. Take your time, and please take a long, hot shower! You'll feel better after that."

"Have you heard about Sandy's niece?"

"Very sad. We're discussing it now."

Of course, Dana had heard; Dana knew everything that happened in the town of Kodiak, if not on the entire island. She would know all the latest information, and that, if for no other reason, made me decide to get cleaned up and head to dinner.

Forty-five minutes later, I walked into the Rendezvous. My friends were easy to spot in the small restaurant, but instead of the raucous laughter that was normal during these get-togethers, their mood was somber, their heads bent close together as they conversed in low voices. Dana looked up and smiled when she saw me. She waved me to an empty chair. I took off my raincoat and sat, and the other ladies stopped their conversation to say hi. The group present included Cassie Thomas, a nurse at Kodiak Providence Hospital, Carolyn Reft, my accountant, and Linda Bragg, an English teacher at the high school. I'd met Dana soon after I'd moved to Kodiak two years earlier, and I'd gotten to know Cassie and Carolyn fairly well over the past year. Linda Bragg, though, was only a casual acquaintance. Linda and Cassie were good friends, and Linda worked at the high school with Sandy Miles, the woman whose niece was missing. Unlike the rest of us, though, Linda was married with two kids, so she usually had better things to do than to hang out with the girls on a Friday evening.

"Have you heard anything else about the search?" I asked.

Dana shook her head. "No, and with each passing hour, the likelihood of a rescue fades. I don't know what it's like on the west side of the island, but if it's anything like it is here in town, it's too foggy for the Coast Guard chopper pilots to see anything."

"I was on the west side today," I said, "and it wasn't foggy out there then, but we did run into fog on our way back to town."

Dana grinned. "I bet you enjoyed that flight." She knew how much I hated flying in small floatplanes.

"Trust me," I said, "the flight wasn't the worst part of my day."

"Did you see anyone searching for Deanna when you were out there?" Linda asked.

"When we were leaving to come back to town, we saw the Coast Guard chopper, and the chopper pilot told our pilot to keep a lookout for an aluminum skiff adrift. I had no idea the lone occupant of the skiff was a 17-year-old girl."

"She was old for her age," Linda said, "and her family has fished that site since Deanna was a toddler, so she grew up around boats. I'm not sure she'd know how to fix one if she had engine problems, though."

Dana grunted. "Who does? These four-stroke engines are nice until they have a problem, and then it's nearly impossible to fix them yourself. A couple years ago I was by myself in the middle of Karluk Lake when the outboard suddenly quit. It was purring along fine and then nothing. It was getting windy, and I needed to get back to shore. I fumbled through the toolkit and found the service manual neatly placed in a Ziploc bag, so I open it up to the trouble-shooting guide, and do you know what assistance the guide offered? It told me to take the engine to my nearest authorized Honda dealer!"

We all laughed.

"So what did you do?" Cassie asked.

"I called Camp Island on my radio and asked for someone to come tow me to shore. It was totally humiliating, and I still get razzed about it. My point is that if something like that happened to Deanna, she wouldn't know what to do."

"Didn't she have a radio?" I asked.

All three women shook their heads. "Sandy told me Deanna forgot to take the handheld VHF. Jody – that's Deanna's mother – is blaming herself for not making sure Deanna had her radio. They were so busy getting ready for the Fourth of July party, no one thought about it," Linda said.

"Why didn't they go to the party together?" I asked.

"Deanna wanted to stay later and hang out by the bonfire with her friends. This was the first time her parents let her take the skiff that far on her own. She followed her parents to the party, but they left at 3:00 pm, and she stayed later. She was supposed to leave the party by 5:00 because her parents knew the forecast was calling for 25-knot winds last night, but according to her friends, she left the party a little after six," Linda said. "By then, it was already blowing pretty good."

"That poor kid must have been terrified if her engine died when she was in big seas," I said.

The women all nodded.

"If it turned sideways, and she started taking waves over the side, the boat might have filled up with water and sunk," Dana said in a hushed voice. "They may never find any sign of Deanna or the boat."

No one said anything for a few minutes, and I was still lost in thought when a glass of Merlot magically appeared on the table in front of me. I turned around and looked into the smiling face of Toni, the owner of the Rendezvous.

"Wow, you remembered what I drink," I said. Is this a sign I've been hanging out at your bar too much?"

"I heard you had a rough day digging through the intestines of a rotting whale, so I thought you'd need this."

"You heard about the necropsy?"

Toni was the only person in Kodiak who was more connected than Dana.

"Can I get you anything to eat?"

"I'd kill for some of your clam chowder."

Toni's clam chowder was legendary, and a bowl of it was sure to improve my mood.

"I'll be right back," she said.

"Is there any news on Deanna?" Dana asked.

Toni pursed her lips and shook her head. A life-long resident of Kodiak, I was sure that Toni knew how these dramas usually ended, and as more time passed, the more certain the ending became.

"Did the police figure out who killed that woman in May? You know, the one they found in the boat harbor with her throat cut?" Cassie asked after Toni left the table.

"I haven't heard much about it lately," Dana said.

"Debbie Sidle," Carolyn said. "She was a prostitute. I went to high school with her, and she was wild even back then. Her dad left when she was in grade school, and her mother worked at the grocery store. Debbie did whatever she wanted; her mother had no control over her. She ran with the 'druggie group' when we were in high school."

"She lived a high-risk lifestyle," Cassie said. "It won't be an easy case for the police."

Toni appeared with my clam chowder, and I devoted the next several minutes to my taste buds. Around me, my friends discussed how they'd spent their Fourth of July. I listened without commenting; I couldn't stop thinking about the missing girl and wondering if she would be found soon.

"Well, ladies," Linda said several minutes later, "I'd better get home to the family. I promised my youngest I'd play his latest video game with him, even though he will slaughter me as he always does."

Carolyn stood. "I've got to get too."

I drained my wine glass. "I'm headed to bed," I said, "where I will undoubtedly dream about exploding whales."

Chapter Two

Monday, July 8th

I hunched over my desk, trying to decipher the rough draft of a Master's thesis written by one of my graduate students. Kim was Korean and brilliant, but he had not mastered the English language, and it was painful to read anything he wrote. The knock on my office door was a welcome break. I leaned back in my chair.

"Come in."

Geoff Baker, one of my favorite people at the Marine Center, let himself into the office, gently closed the door, and folded his lanky form into the chair in front of my desk. Geoff had been a graduate student when I was first hired at the center, but he'd received his doctorate in May and Peter Wayans, the director of the center, immediately offered him a job as a biochemistry instructor and researcher. Geoff was good natured and usually had a broad smile on his face, but today he looked grim.

"What's up?" I asked.

"They found the skiff," he said.

"What skiff?"

"You know, the girl who went missing a few days ago."

"Deanna Kerr?"

Geoff nodded. "The Coast Guard found it still floating in Shelikof."

"How did it get out there? Wasn't the wind blowing the other direction the last time she was seen?"

"You know ocean currents," Geoff said. "They're complicated."

I nodded. "I gather Deanna was not in the boat."

"No. There's no sign of her. Maybe she was washed overboard."

"Her poor parents," I said. "I'd better call Sandy tonight."

"Sandy?"

"Sandy Miles, Deanna's aunt. She's a friend of mine."

"Ah, the math teacher at the high school."

I nodded again. "Come to think of it, Sandy's probably still out in Uyak at the fish site. When Deanna went missing, Sandy flew out to the Kerrs' fish site to stay with her sister, Deanna's mom."

"I bet they're not having a happy day out there." Geoff reached back and tugged on his bushy, red ponytail. He slowly stood. "I have a class to teach in 10 minutes," he said. "Let me know if you hear anything."

As soon as Geoff left my office, my cell phone rang.

"Have you heard?" The sorrow in Dana's voice was evident.

"I just got the news; it's so sad."

"Sandy must have her hands full out there."

"I was planning to call her, but then I remembered she flew out to the fish site. Is she still out there?"

"As far as I know," Dana said. "I'm sure she'll fly back to town in a day or two now, though."

"Do you think they'll have a memorial service for Deanna?"

"I don't know," Dana said, "but I doubt they will hold a service for a while unless her body is found. There's always that tiny chance she somehow made it to shore and survived."

"That would be a miracle."

"It didn't happen, but it probably will take her parents a few weeks to accept Deanna is gone."

I didn't talk to Sandy until a week later when she called to let me know she had flown back to Kodiak that day.

"I was so sorry to hear about your niece," I said. "How are you?"

"I'm okay," she said, "but my sister is a mess. I probably should have stayed with her longer, but I had to get away. Now that I'm back in town, I feel guilty."

"You shouldn't feel guilty. You were there for Jody when she really needed you, and I'm sure she appreciated it. How's the rest of the family doing?"

"Jack stays busy, and at first, he was out searching every day. The kids are sad, but they'll be fine. It's Jody I'm the most worried about. When the Coast Guard first found the skiff, she was certain Deanna would be found sitting on a beach somewhere. She was in complete denial. Once she began to accept Deanna was gone, she sank into a horrible depression and wouldn't even get out of bed. I don't know how she'll recover from this tragedy. Her kids are her life."

"Maybe it will be easier if Deanna's body is found."

"Definitely. Both Jody and Jack say they won't have a funeral or a memorial service until they have her body. I tried to tell them she may never be found, but they didn't want to hear that."

"What do you think happened?" I asked.

"I think she had engine trouble. The outboard wasn't working when they found the skiff, and the hood was off. I can see Deanna bending over the outboard in heavy seas. She probably got hit by a wave and swept overboard. It's a miracle the boat didn't fill up with water and sink. If she'd stayed inside the boat, she would have survived."

"That's so tragic. I'm sorry, Sandy. Please let me know if I can do anything to help, and I mean anything."

"Thanks, Jane. I don't think there's much any of us can do right now, but I'll keep your offer in mind."

Chapter Three

Sunday, October 13th

Alaska State Trooper Sergeant Dan Patterson knew his night was about to take a turn for the worse. He had just finished his shift and walked into his house when his phone chirped. His wife was dishing up a plate of spaghetti for him, but when the phone rang, she stopped, knowing she would be reheating his meal in several hours.

"I'm on my way," he said into the phone. He looked at his wife. "Sorry hon, this sounds like a bad one. Don't wait up for me; I have to drive to Chiniak."

He hurried to his car in the driving rain, fastened his seat belt and began the 42-mile drive down the Chiniak Highway. On a sunny day in July, this drive rivaled any in the world for its scenic beauty, but this was not a sunny day in July; it was a rainy night in October. The road was dark and curvy, and Patterson gripped the steering wheel as he concentrated on the pavement in front of him. Staying on the road was not his only concern. He had to watch for deer and possibly even bears running across the highway. The trooper who had called told him to park at the post office in Chiniak, and they would cover the final mile of their trek on four-wheelers. All Patterson had been told was that a body had been discovered in the woods. He didn't know whether the victim was male or female or whether it had been there a day or a year. If he'd understood Trooper Ben Johnstone correctly, the trooper himself had found the body while deer hunting on his day off. The usually calm and organized Johnstone, however, had sounded rattled so Patterson may have misunderstood him. He'd get the details soon enough.

Patterson had only been stationed on Kodiak for six months, and he had only been to Chiniak once before, but it was a town with a population of 50 people, so finding the post office was not difficult. By the time he parked the car, the blinding rain pelted the windshield in sheets. Patterson pulled on his raincoat, stepped out of his vehicle, and shook hands with Trooper Ben Johnstone.

"I see the weather isn't going to be our friend tonight," Patterson said.

"No, sir. If there were tracks near the body, they won't be there now."

"So the body is fresh?"

"Yes, sir. No more than a day or two old. She was murdered."

Patterson felt a headache coming on. This would be a very long night. "You're sure it wasn't a hunting accident?"

"This was no hunting accident, sir. I'm certain of that. It's pretty hard to accidentally cut someone's throat."

The headache spread into Patterson's neck. "You are the one who found the body?"

"Yes, sir, I was walking through the woods. I'd been hunting about two hours and was heading back to my cabin because it was starting to rain hard. I caught a glimpse of something strange on the ground, and after a few more steps, I realized it was a body. I took some photos and checked around the area for footprints or four-wheeler tracks, but I didn't see anything. She must have been murdered before the rain started."

"How are you doing?" Patterson asked. "This must have been quite a shock."

"Yes sir, it was. I'm fine, though. It's just that you don't expect to find a dead girl in the woods when you're deer hunting."

"A girl?" Now his stomach was beginning to hurt.

"A teenager, sir."

"Okay, let's go take a closer look."

Patterson followed Johnstone through the woods, each man riding a four-wheeler that Johnstone had somehow managed to procure. They had to travel slowly through the Sitka spruce rainforest to avoid smashing into a tree, but at least the large trees shielded them from some of the rain.

Fifteen minutes later, Patterson spotted the red beam of the light Johnstone had left to mark the location of the body. They parked their four-wheelers several yards away and approached the body on foot.

The naked body was sprawled on the ground, arms out to the side and legs spread wide. It had been posed for maximum effect. Her throat had been slashed so deeply she nearly had been decapitated. Her brown eyes stared sightlessly up at the trees. Patterson noted what looked like bite marks on her breasts, but otherwise, her slim, pale body appeared unmarred.

Patterson recalled a similar murder on Kodiak only a few months earlier. In May, a 36-year-old prostitute had been found floating in the boat harbor, and her throat had also been cut. Since that victim had been found within the city limits, the crime fell under the jurisdiction of the Kodiak Police Department, and Patterson did not know the specifics of the case. While the first victim was older than this girl, Patterson felt the similarities between the two cases warranted further investigation.

"We need to get a tarp over the scene right away," Patterson said.

"Yes, sir. I brought one with me. I'll get on that. Are the crime scene people on their way?"

"I'll send them tomorrow when it's light, but I don't think they'll find much. If there ever was any evidence here, it has been washed away by now. I don't see much blood, so I'm guessing this is only where the body was dumped, not where she was killed. Once you get the tarp set up, go back to town and see if you can borrow a trailer or a sled or something we can use to transport the body back to my vehicle. After I take photos, I think we should get her packaged and transported back to Kodiak. The only hope we have of preserving any evidence on her body will be to get her out of this weather."

It was 3:00 am by the time Patterson finally returned home and ate his spaghetti dinner. He and Johnstone had packaged the body, and it was ready to ship to Anchorage to the state medical examiner's office on the morning Ravn flight.

Patterson had a bad feeling about this crime and the woman found floating in the boat harbor. On an island where few murders occurred, two women killed in the same manner in the span of six months suggested to him they were killed by the same perpetrator or perpetrators. Was a serial killer hunting women on the island?

Chapter Four

Monday, October 14th

The girl's body was flown to Anchorage to the State Medical Examiner's Office the following morning. The autopsy would be performed later that day, but Patterson doubted it would yield much information. Meanwhile, he focused on identifying the victim. He started this process by showing the photo to the dispatcher in the trooper's office. Patterson doubted Irene Meadows knew all 15,000 inhabitants of Kodiak Island, but from what he'd observed, she knew most of them.

Irene took one look at the photo, clicked her tongue, and said, "That poor girl. She really never had a chance."

"You know her?" Patterson asked.

"Sure, that's Tasha Ayers. Her mama is Hope Mills. Not much of a mother, that one. She works at the Fresh Seafoods cannery, but rumor has it she makes extra money by running a prostitution business out of her home."

"Do you know anything about Tasha?"

"Again this is just a rumor, but I hear she is – or was – into drugs. There was also some speculation that she worked for her mother."

"As a prostitute?"

"Mmm hmm, but again, I don't know if the rumors are true."

"How old was Tasha?"

"She's a senior I believe, so she must be 17 or 18."

"Okay, she's in school. That gives me a place to start."

"I don't think she was much of a student, but as far as I know, she was still enrolled in school."

"Thank you, Irene, I owe you lunch."

"Yes, you do."

As Patterson sat in a chair outside of Principal Jeannie Daniel's office, he flashed back to his own high school days. He was a good kid and didn't get in much trouble, but he had made two memorable trips to the principal's office, and while the meetings with the principal had been bad, they were nothing compared to the lashing his father gave him when he got home. He rubbed his hand over his short-cropped hair and smiled. *If Dad had lived long enough to see his only son become an Alaska State Trooper, he would have been surprised and proud.* Patterson's father had been an Anchorage police officer who had died on the job. He wasn't shot or killed in a high-speed chase, he simply keeled over at his desk from a heart attack at the age of 44.

"Detective Patterson, I'm sorry I kept you waiting."

Patterson looked up at a slim, petite woman wearing a flowered dress. She held open the door to her office and ushered out a pimply faced teen, his gaze locked on the floor.

Patterson stood and held out his hand. "Principal Daniel, I presume."

"Please call me Jeannie." She shook his hand. "Come into my office where we can talk in private." She led him into her office, and he sat in the chair in front of her desk.

Principal Daniel was in her late thirties, and she obviously took good care of herself. Her frame was lean, but he could see the muscles in her calves. Her shoulder-length blonde hair was curled and hair-sprayed into place, her makeup subtle and flawless.

"How can I help you, today?" she asked

"I'm afraid I have some bad news about one of your students."

"Yes?" Her smile faded into a concerned frown.

"Tasha Ayers is a student here, correct?"

"Yes, she is."

"I have a photo I need to show you," Patterson said. "I must warn you, though, the girl in this photo is dead, and the photo is disturbing. I'm sorry to put you through this, but I need to know if this is Tasha Ayers." Patterson removed a photo of the murder victim from a folder.

Jeannie Daniel's hands flew to her mouth. "Oh, my! What happened to her?"

"Is this Tasha Ayers?"

"Yes. Was she murdered? It looks like her throat was cut."

"I can't really get into the details of the case at this point."

"Have you notified her family?"

"Not yet. I wanted to be sure this was Tasha before I told her mother. Do you know her mother?"

"I've talked to her on the phone and tried to get her to come here to meet with me, but she doesn't," she sucked in a breath, "I mean she didn't take much interest in her daughter's life."

"Was Tasha in trouble often?" Patterson asked.

"Mostly she was absent. She skipped school more than she didn't. She did get caught smoking pot once, though. She wasn't a bad kid; she just didn't seem to care. She was in a downward spiral, but I never expected this."

"Was she close to any of the teachers?"

"I doubt it, but I'll print off her class schedule for this semester, so you can talk to them. Most of the teachers stay in the building for an hour or two after classes end, so that would be a good time to interview them."

Patterson left with Tasha's schedule in his folder. He checked his watch; it was 10:15 am. He'd scheduled a meeting with Kodiak Police Chief Howard Feeney and Detective Maureen Horner at 1:00 pm, but he had plenty of time between now and then to do the dreaded task of informing Tasha's mother her daughter was dead.

The rain had subsided to mist and fog. It was unseasonably warm for October, but according to the forecast, it was about to change. A huge storm system was hovering in the Aleutians, moving slowly toward Kodiak. Snow was predicted in two days, and if the weatherman had it right, the snow would be accompanied by 50-knot winds. The roads would be not only wet, they would be snow-packed and icy.

Patterson checked his file folder for the address of Hope Mills. Mrs. Mills lived in a run-down trailer park in the middle of town, and her trailer was one of the worst looking of the bunch. He climbed the aluminum steps of the dirty, white structure and knocked on the door. There was no answer. He knocked again, louder this time. Still nothing. He was about to knock a third time when the door to the adjacent trailer opened, and the elderly woman called, "She's not there. She's at work. Works at Fresh Seafoods."

"Thank you, ma'am," Patterson said. He sighed. He hated notifying next of kin, but it was much better when the task could be done at the relative's home instead of at the workplace. He didn't have much choice, though.

He drove down Marine Way and pulled into the parking lot of Fresh Seafoods. He located the main office and asked to speak to Hope Mills. Five minutes later, a thin woman with short-cropped black hair and a face that had seen a hard life appeared in front of him.

"What's she done now?" The woman crossed her arms in front of her.

"Mrs. Mills?"

"That's right. This about Tasha?"

"Why do you ask?"

"'Cause she's always getting herself in trouble."

"I'm afraid it's more serious than that, ma'am."

"Well, spit it out. I ain't got all day. I have bills to pay, and having a state trooper stop by your workplace ain't the best way to keep your job."

"Tasha is dead, ma'am." *If she wants me to spit it out, I'll oblige.*

Hope Ayers stared at him, mouth agape. "Dead?" A tear seeped from her right eye, and she angrily brushed it away.

"I'm sorry, ma'am."

"How? A car wreck?"

"No ma'am, she was murdered."

Hope backed against the wall and then slid down it, sitting hard on the floor. "Murdered? Who would want to kill her?"

"I was hoping you could help me with that. Did Tasha have any enemies or anyone who would want her dead for any reason?"

"She was a kid!" What kind of enemies could she have?"

He wasn't getting anywhere here. "Can you give me the names of her friends?"

"She didn't have friends that I knew about. She didn't tell me anything, and she was rarely ever home. She ran wild, and I couldn't control her."

"Did she take drugs?"

"I don't know. Probably." She slowly pushed herself back up the wall until she was standing. "Listen, are you through with me? I need to get back to work."

"Mrs. Ayers, I'm sure under the circumstances your boss would understand if you wanted to go home."

"Why would I want to do that?" She turned and marched away, leaving Patterson to stare at her retreating form.

Patterson returned to trooper headquarters and sat at his desk. He'd sent Johnstone and another trooper to Chiniak to interview everyone in town to find out if anyone had seen anything suspicious in the hours before Tasha's body had been found. Another trooper was photographing and analyzing the crime scene. According to Irene, none of the troopers had called in to report anything. Patterson didn't think there was much else he could do on the case until he heard either from the troopers or the medical examiner or until 4:00 pm when he could interview Tasha's teachers.

A few minutes before 1:00 pm, Patterson parked in the Kodiak police station lot. As soon as he entered the building, he was directed toward the conference room, and a few minutes later, Police Chief Howard Feeney and Detective Maureen Horner entered the room. Horner closed the door behind her, and she and Feeney shook Patterson's hand. Horner sat across the table from Patterson, and Feeney sat at the head of the table. They wasted no time with small talk.

"Heard you caught a bad one," Feeney said.

Patterson nodded. "A teenager with her throat cut. Nearly decapitated. Name is Tasha Ayers."

Horner nodded. "I'm familiar with Tasha. She's had a few run-ins with the law."

"Such as?" Patterson asked.

"She was caught shoplifting at Wal-Mart, and then when the patrolmen located her, they found crystal meth on her. I think she was caught with drugs another time or two, but I'd have to check her file."

"I heard a rumor she may have been involved in prostitution. Do you know anything about that?"

Horner shook her head. "Not as far as I know."

"We'll get her file to you right away," Feeney said.

"Look," Patterson said. He put his elbows on the table, laced his fingers, and rested his chin on his hands. "I'm concerned this homicide may be related to the one you had in May. The body in the boat harbor. Wasn't her throat cut too?"

"Yes," Horner said. "I have a few leads on that one but nothing concrete. You think Tasha's murder might be related?"

"I'm concerned," Patterson said. "Two murders in six months. Both victims had their throats slashed, and from what little I've learned about this Ayers girl, they both lived high-risk lifestyles. It could be a coincidence, but for an island with 15,000 people, it would be a big coincidence."

"Are you suggesting both women were killed by the same perpetrator?" Feeney asked.

"I think he's suggesting we have a serial killer on our island." Horner sat back in her chair and ran her hand through her straight, shoulder length chestnut hair.

Patterson shrugged. "That's my concern."

"There have to be three murders before the perpetrator is classified a serial killer," Feeney said.

"Technically yes," Patterson said, "but I don't think we should wait for another woman to die before we contact the FBI."

"The FBI?" Feeney sat straight, his face reddening.

"Sir," Patterson said, picking his words carefully, "they're the experts on serial killers. I think it would be a good idea to ask for their help, and I believe it would be wise to ask for it now."

"What do your bosses think?" Feeney asked. His voice remained calm, but the trail of sweat running down his red face suggested he wasn't fond of Patterson's idea to involve the FBI.

"I haven't talked to my bosses yet, sir. I thought it would be best to talk to you first."

Feeney pursed his lips and stared at the wall at the far end of the room for several moments. Finally, he said, "I won't rule out the FBI, but I don't want to contact them yet. It looks like we can't handle the investigation of two murders on our island, and I think that makes us appear incompetent. If the FBI rushes in here and the case is solved, they'll be the heroes, and we're left looking like the local yokels."

"Yes sir," Patterson said. His opinion was that calling the FBI into the case early would make the Kodiak police and the troopers look not only competent but wise enough to know when to ask for assistance from an agency that had spent a great deal of time and money learning how serial killers ticked and knew how to apprehend them. The way Feeney wanted to approach the case was akin to your family doctor refusing to send you to an oncologist because he felt it would make him look as if he couldn't cut the cancer out of you himself. No matter what profession you were in, there were times when you needed to call on those with more expertise in a particular situation. Without Feeney on board, Patterson knew there was no point in approaching his superiors about involving the FBI. He would just have to hope they could solve the case before more women were murdered.

By the time Patterson left headquarters to return to the school at 4:00 pm, he still hadn't heard from the troopers in Chiniak nor from the medical examiner. He had reviewed Tasha's class schedule and knew which teachers he needed to interview. He had phoned Principal Daniel and requested she ask each of Tasha's teachers to remain in their respective classrooms until he could talk to them. Patterson interviewed the teachers in order, beginning with Sandy Miles who taught algebra, Tasha's first class of the morning and ending with Linda Bragg who taught English Literature, Tasha's last class of the day. The results of the first five interviews were discouraging. None of the teachers really knew Tasha. The overall picture Patterson got was that Tasha was bright enough, but she put little effort into her school work. She often skipped school altogether or cut at least a part of the day. When she was in the classroom, she seemed sullen and withdrawn, adding nothing to class discussions, and when she bothered to hand in class work, it was often incomplete. Her grades were poor; she was failing history and earth science, had Ds in algebra and accounting, and a C in sociology.

The last teacher Patterson interviewed was Linda Bragg, Tasha's English Literature teacher. Her classroom door stood open, and when Patterson entered her room, he saw her at her desk, head bent, grading papers. He watched her for several seconds while she scribbled in the margin of a paper in red ink. She appeared to be consumed with her task. Like the other classrooms Patterson had just visited, this room was brightly decorated. Student artwork covered the walls, and although Patterson remembered little from his own, brief relationship with William Shakespeare, he recognized the drawing of the balcony scene from Romeo and Juliet and the portrayal of the witches from Macbeth. Interspersed between the artwork, Linda Brag had posted famous quotes from Shakespeare: *"By the pricking of my thumbs, something wicked this way comes"*; *"To thine ownself be true"*; *"To be or not to be; that is the question"*; *"Good night, good night! Parting is such sweet sorrow"*; and *"What is in a name? That which we call a rose by any other name would smell as sweet."* Patterson smiled. His personal favorite was missing: *"The first thing we do, let's kill all the lawyers."*

Linda Bragg glanced up from the paper she was grading and shook her head. "They think they hate Shakespeare, but next we tackle Milton and Chaucer, and they will beg me to return to the works of the bard."

Patterson smiled at Ms. Bragg and introduced himself. Linda Bragg was in her late 30s or early 40s. She had shoulder length blonde hair, thin lips, a perfectly straight nose and wide, intelligent, brown eyes. When she stood to shake Patterson's hand, he guessed her height at 5'2" and her weight at 100 pounds.

"Principal Daniel said you wanted to ask me some questions. Is this about one of my students?"

"Yes, ma'am. I would like to ask you about Tasha Ayers."

"Why, is she in some sort of trouble?"

Patterson sighed. He wished he had gathered the teachers together and told them all about Tasha at the same time. It was brutal to have to repeat this tragic news over and over. "I'm sorry to tell you Tasha is dead. She was murdered sometime yesterday evening."

Linda Bragg burst into tears and sat down hard in her desk chair. She sobbed for several minutes and then dabbed at her eyes and nose with a tissue and said, "I knew something bad was going to happen to her, but I thought it would be trouble with the law. I never imagined she'd be murdered."

"Why is that, Ms. Bragg? Why did you think something bad would happen to her?"

"She's been in a bad place all semester. I've had Tasha as a student since she was a freshman. She liked to write, and I encouraged her. She's one of those students I felt I could help, and for her first three years in high school, she seemed to crave my encouragement. I don't think she got much encouragement at home. But, this year it has been a different story. She has been depressed, hasn't been turning in her work, skips class, and doesn't seem to care about anything. I tried talking to her several times, but it didn't help. And then ..." A fresh torrent of tears burst from Linda's eyes, and she wiped them with her tissue.

"Yes, ma'am?"

"Yesterday I asked her to stay after school. I decided I'd try the tough-love approach, so I told her she was failing English Literature." Linda sobbed and buried her face in her hands. "Why did I do that?"

"What time was this ma'am?"

"I don't know, around 4:00 pm."

"And what did she say?"

"Nothing. She just shrugged and turned and walked out the door, but I could tell I'd hurt her. She thought I liked her and would give her a passing grade no matter what."

"Did you see her after that?"

"No, I watched her drive away. What time was she murdered?"

"Sometime after you saw her and before her body was discovered just before it got dark last night," Patterson said. "Can you tell me who Tasha's friends were? Did she have any friends in your class?"

"No, I don't think so. I never saw Tasha talking to anyone, and she always seemed to be alone. Sometimes I'd see her outdoors hanging around with the, well, I hate to stereotype kids, but she hung out with a rough crowd. Even so, I never saw her talk to any of those kids. She didn't seem to fit in well anywhere. I believe Tasha was a girl with serious problems. You should speak with Paul Mather, the school counselor. As much as Tasha skipped school, I'm sure Paul spent a great deal of time talking to her."

Patterson asked Linda if she would be okay, and she assured him she would. She also promised to call him if she thought of anything else.

Patterson followed Ms. Bragg's directions to the school counselor's office and knocked on the door without much hope of a response; it was after 5:00 pm, and he figured Mather would be gone for the day. He was pleasantly surprised when the door opened, and a man with dark hair wearing wire-rimmed glasses looked inquisitively at him.

"Are you Paul Mather?" Patterson asked.

"I am."

Patterson held out his hand and introduced himself.

Mather pushed the door open wider and invited Patterson into his office. Patterson guessed Mather was in his mid-thirties. He had an athletic build, an olive complexion, and dark hair cut short. Mather's office was larger than Patterson expected. His desk sat in the far corner of the office under a window that looked out onto the school parking lot. Framed diplomas and other credentials decorated the wall behind the desk, and two empty chairs sat in front of and faced his desk. The rest of the office space was less formal. A sitting area occupying the area to the right of the door included four comfortable chairs and a coffee table holding a stack of magazines. Several mobiles with glass crystals, chimes, and butterflies dangled from the ceiling, and the walls were decorated with pro football posters, a poster of a kitten, and a poster of a unicorn.

Patterson gestured to the chairs. "I assume this is where you talk to troubled teens?"

Mather nodded. "This is what I call 'the pit.' My goal is to put kids at ease, so they don't feel as if they are being interrogated or scolded. They get enough of that from their visits to the principal's office. My job is to help them work through their problems and hopefully help them become better students and better citizens."

"Please, sit down." Mather gestured to the sitting area.

Patterson hesitated but then settled onto one of the chairs. Patterson guessed Mather's pit appealed more to kids than it did to him; he found the small area claustrophobic.

Mather reached up, pulled on a brass chain, and a bright light filled the space. "Some kids have problems, get depressed, or act out simply because it's dark here during the short winter days. This is a full-spectrum light that simulates daylight as nearly as possible. I'm not saying it will turn their lives around, but I hope it will cheer them up while we're discussing solutions to their problems."

"Was Tasha Ayers one of the students you tried to help?"

Mather sighed and sat in a chair across from Patterson. "Tasha needs more than a bright light to solve her problems. Since you are here asking about her, I can only assume she's in some sort of legal trouble?"

"Tasha Ayers is dead," Patterson said. "Her body was discovered late yesterday near Chiniak. She was murdered."

Mather recoiled as if he'd been slapped. He removed his glasses and rubbed the bridge of his nose. "Damn," he said. "I liked Tasha. She was a bright kid, but she had big problems. She was smart enough, but she wasn't motivated." He shook his head. "No, it was more than that. It was as if she was trying to sabotage herself and set herself up for failure."

"Why would she do that?" Patterson asked.

"Tasha is not one of my success stories. I couldn't get her to open up to me, but from what she did say, I know her home life wasn't happy. Her dad hadn't been in the picture for a long time, if he ever was, and I got the idea that her mother, who has a job at a cannery, is a part-time prostitute. I don't have any proof of this, but I suspect Mama may have encouraged Tasha to have sex for money too, or maybe she forced her against her will. What little Tasha did say about her mother wasn't good, and she certainly didn't respect her mom."

There it was again. Irene had also mentioned she'd heard Tasha's mother had forced Tasha to turn tricks. Of course, the rumor may not be true, but Patterson found it interesting he'd already heard it from two different sources.

"What about the rest of her family?" Patterson asked.

"She has one brother – Tim. He graduated from high school three years ago, a year before I took this job. Tasha never really spoke about him, so I assumed they weren't close. You should also probably know that Tasha had some substance-abuse problems," Mather said. "A teacher sent her to my office last year because she was drunk in class. She really should have been sent to the principal's office, but Principal Daniel would have suspended her for at least three days, and neither the teacher nor I wanted that. Tasha needed to be encouraged, not punished. This year, Tasha was caught smoking pot, and she was suspended for three days. I suspect she was into harder stuff as well."

"Such as?" Patterson asked.

"Oxycontin or maybe even meth or heroin. I'm sure I don't have to tell you heroin is a problem in Kodiak. I'm not saying Tasha was an addict, but I suspect she used harder drugs, at least occasionally."

"Did Tasha have any friends you know of?"

Mather was shaking his head before Patterson finished the question. "She was a loner. She never talked about friends, and I never saw her with anyone else. She was the kind of girl who walked around with her head down and a frown on her face."

"When was the last time you saw her?" Patterson asked.

Mather looked up at the ceiling, lost in thought for a moment. "It would have been Friday around 11:00 am. I called her to my office to tell her that she was failing Earth Science, History, and English Literature. I told her if she didn't get her act together, she wouldn't graduate. I guess I was a little abrupt with her, but I wanted to make sure she saw the big picture. She only had one more year to go, and I wanted to make her see she only needed to hang in there awhile longer."

"What did she say when you told her she was failing?"

"She said she'd do better, but she'd said that before. She knew what I wanted to hear." He shook his head. "Poor kid."

When Patterson got back to his office, Johnstone and the other troopers were waiting for him, but they had little to report. No one in Chiniak could remember seeing Tasha in town the previous day, and no one could remember seeing anyone in the area who either didn't live there or have a hunting cabin there. The day had been cold and rainy though, so most of the residents had spent the day indoors and didn't notice who came and went from the town. The crime scene yielded no evidence, but Trooper Martin shot numerous photos of the spot where Johnstone had found Tasha's body. It had rained hard all night in Chiniak, and it was still raining today. Any evidence left at the scene was gone.

Irene reported that Dr. Jarod Libby, the medical examiner, had called while Patterson was at the school, and he wanted Patterson to call him back.

Patterson checked his watch. "It's 6:30 pm. How long did he say he'd be at his office?"

"He gave me his cell phone number and said to tell you to call him at your earliest convenience."

Patterson's eyebrows rose. *Did the medical examiner find something significant during the autopsy?* He dialed the number.

The phone rang three times before a breathless voice answered. "Libby."

"Doctor Libby, this is Detective Dan Patterson with the Alaska State Troopers. Did I catch you at a bad time; you sound out of breath?"

"No, no, I'm at the gym. I'm glad you called. I found something significant during the Tasha Ayers autopsy, and there's something else I'd like to discuss with you."

"Okay."

"First of all, the Ayers girl was in her first trimester of pregnancy. I'd say the fetus was two months old."

"Interesting."

"I thought that would interest you. The only other significant finding, and I believe you already noted it, were the four human bite marks on the breasts."

"What about rape?"

"I didn't see any signs of vaginal or anal trauma. She obviously was sexually active, though, so it's impossible to know if she submitted voluntarily to a rapist, hoping he wouldn't hurt her if she did what he wanted, but I found no signs of semen or condom lubricant."

"Will you fax me a copy of your report in the morning?"

"Will do, but there's something else here that bothers me. I also performed the autopsy on Deborah Sidle who was murdered in Kodiak in May. I believe the Kodiak Police are handling the Sidle investigation. Anyway, she also died from exsanguination when her carotid artery was cut."

"Yes, I know that."

"Did you also know she too had bite marks on her breasts?"

Patterson leaned back in his chair. "No, doctor, I didn't know that, and I appreciate you pointing it out."

"I hope I'm wrong, but if I had to guess, I'd say both of these women were killed by the same person."

"Doctor Libby, would you be willing to repeat that remark to my commander? I would like to ask the FBI for assistance, but two murders, even if committed by the same perpetrator, don't make this a serial-murder crime, and Police Chief Feeney doesn't want to bring in the FBI unless we have a third, similar homicide. I'd like to call them now."

"Detective, I will be happy to relay the similarities between the two cases to your commander because I think you will have another victim down there with her throat cut, and I would like to do everything I can to find this maniac before another woman dies."

Chapter Five

Tuesday, October 22nd

"I'm Russell Wilson, and you're Tyler Lockett. Go long!" Six-year-old Trevor Nilson raced down the rocky beach while looking over his shoulder, waiting for his nine-year-old brother, Herman, to pass the football to him.

When Herman finally did release the ball, it sailed a foot above Trevor's outstretched fingertips and into the surf at the edge of the beach.

"You have to jump for it!" Herman yelled.

"I did," Trevor called back. "It was a bad pass."

"Shut up and get the ball."

Trevor hurried down to the water's edge, where the ball had become entangled in a pile of orange rockweed nearly the same color as the football. The late October day felt chilly, but at least the rain had stopped, and the boys could play outdoors and get some exercise after a day of sitting in the classroom at the Larsen Bay school.

Trevor picked up the football but then became distracted by a hermit crab scurrying along the beach, sporting a shell that had once belonged to a moon snail. The crab ran under the rockweed, and Trevor began parting the kelp to look for the tiny creature.

"What are you doing?" Herman yelled. "Knock it off and get back here with the ball. If we don't do something in two more downs, the Patriots will get the ball back."

Trevor stood, abandoning his search for the hermit crab and was just turning to run back to his brother when something caught his eye. At first, he thought it was driftwood wrapped in a huge section of bull kelp, but it looked strange, like several sticks of driftwood connected to each other at odd angles. He approached the bull kelp and pulled back the large bladder of the kelp to get a better look.

Trevor's piercing scream sent his brother running toward him, and when he saw what Trevor had found, they both sprinted up the beach toward their house, seeking the protection of their mother.

Two hours later, Detective Dan Patterson and Trooper Ben Johnstone arrived in Larsen Bay. Public Safety Officer Jack Stupe, met them at the airstrip and drove them to the Nilson residence. A very excited Trevor Nilson and his brother, Herman, told the troopers the story of how they discovered the skeleton, and then Stupe led the troopers down the beach to view the remains. Since the tide had been receding, Stupe left the skeleton where it lay. While Patterson appreciated this show of expertise by the public safety officer, he doubted if it would have mattered if Stupe had moved the remains. The skeleton had washed up on this beach, moved by the wind, tide, and powerful North Pacific currents. Where the skeleton was now had little to do with where it had started.

The first question that needed to be answered was how old was the skeleton? At one time, thousands of Alutiiq people had lived in this bay, and there were numerous burial sites around the bay. In all likelihood, this skeleton had been washed out of a bank and was several hundred, if not several thousand, years old. Nevertheless, until proven otherwise, Patterson would treat this as a recent death. The remains were skeletal, but in the ocean, it didn't take long for flesh to be stripped from a body. A corpse in the ocean created a banquet for a large variety of organisms, including the lowly sand flea, and a swarm of sand fleas could strip a carcass of its flesh in a matter of days.

"Let's get some photos and get this packaged. I'd like to ship it up to Anchorage tonight if possible," Patterson said.

"Yes, sir," Johnstone said.

Stupe and Johnstone stood back while Patterson snapped photos, and then they both walked toward the corpse. Johnstone carried a body bag.

"Okay, let's be careful here. We don't want it to fall apart if we can help it. Jack, you get the skull, and Ben you grab the feet. I'll try to support it in the middle." Patterson said.

"I can't believe it's still together like this," Stupe said. Maybe there's still some connective tissue on it."

"If there is, then it's a recent death," Paterson said.

Johnstone got the body bag as close to the skeleton as possible. Patterson counted to three, the men lifted, and the skeleton fell apart.

"Damn!" Patterson said. "Well, pick up the pieces. Make sure you get all of it."

"Sergeant, I think you need to look at this," Johnstone said.

Patterson knelt beside Johnstone and studied the skeleton. The two ankles were attached to each other, the bones loosely bound by wire. Two feet of wire trailed from the ankles.

"It looks like someone wired his ankles together and then attached the wire to something else like an anchor or a rock. When the wire started to disintegrate, the skeleton floated free," Johnstone said.

"The only problem with that theory is skeletons don't float, but the bones probably could be rolled along by a storm surge, or maybe the body became entangled in the kelp before the flesh decayed, and the bull kelp kept it afloat." Patterson leaned closer to study the ankle bones. "The wire is suspicious; we'll see what the medical examiner thinks. This looks like the skeleton of a child or a woman. It's too small to belong to a man."

"Sir," Stupe said, "we don't have all the bones here. It looks like we have the skull, some rib bones, the pelvis, one arm, and the legs and feet."

"Let's scour the area and see if we can find anything else, but I think we're lucky to have this much." Patterson said.

An hour later, they gave up the search for more bones. Patterson wanted to get the remains back to Kodiak and possibly even up to Anchorage that night, so they would have to fly back to Kodiak before dark. The mountainous terrain of Kodiak made flying a small plane around the island safe only when the pilot could see where he was going. Flying after dark was not only illegal but also stupid. Patterson was a good pilot who did not like to take unnecessary chances.

Chapter Six

Wednesday, October 23rd

Late Wednesday afternoon Doctor Jarod Libby called Patterson.

"Doctor Libby," Patterson said. "I'm glad you're on this case."

"I asked for it when I heard it was from Kodiak. I will need some help from the anthropologists, though, before I have a final report, but I wanted to let you know what I have so far. This is a recent death. The forensic anthropologist will be able to pinpoint the date of death within a number of years. In other words, we'll know whether she died this year or three to five years ago or 10 years ago, but that will probably be as close as they can get, and even then, it's just an educated guess, especially for a submerged corpse. All those sea critters strip the flesh from the body in short order. They probably were on her as soon as she hit the water."

"Doctor, did I hear you right? Did you say 'she'?"

"I'm fairly certain this is the skeleton of a teenage girl or a young woman in her early twenties. Again, the anthropologists will be able to narrow down the age range."

"What about the ankles?"

"Your guess is as good as mine, but I think her ankles were bound together, and I suspect the other end of the wire was tied around something heavy."

"But her ankles would have had flesh and tissue on them when she was bound. The wire was loose, but it was still tight enough that it didn't slip off."

"I think she was a petite young woman or girl who didn't have much fat. Her ankles probably were bound tightly, to begin with, and once all the tissue decayed, the wire was still tight enough to remain in place."

"Anything else?" Patterson asked.

"One more thing. The right tibia has three separate healed fractures. That's unusual enough to be an identifying feature. If we can make a probable ID and get DNA from her likely parents, we should be able to test their DNA against hers and hopefully get a match. We will use her bone marrow for that."

"Good to know," Patterson said. "We had a young girl go missing in a skiff accident a few months ago, so I can check with her parents to see if she ever broke her leg."

"If this is your missing girl," Libby said, "I don't think her death was accidental. At least that's not what I plan to write on her death certificate."

Patterson sighed. He didn't need another murder to solve. "I don't suppose there's any way to determine how she died?" he asked.

"No way to be certain," Libby said, "but her skull was crushed, and that would have done the job. The only problem is that I can't determine whether her skull was crushed before or after she died."

Patterson grabbed his keys and headed for his truck. *This won't be a pleasant task, but if the bones are those of Deanna Kerr, at least her parents will have something to bury. They can finally have a funeral service.* Patterson thought the word "closure" was overused, but in this case, it might apply. Deanna's family had been left in limbo. They had to know Deanna was dead, but they had still not had a memorial service for her, and he'd heard that Deanna's mother, Jody, was still very depressed.

Patterson drove out Mill Bay Road, cut over to Rezanof, and turned down onto Spruce Cape Road. He pulled into the driveway of the lovely log home perched on a cliff overlooking Spruce Cape. He walked up to the front porch, admiring the stained-glass door depicting a red salmon jumping up a waterfall. He rang the doorbell, took a deep breath, and stood, hands clasped in front of him.

Moments later, Jack Kerr opened the door. "Sergeant Patterson," Jack Kerr's eyebrows rose. "Please, come in."

Patterson stepped into the tiled entryway.

"Come in; have a seat," Jack said.

Patterson untied his boots, slipped out of them, and then followed Jack into a cozy great room. A large picture window offered a breathtaking view of the North Pacific Ocean. Today the ocean looked angry and dark. Large waves and a heavy swell crashed against the cliffs, and in the distance, a fishing boat rolled and bobbed as it made its way to port.

"Have a seat." Jack motioned to a couch near the fireplace and went to sit in an overstuffed chair situated directly across from Patterson. A glass coffee table spanned the space between them.

"Before you sit," Patterson said, "is your wife here?"

"I think she's taking a nap," Jack said.

"I need to talk to both of you."

"Okay, I'll call her."

Patterson waited five minutes, staring into the fire and thinking about what he would say. He decided it was best just to spit it out, but he wouldn't mention the bit about the wire on the ankles. He wanted to think about the wire for a while.

Patterson stood as Jack issued his wife into the living room. Jody Kerr wore a yellow bathrobe over flannel pajamas. Her hair was uncombed, her eyes red, and her face pale.

"Mrs. Kerr," Patterson held out his hand.

She placed her cold palm in his but made no effort to shake hands.

Patterson wondered if she was sedated.

Jack issued Jody to the chair closest to the fire. He took the chair to her right. They both looked expectantly at Patterson.

"There's no easy way to say this," Patterson said. "Two young boys in Larsen Bay discovered a skeleton on the beach yesterday, and the medical examiner in Anchorage believes it is the skeleton of a young woman." He looked from Jack to Jody.

Jack's expression remained fixed, but tears bubbled from Jody's eyes as she sat slumped in the chair.

"The medical examiner noted the deceased had at one time broken her right leg in three places. Did Deanna ever break her leg?"

This last question made an impact. Jody let out a whimper, while Jack buried his face in his hands. Patterson waited until Jack regained his composure.

Jack dropped his hands from his face and sat straight. "Yes," he said, "Deanna was in a car wreck three years ago and broke her leg in three places."

Patterson nodded. "I'd like to get a mouth swab from both of you, so we can compare your DNA to the DNA from the remains," he said quietly.

Jody's sobs grew louder.

"The coroner said he'll use a bone-marrow sample from the skeleton for the DNA test, but it would also be helpful if you have a hairbrush or toothbrush that belonged to Deanna," Patterson said.

"I don't understand," Jack said. "How did she wind up on the beach? Skeletons can't float, can they?"

"I don't know, sir. Our guess is she was carried there by a storm surge. She was wrapped in bull kelp, and it would have been enough to float her remains."

"What are the chances of that? It seems impossible." Jack's face was red

Patterson nodded. "Bodies lost at sea are usually never found. We're very lucky in this case."

Tears ran down Jack's face, and he wiped them away. He reached over and put his hand on Jody's arm. "We can finally bury our little girl, Mama."

Jody bent her head and sobbed into her Kleenex, "When?" she asked.

"If the medical examiner will accept the broken leg bones as a positive identification and release the remains, we'll have them flown back to Kodiak, and sent to the mortuary here."

"We want her cremated," Jack said.

"The mortuary will call you when she arrives," Paterson said.

Chapter Seven

Saturday, October 26th

I sat with my friends Dana Baynes, Carolyn Reft, Cassandra Thomas, and Liz Kelley, the park ranger at Fort Abercrombie State Historical Park near Kodiak. Linda Bragg and her husband sat nearby. I didn't know the Kerrs, but Deanna's Aunt Sandy was a good friend of mine, and I wanted to be at the funeral to show my support for her. Attending the funeral of a 17-year-old girl is not the way anyone wants to spend her Saturday afternoon, but I was glad the Kerrs finally had something to bury. They may not know what had happened to Deanna, but they had her remains and hopefully could move forward with their lives.

We sat two rows back on the right side of the church, and the family occupied the front two rows on the left side of the church. While I knew it was impolite to stare at the bereaved, I couldn't help myself. It was like driving past a bad car wreck and not looking at it; I couldn't help but glance at them periodically throughout the service. Jody Kerr sat the furthest from the aisle, and I could only see the back of her head and her right hand, which was holding a tissue to her face during the bulk of the service. Next to her sat Deanna's sister, Evelyn, and next to Evelyn, leaning against his father sat little brother, William. Jack Kerr sat by the aisle and stared straight ahead during the entire ceremony. He remained stoic but seemed to be in a daze, determined to make it through the day.

Sandy had told me when I'd called her the previous evening that her sister, Jody, was sedated and had been taking sedatives since Deanna first disappeared. Sandy hoped once the funeral was over, Jody would stop taking the medication and return to her life. Evelyn,

14, and William, 8, needed their Mom. Both Jack and Jody were real estate agents and had their own firm. They closed their agency during the summer salmon-fishing season and then re-opened it in the fall when they returned to town. Since Deanna went missing, though, Jody had been too depressed and medicated to work, so Jack was forced to do both their jobs. Sandy said everyone was stressed, and she didn't know what would happen to the family if Jody couldn't pull herself together and move past this tragedy.

When the pastor finished his eulogy, he asked if anyone would like to share memories of Deanna. I looked around the packed church, filled with adults and kids, probably Deanna's friends and perhaps some of Evelyn's and William's friends as well. No one rose and walked forward to the pulpit. I didn't blame them. The atmosphere was too dark and gloomy to share a funny or heartfelt story about the deceased, and anything anyone could say would just make the family sadder. I think everyone wanted to get this service over with and get out of the church.

I chanced another glance at the family as the choir sang "Amazing Grace," which I thought was an odd song choice for a child's funeral. Jack still stared straight ahead, his expression blank. Little William cried. Evelyn's face was buried in her hands, and I could hear Jody's sobs. What a depressing afternoon!

Chapter Eight

Monday, November 18th

P ark Ranger Liz Kelley was alone on patrol at Fort Abercrombie State Historical Park, but since she was the only ranger who worked at the 182-acre park, this was business as usual for her. Fort Abercrombie was a beautiful park, rich in history and nestled in a Sitka spruce forest. The park was bordered on its front edge by steep cliffs that plunged into the heavy surf of the ocean. The park had a small lake containing trout, and in the summer, small meadows burst with wildflowers of every hue. There were numerous campsites designed primarily for tent campers, and in the summer, the park was full of tourists.

This was not summer, though. It was a snowy, blustery November evening. Liz sometimes patrolled the main area of the park on foot when the weather was nice, but when it wasn't, she made her rounds in the beat-up pickup with the state park insignia on the door. In the summer, she spent most of the day out on the park grounds, answering visitors' questions and making sure they obeyed the park's rules. This time of the year, she spent most of her time huddled in the ranger's station with her computer, a small TV, and most importantly, a coffee maker. Liz had last driven the main roads of the park at 5:00 pm, and she hadn't seen a living soul. She had seen several deer huddled under the protection of the spruce trees, but she saw no trucks, cars, nor tents. When she got back to the ranger's station, however, she noticed headlights pulling into the park. It was too dark to determine the make or model of the vehicle, let alone see who the driver was, but it had to be teenagers. Who else would be out in the park on a snowy, November night? She hadn't seen the vehicle leave the park, but she assumed it had driven past while she was deep in concentration, working on her computer.

At 7:00 pm, Liz locked the ranger's station and climbed into the truck to make her final rounds for the evening. She was anxious to get home to her husband and dog, so this would be a quick trip down the main road. She wanted to make sure the vehicle she'd seen entering the park earlier hadn't slid off the slick roads. She hoped the driver had enough sense not to drive down one of the side roads in this weather, and she wasn't willing to drive down every small road looking for a phantom vehicle.

Liz thought about her husband, Dave, and Cholla, their golden retriever. In 20 minutes the three of them would be settled in front of a roaring fire listening to music. Maybe she should call Dave now and tell him to start heating the water for hot buttered rum.

Liz drove slowly in the blizzard conditions. Four inches of snow covered the ground, and the large, heavy, wet flakes were quickly adding to the amount. Liz estimated the wind was blowing 35 knots or more, causing the snow to whiz horizontally past her windshield. For a moment, she considered abandoning her last rounds and heading home, but she continued at a snail's pace, stopping every few feet to look left and right into the forest. *Only an idiot or an overzealous park ranger would be out here on a night like this.*

She reached the end and the concrete barrier where people could stand and look out over Spruce Cape and was happy to see there were no vehicles parked there. She did a U-turn and was starting back toward the park entrance when her headlights illuminated something bright pink a few feet off the road. At first, she thought it was a plastic bag, but it was too big. *Should I stop and check it or pretend I didn't see it and keep driving?* She sighed deeply, shifted into park, grabbed a flashlight from the glove compartment, and crawled out of the truck. She cinched her hood tight and slogged through the snow toward the pink object. After only a few steps, she realized she was looking at a pink, down coat. After several more steps, she saw there was someone in the coat. She hurried toward the fallen form, all thoughts of her husband and dog and their cozy family room vanished from her mind, and she began running through first aid protocols in her head. *Will I have to perform CPR? Do I have my rescue-breathing mask in my pocket? Should I put on rubber gloves before I touch the person?*

"Ma'am," she called, "can you hear me?" Liz slowed her pace as she neared what she assumed was an unconscious woman. "Ma'am?"

The woman was on her side facing away from Liz. Liz touched her arm and called to her again, and when the woman didn't reply, Liz rolled her onto her back. She took one look at her and stepped away from the body. She switched the flashlight to her left hand, and her right hand instinctually unsnapped her holster. She put her right hand on the butt of her gun while she swung the flashlight in a wide arc. She had seen a vehicle enter the park around 5:00 pm, but she had not seen it leave. Was the murderer still in the park? Was he watching her? She felt sweat run down her back, and she fought to control her emotions. It was no time to panic. She had to think clearly and act professionally.

Liz removed her hand from the butt of the gun and pulled her cell phone from her right rear pants' pocket. She dialed the trooper's office and talked to the night-duty dispatcher. She was proud her voice sounded steady as she reported she had found a dead body in the park and was certain the corpse was a victim of a homicide. *You can't cut your own throat, can you?*

The dispatcher told her he had been instructed to immediately call Sergeant Patterson if anyone called to report a homicide. Patterson wanted to be the first law-enforcement officer at the murder scene. The dispatcher asked Liz to stay with the victim until Patterson could get there.

"How long will that be?" Liz asked.

"Probably 15 to 20 minutes."

Liz agreed to remain near the corpse, but she wasn't about to stand out here in a blizzard, especially when she couldn't be certain the murderer wasn't still in the park, perhaps standing behind a tree watching her. She returned to her truck, turned up the heater, and turned on the radio to a country music station. A few moments later, she turned off the radio. She couldn't afford to compromise her senses. She needed to stay watchful and alert.

She did not believe the murderer was still in the park. He had probably left hours ago, cruising past the ranger's station with his headlights off so he wouldn't draw her attention. Nevertheless, she didn't know he was gone, and her life might depend on remaining watchful.

The 15 minutes she waited until she saw the headlights of the trooper SUV seemed like hours, but when the vehicle parked beside her truck she felt the tension drain out of her body. She opened the door, climbed from the truck, and shook hands with Trooper Sergeant Dan Patterson and Trooper Mark Traner.

"What do we have here, Liz?" Patterson asked.

"It's a bad one," she said leading them to the corpse that was now covered with a layer of snow. "Her throat was cut. I knew CPR wouldn't help her."

"Did she have much snow on her when you found her?" Traner asked.

A slight waver in his voice betrayed the young trooper's attempt to maintain a professional demeanor, and Liz realized this was probably his first murder victim too. "She had maybe half an inch on her, but there was snow underneath her too."

"So she was dumped here sometime this evening," Traner said.

"I drove this road at 4:00 pm, and I didn't see anything," Liz said. "She's off the road, so I may have missed her, but I don't think so. Also, a vehicle entered the park at 5:00 pm. I didn't see it leave, but it must have."

Both Patterson and Traner swung their flashlight beams in wide arcs, suddenly alert to the fact the perpetrator may still be in the area.

"Could you make out the type of vehicle?" Patterson asked.

"No," Liz said, and she felt as if she had failed to do her duty. "It was dark and snowing so hard by then I couldn't see much of anything. From the height of the headlights, though, I think it was either a pickup or an SUV."

"You said the vehicle entered the park at 5:00 pm, but the corpse only had half an inch of snow on it when you found it at 7:00 pm?" Traner asked.

Liz understood what Traner was thinking, and she had to admit the situation didn't make sense. "If she was dumped at 5:00 pm," she said slowly, "she should have had more snow on her."

"She wasn't killed here," Patterson said. "There's not enough blood."

"Maybe he killed her in his truck," Traner said.

"Possibly, but think what a mess that would make. He slit her throat; there would have been a lot of blood."

"Maybe she was already dead when he drove into the park, but he wanted to spend some time with her before he dumped her," Liz said quietly.

Both troopers turned and looked at her. "That's an unsettling thought," Traner said.

Liz shrugged. "It would take a monster to slit someone's throat, and I think spending quality time with a dead body is just the type of thing a monster would do."

Patterson knelt down and began examining the body. "She's fully clothed," he said. "Maybe he redressed her. That would have taken some time." He studied her face. He looked up at Liz and Traner. "Do either of you know who she is?"

They both shook their heads.

"I've never seen her," Traner said.

"I don't remember seeing her in the park," Liz added.

Patterson grunted. "I'll show her photo to Irene. If she's from Kodiak, Irene will know who she is. Why don't we get some photos and get her out of here? I think it's obvious this was a body dump, and with this snow, there's no point trying to find footprints."

"Maybe the killer waited until it started to snow to dump her so his tracks would disappear," Liz said.

"That's possible," Patterson said, "and if that's the case, it means he's had her stored somewhere until now. Hopefully, the medical examiner will give us some answers."

Once Patterson finished taking photos, Traner and Liz helped him lift the body into the back of the trooper SUV. "I'm beginning to feel like a hearse driver," Patterson said. "This is the second dead woman I've had in the back of my vehicle in the past few weeks. I hope this doesn't become commonplace."

Patterson asked Liz not to tell anyone about finding the murder victim. "I don't want to start a panic," he said. "I know we'll have to release the information soon, but I would like to talk to my superiors and get permission to contact the FBI before we release this to the public. Also, Liz, I think you should be brought in on this investigation, at least for a few days. He has been in the park once that we know of, and he may come back here. I'd like you to come over to trooper headquarters tomorrow at 1:00 pm for a meeting."

Liz nodded and crawled into her truck. She'd called her husband an hour earlier to tell him she would be late. She didn't tell him what had happened, but she would tell him when she got home. *I can trust him not to tell anyone.* She didn't think she would ever get the image of blonde hair, a pink parka, staring eyes and a slit throat out of her head. That vision was sure to haunt her nightmares.

Chapter Nine

Tuesday, November 19th

The following morning, Patterson transported the body to the airport where it was shipped to Anchorage. The previous evening, he had called Dr. Libby's personal cell number and requested he perform the autopsy on the latest victim.

"Was she killed in the same way as the other two?" Libby asked.

"Exactly the same," Patterson said.

"You've got a problem down there. As I told you before, I'll be happy to share my opinion with your boss if it will help get the FBI on this case. They know more about this type of murderer than the rest of us do."

"Thanks," Patterson said. "Let me know what you find during the autopsy, and then I'll decide what to do."

Patterson was already setting the wheels in motion, though. He'd talked to his boss, and they both agreed they needed to contact the FBI. He now phoned Kodiak Police Chief Howard Feeney and told him about the latest body. Feeney wasn't happy, but he agreed it was time to ask for help from the "big boys", as he called them. Feeney said he and Detective Horner would be at the 1:00 pm meeting, and he agreed not to tell any of his other officers about the latest victim.

"You won't be able to keep this quiet long," he said.

"I realize that," Patterson said. "I'd just like to keep it out of the papers until I can contact the FBI and get a task force organized."

Patterson closed his office door and considered who he would like to appoint to the task force for this case. He wanted to include two troopers besides himself. He knew Kodiak Police Detective Maureen

Horner would be an asset, and although Feeney would not be an asset, he could not very well exclude the chief of police. Liz Kelley would not be an active member of the task force, but she should attend the meetings, at least for a while. By noon, Patterson had his list.

Present at the 1:00 pm meeting were Patterson, Feeney, Horner, Trooper Johnstone, Trooper Traner, and Liz Kelley. Both Johnstone and Traner were young, and neither would bring much experience to the task force, but both troopers had impressed Patterson in the few months he had worked with them. Johnstone thought outside the box and often brought a unique perspective to an investigation. Mark Traner offered boundless energy and enthusiasm; traits Patterson considered valuable in an investigation that would likely force them all to work many hours of overtime.

Patterson brought everyone up to speed and then said he would like to form a joint task force with the Kodiak Police. Feeney agreed and asked Patterson if he would like to include another Kodiak police officer on the task force.

"At this point," Patterson said, "I'd like to keep the task force fairly small, but if the murders continue, we will need more of your detectives. Liz, here, isn't really part of the task force, but since one of the bodies was dumped in Abercrombie, I think it's important to keep her in the loop. She'll keep her eyes and ears open for any suspicious vehicles in the park." Patterson looked at Liz. "I think, for the time being, you should increase your patrols to at least once every two hours. Can you do that?"

Liz nodded. "Sure," she said, "but I don't know what I'm looking for."

"Neither do I," Patterson said. "Just keep your eyes open."

"Have you contacted the FBI yet?" Detective Horner asked.

"I've made a formal request, but I haven't spoken with an agent yet."

"Where do we start with this investigation?" Traner asked.

"I have no idea," Patterson said, "but this is an island, and as long as the perpetrator stays on this island, we should be able to find him."

"But if he jumps on a plane to Anchorage, we're screwed," Johnstone said.

Patterson nodded. "We need to identify the latest victim, so that would be a good place for you to start, Mark. I'll let all of you know what I hear from the coroner and the FBI, and we can start from there."

Three hours later, Patterson received a call from Liz Kelley.

"I was making my hourly rounds a few minutes ago and saw a red pickup truck stopped near where I found the corpse last night. I was quite a ways away on a side road, and before I could get to the main road, the truck sped away. I'm sorry, I didn't see the license plate."

"That's okay, Liz. Good work. Do you know what type of truck it was?"

"I think it was a Ford F-150. An older model. Dark red."

"This may be the clue we need to break this case wide open," Patterson said. "I'll send a trooper out there to put up a trail cam focused on the spot where we found the body. We'll aim another one at the park entrance."

"Okay," Liz said, "but I think the driver of the truck saw me driving toward him, and that's why he sped out of the park. I doubt he'll be back."

Just as Patterson was disconnecting with Liz, Traner knocked on his door.

"We have a name for the victim," Traner said. "Irene didn't recognize her, but her prints were in the system." He looked down at his notebook. "Her name is Amy Quinn. Her last known address was Anchorage, so she must have come to Kodiak only recently."

"Why were her prints in the system?" Patterson asked.

"She was arrested for solicitation."

"How many times?"

"Only once," Traner said.

"See if you can get any more information from the arresting officer."

"Will do," Traner said.

Chapter Ten

Friday, November 22nd

I poured myself a glass of Merlot and placed it and a peanut butter sandwich on the table in front of me. I tore open the bag of quinoa chips and poured a few on my plate. My cell phone buzzed in my purse. I considered ignoring it, but a call in the evening was most likely from one of my friends or my father, and I shouldn't really ignore any of those people. I fished the phone out of my purse and answered without looking at the display. The voice on the other end caused me to sit down hard on the couch.

"Jane, it's Nick Morgan. How are you?"

I didn't say anything for several seconds. I hadn't heard from FBI Special Agent Nick Morgan in nearly a year, and I hadn't expected to hear from him ever again. He had come to Kodiak a year and a half earlier to investigate the bombing of a floatplane. Since my young assistant had been killed in the bombing, I was also involved in the investigation. Nick and I became friends, and I thought our relationship might develop into something more than that, but he decided to give his marriage one more try, and when the investigation ended, he returned to Virginia. He had called me the previous November to relay some follow-up details about the investigation of the floatplane crash, but we'd kept the call formal, devoid of any personal details.

I pulled myself together and tried to sound cool and detached. I was glad he couldn't hear my thudding heart. "I'm fine, how are you?"

"Hanging in there. I've wanted to call you several times, but I didn't know what to say."

I didn't know what to say to that, so I remained silent. The image of Nick Morgan flooded my mind. I saw his athletic build, his black hair graying at the temples, the few lines on his face, and his strong hands. What I remembered most though, were his dusty blue eyes. When I'd first met him, intelligence blazed from those eyes, but after I got to know him better, I also saw the compassion they revealed.

"I wanted to let you know I'm coming back to your neck of the woods."

"Oh?" I hoped I sounded more casual than I felt.

"The Alaska State Troopers and the Kodiak Police Department contacted the FBI to request our assistance in solving a string of murders there. Since I'd recently been to Kodiak, my boss asked if I would be interested in taking the case." He paused for a moment. "I thought I should let you know I'll be on your island in a few days. Otherwise, it might be awkward if we run into each other. Kodiak isn't very big, so we're bound to bump into each other somewhere."

"A string of murders? I've heard of two murders in the past year."

Morgan remained silent for so long I thought the call had dropped, but then he said, "You know I shouldn't tell you this, but you have a sharp mind and undoubtedly know some of these people, so maybe you can be of some help. You've had four murders in the last few months on your little island."

"Four?"

"Deborah Sidle, a local prostitute, was murdered in May. Her body was dumped in the boat harbor. Deanna Kerr was murdered in Uyak Bay, presumably on the Fourth of July. Tasha Ayers, a high school senior, was killed in October, and the body of Amy Quinn, a prostitute from Anchorage, was found in Abercrombie Park four nights ago."

"Wait a minute," I said. "First of all, Deanna Kerr's death was an accident. I know her aunt."

"Not according to the medical examiner," Morgan said.

"How could he tell? I thought just a few bones were found."

"Yes, but her skull was bashed in, and the M.E. thinks from the angle and force of the impact, she was hit on the head with something very heavy."

"She was swept out of a boat in heavy seas. Couldn't she have hit her head on the boat or a log or a rock?"

"I doubt we could prove it in court, but our forensic experts say it's unlikely she could have accidentally hit her head in this way." He paused again and seemed to be debating whether to say more. Finally, he said, "I really shouldn't tell you this, but when the skeleton was found, her ankles were wired together. Our guys think the wire on her ankles was tied to something heavy and she was thrown overboard. Either the wire disintegrated or broke, but the body parted from the heavy object, and her remains eventually washed ashore. I'm sure whoever threw her overboard believed she would never be found, and it's a miracle she was."

"Does her family know about this?" If so, Sandy hadn't mentioned it to me.

"No, the family doesn't know Deanna was murdered. I imagine I will have the joy of informing them."

"I'm sorry," I said. "I could never do your job."

Morgan chuckled. "It's not all fun and games."

"The fourth victim," I said, "I haven't heard anything about her."

"It will be in your newspaper tomorrow. The police managed to keep it quiet for four days while they contacted us. They wanted help with the profile of the killer before the news went public. They are afraid a newspaper report of the crime might spook the killer, but I don't think he'll leave the island quite yet. He's the type of killer who is narcissistic and thinks he's smarter than the police. Why should he leave Kodiak? He hasn't been caught so far."

"Who found the body in Abercrombie?"

"The park ranger, why?"

"Liz Kelley, the park ranger, is a friend of mine."

"Jane, you can't tell her I told you anything about this murder. It will be public knowledge tomorrow, and then you can tell her you read it in the paper. Until then, you're not supposed to know about it."

"I understand," I said. "I feel terrible for Liz, though. This must have been a rough four days for her, and she hasn't been able to confide in anyone."

"I'm sure you're right," Morgan said.

"And you think all of these murders are related?"

"I can't be certain, but I find it difficult to believe there's more than one murderer running around Kodiak slitting women's throats."

"So they were all killed in the same way?"

"We know three of them had their throats slashed. We don't know how Deanna Kerr died. I think Deanna's murder might be the key to solving this case, though."

"Why is that?" I asked.

"The other bodies were found in or near Kodiak on the road system, but Deanna's was found during the summer on the other side of the island in Uyak Bay. I think it's likely the perpetrator had a summer job in Uyak, either as a fisherman or a cannery worker. We're looking for someone who lives in Kodiak part of the year but was in Uyak Bay on the Fourth of July, and that fact should narrow down any list of suspects we develop."

Morgan was smart. He was already working the case, and he hadn't even arrived in town yet. I had no doubt he would help solve it.

"Do you have any other evidence?"

"Not much, I'm afraid, but we're just beginning the investigation. The Kodiak Police have been investigating the murder of the victim found in the boat harbor, and the troopers were investigating the murder of the high school senior. No one was investigating the death of Deanna Kerr because until recently, they didn't know she had been murdered. Now we can put all these cases together, and the picture should become clearer."

"What if they aren't all related, though?"

"If the murders weren't all committed by the same person or persons, that fact should become obvious early in the investigation."

I paused a moment. "You have my number. If you have some spare time while you're in town, give me a call, and we'll catch up."

"I'd like that," Morgan said.

I disconnected and leaned back on the couch, my dinner forgotten. *Nick Morgan is coming back to Kodiak. I don't know if that is good or bad news.* I'd had feelings for the man and had been disappointed when he had reunited with his wife, but a relationship with him could never work. He lived on the other side of the country and was married not only to his wife but also to his job. He was a workaholic, and his work had created many of the stresses in his marriage.

I had been married once to a doctor, and I had thought we were happy until he left me for his nurse; what a sad cliché. After that, I decided never to enter another romantic relationship unless I fully trusted my partner and believed the relationship had a realistic chance of making it. Of course, how can you ever completely trust another human being? I hadn't been in a serious relationship since my divorce. Lately, I had dated Brad Simpson, a fish and game biologist, a few times. Brad was funny and made me laugh, but sparks weren't flying. On the other hand, just the thought of Nick Morgan set off rockets in my brain. *Rockets are never good.*

Chapter Eleven

Monday, December 2nd
10:00 am

M organ barely could see the runway as the Dash 8 descended through the thick clouds and heavy snow toward Kodiak. Wind buffeted the plane from side to side, and he wondered how the pilot would manage to control the plane and hit the runway with this poor visibility and turbulence. It seemed like only seconds between the time they popped out under the clouds and the plane touched down on the runway, bounced once, and then screeched to a stop in front of the small terminal.

Morgan grabbed his bag and briefcase and headed down the stairs of the plane. With all the traveling he did, he had learned to pack light. Snow and wind pummeled him as soon as he stepped out of the plane; he pulled the hood of his parka over his head and rushed toward the door of the airport. When he stepped inside the terminal, an Alaska State Trooper walked toward him and held out his hand.

"Agent Morgan, I'm Dan Patterson. It's nice to meet you."

Morgan shook Patterson's hand. "Please, call me Nick."

Patterson nodded. "Do you have luggage?"

"No, this is it," Morgan said. "I probably should get a rental car, though."

"Why don't you wait on that. You won't want to drive a rental car on these roads. We can chauffeur you around until the weather improves."

The men left the airport and hurried to the trooper's SUV. As they pulled out onto the highway, Morgan said, "I'm sure this weather isn't making your investigation any easier."

"Forget forensic evidence," Patterson said. "If you want to murder someone, winter in Kodiak is the time and place to do it. We've got zip for footprints or tire tracks."

"What about for the Ayers girl? It wasn't snowing then, was it?"

"For that one, we had heavy rain to conveniently wash away any evidence."

"The M.E. thinks the last victim was sexually assaulted, but he has no semen?" Morgan asked.

"Right. He found residue from a condom in the last victim, but no residue in the Ayers girl. He suspects the first victim was also sexually assaulted, but he couldn't be certain, and of course, there is no way to know what happened to Deanna Kerr."

"Her family still doesn't know she was murdered?" Morgan asked.

"No, we thought you would want to be there when we break the news."

"Do you think anyone in her family is capable of committing these crimes?" Morgan asked.

"Not really, but you said we should concentrate on individuals who spent the summer in Uyak Bay, or at least were on a boat in Uyak Bay around the Fourth of July and spent the remainder of the year in or around town. No one fits that picture any better than the Kerr family."

Morgan liked the way Patterson thought. He was already forming an opinion of the trooper as a sharp investigator. He was impressed Patterson had called the FBI so early in the investigation. Too many cops hated to ask for help, especially from the FBI; they wanted the glory of solving the case by themselves. Patterson, though, seemed more interested in catching the perpetrator before more women were killed. He wasn't thinking about his own career or his pride; he wanted only to utilize the best resources he could find to catch the killer.

They drove past a large tree; the leaves had long fallen from its branches, replaced instead by at least 20 bald eagles, standing wing to wing, occupying every free piece of real estate. Fifty feet away, another two dozen eagles perched on the ridge lines of two metal buildings.

"I remember seeing lots of eagles when I was here before," Morgan said, "but not this many in one place."

"It's because the cannery effluent is full of ground-up fish," Patterson said. "Eagles migrate to Kodiak from the mainland for easy, winter food. You see them everywhere this time of year, even perched on the back of pickup trucks."

"I can certainly smell the processing plant," Morgan said.

Patterson nodded and laughed. "I already have you registered at the Baranof Inn. Do you want to drop off anything there or go straight to our headquarters? I have a task force meeting planned to begin in half an hour. I wasn't sure your plane would be able to land in this weather, so I should call the other task force members and let them know you're here and the meeting is a go."

"I don't need to stop at the hotel," Morgan said. "Let's go to your headquarters, and I'll get organized."

At 11:00 am, Morgan followed Patterson into a conference room, and Patterson introduced him to Trooper Mark Traner, Trooper Ben Johnstone, Police Chief Howard Feeney, Detective Maureen Horner, and Park Ranger Liz Kelley.

"Liz is keeping an eye on things at the park for us," Patterson explained. "Thanks to her, we now believe the suspect drives a red Ford F-150 truck."

Morgan nodded. "It's smart to keep Liz in the loop. If he's used the park once, he may use it again. A serial murderer sometimes returns to either the kill location or to where he dumped the body, so he can relive the experience of the thrill of the crime."

"We placed surveillance cameras at the park entrance and where the body was dumped. The cameras are concealed, so I don't think they'll be detected."

"Excellent." Morgan nodded his approval. "What else do you have?"

"We've tried to run down the pickup truck," Patterson said, "but we haven't had much luck. There are more red pickups on this island than you would think, but none of them belong to anyone connected to the dead women, at least not as far as we can tell."

"The pickup may not be registered here," Morgan said.

Patterson nodded. "That's very possible." He looked at his notes. "So far we have three possible suspects. Let's see," he studied his notebook for several seconds. "Maureen, the first one is yours; why don't you tell us about him."

Detective Horner stood. She was at least 5'8" tall with shoulder-length, brown hair, and an angular face. Her dark blue eyes pierced Morgan as she spoke directly to him. He could tell she was not pleased to have the FBI involved in her investigation. Her voice was strong and confident as she relayed the facts.

"Caden Samuels is a local Kodiak fisherman. He owns the *Sea Mistress,* a 32-foot, wooden boat that has seen better days. Mr. Samuels has a lengthy record for bar fights, spousal abuse, and writing bad checks." Horner did not need notes as she recited Samuels' misdeeds. Her eyes never wavered from Morgan's face. "He has also been arrested numerous times for heroin possession and dealing drugs. He was seen talking to the first victim, Deborah Sidle, the night before her body was found floating in St. Paul Boat Harbor." She paused a few moments and then continued. "When interviewed, he claimed that he and Ms. Sidle were friends and stated he had nothing to do with her death. Mr. Samuels has no known ties to the other victims."

Once Morgan was certain Horner had finished her recitation, he said, "Tell me more about Mr. Samuels. Is he still using drugs?"

"I can't be certain," Horner said, "but I believe he is. His last arrest for drug possession was 13 months ago."

"The perpetrator of these crimes is a highly-organized individual. I doubt a drug user would be able to commit four murders and not leave any evidence," Morgan said. "Do you think Samuels is organized enough to pull off these murders?" He returned Horner's direct gaze.

Horner sighed and looked down for the first time since she began her recitation. "I find it hard to believe he's smart enough to outwit the police and the troopers, but I don't think we should mark him off our list just yet."

Morgan nodded. "Thank you, Detective Horner." He looked at Patterson. "Who else do we have?"

Patterson looked at Trooper Johnstone and nodded his head. "Ben?"

Johnstone stood and cleared his throat. "The latest victim, Amy Quinn, was last seen with," he looked down at his notepad, "Jerome Collins, a high-line crab fisherman, and tender operator. The night before Liz found Amy Quinn's body at Abercrombie, Amy was seen with Collins at The Anchor, a bar here in town. According to the bartender, Mr. Collins bought Ms. Quinn two drinks, and then they left the bar together. We interviewed Mr. Collins by phone, and he admitted he paid her for sex, but he claimed that when she left his car, she was still alive and well." Johnstone consulted his notes again before continuing. "Mr. Collins denied knowing the other victims, but according to the bartender, Collins liked prostitutes, and he had seen Collins with Ms. Sidle on several occasions."

"Not only that," Patterson said, "but Collins runs a tender for Uyak Cannery in the summer, and I checked with David Sturman, the superintendent of the cannery. Collins often picked up salmon from the Kerr's fish site, so it is likely he knew Deanna Kerr."

Morgan leaned back in his chair. This suspect had his interest. *Not only did Collins know the two prostitutes, but he likely knew Deanna Kerr and was in Uyak during the summer.* "Do you know if Collins was in Uyak over the Fourth of July?"

Patterson nodded. "According to Sturman, Collins and his boat, *Arctic Raider*, were in Uyak Bay over the Fourth."

"Give me more details about Mr. Collins," Morgan said.

Johnstone studied his notebook. "He's the divorced father of two sons – teenagers that live with his ex-wife. He has a house here in Kodiak, but he spends most of his time either on his boat or at his condo in Ixtapa, Mexico."

"You said you interviewed him by phone. Does that mean he is not in Kodiak now?" Morgan asked.

"He's in Dutch Harbor, getting ready for the Bering Sea Tanner crab fishery. Sturman gave me his cell phone number, and I was lucky to catch him before he headed out on his boat and out of cell-phone range."

"But he was in town when the latest body was found?"

"Yes. He left for Dutch Harbor the day after Amy Quinn's body was discovered."

"Does he have a red truck?"

"Not according to him."

"Does he have any connection to Tasha Ayers?"

Johnstone shrugged. "He said he doesn't know the girl, but she was in the same class as his oldest son so he may have been lying."

"We need to get him back to Kodiak and interrogate him further," Morgan said. He looked at Patterson.

Patterson nodded. "I'll contact the cannery he delivers to in Dutch, and they can get a message to him. He won't be happy."

"One more question," Morgan said. "When you say a crab high-liner, I picture one of those boats on the 'Deadliest Catch.' Do I have the right picture in my mind?"

"You do," Johnstone said. "The *Arctic Raider* is 130 feet long. It's a beautiful boat."

"And you said Collins uses his boat as a tender in the summer. A tender picks up salmon from the commercial fishermen and delivers the fish to the cannery, correct?"

Johnstone nodded. "Yes."

"So this is a guy who is organized, successful, and has resources," Morgan said. "This individual fits the profile I've developed much better than your first suspect. Do you have any other possible suspects?"

"At this time, we have one more suspect who interests us," Patterson said. "His name is Bobby Saunders, a Kodiak man who worked at Uyak Cannery this past summer. When we called Sturman to ask him about Collins, he told us about Mr. Saunders. According to Sturman, a female worker at the cannery claimed Mr. Saunders tried to rape her, but she managed to escape. Sturman said he immediately fired Saunders, but this all happened a month after Deanna Kerr went missing."

"Can you tie Saunders to the other victims?" Morgan asked.

"Not really," Patterson said, "but Saunders lives in Kodiak, so it's possible he knew the other victims. He says he didn't know them, but Mr. Saunders has had several run-ins with the police including some for assault and one arrest for attempted rape, so I'm not sure we can believe what he says."

"Is Saunders working now?" Morgan asked.

"He has a job at a cannery here in Kodiak. He manages to stay employed most of the time, and according to his boss here in Kodiak, he's a good worker."

"I suggest getting all three of the suspects in here for more in-depth interviews," Morgan said. "From your reports and the photos of the crime scenes, I believe the perpetrator of these crimes is a successful male in his late 20s or 30s but possibly younger. He not only has a job, but he excels at his job. He is narcissistic and believes he is smarter than the police, and this works to our advantage because he doesn't believe we'll catch him. In all likelihood, he will stay in this area and continue to prey on women, at least for a while." Morgan cleared his throat. "I also believe he is the type of predator who collects trophies. He may keep a victim's earrings, necklace, scarf, underwear, or something else. We need to go to the victim's families and find out if a favorite necklace, something the victim always wore, a ring, or anything else, was missing from the victim's body when she was found. If the perpetrator was the guy in the red truck Liz saw at Abercrombie, then he likes to re-visit the places where he dumped his victim's bodies, so we should get a camera set up near Chiniak where the Ayers girl was found and maybe another camera pointed at the boat harbor where the first victim was found. Since the first victim could have been dumped anywhere in or near the harbor, though, it's less likely he will visit the spot where she was found. Sergeant Patterson, perhaps you and I can come up with a game plan for re-interviewing everyone. I would like to talk to Deanna's and Tasha's friends, teachers, counselors, and the principal at the school, and of course the victims' families. Do we know anything about the families of Deborah Sidle and Amy Quinn?"

"I've talked to Deborah's father," Horner said, "Her mother has been dead for 15 years, and the father had very little to do with his daughter. I found out more about her from two of her friends here in town, but even they didn't seem to know much about her life."

Johnstone said, "I'm trying to track down Amy Quinn's next of kin, but I haven't had much luck. According to the Anchorage police, she came to Alaska from Seattle, but I haven't been able to get any further than that yet."

"Let me know if you find out more," Morgan said. "There's one more thing," he added. "I received a text message from the FBI lab, and the forensic experts think the throats of victims one, three and four were slit with a long knife, like a fillet knife."

"Brilliant," Chief Feeney said. "You've just narrowed the suspect pool to the entire island. Everyone on Kodiak owns at least one fillet knife."

After the rest of the group had filed out of the conference room, Patterson turned to Morgan. "Shall we drive out to the Kerr residence and let them know their daughter was murdered?"

Morgan nodded. He would have preferred to talk to Deanna's and Tasha's teachers before interviewing the parents, but he knew the authorities should inform Deanna's parents that her death had been ruled a homicide. If they heard this news from someone other than the police, they would not be happy. As much as Morgan hated passing along bad news to victims' families, he wanted to watch Deanna's parents' reactions when they heard their daughter had been murdered. Morgan knew parents killed their children all the time, all over the world. This case had the feel of a predator stalking young women, but he couldn't afford to have tunnel vision. At this point, everyone was a suspect.

He followed Patterson to his SUV.

"How do you want to handle this?" Patterson asked.

"This is your case," Morgan said. "I'm just here for assistance. I think you should tell both parents at once, though. I would like to see how they react to the news."

Patterson nodded and started the engine. He drove slowly out the road while large snowflakes whipped past the windshield. He pulled into the Kerr's driveway, and he and Morgan stepped out of the SUV. Morgan bent his head against the wind as they walked up to the porch. Jack Kerr opened the front door and ushered Patterson and Morgan into the foyer.

Patterson introduced Morgan and then said, "We're sorry to bother you again, Jack, but we need to speak with you and Jody for a few minutes."

"I think Jody is asleep," Jack said. "Is it necessary to bother her?"

"I'm afraid so," Patterson said.

"I'll get her," Kerr said. "Show yourselves into the great room. It's warmer in there by the fire."

Morgan and Patterson removed their boots, walked into the great room, and sat in the two chairs facing the couch. They didn't speak as they waited for the Kerrs to return. Jody Kerr was again dressed in a bathrobe, and Morgan could tell she had been sedated as she shuffled into the room and Jack helped her sit on the couch.

Morgan and Patterson both stood as the Kerrs seated themselves. Morgan introduced himself to Jody, and she acknowledged him with a faint nod.

"I'm sorry to bother you folks again," Patterson said, "but we need to inform you that Deanna's death has been ruled a homicide."

Jody sat back hard on the couch, her arms wrapping her in an embrace. Morgan studied Jack, whose face turned a blotchy red.

"That's ridiculous," Jack said. "People saw her leave the party. She was alone in her skiff. She got caught in heavy seas. Her engine probably died. She somehow fell or got swept overboard. How could that be murder?"

Patterson exhaled a deep breath. "I know this is difficult to hear, but her ankles were wired together, and it is unlikely she did that to herself. I suppose we can't rule out suicide, but there's no reason to suspect she killed herself is there?"

At the mention of suicide, Jack Kerr stood, his face now beet red. "No!" He bent over and yelled into Patterson's face. "Deanna would never do that. She was a happy girl."

Morgan looked at Jody Kerr. Her mouth gaped, and large tears slowly rolled over her cheeks.

"Ma'am," Morgan said, "do you agree with your husband? Would there be any reason your daughter would want to harm herself?"

Jody Kerr slowly shook her head. Her mouth moved as if she was trying to say something, but no words came out.

"Of course she would never harm herself," Jack said.

"Why don't you sit down, Jack," Patterson said. "I know this is difficult, but we have to ask these questions. Something apparently happened to Deanna sometime after she left the Fourth of July party, and we need to find out what that was."

Jack stood rigid for several more seconds, and then he seemed to deflate as the anger seeped out of him. He sank onto the couch, put his head in his hands, and sobbed. Patterson and Morgan waited patiently for him to recover. After several minutes, he sat up, pulled his handkerchief from his pocket and wiped his face. His wife never moved or even glanced at her husband. Her gaze remained fixed as tears continued to trickle from her eyes.

"If Deanna's death was anything other than an accident, then someone killed her. My baby would never take her own life," Jack said.

"We are treating this as a murder investigation," Patterson said. "We'll do everything we can to find out who murdered your daughter. Is there anything you can tell us?"

"What do you mean?" Jack asked.

"Was there anyone at the Fourth of July party or anyone in Uyak Bay last summer who took an unusual interest in Deanna?"

Jack thought for a moment. "No one that I know of. She was hanging out with the other kids at the party. To be honest, I didn't pay much attention to them, but when we left, Jody waved to Deanna to let her know we were leaving, and Deanna was all smiles. She was sitting around a bonfire with her friends, laughing and talking."

"Did you know everyone at the party?" Morgan asked.

"No, of course not," Jack said. "I knew all the set-netters, and there were some cannery people and tender operators there I knew, but I didn't know all the crew members. Crews change from one year to the next, so I rarely bother to get to know another fisherman's crewmen."

"Could you make a list for us of everyone you can remember who was at the party? We'll contact each fisherman and get the names of their crew members," Patterson said.

"Sure," Jack said, "but it will take me a while."

"I'll send someone over to pick it up tomorrow," Patterson said.

"What about you, Mrs. Kerr," Morgan asked, "do you know anyone whom your daughter was having trouble with?"

Jody Kerr looked like a zombie. She didn't seem to know she had just been asked a question. Her gaze remained fixed, staring straight ahead. The tears had stopped, but her face was still wet. Morgan's question seemed to remind Jack his wife was in the room. His head jerked toward Jody, and he reached over and put his hand on her arm.

"Jody's having a tough time with this," Jack said. "The doctor gave her sedatives."

Morgan thought Jody looked as if she had taken too many of those sedatives. He would have liked to chat one-on-one with Deanna's mother because teenage girls sometimes tell their mothers things they don't tell their dads. That chat would have to wait, though, until Jody was less medicated.

"Did Deanna have a computer, an iPad, or a smartphone?" Morgan asked.

Jack nodded. "She had a laptop and a smartphone."

"Would you mind if we take a look at those?" Morgan asked.

Jack began shaking his head as soon as Morgan began asking the question. "We got rid of them," he said. "We don't let the kids take their computers and phones to the fish site. There's no internet out there, and we want our summers to be family time. But, when we got back to town, the first thing I did was destroy Deanna's phone and computer." He shrugged. "I couldn't stand to look at them. I shouldn't have gotten rid of them so soon, I know." He shook his head again. "I'm sorry they're gone."

Morgan was surprised Jack had thrown away Deanna's computer. *Why didn't he given it to one of the other kids?* Still, he could only guess at how anguished Jack must have been after Deanna's death. Maybe throwing away Deanna's things had made him feel as if he were moving forward with his life.

Patterson stood and looked from Jack to Jody and back to Jack. "If you think of anything to aid us in this investigation, please call us immediately. Deanna was one of four women murdered on Kodiak in the last few months. These murders may or may not be related, but we are considering all possibilities."

"You think a serial killer murdered Deanna?" Jack asked.

"I don't know, Jack," Patterson said, "but at this point, we can't rule out that possibility."

"What did you think?" Patterson asked Morgan when they were back in the SUV. Patterson gripped the steering wheel and stared out the windshield through the heavy snow.

"Both parents seem to be distraught over their daughter's death," Morgan said. "I would like to interview the mother again, by herself if possible, but she'll have to be less sedated than she was today."

"She was sedated when I dropped by to tell them we'd found Deanna's remains, but she wasn't as out of it as she was today. I could at least talk to her then, and she would respond."

"Let's give her a few days and try again," Morgan said. "I'd like to interview Deanna's and Tasha's teachers as soon as possible."

"When we get back to headquarters I'll call Principal Daniel and set up a time to go over to the school. We did talk to Tasha's teachers already."

"I know you did," Morgan said, "but let's do it again. If they know both Deanna and Tasha were murdered, maybe they can point out any connections the girls had."

Chapter Twelve

Monday, December 2nd
4:00 pm

M organ and Patterson arrived at the school at 4:00 pm. They decided to interview Sandy Miles first. Not only did Sandy have both Tasha and Deanna as students, but Sandy was also Deanna's aunt and might be able to provide insight into Deanna's family dynamics.

Patterson knocked on the door to the mathematics classroom, and it was opened by a woman in her early thirties with close-cropped brown hair, piercing blue eyes, and the lithe build of a runner.

"Sergeant Patterson, please come in," Sandy Miles said.

"Ms. Miles, I'd like to introduce Special Agent Nick Morgan with the FBI."

Sandy shook Morgan's hand. "Please call me Sandy. Come in and sit down." She gestured to two of the student desks, and she settled in another desk across the aisle from them. "Do you have more questions about Tasha?"

"Yes, and we also have another matter to discuss," Patterson said.

Morgan glanced around the classroom, intrigued by all the decorations. He had never given the idea of decorating a math classroom any thought, but Sandy Miles had gone to great lengths to brighten the atmosphere for students studying what he assumed many considered a tedious subject. Mathematical equations, ranging from simple addition problems to what he assumed were advanced calculus equations, covered the walls, and geometric figures from triangles to pyramids to spheres to squares to others whose names he couldn't recall dangled from the ceiling. There was no question what subject was taught in this classroom.

"I'll be happy to help you in any way I can," Sandy said.

"First of all, ma'am, this first bit of news may be difficult for you to hear." Patterson said.

"Oh," Sandy sucked in a breath, and Morgan imagined her spine stiffening as she sat straighter in her chair.

Patterson lowered his voice. "The coroner has ruled your niece's death a homicide."

"Deanna? Weren't there only bones left so how could they tell she was murdered?"

"Her ankle bones were wired together. We believe the wire was attached to a rock or an anchor. The wire apparently broke, allowing ocean currents to move Deanna's remains to shore," Patterson said.

"Oh my God!" Sandy's hand flew to her mouth, and tears rolled out of her blue eyes.

"I'm sorry. I know this is rough," Patterson said.

"Do Jack and Jody know?"

"Yes ma'am, we talked to them earlier today," Patterson said.

"Jody won't survive this," Sandy said. She pulled a tissue from her skirt pocket and wiped her eyes.

"Jody appeared to be heavily sedated," Morgan said. "Do you know anything about the medicine she's taking?"

"No, but I think Jack gives it to her." Sandy shook her head. "It's easier for him to keep her sedated, but it isn't good for her. She'll never work through this grief if she's drugged all the time, and her kids need her. I've talked to Jack about it, but he just keeps giving her the pills."

"It's a sad situation," Patterson said. "No parent should have to bury a child."

"I don't understand how Deanna could have been murdered," Sandy said. "Her friends watched her leave the party alone. It was windy, so everyone assumed she had an accident. Where would she have met someone who could have murdered her?"

"When the Coast Guard found her boat, the cowling was off the outboard. It looked as if Deanna may have had outboard problems.

Originally, we believed she was bending over the outboard trying to fix the engine when a wave slammed into her and knocked her out of the skiff." Patterson shrugged. "It is also possible, though, that someone stopped to offer assistance."

"And, what? This good Samaritan killed her?"

Patterson nodded. "Right now, that's the only scenario we can imagine. As you said, she was out in the middle of the bay in a skiff by herself. How else would she have come into contact with another person?"

"There is one other possible explanation, Sandy," Morgan said. "Deanna could have done this to herself. Do you think that's a possibility?"

Sandy's right hand slapped the desktop. "Absolutely not! Deanna was a happy girl. She would never commit suicide."

"That's what her parents said," Morgan said, "but we have to ask these questions."

Sandy sighed. "I know; I understand. I didn't mean to get upset; this is just a lot to take in."

"Tell us about Deanna," Morgan said.

Sandy stared at the ceiling for a moment, lost in thought and then said, "Deanna was a good girl, a sweet girl. She was an excellent student and active in student politics. She was also a good athlete; she played volleyball, basketball, and was a hurdler in track. Don't get me wrong," Sandy leveled her gaze at Morgan. "I'm not naive. Deanna was popular, and I know she probably drank some alcohol at parties and did a few other things she didn't want her parents to find out about, but she was well-grounded, and her parents had very little trouble with her."

"Did Deanna and Tasha Ayers have anything in common with each other?" Patterson asked.

"Why? Do you think their deaths are related?"

"We don't know yet," Patterson said," but we're trying to cover every angle."

"I don't remember ever seeing Deanna and Tasha have a conversation. Tasha didn't talk to many people, and she particularly avoided the popular kids. I don't know that she had any animosity against those kids, but she seemed to want to stay away from them. Tasha was a year older than Deanna, and I never had the two of them in the same math class. Tasha took pre-algebra; that class is required for all freshmen. My other math classes are optional, and Tasha wasn't interested until this year when she surprised me by signing up for algebra. She was bright enough, and as I recall, she got decent grades in pre-algebra, but she rarely attended the algebra class. I don't think math was her thing."

"And Deanna?" Patterson asked.

"Deanna loved math and science, and she took every math class she could. Deanna took tough classes and got As and Bs. She would have done well in college." Sandy's gaze dropped to the floor, and Morgan thought she was about to start crying again.

"Tell us more about Tasha," Morgan said.

Sandy shrugged. "I was aware she frequently skipped school, and I knew her grades were poor this year. As I told Sergeant Patterson when he questioned me after Tasha's murder, Linda Bragg, the English teacher, knew Tasha better than I did. Also, the school counselor, Paul Mather, could probably give you some insights into Tasha's short life."

"Sandy," Patterson said. "I don't want you to be offended by this next question, but since you were Deanna's aunt, you probably have some idea what her home life was like. Did she have a good relationship with her parents and siblings?"

Sandy took a deep, steadying breath. "Deanna seemed very close to her parents, and she adored her little brother and sister. Of course, they had spats, and Deanna was a teenager, so she had a few arguments with her parents, but they were a loving family, and they all looked forward to their summers out at the fish site."

"I think that's all we have for now," Patterson said. All three stood, and Patterson and Morgan shook Sandy's hand. "If you think of anything else about either girl, no matter how insignificant it seems to you, please give us a call."

Morgan followed Patterson from the mathematics room down the hall to the English room.

Patterson chuckled when they walked in the room. "I see we've moved from Shakespeare to Chaucer and Milton," he said.

Morgan glanced at the drawings on the walls and immediately understood Patterson's reference. Some of the artwork depicted scenes of pilgrims from Chaucer's work while other fiery images must represent hell and the writings of Milton.

Linda Bragg looked up from the pile of papers on her desk. "Sergeant, I'm impressed. You remember your English literature."

"Not well, I'm afraid, but I feel your students' pain."

This brought an even bigger smile to her lips. "And they call water-boarding torture."

Patterson introduced Morgan, and Linda Bragg stood, grabbed two foldable chairs from the corner of the room and set them in front of her desk. She invited Patterson and Morgan to sit and returned to her chair behind her desk.

"Ms. Bragg," Patterson said. "The coroner has ruled the death of Deanna Kerr a homicide."

"I don't understand," she said, "I thought she was in a boating accident."

"No," Patterson said. "We think she was hit on the head, her ankles wired together and tied to a rock, and she was thrown overboard."

Linda Bragg stared at Patterson, her mouth agape. "Who would do something like that?"

"That's what we're trying to figure out, ma'am. We're also trying to find out if Deanna's murder is in any way related to Tasha's murder."

"Why would it be?" Linda asked. "They were murdered months apart and on different sides of the island."

"Their murders may not be related," Morgan said, "but we're trying to determine if they had anything in common or if they were associated with any of the same people."

"I see," Linda said. "You think the same person murdered both of them?"

"We don't know, ma'am," Patterson said. "Did you ever see Deanna and Tasha together?"

"Never," Linda answered immediately and shook her head for emphasis. "I had both girls in my creative writing class last year. Deanna sat near her friends, and Tasha sat alone in the back of the class. Deanna was a better student, but Tasha was the more talented writer of the two. As I explained to Sergeant Patterson the last time he interviewed me, English, and more precisely writing, was Tasha's favorite subject. She got decent grades in my classes until this year, but this semester I couldn't inspire her to write. On the few occasions she actually showed up for class, she seemed distant and distracted."

"Did she write about anything in particular?" Morgan asked.

Linda leaned back in her chair. "I've been thinking about what she wrote. Most of her papers were creative. She was into dragons and castles; some of her stuff was very graphic, but she had a vivid imagination. I was alarmed by some of the vivid sex scenes she wrote, though. I try not to censor my students as long as their words don't harm anyone else, but Tasha seemed to know too much about sex. I realize many of my high school students are sexually active, but Tasha seemed to have too much knowledge about aberrant sexual behavior. Some of her stuff made me blush."

"Did you talk to her about it?" Patterson asked.

"Not really, although I did tell her that I personally would like her to tone things down a bit, and she did. I have been thinking about one assignment I gave my students, though. I asked the kids to write a biographical piece, and I felt Tasha was trying to play me. I wasn't sure what to make of it. I talked to Tasha, and she admitted she'd made up most of it. I didn't give it much more thought, but after she was murdered, I remembered it and wondered if there was some truth to it. I thought about calling you, Sergeant, but I gave the paper back to her, and it's been a year; I only vaguely remember what she wrote."

"Anything you can remember might help us, ma'am."

Linda let out a deep breath. "Well, I remember Tasha wrote that her father left when she was a baby, and her mother has had a string of boyfriends since then. According to Tasha, some of her mother's boyfriends abused Tasha. She didn't describe the abuse, so I don't know if it was physical, sexual, or both. Tasha did say her brother sexually abused her, and that's when I became suspicious I was reading a work of fiction instead of a memoir."

"Why is that?" Patterson asked.

"I had Tim Ayers as a student. He's been out of school three years now, but he was a good kid. He was a wrestler and a swimmer, and he got fairly good grades. I find it hard to believe the kid I knew would sexually abuse his little sister."

Morgan knew monsters were often difficult to identify. *They walk among us and act like normal, respectable people.* "Do you know where Tim Ayers is now?"

"He's still in Kodiak," Linda said. "I ran into him in the grocery store the other day. He works as a hunting and fishing guide in the spring, fall, and summer, and I think he does part-time jobs here in town in the winter."

"What about Deanna?" Morgan asked. "Did any of her papers tell you much about her life?"

Linda shook her head. "As I said, Deanna was a good student; she got mostly As and Bs on her tests, and her writing was fine, but nothing exceptional. She seemed like a happy, normal high school student."

Patterson thanked Linda Bragg and reminded her to call him if she thought of anything else.

Jonathan Grand, the history teacher, looked as if he was approaching retirement age, and his classroom was old-school. The walls were mostly bare except for a map of the United States depicting Civil War battles, a map of Germany showing battles from WWI and WWII, a map of the South Pacific, also designating locations where WWII battles had taken place, and a map of the Middle East, depicting more recent conflicts. This classroom reminded Morgan of his high school history classroom with nothing frilly there, just the facts.

Jonathan Grand was not happy to have his test grading interrupted. He did not offer Patterson and Morgan seats, and he did not stand and shake their hands. He simply glared at them over his reading glasses. He didn't even blink when Patterson told him that Deanna Kerr's death had been ruled a homicide, and he seemed reluctant to divulge any information about Deanna or Tasha.

Finally, he said, "I had both Deanna and Tasha in my U.S. History class last year. I remember they worked in the same group on one of my group assignments."

"Do you remember them interacting much?" Patterson asked.

"No I do not," Grand said. "Deanna put in a reasonable amount of effort on the project, but when Ms. Ayers graced us with her presence, she sat quietly and offered little to the group. Jake Small, the group leader, complained to me that Tasha did not do her share of the work, so I failed her and gave the rest of the group a B- on the assignment."

Morgan wasn't surprised this old crank could remember a grade he'd given on a project a year ago. *Grades are probably all the old guy thought about. If there is a Mrs. Grand, she has my sincere sympathy.*

"I wouldn't want that old geezer as my history teacher," Patterson said after they had left Grand's room and were walking down the hall.

"He reminded me exactly of my high school history teacher," Morgan said. "It is interesting, though, someone finally put Tasha and Deanna in the same place at the same time. It's probably a long shot, but maybe we should find out who else was in that history group."

Patterson grunted. "I hope we get better leads than that." He looked at his watch. "It's after 5:00 pm, and I assume the teachers will be heading home soon. What do you say we leave the rest of Tasha's and Deanna's teachers until tomorrow and instead talk to the guidance counselor next?"

Morgan nodded. "Lead the way."

Paul Mather was on the telephone when they knocked on his open door. He waved to them and invited them into his office. They walked past the conversation pit toward the window where Mather sat behind his desk.

"Someone just walked into my office, hon, so I'll see you in a little while." He disconnected, stood, and held out his hand. "Sergeant Patterson, nice to see you again."

Patterson introduced Morgan and again explained that Deanna's death had been ruled a homicide and they were at the school to learn more about both Tasha and Deanna and to find out if the girls had any connection to each other.

"That is very sad news about Deanna Kerr," Mather said. "She was a sweet kid with a bright future. You think she and Tasha were killed by the same individual?"

"We don't know," Patterson said, "but we are trying to determine if the girls had any links between them."

"Didn't Deanna die on the other side of the island?" Mather asked.

"Yes sir, she did, but we still think there is a possibility her murder could be linked to Tasha Ayers' murder."

"I'm not sure how I can help you," Mather said. "I don't know of any link between the two girls. Tasha was a loner, and Deanna had a large group of friends."

"So as far as you know, they did not have any of the same friends?" Morgan asked.

"I counseled Tasha," Mather said, "and I am fairly certain she did not have any friends at this school. She certainly didn't run around with the popular kids."

"Did you also counsel Deanna?" Morgan asked.

"I'm sure I offered her some career counseling, but I'd have to check my files to see what we talked about. She didn't need much from me, so it was probably a short session. I'm required to evaluate every freshman, and then I talk to them again when they are juniors and seniors. Deanna did not have any behavioral problems requiring my intervention, so we just had the usual generic 20-minute conversation."

"But you were her basketball coach?" Patterson asked.

"Yes, that's right. Deanna was on my basketball team. She wasn't a starter, but she played a few minutes every game. She was actually a much better volleyball player than she was a basketball player."

"And you don't coach volleyball?" Patterson asked.

"No, Gordon Small is the girls' volleyball and the boys' basketball coach. He probably knew Deanna better than I did, because he thought she had a great deal of potential as a volleyball player. I know he coached her in strength and endurance training. He's also the girls' track coach, and Deanna was on the track team. I think she was a hurdler."

"Thank you," Patterson said. "We'll talk to him. What about Deanna's friends? Do you know who she hung out with?"

"I know a few of them, but I couldn't give you an extensive list. I'd suggest starting with her volleyball and basketball teammates. Those girls are tight."

Patterson and Morgan shook hands with Paul Mather. "I hope you find the monster responsible for the deaths of these girls soon," he said. "I recently brought in a grief counselor to talk to some of the kids. The girls, in particular, have been very upset about the deaths of Tasha and Deanna. When they find out Deanna was murdered and didn't die in an accident, I'm sure I will have another crisis on my hands."

"Is there anyone, in particular, having trouble dealing with these deaths?" Morgan asked.

"No, as I said, it's mainly the girls who are scared. Deanna was popular, so her friends miss her. She's been gone since July, but finding her bones in October, just a few days after Tasha was found murdered, was quite a shock for all of us. It hits high school kids hard when one of their friends die. It's bad enough to have a friend die in an accident, but to have a friend murdered is unthinkable." Mather shook his head.

Mather told Patterson and Morgan that Gordon Small's office was next to the locker room in the gym. It was 5:20 pm but Mather said Small usually stayed late. Even if he didn't have practice, he often had to supervise kids who were working out in the weight room after school.

The door to Small's office was closed, and Patterson knocked softly on it. Several seconds later, the door flew open. A short, balding man in his mid-forties looked up at Patterson, startled.

"Oh, I thought you were one of the kids returning some gear. I'm trying to get out of here and go home."

"Mr. Small, I am Sergeant Patterson with the Alaska State Troopers, and this is Special Agent Nick Morgan with the FBI. Can we steal a few minutes of your time before you leave for the day?"

Small ran a hand over his balding pate. "The troopers and the FBI; this must be serious. Sure, sure, come in and have a seat."

Morgan was first to follow Small into his office. The room was decorated with posters of sports figures, including football players, basketball players, and Olympic champions. Small had a gym locker behind his desk, and he hurried to the locker and shut the door, but not before Morgan glimpsed a poster of a *Sport's Illustrated* swimsuit model taped to the inside of the locker door. This wasn't the raciest swimsuit photo ever to grace the pages of the magazine, but Morgan thought not only did it seem odd a man in his forties would tape a photo of a swimsuit model to his locker, but this was a man who coached high school girls. The photo was inappropriate for any coach or teacher to have in his office, and Morgan guessed Principal Daniel did not know it existed.

Now was not the time to talk about the poster, though. Patterson and Morgan wanted Coach Small to tell them more about Deanna and her friends, and antagonizing him by mentioning the poster would not further that goal. Morgan and Patterson settled into two folding chairs in front of Small's desk, while Small sat in his desk chair.

"What can I do for you?" Small asked.

Patterson told him Deanna's death had been ruled a homicide and said they were trying to get a feel for what Deanna had been like and who her friends had been. "Paul Mather said you probably knew her better than he did."

Small picked up a red hair ribbon from his desk, folded it, stuffed it in his top desk drawer, leaned back in his chair, and shrugged. "I'd agree with that statement. I had her on the volleyball team for two years, and I think she only played basketball one year."

Morgan noted Small did not seem surprised to hear Deanna had been murdered. Of course, by now, he could have heard the news from one of the teachers they had interviewed earlier.

"I understand Deanna was a good volleyball player," Patterson said.

Small nodded. "She was very good. I began starting her on varsity toward the end of her freshman year, and she started every match as a sophomore. We missed her this season." As soon as the words were out of his mouth, he wrinkled his nose and shook his head. "That didn't come out right. The entire team was shocked and saddened by her death, and because of that, we weren't very good this year. Deanna was more than a good player, she was a motivator, and she was nice to everyone. Without her, the team seemed to fall apart. No one wanted to play without her, and I have to admit I couldn't blame them. It's hard to get excited about a silly game when one of your friends, and for me, one of my kids, has died. The team will be extremely upset to hear she was murdered."

"Do you think you could assemble her teammates after school tomorrow, so we could talk to them?" Patterson asked.

"Sure, I can do that," Small said.

"We'll try to get the basketball players together too," Patterson said.

"Most of them will be the same girls, but there might be a few on the basketball team that weren't on the volleyball squad," Small said. "I'll try to get them all together tomorrow afternoon."

"What can you tell us about Deanna?" Morgan asked.

"Like I said, she was a good volleyball player, and she kept her grades up, so I never had to worry about her eligibility. She was always positive. There was no drama with Deanna. High school girls can be full of drama, but there was none of that with Deanna. She was a great kid." He shook his head. "I can't imagine who would want to kill her."

"In addition to coaching girls' volleyball, you also coach boys' basketball and track, and you're the P.E. instructor. Is that correct?" Patterson asked.

"Pretty much, but I'm mainly the boys' track coach. Vivian Lyne coaches the girls. Deanna was also a member of the track team."

"Did you have Tasha Ayers for P.E.?" Patterson asked.

"Every freshman is required to take P.E. It's an elective after that. I had Tasha as a student when she was a freshman, but gentlemen, I have had a lot of freshmen in my P.E. classes over the years. A few stand out in my mind, but most don't. I can't tell you anything about

Tasha Ayers. I could check her records to see what grade I gave her, but other than that..." He shrugged.

Patterson and Morgan stood and shook Small's hand. "When would be a good time for us to interview the girls tomorrow?" Patterson asked.

"How about 3:00 pm? I'll assemble them a few minutes before the end of school."

Patterson thanked Small, and he and Morgan stepped out of the high school and into a raging blizzard.

"Wow," Patterson said. "I didn't expect the snow to be this bad."

Morgan pulled his hood over his head. Daylight had long since departed, and Morgan felt hypnotized by the snow dancing in the glow of the lights illuminating the high school parking lot. Between the howling wind and the need to bury his face in his coat, he didn't attempt to hold a conversation with Patterson. Once they were in the SUV, Patterson turned the heater to high and grabbed the ice scraper, using the brush end to clear the snow from the window. He climbed back in the vehicle and rubbed his hands together while he waited for the interior to warm.

"Did you see the poster Coach Small had in the locker behind his desk?" Morgan asked.

"No," Patterson said. "I saw him shut the locker door, but I didn't see anything in the locker."

"He had a poster of a *Sport's Illustrated* swimsuit model taped to the inside of his locker door."

"You're kidding!"

"No," Morgan said. "I got a clear look at it."

Patterson looked at Morgan and groaned. "That's not a crime, but it should be," he said. "The creep coaches young girls. Maybe I should have a talk with Principal Daniel and let her know what you saw."

"That might be a good idea," Morgan said, "but don't do it yet. We may need Small's help with this investigation. Besides, if he has any brains, the poster has been ripped to shreds by now."

"I would like to see what else he has in his locker," Patterson said.

Morgan nodded. "I think we should keep an eye on him. He didn't seem surprised when you told him Deanna had been murdered."

"Yes, and before he caught himself, I thought he was going to say Deanna ruined their volleyball season by dying," Patterson said.

Patterson dropped Morgan at the front door of the Baranof Inn, and Morgan was glad to get checked into the hotel and order room service. He settled at the desk in his room, devoured the steak, and sipped the scotch. He considered calling Jane but fought the urge. Until he called her the other night, they hadn't spoken to each other in a year. *She's probably involved in a serious relationship by now, and I don't want to make a fool of myself by acting too interested.* The last thing he had told her about his private life was that he and his wife had decided to give their marriage another try. The reconciliation had lasted less than a month. When he returned home from an assignment in St. Louis where he had been assisting the police with identifying and arresting the serial killer of at least nine, young women, he'd found his bags packed and sitting in the foyer. His wife had left him a note saying she was on a shopping trip in New York, would be home in three days, and wanted him and his stuff out of the house by then. She'd always accused him of putting his career ahead of her, and in her mind, when he accepted the assignment in St. Louis, he proved her right. He knew she was right. *I wasn't a great husband, but she wasn't a great wife either. Perhaps we were just a poor match.* He had no animosity against her and hope she would find happiness. She refused to take his calls, though. Maybe someday she would forgive him; he hoped so.

He had thought about calling Jane when it was clear his marriage was over, but he decided he wasn't relationship material, and it would be stupid to get involved with a woman who lived thousands of miles away. Then he had talked to her the other night and hadn't been able to stop thinking about her since. He pushed his plate aside and rubbed his head. *It's best if I don't call Jane at all while I am in Kodiak. She deserves better, and I don't need the inevitable heartbreak any attempt at a relationship with her is sure to bring. Maybe we can remain friends, but I know I want more than that.*

Morgan tried to concentrate on the case. He'd brought back copies to his room of the reports of the Kodiak police department's investigation into the murder of Deborah Sidle and the trooper's investigations of the murders of Tasha Ayers and Amy Quinn. All the file folders were thin. So far, the only decent leads were the red pick-up truck and eyewitness accounts of Jerome Collins and Caden Samuels each talking to one of the prostitutes the night before her body was discovered. Morgan was more interested in Jerome Collins than he was in Samuels. Samuels didn't sound smart enough or sober enough to pull off four murders without getting caught. Jerome Collins, on the other hand, was a successful crab fisherman, a job that required guts, skill, and brains. Morgan hadn't met Collins yet, but from what little he had been told, he believed the man could be a viable suspect.

Chapter Thirteen

Tuesday, December 3rd

Trooper Mark Traner picked up Morgan at the hotel and drove him to trooper headquarters. A foot of snow blanketed the town, and a fierce wind whipped it into drifts on the side of the road. The sky had cleared, and the temperature had plummeted into the teens. At 7:45 am on a December morning, it was still not light.

When Traner and Morgan walked into the conference room at 8:00 am sharp, Sergeant Patterson, Detective Horner, Trooper Johnstone, Liz Kelley, and Chief Feeney were already seated, each with a Styrofoam cup of coffee in hand. A box of sweet rolls lay open in the center of the conference table. Patterson poured coffee for Traner and Morgan and handed it to them.

"You might as well start, Ben," Patterson said.

Trooper Johnstone cleared his throat and opened the file folder on the table in front of him. He pulled a glossy 8 x 10 photo from the folder. He tapped the photo. "This is Amy Quinn's high school graduation photo. She graduated from high school in the tiny town of Fern, Washington three years ago. I was able to track her through her social security number. She worked at the grocery store in Fern when she was in high school. I talked to the local police chief, the principal of the high school, and some of her teachers. She was apparently a good kid and an average student, but she had a horrible family life. Her dad was arrested for child molestation when Amy was seven. He molested Amy and one of her little friends, and when the friend told her parents what had happened, they contacted the police. For some reason, Amy's mother blamed Amy for the father being thrown in jail, and when

Amy was 14, the mother died from a drug overdose. Amy moved in with an aunt who didn't want her and then moved out on her own when she was 16. She stayed and finished high school, but she left town the day after graduation, and none of the people I talked to knew where she had gone. None of them had heard from her since then."

"Did you interview the aunt?" Morgan asked.

"I did, and she didn't seem too upset Amy was dead. She said she knew something bad would happen to that girl."

"Sounds like a lovely lady," Maureen Horner said.

"Why don't you put her photo up on the board, Ben," Patterson said. "Do you have a photo of Deborah Sidle we can put on the board, Maureen?"

Maureen slid a 6 x 8-inch photo across the table to Johnstone.

"I have Tasha Ayers here," Traner said, sliding another 8 x 10 photo to Johnstone to add to the magnetized white board.

"What about Deanna Kerr?" Patterson asked.

"I have it, sir," Johnstone said, lining the photos up one after the other. He wrote each victim's name under her photo.

"Except for the Kerr girl, all of the victims look alike," Chief Feeney said.

"Good observation," Morgan said. "They all have shoulder-length dark hair and slender builds."

Feeney glared at Morgan, but Morgan's attention was focused on the photos, and he didn't seem to notice Feeney's irritation.

"They also all have their hair parted in the middle," Feeney said, the rancor in his voice so obvious it caught Morgan's attention.

"Right," Morgan said. *Eggshells. No cop wants to be patted on the head by the FBI.*

"Liz do you have anything?" Patterson asked

Liz Kelley shook her head. "I had three cars in the park yesterday, and one slid off the road. None of them were red pickups or pickups of any color. They were all kids."

Patterson nodded. "It's a long shot, but keep watching."

"Back to the photos," Detective Horner pointed toward the board. "The prostitutes and the Ayers girl all had straight shoulder-length black or dark-brown hair, but Deanna Kerr looked nothing like that. She had blonde hair."

Morgan nodded. "That difference may be important, but maybe not. It's possible the killer knew Deanna would be leaving the Fourth of July party alone in her skiff and simply seized the opportunity, even though she didn't look like his preferred type."

"What was wrong with her outboard, anyway?" Feeney asked. "Did anyone ever figure that out."

"Jack, the dad, thought there must have been some water in the fuel line," Patterson said. "He said Deanna knew enough to check the fuel line, but maybe she panicked in the rough seas."

"Or maybe someone stopped to offer her help before she had the chance to check it," Horner said.

A chorus of nods followed Horner's statement, and Morgan knew every individual at the table was imagining a possible scenario in his or her head.

"I finally talked to Jerome Collins, and he is flying back to Kodiak tomorrow afternoon to be interviewed. Patterson said. "He wasn't happy about leaving the Bering Sea, but he agreed to talk to us as long as he could fly back to Dutch Harbor the following day."

"Good," Morgan said. "Would it be possible to fly out to Uyak Cannery tomorrow morning and interview the superintendent before we talk to Collins?"

"If we get the weather for it," Patterson said. "It would be too windy today, but it is supposed to be a little calmer tomorrow. Our floatplane is down for maintenance, but I'll set up a charter with one of the flight services here in town for first light tomorrow morning. Detective Horner, would you like to join us?"

Maureen Horner looked surprised. "Sure," she said.

"What about Caden Samuels and Bobby Saunders, the other preliminary suspects?" Morgan asked. "Do we know where they are? We should re-interview them."

"I know where Samuels is," Horner said. "I can talk to him again."

"Would you mind if Ben here accompanies you?" Patterson asked. "I think it would be good to have someone from both of our agencies talking to these suspects. We all know our own cases best, and the slightest comment might trigger a link to one of the other murders."

"No problem," Horner said, but the scowl on Feeney's face suggested he felt one of his best detectives was being second-guessed.

"As of a week ago, Saunders was still here in Kodiak," Johnstone said.

"If you can get him in here tomorrow afternoon," Morgan said, "we can interview him after we finish with Collins. If possible, it would be good if you could join us for both of those interviews, Detective Horner."

"I can do that," Horner said.

"Maybe you and I and Agent Morgan can sit down and discuss our interviews for tomorrow," Patterson said.

"I need to make a few calls, and then I'm all yours," Horner said. "Ben, would you be available after lunch to go talk to Samuels?"

"Yes ma'am, anytime," Johnstone said.

"Mark, why don't you track down everyone you can who knows Jerome Collins. See if anyone can place him with Deborah Sidle, Tasha Ayers, or Deanna Kerr. Find out how well his sons knew Tasha and Deanna. Any information you can find on Collins may help us with our interview tomorrow. Agent Morgan and I will re-interview Tasha's mother, and we hope to talk to her brother as well. This afternoon we have a meeting scheduled to talk to the girls' volleyball team." Patterson looked at Morgan. "Coach Small called before I left the office last night and told me the meeting has been arranged."

Morgan nodded. "I think Coach Small deserves a closer look as well."

"Right," Patterson said. "Very discretely, Ben, check into Coach Small's background. It's probably nothing, but Agent Morgan and I picked up a strange vibe from him yesterday."

"Sure," Johnstone said. "I'll see what I can find."

Patterson looked at Morgan. "After we talk to Deanna's teammates, we can finish interviewing the teachers we missed yesterday."

Morgan nodded in agreement, and Patterson adjourned the meeting and told Morgan he would be back in half an hour to plan their interviews for the next two days. Morgan made a few notes in his spiral notebook and then wandered to the front of the room to take a better look at the photos on the white board.

The photo of Deborah Sidle was a blow-up of a snapshot that had probably been taken within the last year. Deborah was 38 years old when she was murdered, but the woman depicted in this photo looked 50. Her hair was black, streaked with gray at the temples. Deep lines radiated from the corners of her sunken brown eyes, and the lines sprouting from the margins of her lips suggested she had been a smoker. In this photo, her complexion looked pale and blotchy. Her lips formed a straight line, her hard eyes stared at the camera, and her nostrils flared as if she was angry. Morgan knew it was impossible to determine someone's personality from a single snapshot, but Deborah Sidle did not look like someone you would want to mess with, and he bet she went down fighting. Unfortunately, no DNA was found underneath her fingernails or anywhere else on her body. Of course, she had been submerged in the ocean for several hours, so any trace evidence probably had been washed away. In this photo, Deborah wore a long-sleeved, V-necked sweater and blue jeans that hung on her rail-thin figure. *Had she recently lost weight, or had she bought secondhand jeans that were too big for her?* Large, gold, hoop earrings and a gold chain with a deep purple stone completed her outfit.

The next photo was of Tasha Ayers. It was also a snapshot, and Tasha looked like a younger, softer version of Deborah Sidle. Tasha did not yet have the sunken eyes or the lines around the eyes and mouth, but she had Deborah's scowl and hard stare. Tasha's eyes were big and blue, and like Deborah, her black hair was parted in the center, but Tasha's hair was pulled back into a ponytail with a red, tie-dyed ribbon. In this photo, Tasha wore a black turtleneck and black pants. Sharp studs pierced her ears, and a necklace that looked like a dog's collar ringed her neck on the outside of her turtleneck. Her skin gleamed ghostly white, but the hue may have been the result of makeup. Black eyeliner rimmed her eyes, and her lips were painted ruby red.

The next photo was a headshot of Deanna Kerr, her blonde hair ruffled by the breeze. A wide smile graced her lips, and her deep, blue eyes sparkled in the sunlight. In stark contrast to Tasha Ayers, she looked like a kid who didn't have a care in the world. This was a great photo, and Morgan knew it was probably one of her parents' favorites. It would be far too simplistic to compare this photo of Deanna to the one of Tasha Ayers. This was a photo taken when Deanna was happy and smiling, but that may or may not have been the exception to her personality. No one they had spoken with had portrayed Tasha's disposition as sunny, but it was also not fair to think of her as sullen and angry all the time. The temptation was to classify Deanna as a happy teenager with few problems and Tasha as a troubled teenager with a hard life. Most of what they had heard so far supported those portrayals, but it would be a mistake to categorize the personalities of any of the victims this early in the investigation. In the photo, Deanna wore a plaid, button-down shirt. A silver and pearl chain ringed her neck, but no other jewelry was visible.

The last photo was a high school yearbook photo of Amy Quinn. She wore a turquoise, scoop-necked sweater, a gold locket on a gold chain, and small, gold earrings. Her dark brown hair was parted in the middle and hung past her shoulders. She had voluptuous lips curved into a sweet smile, a rosy complexion, a slender nose and small, brown eyes. Of all the photos, this one made Morgan the saddest. This young woman looked full of hope and possibilities. *Why had she turned to prostitution?* According to Johnstone, she'd had a terrible family life, but she had graduated from high school and had held a job at a grocery store in Fern. *What had happened between then and when Liz had found her lifeless body in Abercrombie Park?*

Morgan backed away from the whiteboard and studied the four women from a distance. Deanna Kerr's photo did not belong with the others. She looked nothing like the other three victims, and she was also the only victim killed on the other side of the island. Morgan felt Deanna was key to solving these murders. *If she was simply a victim of convenience, then which of their suspects was in Uyak Bay over the Fourth of July? Also, why had the killer chosen the other three victims? Was it possible the murderer had a past girlfriend, wife, or even a mother who'd had straight, dark hair parted in the center, and when he murdered a victim, he was killing this woman from his past over and over again?*

The door opened behind Morgan, and he turned to see Maureen Horner enter the conference room.

She nodded at the photos. "It is interesting how much three of the victims resemble each other," she said.

Morgan took in Maureen's shoulder-length brown hair, her angular face, and piercing blue eyes. It struck him how much the detective resembled the victims. *Has this thought occurred to her?* "He does seem to have a certain type," Morgan said, "and as you mentioned, Deanna Kerr looks nothing like the other victims. As I said, she was probably a victim of convenience, but if he chose her for a particular reason, that reason might be important to solving this case."

"Or she was murdered by someone else," Horner said.

Morgan nodded. "That is always a possibility, and we don't want to get so caught up making her murder fit with the others that we overlook something. If she was murdered by the same individual, though, the fact she looks different from the other victims and the fact she was murdered on the other side of the island could be important to solving this case."

"Jerome Collins may have known all the victims, and he was in Uyak Bay when Deanna went missing," Horner said.

"Mr. Collins intrigues me," Morgan said. "By all accounts, he is smart and organized, and as far as we know, he was in the right place at the right time to murder each one of the victims. We know he knew Amy Quinn, and he must have at least known who Deanna Kerr was. There is also a high degree of probability that he knew Deborah Sidle, and he possibly also knew Tasha Ayers, since she was in his son's class. Tasha could not have lived in a vacuum. She must have had some friends or at least acquaintances. I think it's important that we find out who those were."

"Maybe you'll get some leads when you talk to the girls on the volleyball team," Horner said.

Patterson entered the conference room at a brisk pace. "Sorry I'm late," he said. "Unfortunately this isn't the only case we have right now. The winter restlessness seems to be starting early this year. Yesterday we had a fatal stabbing in Bell's Flats, a guy shooting at his neighbors in one of the villages, and we busted a meth lab in an isolated cabin out near Chiniak."

"Your resources are spread thin considering you have to cover the entire island outside the city limits," Morgan said.

"Tell me about it," Patterson replied.

Morgan, Patterson, and Horner spent the next two hours planning their interviews with Samuels, Saunders, and especially Collins. They also covered the questions they wanted to ask David Sturman, the superintendent of Uyak Cannery. At noon, they broke for lunch. Patterson drove Morgan to King's Diner where they ate lunch, drank coffee and talked about anything other than the investigation. Patterson told Morgan about his wife and his son who was serving in the Marines. Morgan told Patterson about some of his cases and life in the big city.

Patterson said according to Hope Mills' boss, Hope's shift would end at 1:00 pm. Patterson and Morgan decided to wait until Tasha's mother was at home to talk to her. Patterson hoped she might be more willing to talk about her daughter's life in her home environment. They also wanted to get a look inside Tasha's home and hoped the mother might let them look at Tasha's bedroom. If they were really lucky, Mrs. Mills would grant them permission to inspect Tasha's personal computer, if she had one.

After lunch, Patterson and Morgan went back to trooper headquarters to return calls and do other office work. Morgan made himself at home in the conference room and spent most of the time on the phone consulting on other cases. At 1:30 pm, Patterson knocked on the conference room door and asked Morgan if he was ready to talk to Hope Mills.

The wind had calmed, but the temperature still hovered in the mid-teens. Morgan pulled his hood over his head as soon as he walked out of trooper headquarters. The drive to Hope Mills' rundown trailer took less than 10 minutes. A beat-up, blue van sat in front of the trailer, and Morgan hoped the presence of the van meant the Mills woman was home.

Patterson knocked on the front door, and it was opened a few seconds later by a thin, weather-beaten woman smoking a cigarette. She was dressed in a sweatshirt and sweatpants. Hope Mills looked exactly as Patterson had described her. She sucked in a breath when she saw Patterson.

Patterson introduced her to Morgan and then asked if they could come inside and talk to her for a few minutes. She stood back and ushered them into the trailer. Morgan was surprised by the interior of the small home. In stark contrast to the exterior, the inside of Hope Mills' trailer appeared spotless. Not only was it tidy, but the surface of the wood coffee table had been polished to a glossy shine. The linoleum floor had also been waxed and buffed, and the throw rugs were clean and artfully placed. Morgan followed Patterson's example and removed his boots, leaving them on the mat inside the door. Both men accepted the cups of coffee Hope offered, and they set the cups on coasters on the coffee table in front of where they sat on the couch.

The air smelled faintly of cigarette smoke, but Hope had tried to cover the smell with a lilac fragrance. She extinguished her cigarette and put the ashtray in the kitchen before settling onto a chair across from Morgan and Patterson. She folded her arms and sank back into the chair. Rather than the confrontational attitude Morgan had expected, her demeanor seemed resigned. Since Morgan had a Ph.D. in psychology, Patterson had asked him to take the lead with Hope Mills. Patterson said his first interview with the woman when he had informed her of her daughter's death had not gone well, and he suggested perhaps Morgan could figure out a better way to approach this particular subject. As it turned out, she seemed ready to talk this time.

"Mrs. Mills," Morgan began, "I am very sorry for your loss. I know it is extremely difficult for a parent to lose a child, but the death is even tougher to accept when the child is murdered."

Hope Mills said nothing, but tears streamed down her face.

"Detective Patterson and I are hoping you can give us a better picture of who Tasha was. We've talked to her teachers at school, and to be honest, they didn't know her very well."

Hope exhaled an exasperated gasp. "Of course they didn't know her very well. She wasn't the doctor's or the lawyer's or the mayor's kid. She didn't even have a dad. They thought of her as white trash and didn't even try to help her."

"Tasha's English teacher, Mrs. Bragg, was quite fond of Tasha. She felt Tasha had a talent for writing and said Tasha was doing well until this year when she seemed to lose interest in everything. Do you agree with that assessment?" Morgan asked.

Hope Mills sighed and stared at the ceiling for several seconds. "I don't know what was going on with Tasha. She started acting strange, or maybe I should say stranger than usual, in late July. One day she'd be cheerful, and that by itself was unusual for Tasha, the next day she'd be so sullen and angry she wouldn't even look at me. I asked her what her problem was, but I was the last person she'd ever confide in."

"Did you have many problems with Tasha?" Morgan asked.

Hope shrugged. "Just the usual teenage things. She tried drugs and alcohol." Hope laughed. "After talking to her brother, we decided much to Tasha's dismay, she didn't like drugs and alcohol. I know she got caught at school a couple of times with drugs, but nothing like that had happened in quite a while, and I don't know when the last time was I smelled alcohol on her breath." She held up a hand. "I know I could have been missing something, but Tasha was a much better girl than she wanted people to think she was."

"What about boyfriends?" Morgan asked.

"Well, I know she had boy problems, but I don't know who he was."

"She never mentioned anyone?"

A fierce shake of the head. "Never. Not to me, anyway."

"Why do you think she was involved with someone?"

"Those mood swings. I can't come up with any other reason for them. Tasha was never a happy child, and sometimes she was sullen, but lately, there were times when she had a big smile on her face and other times when she was so depressed, I was worried about her. When Sergeant Patterson here told me she'd passed, I immediately thought she had taken her own life. That's how depressed she was at times. Only a man or a boy can cause that kind of grief."

"Mrs. Mills, what did you think when you learned Tasha was nearly three months pregnant when she died?" Morgan asked. He watched her reaction and saw nothing but a fresh trickle of tears.

"I never suspected, but it makes sense," Hope said. All those emotions were fueled by raging hormones. My poor baby."

"You have no idea how she got pregnant, though?" Patterson asked.

"Well, of course, I know how she got pregnant, but I don't know who got her in that condition if that's what you're asking." Hope leveled her gaze at Patterson. "Listen here, I know the rumors around town about me, so I'm going to lay it on the table for you. Have I ever been paid for sex? Yes I have a few times, and I'm not proud of that, but when you have kids to feed, you do whatever it takes. I have a good enough job now to pay the bills, and I haven't had to resort to selling myself in a long time. I'm sure you've also heard Tasha worked for me as a prostitute. That is a lie. I may not be mother-of-the-year material, but I would never make my little girl sell her body. That's a despicable rumor."

"Did you know Tasha was sexually active?" Morgan asked.

"I did not, but I suspected she was. I made sure she got on birth control, and I told her to always make her partner wear a condom. I also told her to wait until she found someone special, but she laughed in my face. She knew what I'd done at times, and she didn't have much respect for me. I think most of the time she hated me." A fresh flood of tears poured from Hope's eyes, and she rose and walked into the kitchen, returning with a Kleenex.

"Why did you think she was involved in a sexual relationship?" Morgan pressed.

"Because she started staying out all night, and once, she was gone for an entire weekend. I was frantic and furious with her when she walked through the door on a Sunday night, but she told me not to worry about her and said it was none of my business where she was. I admit I had no control over her, but she wasn't wild."

"Would you mind if we look at her room? It might give us a better feel for who she was." Morgan said.

"Okay," Hope said, "but can I ask you something first?"

"Sure." Morgan nodded.

"Did the same guy kill Tasha that killed those other women?"

"We don't know, ma'am, but it is one theory."

Hope nodded and stood. Morgan and Patterson followed her down the narrow hall of the trailer. She pushed open a door and stood back, and Morgan and Patterson entered the small bedroom that had belonged to Tasha Ayers.

Tasha's bedroom had very little personality. Nothing suggested it had been the bedroom of a teenage girl. There were no posters of rock stars or handsome actors on the walls, no stuffed animals on the bed, and no jewelry or makeup scattered across the dresser top. The bed was neatly made with a plaid quilt that appeared to be decades old and was ripped in several places. A single pair of tennis shoes peeked out from under the bed, but no other shoes or clothes were in sight, and Morgan assumed they were all either folded in the dresser drawers or on hangers behind what he guessed was the closed closet door.

The only part of the room that looked lived in was the small desk in the corner. There was no computer in sight, but two spiral-bound notebooks were stacked in the upper right-hand corner of the desk, a sketchbook lay in the center, and a jar full of pens and pencils sat toward the back, near the wall. A corkboard hung on the wall behind the desk, and this immediately drew Morgan's attention.

Tasha had pinned several drawings on the board. If these were Tasha's drawings, she'd been a talented artist. Most of the drawings were of dragons and wizards and other mythological characters, but two drawings were different, and Morgan focused on those. One was a baby wrapped in a blanket and lying in a crib. The baby looked chubby and healthy, a slight smile curved its little lips. Another drawing depicted two adults and a small child. The woman in the drawing was, without question, meant to portray Tasha. The child could have been a girl or a boy and had Tasha's features. The man in the drawing had no features at all and was little more than a stick figure. There were no clues as to who Daddy was in the drawing.

Why is that? Morgan wondered. *Was Tasha trying to keep the identity of her lover, the future father of her child a secret? Most teenage girls want the world to know whom they are dating. Why had Tasha been so secretive about this matter, and did this secret boy or man have anything to do with her death? Maybe she told him she was pregnant and planned to have his baby, and he killed her to stop that from happening.*

Morgan heard a sob behind him and turned to see Hope Mills, her eyes wide and her hands covering her mouth. "She was always drawing, but these," she gestured to the drawings of the baby and the family, "didn't mean anything to me until I learned she was pregnant. "If only she had told me what was going on, maybe I could have done something."

Morgan let his gaze wander from the drawings to the half dozen or so photos pinned to the board. One was a man standing on the back deck of a fishing boat, another showed a small girl Morgan assumed was Tasha, a third photo pictured the girl a few years older standing next to an older boy, and together, they were holding up a large salmon. The next photo portrayed Tasha at approximately age 12 with two other girls, arms around each other, smiling at the camera. The last two photos were of Tasha a year or two before her death. In one, she must have been dressed for a Halloween party. Her skin was pasty white, her lips blood red, and her eyes dark with heavy makeup. She wore a cape with a hood, and her mouth scowled, the fangs from her fake teeth clearly visible. The last photo was a group photo of Tasha with a bunch of other kids standing around a camp fire. Several kids held beers, and others held soft drinks while they posed for the photo. Tasha stood apart from the group with nothing in her hand.

She looks sad and alone, but for some reason, she pinned this photo to her bulletin board. "Mrs. Mills, can you tell me about these photos?" Morgan asked.

Hope Mills still had tears running down her cheeks. She slowly pulled her gaze away from the drawing of the baby and focused on the photos. "That one there," she stabbed a finger at the man on the fishing boat, "was Tasha's no-good father. She never met the man, and he never paid a dime of childcare for her and her brother, but of course, Tasha cast him in the role of a saint and was certain I had driven him away from the family. She badgered me until I showed her this photo, and then she took it and pinned it up in her room." Hope shook her head in disgust.

"And I assume the little girl is Tasha?" Morgan asked.

"Yes, at age three. The next one is her and her brother, Tim." She laughed. "They were so proud of that salmon. Tasha hooked it, and her brother reeled it in. Bob and me – Bob Mills was my second husband – we told them they both caught it."

"You divorced Mr. Mills?" Patterson asked.

Hope shook her head. "He died in an accident at the cannery. A forklift rolled over on him. Bob was a good man. He was a good dad to the kids, but after he died, things fell apart."

"I assume this was a Halloween party." Morgan pointed to the next photo.

"Yes," Hope said. "She got all dressed up to go to that party, had me take her photo, and then she never went."

"When was that, ma'am?" Morgan asked.

Hope Mills ran her finger over the photo. "Just last year," she said.

"And this last photo. Do you know who these kids are?" Morgan asked.

"That is my son, Tim." Hope pointed to a tall, stocky kid with dark brown hair who was standing at the back of the group. He had a slight smile on his face and held a can of Budweiser. Hope pointed to two more kids. "That's Tim's buddy Eric and Eric's girlfriend, Samantha. I think this kid is named Shep, or at least that's his nickname. These are all Tim's friends, but I don't know their names. You'd have to ask him. Unlike Tasha, Tim has lots of friends."

"Does Tim still live with you?" Patterson asked.

Hope shook her head. "He has a little apartment out in Bell's Flats. Tim is a hunting and fishing guide. In the winter he works for a contractor here in town. They mostly do indoor projects in the winter. Tim is a talented woodworker, and he makes good money. He helps me out with my bills when I need it."

"Were he and Tasha close?" Morgan asked.

Hope pursed her lips and thought for several moments. "They were close when they were young, but once Tasha got into high school, she didn't have anything to do with her family. I doubt he knows any more about who she hung around with than I do." She shrugged. "You're welcome to ask him, though. I'll give you his address. He's home most nights."

"Ma'am, would you mind if we borrow this photo of the kids at the party, so we can ask him about it?" Morgan asked.

"If you think it will help, take it and anything else."

Morgan picked up the sketchbook and the two notebooks. With Hope's permission, they went through the desk drawers, the dresser drawers, and Tasha's closet. They found one more notebook in the desk, but they found nothing else of interest.

"Did Tasha have a computer?" Morgan asked.

"No, we can't afford things like that. She did have her phone, though, and I would like it back when you're done with it."

Patterson blinked. "Ma'am, we didn't find a phone on Tasha's body."

"Oh!" Hope said. "I just assumed you had it."

"What kind of phone did she have?" Patterson asked.

"It was just a cheap flip phone, not one of those smartphones. Like I said, we can't afford anything fancy like that, but Tasha wanted a phone, and I thought it was a good idea for her to have one."

"Mrs. Mills," Morgan said, "Do you know if Tasha was wearing any jewelry the last time you saw her?" None was found on her body."

Hope sat on the edge of Tasha's bed. "I should have thought of this sooner," she said. "Last summer she started wearing a copper bracelet. It was more of a cuff than a bracelet. It was wide and shiny; it was very pretty. Over the last few months, I never saw her without it. I haven't seen it around here, so she must have been wearing it when she died."

"Anything else?" Morgan asked.

"She usually wore earrings, but nothing special. I'm sure she would have been wearing the bracelet, though."

"Do you have any idea where she got the bracelet?" Patterson asked.

Hope shook her head. "She told me she bought it somewhere. I asked where she found the money to buy something like that, and she stalked away as usual."

Morgan and Patterson thanked Hope for her time, and just as they were walking out of her house she asked, "Was it a boy or a girl? No one ever told me."

"Ma'am?" Patterson asked.

"The baby, was it a boy or a girl?"

"A girl," Patterson said quietly.

Fresh tears sprang from Hope's eyes. She stood in the doorway and watched Patterson and Morgan leave. Morgan couldn't help but feel sorry for the woman. Her life had been tough, but it seemed as if she had done the best she could. He didn't question she had loved Tasha.

"That was not the same Hope Mills I interviewed when I informed her of her daughter's murder. That woman seemed like an absentee mother who cared about no one but herself. This was a grief-stricken mother brought to her knees because her teenage daughter had been murdered," Patterson said when he and Morgan were back in the SUV.

"Which version of Hope Mills did you find the most believable?" Morgan asked.

Patterson shook his head. "They both seem believable to me."

"Mrs. Mills probably was shocked when you first told her about Tasha, and her defenses were up. She is a woman who has lived a hard life and has had to deal with a great deal of adversity. When something traumatic happens to her, her first reaction may be to act tough and pretend nothing bothers her and as if there's nothing she can't deal with. She can't sustain the tough persona for a prolonged period of time, though, so eventually, the woman with feelings, with hopes and dreams, anger and disappointment, bitterness, and despair emerges," Morgan said.

"Or she could have been putting on a show for us today," Patterson said.

Morgan nodded. "Or that," he agreed.

"It would have been helpful if Tasha had given the daddy in her drawing a face and a few other features," Patterson said.

"I've been thinking about the drawing," Morgan said. "I can imagine several reasons for leaving Daddy as a stick figure instead of drawing him as a real boy or man. Maybe she didn't know who the father of her baby was. Just because her mother said she didn't push Tasha into prostitution doesn't mean it's true, or Tasha could have gotten into the business on her own to make some money. It's also possible by the time Tasha made the drawing, she and the baby's father were no longer together, and the drawing was meant to represent Tasha's hopes of finding someone who would be the father to her child."

"I wondered if the drawing represented Tasha's own father leaving her," Patterson said.

"Maybe," Morgan said, "but the young woman in the drawing bore a striking resemblance to Tasha, and Tasha did not look much like her mother. Still, you could be right." Morgan paused a moment. "I'm looking forward to talking to Tim. I have a feeling he knows more about Tasha's relationships than his mother thinks he does."

"I would like to believe the stick man in the drawing is our murderer," Patterson said.

"So would I," Morgan said, "but why the long-term relationship with Tasha? I assume Deanna, Deborah, and Amy were murdered after one brief encounter, but the man Tasha was involved with must have been in her life several months. She was two months pregnant, and according to her mother, her mood had been bouncing from happy to depressed for the last several months."

"Learning who Tasha was involved with may well be the key to solving this."

"Yes," Morgan said, "unless her murder had nothing to do with her pregnancy."

Chapter Fourteen

Tuesday, December 3rd

It was 3:25 when Patterson parked the SUV in the high school parking lot. He and Morgan rushed through the school to the gymnasium where they found 17 girls sitting quietly on the bleachers. Coach Small walked to the door to shake their hands.

"This is most of the volleyball squad along with a few girls from the basketball team," Small said. "One of the girls is home sick today."

Patterson thanked him for gathering the team and then asked Small if he minded if he and Morgan talked to the girls alone. "They may feel more comfortable talking to us out of the earshot of coaches, teachers, or parents. They won't want to say anything in front of you that could get them in trouble."

"Sure," Small said, "but do you need their parents' permission to talk to them?"

"No," Patterson said. "This is simply a fact-finding conversation. We in no way suspect any of these girls were involved in the deaths of their classmates. We just want to get to know who Deanna and Tasha were, and who better than their peers to help us understand what they were like? I assure you we will shut down this interview immediately if things take an unsuspected turn, but I don't see that happening."

Small nodded. "I'll be in my office if you need me."

Patterson introduced himself and Morgan to the assembled group of girls, and then he again let Morgan take the lead.

"I know this has been a rough few months for all of you," Morgan said. "Deanna went missing in July, and now I'm sure you've all heard the evidence shows she was murdered."

A few of the girls shifted on the bleachers, but no one said a thing.

"Deanna was your teammate and your friend. What Sergeant Patterson and I would like this afternoon is for you to tell us about your friend. By getting to know more about her and her life, we may be able to figure out who killed her."

"But she was killed on the other side of the island," a lanky girl with short, curly, red hair said. "How could her murder have anything to do with school and her life in town?"

Morgan nodded. "That's a fair question and her murder may have nothing to do with her life at school or her life in town, but I won't lie to you today. We think one person may have murdered four women on Kodiak Island, and we believe Deanna was one of his victims. The other three women were murdered in or near town so Deanna may have been murdered by someone she knew who lives in town. It could have even been someone she knew and liked."

"Was she murdered by the same guy who killed Tasha?" an athletic girl with long black hair and black eyes asked.

"We think it's possible," Morgan said. "Did Deanna and Tasha ever hang out together or have the same friends?"

The girls all shook their heads.

"Tasha didn't hang out with anyone," a stalky girl with blonde and pink ponytails said. "She barely ever came to school, and when she did, she didn't talk to anyone. She wasn't friendly."

"She was scary," the red-haired girl said, and several of the other girls nodded their heads.

"How is that?" Morgan asked.

"She wore black everything: clothes, make-up, fingernail polish, and she glared at you if you looked at her," a small girl with short black hair said.

"Did Tasha have a boyfriend?" Morgan asked.

Head shakes all around again.

Morgan sighed. *Tasha is going to be a hard one to crack, but someone must know what she spent all her time doing. Kodiak is a fairly small town, and eventually, we will find someone who knows where Tasha went when she skipped school.*

"Let's get back to Deanna," Morgan said. "Which one of you wants to tell me about her?"

A hand shot up in the front row.

"Yes," Morgan pointed to the girl. "Please tell me your name and what you remember about Deanna."

The petite blonde had hair that hung to her waist. Tears rolled from her big blue eyes, and her voice shook as she began to talk. She soon sat taller, though, and got her voice under control. "My name is Julie Paige, and Deanna and I were best friends. We did everything together. Deanna was smart, fun, nice to everyone, and a good friend."

Several other girls nodded their heads in agreement. "And a good volleyball player," one of them said.

"Sounds as if she was a great, young woman," Morgan said, well aware that he was unlikely to hear anything bad about Deanna unless he had the opportunity to interview each girl individually. It might come to that, but if it did, parents and lawyers would get involved, and he hoped to avoid that situation if possible.

"Did Deanna have a boyfriend?" Morgan asked.

"She had a crush on Brad Wells," Julie said. "His family fished in Uyak too, so she sometimes saw him in the summer."

Morgan's ears perked up at this comment that Deanna had liked a boy who potentially had been in Uyak Bay when Deanna went missing.

"Did Brad like Deanna?" Morgan asked.

"I don't know," Julie said. "He's very popular, and he's dating Marcia Roberts this semester."

"Marcia is a cheerleader," the petite black-haired girl said and wrinkled her nose.

"Do any of you know if Deanna spent time with Brad in Uyak this past summer?"

"I spent two weeks in June visiting Deanna at her fish site," Julie said. "We saw Brad once when we went to the cannery, but Deanna just said hi to him. She didn't know him very well."

"His family only moved here two years ago," the redhead said.

"Were there any other boys or men Deanna talked about?"

Morgan watched Julie and the girl she was sitting next to lock eyes. He waited expectantly, and finally, Julie said, "This is probably nothing, but there was someone. I don't know anything for sure, though, so I don't want to get him in trouble."

"Tell us what you know," Morgan said. "If he didn't do anything, he won't get in trouble."

Julie and the other girl again shared a look, and then Julie said, "There's this kind of creepy guy who paid too much attention to Deanna. She said it was nothing, but I think he's strange."

"I think he's into young girls," the other girl said.

"Tell me about him," Morgan said.

"We all know him," Julie said, "because he sometimes helps Coach Small, but something about him is just creepy."

Now the other girls began to nod, and the redhead said in a hushed voice, "He watches us too closely."

"And likes to touch our arms and stuff," one of the other girls said.

"Once he touched my leg," the girl with the blonde and pink ponytails said.

A chorus of "ooooh" and "yuck" emanated from the bleachers.

Morgan's interest was piqued, and behind him, he heard Patterson shuffle and move forward a step.

"What is this man's name?" Patterson asked.

"Mr. Carson," Julie said. "Rick Carson."

"Did he seem particularly interested in Deanna?" Morgan asked.

Julie nodded. "He's known Deanna since she was a baby. He's good friends with her parents, and he also has a fish site in Uyak Bay."

"Was Deanna afraid of him?" Morgan asked.

"Not really," Julie said. "She called him Uncle Rick and said he was harmless, but when I was out in Uyak in June, he came by to visit a lot, and he was always looking at Deanna and putting his arm around her. It wasn't right."

This was better information than Morgan had hoped to get from these girls. Rick Carson had just moved to the top of Morgan's interview list. "Does Mr. Carson help with the basketball team too?"

"Not anymore," the redhead said. "He did once or twice, but I think he's Coach Small's friend. He helps Coach Small with boys' basketball and track too."

"Did you tell Coach Small how you felt about Mr. Carson?" Morgan asked.

"No," the girls said in unison.

"He is mostly harmless," Julie said. "He's just too touchy-feely, and that's a little creepy."

"Is there anything else you can tell me about Deanna? Did she have many friends outside her school friends?" Morgan asked.

None of the girls had anything else left to offer, so Morgan thanked them for their time, and he and Patterson walked to Coach Small's office. Small opened the door a few seconds after they knocked, and Morgan noted the door to his locker was shut. Small sat behind his desk, and Morgan and Patterson sat in the two chairs they had occupied the previous day.

"Did the girls tell you anything of interest?" Small asked.

"They mentioned Rick Carson," Morgan said. "They said he is creepy."

"Rick?" Small seemed genuinely surprised. "Why would they say that? Rick is very generous with his time. He doesn't get paid to help me coach. He's a great asset, and they shouldn't be saying bad things about him." He shook his head. "That's crazy talk. You know how kids are."

"Mr. Small," Morgan said, the contempt in his voice barely concealed. "I know kids are usually able to pick up on inappropriate signals from an adult. Did it ever occur to you that Mr. Carson helps you for free because he likes being around young girls?"

"No way!" Small said. "I've known Rick for a long time. He's not a pedophile if that's what you're trying to say."

Morgan thought about the poster in Small's locker and wondered what he was dealing with here. He reminded himself it could be nothing more than bad judgment or a misunderstanding. He would need to tread lightly. "We have no intention of accusing an innocent man of something he didn't do," Morgan said, "but we will need to interview him. Does he have an office here at the school?"

"He does," Small laughed. "It's really a closet that we converted into an office for him, but he only uses it occasionally. He isn't at the school now."

"We would appreciate it if you didn't contact him until after we've had a chance to talk to him," Patterson said.

Small took a deep breath and sat back in his chair. "Of course," he said. "I understand. Rick is a good guy, but he is a little different. He has never been married, and I think he's always wanted kids. He's quirky, and I'm sure that's why the girls think he's strange."

Once Morgan and Patterson were back in the school hallway, Morgan said, "I'd like to find out what some of the other high school staff think of Rick Carson."

"Why don't we see if Sandy Miles is still here," Patterson said. "Not only is she a teacher, but she was Deanna's aunt, so she should have an opinion of Mr. Carson."

Sandy Miles' door was open, and she sat behind her desk writing in a notebook. She looked up when Patterson knocked on the door frame. "Sergeant Patterson and Agent Morgan, come in. What can I do for you today?" She remained sitting as the two men approached her desk.

They sat at two of the student desks in the front row.

Patterson said, "We just talked to the girls on the volleyball squad, and they told us about a man named Rick Carson. Do you know Mr. Carson?"

"Sure, I know Rick. He's friends with Jody and Jack." Sandy crossed her arms in front of her and looked warily at Patterson.

"Can you give me your impression of Mr. Carson?" Patterson asked.

Sandy braced her elbows on her desk and dropped her head into her hands for several seconds, and then she looked at Patterson. "What did the girls say about Carson?"

"We'd like to hear your impression first, ma'am," Morgan said.

"Well, I suspect he's harmless, but he is strange. I talked to Jody about him once and asked her if she thought he paid too much attention to Deanna."

"What did she say?" Patterson asked.

"She laughed at me and said Rick loved Deanna and the other kids and had known them all since they were babies. She said he was their kindly, spinster uncle, and the kids adored him."

"Do you think that's true?" Morgan asked. "Did the kids adore him?"

"From what I saw, yes, but I'm a teacher, and I've been trained to watch for predators who prey on children. Rick Carson sets off a few alarm bells." She shrugged. "Still, I have nothing but the utmost respect for Gordon Small, and I'm sure he wouldn't allow Rick to help him coach if he thought Rick had inappropriate feelings toward the kids."

Morgan considered telling Sandy about the poster in Small's locker, but he decided not to bring it up at this point.

"We were told Rick Carson has a fish site in Uyak Bay near the Kerr's site; is that correct?" Patterson asked.

"He does," Sandy said. "That's where Jack and Jody first met him. When they bought their site, they didn't know much about set-netting, and Rick helped them get started. They've been friends ever since." She paused. "I have to know; do Deanna's friends think Carson did something to her?"

"They thought Carson was creepy and that maybe he paid too much attention to Deanna," Morgan said. "Coach Small said Carson is a little different but harmless. We just wanted to see what you think about him. Kids are sometimes better than adults at picking up on certain vibes." He shrugged. "But kids also have big imaginations, and they are greatly influenced by movies, books, video games, and songs, so we don't want to jump to any conclusions."

Sandy sighed. "To be honest, I agree with Gordon. Rick Carson is odd but well-meaning. I can't believe he would do anything to hurt Deanna."

"Is there anyone else at the school that spent time with Carson; any teachers or staff?" Patterson asked.

Sandy Miles thought for a moment. "I think he helped with the basketball team sometimes," she said. "You might talk to Paul Mather. Paul has a degree in psychology, so maybe he can give you more insight into Carson."

Morgan and Patterson thanked Sandy and walked down the hall to the counselor's office. Mather, dressed in a heavy down jacket, was just locking his office door as they arrived. When they asked if they could speak to him for a few minutes, he told them he was in no hurry, unlocked the door, and ushered them into his office. They followed him to his desk and took seats.

"I was planning a short winter fishing trip this afternoon," Mather said, "but I'm not going anywhere in this weather."

Patterson broached the subject of Rick Carson and asked Mather if he knew the man very well.

"Not well," Mather said. "He helped me out with the girls' basketball team a few times when I first took over, but after a few weeks, I told him I wouldn't need his assistance anymore."

"And why was that, sir?" Morgan asked.

"Look," Mather said, "I know Gordon Small and Carson are friends, but frankly, I felt there was something off about the guy."

"In what way?" Morgan asked.

"Let me be clear about this." Mather held up his hands. "I don't believe Rick Carson is a pedophile if that's where you're headed, but I could tell some of the girls were uncomfortable around him. He touches them too much, and he tries too hard to be their friend. I'm sure I don't have to tell you gentlemen this, but when a man acts that way around kids, it makes me nervous. When you are an authority figure in a school setting, whether you're paid or a volunteer, you must be careful about the relationships you form with your students. You can't afford to get too close to the kids, and I felt as if Rick Carson was walking the line between acceptable and not-acceptable behavior. I wanted to distance myself and my team from him."

"Did you talk to Coach Small about him?" Patterson asked.

Mather nodded. "I did. Gordon thought I was over-reacting, but he promised to keep a close eye on Carson, and none of the girls have ever complained about Carson to me, so I let it slide. I probably was over-reacting." Mather stared at the ceiling and seemed to be debating about saying something.

"Anything you can tell us about Rick Carson would be helpful," Patterson said.

Mather laughed. "I just had this strange picture pop into my mind. In November, I went to Anchorage to a conference with several middle school and high school coaches. Some of us took the ferry, and on the way back to Kodiak, I walked around a corner on the ferry and saw Rick Carson surrounded by a crowd of little kids. He was reading them a story."

"Did he know the children?" Morgan asked.

"That's just it," Mather said, "I don't think he knew any of them." Mather shrugged. "It seemed strange to me."

"Mr. Mather," Morgan said, "what do you think of Coach Small?"

"Gordon? He's first class. Why do you ask?"

"No particular reason," Morgan said. "What does Mr. Carson do for a living?"

Mather shrugged. "He's a fisherman in the summer, but I don't think he does anything else. For some reason, I think he has money from some other source. Either he earned enough to retire at a very young age, or he inherited money."

Morgan and Patterson stood, shook hands with Mather, and thanked him for his time. They spent the next 45 minutes interviewing the few teachers they had missed the previous afternoon, but they learned nothing new about either Deanna or Tasha.

When they'd finished their interviews, they headed out to the parking lot, and as Patterson started the SUV, he looked at Morgan. "I don't know about you, but I want to learn more about Mr. Carson."

"He certainly has my attention," Morgan said, "especially since he had a relationship with the Kerr family and was probably in Uyak Bay when Deanna disappeared."

"What do you think about the boy Deanna was interested in?" Patterson asked.

"Brad Wells," Morgan said. "We should talk to him, but I'd be very surprised if a kid that age could pull off four murders and not leave a trace. You never know, though. Was he one of the kids at the Fourth of July party with Deanna?"

"I'll have to check the list, but I believe he was there," Patterson said.

"It should be easy enough to find out if he left the party soon after Deanna did," Morgan said.

"True," Patterson said. "We don't know when Deanna ran into her murderer, but it was probably within an hour or two after she left the party. The way the wind was blowing, I think she would have been blown into the bay and maybe even pushed up onto the beach after two or three hours. I believe someone pulled her boat out to sea before then."

"But if the boat had remained adrift all night, could it have been pushed out to sea by currents early the next morning when the wind calmed down?" Morgan asked.

"Yes, and we originally thought the boat was swept out into Shelikof the next morning. I was surprised at the time that with all the fishermen in Uyak Bay in July, no one noticed a boat adrift on a calm morning. Now that we know she was murdered, I think she was approached by another boat soon after she left the party. It was very windy, and most of the fishermen were in port or otherwise occupied with the holiday. It's believable no one would have noticed a boat approaching her skiff in those conditions."

"I see what you mean," Morgan said. "If we can tentatively place her encounter with her murderer at one to two hours after she left the party, it will help us eliminate possible suspects. We'll have to be careful, though, to remember the time frame may be longer than that."

Chapter Fifteen

Wednesday, December 4th
7:00 am

M organ ate a bran muffin and sipped his coffee while he watched a boat chug out of the Kodiak harbor. As the only patron in the hotel dining room at 7:00 am, he'd been able to snag a table by the window, but except for the lights of the boat harbor, there was little to see. It was still dark, and Morgan couldn't tell if the weather was good enough for the planned floatplane trip to Uyak Cannery. He felt occasional gusts of wind hit the window, and he wasn't looking forward to what he knew would be a bumpy plane ride to the west side of the island. Still, he hoped they would be able to get out to the cannery this morning because he wanted to interview the cannery superintendent before he talked to Jerome Collins. He needed some insight into how well Collins knew the Kerr girl and if Collins had been in Uyak Bay on the Fourth of July.

Morgan thought the two girls, Tasha Ayers and particularly Deanna Kerr, held the key to discovering the identity of the murderer. The deaths of the other two women were no less tragic, but they had lived high-risk lifestyles, casually engaging with a number of men. It was possible Tasha Ayers had also been soliciting strangers at the time of her death, but Deanna Kerr certainly had not been. She'd been murdered or at least had first encountered her murderer in the middle of a bay in broad daylight. If she'd had engine trouble, she probably would have welcomed assistance from anyone, including a stranger. She did not necessarily know her murderer, but the murderer had to be in Uyak Bay on the Fourth of July, and this fact should narrow down their suspect pool.

Morgan's cell phone buzzed. "Morgan," he responded.

"Nick, it's Dan. The air charter service won't make the final call on the flight until daylight, but I just talked to the dispatcher, and she says it looks like it's a go. They'll want us down at Trident Basin by 8:00 am, so I'll pick you up at a quarter to if that works for you."

"I'll be waiting outside," Morgan said. He disconnected and drained the rest of his coffee. He needed to call his office back in Virginia before he left the hotel.

Patterson was right on time, and Morgan swung into the SUV, a small backpack gripped in his hand. Wind gusts whipped dry snow across the road in front of them as they drove toward the bridge that led to Near Island and Trident Basin, the floatplane dock.

"How cold is it, anyway?" Morgan asked.

"My thermometer at the house said 15 degrees, but the windchill is well below that."

"Not too windy to fly, though?"

"I wouldn't want to fly my airplane in this wind if I didn't have to, but these guys fly in a lot worse every day, so this isn't a problem for them. It will be bumpy, though."

"I'm glad they can do it today," Morgan said. "I want to talk to David Sturman before we interview Jerome Collins."

Detective Horner stood inside the waiting room of the small office for Sea Air. She was dressed in a parka, a heavy wool cap, and ski gloves. She turned toward Patterson and Morgan when they entered and nodded her head. "Lovely out there, isn't it?"

"At least it's clear," Patterson said.

It was nearly 10:00 am before the dispatcher said their pilot was ready and told them they could walk down the ramp to the plane. As they headed down the steep ramp, a gust of wind hit them so hard Morgan had to grip the rail for support.

"This should be a fun flight," Horner said.

The young pilot stood on the float of the plane and motioned for them to climb aboard. They eagerly stepped out of the weather and into the relative warmth of the cabin of the De Havilland Beaver.

Patterson took the front seat, and Morgan and Horner shared the rear seat. The pilot shut the cabin door and then climbed in and shut his door. He turned to look at everyone.

"Hi," he said. "My name is Evan Parker. I'm your pilot today. We have two choices, so I'll let you decide. We can fly around the island and avoid the mountain passes. That route with this wind will take an hour and 15 minutes or maybe a little longer, but it will be calmer. Choice number two is to fly high, straight through the passes. We can do that route in about 45 minutes, but it will rattle your teeth in places and maybe even have you praying out loud a time or two, so what is it?" He looked at each of them. "I know you're a pilot, Sergeant Patterson, so I'm sure you don't mind a little turbulence, but what about you two?"

"I don't mind," Horner said, "let's take the most direct route."

Evan looked expectantly at Morgan.

"That's fine with me," Morgan said. He would have preferred the longer, calmer route, but he wasn't about to admit that in front of the two policemen. He knew if he requested the less turbulent route, for the rest of their careers, Patterson and Horner would tell the story about the wimpy FBI agent who was afraid of a few bumps in a floatplane.

Evan shrugged. "Okay, say your Hail Marys, and please, if you have to scream, push the mike away from your mouth. I have sensitive ears."

As soon as they were off the water, a wind gust rattled the plane. It veered sideways while Evan fought to control it. A few moments later, the plane dropped so hard Morgan banged his head on the ceiling. He cinched his seatbelt tighter and glanced at Horner. She appeared to be casually watching out the window, but he saw that her hands were squeezing the bottom of her seat cushion so tightly her knuckles were white. Patterson calmly watched the dials on the dashboard and Evan's maneuvers to counteract the turbulent conditions. Morgan guessed this flight was probably more difficult for Patterson than it was for Horner or him. They had to trust that Evan knew what he was doing, but Patterson was a pilot forced to sit back and watch someone else fly a plane in turbulent conditions.

Morgan believed Patterson would speak up if Evan did something stupid, but for now, Patterson appeared content to observe Evan in action.

At times, the air seemed to smooth out, and Morgan would begin to relax, but then they'd hit another rough patch. Evan said little during the flight, his attention focused on his duty, but about 40 minutes into the trip he announced, "Okay, folks, we're about to enter Spiridon Pass, and it will be bumpy, so hold on."

Morgan again cinched his seat belt, and he saw Horner and Patterson do the same thing. As soon as they entered the narrow mountain pass, an updraft hit the plane and sent it shooting skyward, followed moments later by a drop of the same magnitude. Morgan pushed the microphone away from his mouth, worried he actually might scream or at least say something embarrassing. The plane veered from side to side in the wind sheer, and Morgan wondered how Evan could possibly keep from ramming a wing into one of the rocky cliffs in this narrow canyon. Morgan's apprehension increased when he saw Patterson stare at Evan, a frown of concern on Patterson's face, his eyes squinted with laser-like precision as he studied the instruments and Evan's demeanor as Evan fought to control the airplane. Morgan sat directly behind Evan so he could not see Evan's face, but the way Patterson was staring at Evan worried Morgan. He gave up any pretense of being the cool FBI guy and closed his eyes.

After what seemed like an hour but was probably less than five minutes, the turbulence lessened, and Morgan opened his eyes. He knew where they were now; he'd visited Uyak Bay on his last trip to Kodiak. All they had to do was clear Amook Island and then land at Uyak Cannery.

"Sorry about that, guys," Evan said as the plane touched down on the ocean and bounced a few times on the waves. "It was worse than I expected. We won't be going home that way."

Morgan allowed a long, slow breath to escape his lips. He looked at Maureen Horner, and she smiled back at him, her face as pale and sweaty as his undoubtedly was.

Evan nosed the plane into a beach covered with rocks. A tall man dressed in a heavy wool coat, a thick stocking cap, wool gloves, and hip boots stood on the beach waiting for them. Patterson and Evan wore hip boots, Maureen wore a pair of knee-high Xtratuf rubber boots, and Morgan wore waterproof hiking boots. Morgan was concerned his boots wouldn't be high enough for him to wade to shore without getting wet, but the beach was steep, so he was able to jump from the float to the shore. The other men helped Evan tie the plane to a dock piling in the lee of the wind, and Evan said he would remain with the plane while they had their meeting.

The man who had met them shook hands with Patterson and Horner, and then he shook Morgan's hand. "Agent Morgan, it's nice to see you again." He paused. "Or maybe not. We only see you when something bad has happened."

"Mr. Sturman," Morgan said. "I'm afraid you're right. Sometimes I feel like the grim reaper. We appreciate you taking the time to talk to us."

"Sure, no problem," Sturman said, "but let's go to my office where it's warmer."

They trudged up the steep beach and stepped onto a snow-covered board walkway. Sturman led them past a warehouse and up two steps to a building that looked more like a house than an office. A welcoming blast of heat engulfed Morgan when he walked through the door.

"Please sit down," Sturman gestured to a sitting area with three upholstered chairs and a couch. Patterson sat in one of the chairs, and Morgan and Horner sat on the couch. Sturman removed his jacket and hat and sat in one of the other chairs.

"I'm surprised you're out here in the winter," Morgan said to Sturman. "I thought this was a salmon processing plant that only operated in the summer during the salmon run."

Sturman sighed. "The new owners want to make this a year-round operation. We're processing cod right now. It's not an easy transition because it was not built for winter operation, and so far, this has been a tough winter. If much more ice builds up, we won't be able to intake enough water to keep things running, not to mention, none of the bunk houses are insulated for winter use, so our fuel consumption for heat has been outrageous. I think they'll have to do some major renovations if they want to make this a full-time winter processing plant. I agreed to help them out this winter, but I don't plan to take a permanent winter position. It's beautiful out here in the summer but not so great in the winter."

"I can't imagine being this isolated in the winter," Morgan said.

"We'll try not to take too much of your time this morning," Patterson said. "I'm worried the weather will deteriorate, and we're on the edge of flyable as it is."

Sturman nodded. "I wouldn't want to be up there today."

"I'm sure you've heard about the three women murdered in Kodiak in recent months," Patterson said.

"I have," Sturman said, "and you think the women were all murdered by the same person?"

"We think it's a possibility, and we've recently added Deanna Kerr to the list of victims."

"I thought Deanna died in a boating accident."

"The medical examiner has determined that she was murdered, and her body was thrown overboard."

Sturman shook his head, "Her poor parents. I know the Kerrs; they fish for us." His eyes widened. "Is that why you flew out here to interview me?"

"It's one of the reasons," Patterson said, "but first we want to ask you about Bobby Saunders."

"You think he killed these women?" Sturman sat forward, his gaze on Patterson.

"He's one of several persons of interest, mainly because of what happened here last summer, and because he was here in the bay when Deanna Kerr disappeared."

Sturman leaned back. "I see," he said, "I don't know if Saunders is a murderer, but he is scum."

"You believe he raped his co-worker?" Morgan asked.

"Absolutely," Sturman said. "Sandra Medina is a good worker and a fine young woman. It was not easy for her to come to me and report what Saunders did to her. She is normally composed, but that day she couldn't quit crying, and that's not all; she had a black eye and claimed Saunders had hit her."

"You reported the crime to the troopers," Horner said, "but then Ms. Medina declined to press charges, is that correct?"

"That's right. Sandra is from the Philippines, and she hopes one day to be a U.S. citizen. She was afraid if she got involved in a court battle, it might weaken her chances of becoming a citizen." Sturman shrugged. "I tried to change her mind, but she wanted nothing to do with the police. She simply wanted Saunders gone from the cannery, and I was happy to grant her wish."

"Do you think Ms. Medina would talk to us?" Morgan asked.

Sturman shook his head. "She's in the Philippines now. She's planning to fly back here this summer, but she is on a limited work visa. I doubt she would tell you much even if you could interview her. She wanted to distance herself from that trauma as quickly as possible."

"What did Saunders say when you asked him about the incident?" Patterson asked.

"The usual," Sturman said. "He said Sandra consented to the sexual encounter, but when he didn't spend enough time with her the following day, she got angry, and she lied about the incident. I, of course, didn't believe him."

"How did he explain her black eye?" Horner asked.

"He said he didn't know she had a black eye and then went so far as to suggest she gave it to herself to make her story more believable. I fired him on the spot and haven't seen him since."

"Do you know if Bobby Saunders knew Deanna Kerr?" Patterson asked

"I doubt it. He may have seen her around the cannery, but I'd be surprised if he ever talked to her. The entire Kerr family visits the cannery a few times a summer, but usually Jack comes to the cannery by himself to take care of business. Jody and the kids probably visit the cannery three or four times a summer, maybe even less. Jack is the boss of the family. Jody isn't meek and submissive, but she follows his lead. I think Jack likes to have Jody and the kids stay at the fish site in the summer. Summer is family time for them."

"What about Bobby Saunders? Was he at the Fourth of July picnic?" Patterson asked.

"No," Sturman said. "The party was just for fishermen, top cannery management and tender captains and their crews. The cannery workers had their own, separate celebration."

"One more thing," Morgan said. "You said you don't think Saunders is a murderer. Why is that?"

"He could be a murderer. I just never saw any signs of violence in the man." Sturman shrugged. "But I guess rape is violence, isn't it?"

"Yes sir, it is," Horner said, her gaze intense, "and a black eye is a sign of violence."

Patterson looked from Horner to Morgan. "Do either of you have any questions about Bobby Saunders you want to ask Mr. Sturman?"

Both Morgan and Horner shook their heads.

"I think we can move on," Morgan said.

Sturman turned his head to one side waiting for Patterson to continue.

"What can you tell us about Jerome Collins?" Patterson asked.

"Jerome?" Sturman looked surprised. "He's first-rate. I've gotten to know him fairly well since he started tendering for us four years ago. Why do you want to know about him?"

"We know he had a relationship of sorts with one of the victims, and he must have known the Kerr family."

"Sure he knew the Kerrs. His boat was their tender. He picked up their fish two times a day," Sturman said.

"Did he ever say anything to you about Deanna?" Patterson asked.

"No, he..." Sturman stopped mid-sentence, and his gaze snapped to a point about a foot above Patterson's head.

When Sturman failed to continue, Patterson said, "Sir? Is there something you want to tell us?"

"I don't want to get him in trouble, but Jerome e-mailed me last night. Mostly, he was just asking me how the winter operation here at the cannery was going. I thought maybe he was looking for a job after the end of the crab season, but at the end of the e-mail, he asked me not to mention to anyone that he was at the Fourth of July picnic." Sturman patted the arm of the chair and then shrugged. "He didn't give any reason, but I guess he thought we were good enough friends I'd lie for him if he asked me to. To tell you the truth, I'd forgotten about his e-mail. I have a lot going on here, and I barely skimmed my e-mail last night or this morning."

"Do you have any idea why he would ask you to lie?" Patterson asked.

"No," Sturman said. "It doesn't make any sense. Nothing happened at the party."

"What time did you get this e-mail?" Patterson asked.

"Last night around 8:00 pm, I guess."

"If I give you my e-mail address, will you forward it to me?"

"Sure," Sturman said, "but Jerome would never hurt a young girl. As I said, he's a stand-up guy; all the fishermen like him."

"Sir, do you know when Mr. Collins left the picnic?" Maureen Horner was in full cop mode, her notebook open on her lap as she scribbled notes.

"I don't know," Sturman said, running his fingers through his thinning hair. "That was several months ago. Let's see; I left at 6:30 pm, and I think Jerome was already gone by then, but I could be wrong. I remember talking to him, and we both had plates of food at the time, so that must have been around 5:00 pm."

"So he must have left sometime between 5:00 pm and 6:30 pm," Horner said.

Sturman shrugged. "I guess so."

"Did you ever witness Mr. Collins spending time with any women, either cannery workers or fishermen?" Morgan asked.

Sturman sat back, sighed, and looked at the ceiling. "No, not that I recall. I don't recall ever talking to Collins about women. I knew he was divorced, and we chatted a few times about his kids, but I don't know if he's dating anyone."

"Thanks, David, we appreciate your honesty, and we won't mention to Jerome Collins that you were the one who told us he was at the party. If we have more questions about him, can we e-mail you?"

"Of course," Sturman said.

"There's a few more people we'd like to ask you about. "Do you know Caden Samuels?"

Sturman thought for a minute and then shook his head. "The name isn't familiar."

"What about Rick Carson?" Morgan asked. "Do you know him?"

"Of course," Sturman said. "He's one of our fishermen."

"What do you think of the guy?"

Sturman shrugged. "He a bit strange, but he's okay. I don't know him well, but he has always been straight with me."

"How is he strange?" Morgan asked.

"Little things," Sturman said. "He stands too close and stares too long. He's just one of those people who are socially awkward. He's not a bad guy, though."

"Was he at the Fourth of July Picnic?" Horner asked.

Sturman leaned his head back and stared at the ceiling. After several moments, he said, "I believe he was. I didn't talk to him, but I think I saw him there."

"But you didn't see him leave?" Horner asked.

"I'm sorry, no. There was a lot going on at the picnic. I didn't really pay attention to who came and went."

"I have one more question," Patterson said. "Do you know Brad Wells?"

Sturman looked confused and started to shake his head again but then said, "Bud and Bridget's kid?"

"That's right," Patterson said. "I believe those are his parents' names. "What can you tell me about him?"

"Brad? He's a kid, the son of one of my fishermen. I never paid much attention to him."

"Do you know if he was hanging out with Deanna Kerr at the Fourth of July party?" Patterson asked.

Sturman shrugged. "I think the older kids were all around the bonfire, but I don't remember. To tell you the truth, I don't even know if Brad was at the picnic. His parents were there, so I assume he was there, but I can't remember seeing him. I did see Deanna Kerr with her mother at one point. Jody Kerr is a nice looking woman. I'd have to be ill not to notice her."

Patterson smiled and stood. "That's all I have for now," he said. He looked at Horner and Morgan. "Did I forget anything?"

Morgan and Horner shook their heads, and Sturman escorted the three detectives back to their plane. As they neared the plane, they saw Evan jumping up and down, trying to stay warm.

"Hey guys, are you ready to get back to town?" Evan asked.

Morgan was not ready for another terrifying flight, but his pride would never allow him voice this opinion. He, Patterson, and Horner all thanked Sturman for his time and then climbed into the airplane, taking the same seats they had occupied on their outbound flight. Sturman helped Evan push the plane off the beach, and then Evan jumped onto the float and climbed into the cockpit.

"Who's for taking a different route to town?" Evan asked.

Patterson, Morgan, and Horner all raised their hands and said, "Me!"

Evan laughed. "It's unanimous. I'll fly around the outside. We'll have the wind at our backs most of the way, so it should only take us 50 minutes or so."

Morgan wouldn't have called the return flight pretty. They hit a few good bumps, and the bleak isolation of the outer shores of the island made him uncomfortable. Sheer cliffs plunged into the sea, and the stormy, black waves crashed into them, sending a wall of frothy water high into the air. Morgan realized there would be no place to land if they had engine trouble and the turbulent ocean would tear the plane to pieces in a matter of seconds. Still, the return flight was much better than their earlier flight had been. Evan appeared to be in control of the plane at all times, and he even seemed relaxed, chatting casually with Patterson about airplanes and flying.

When Morgan stepped onto the floatplane dock in Kodiak, he breathed a sigh of relief, and once he and Patterson were back in the SUV headed for trooper headquarters, Morgan said, "Tell me the truth; were you at all concerned on our flight this morning?"

Patterson laughed. "Concerned? Not at all, I was scared to death. Young Evan never should have flown passengers into that pass in such windy conditions, especially not with the wind from that direction. I assumed he had talked to another pilot who had recently flown through the pass, so he knew the wind was okay in there, but I don't think he gave the situation much thought." He laughed again. "He'll think about it next time, though. He was as scared as we were."

"Nothing is easy up here, is it?" Morgan said.

Patterson smiled. "No sir, and that's why I love it."

Chapter Sixteen

Wednesday, December 4th
1:30 pm

It was 1:30 by the time Patterson and Morgan got back to trooper headquarters. Maureen Horner was right behind them. Irene had ordered sandwiches and chips for the trio since she knew they wouldn't have time to grab lunch. She'd ordered an extra sandwich for Jerome Collins.

"Mr. Collins is in the conference room," Irene said. "He's been waiting for over an hour and is getting a bit cranky."

"Good," Patterson said, "that's just how we want him."

Patterson knocked on the partially-opened conference room door and then entered the room followed by Horner and Morgan. "Mr. Collins," he said, "thank you for flying back here to talk to us." He held out his hand to shake, but Collins didn't budge.

Collins' chair rested on its back two legs, and he leaned against the wall, his arms folded across his chest. Collins glared at Patterson. "I'm losing money every minute I sit here, and I've been here over an hour waiting on you," he said.

Jerome Collins was a big man; not fat, but muscular with broad shoulders and a big neck. His short-sleeved t-shirt revealed strong arms covered with tattoos. His dark hair was cut short over a face that had spent many years battling the weather in storm-tossed seas. He had hard, black eyes, and a broad nose. His lips formed a slash across his angry face.

"I apologize for the inconvenience, Mr. Collins, but we are in the middle of a murder investigation, and we hope you can help us find the perpetrator."

"Like I told you on the phone, I don't know anything about the dead prostitute or the other women."

"You admitted to having a sexual encounter with Ms. Quinn," Patterson said.

"I guess so. I don't know what her name was, but I paid for sex with a prostitute. Left her alive and well, and apparently, someone killed her after that. Didn't see anything, don't know anything, end of story."

"According to the bartender, you and Ms. Quinn talked for a while in the bar before leaving together. Would you mind telling us what you talked about?"

"Why? What does that matter? It's no business of yours."

Patterson exhaled. "Sir," he said, "we know very little about Ms. Quinn, and we are hoping you can tell us more about her. The sooner you cooperate here, the sooner you will be able to get back to the Bering Sea."

Collins eased his chair down onto all four legs. He rested his elbows on the table, folded his hands and stared at Patterson. "What do you think we talked about? We discussed a business proposition. I wasn't interested in learning about her childhood or her favorite color. I wanted sex and she wanted money."

"Did she tell you anything personal about herself, such as where she was from, or why she was in Kodiak?" Patterson asked.

"She'd just arrived in Kodiak on the ferry. She said she got into some trouble in Anchorage and was hoping to make a fresh start in Kodiak. I think she wanted to get a legitimate job, but she needed money to find a place to stay." Collins shook his head. "She seemed like a nice kid, but she was lost and trying to find her way. To be honest, I liked her. I didn't hurt her," he said.

"Did she mention her life in Washington?" Patterson asked

"I didn't know she'd lived in Washington. As I said, we didn't talk about personal stuff. We discussed the weather, she wanted to know about crabbing, and she asked me about cheap places to live in town and other things like that. It was only meant to be a one-time encounter. We weren't trying to start a relationship."

"I understand," Patterson said. "When I spoke with you before, you said you didn't know Deborah Sidle, but the bartender at The Anchor said he'd seen you with Deborah a few times."

"Hank has a big mouth," Collins said. "Okay, I sometimes use prostitutes. Are you planning to arrest me for that?"

"We're interested in bigger things right now, Mr. Collins," Patterson said. "I want you to tell me the truth. How well did you know Deborah, and when was the last time you saw her?"

"I remember getting together with her one time last winter, but I don't recall seeing her after that. She wasn't someone I hung out with. I didn't much like her; she was surly. When we were together, it was all business. That's the way I like it with no strings."

"How long had you known Deborah?" Horner asked.

Collins threw his hands wide and gave Horner an exasperated look. "What does it matter? I've known her for years, but like I said, we weren't friends."

"If you've known her for years," Patterson said, "why did you tell us when we first interviewed you that you didn't know who she was?"

Collins shrugged. "I should have told you the truth, but I didn't want to admit knowing two dead prostitutes. I was afraid you'd haul me off to jail right then."

"Why would you think that, Mr. Collins?" Patterson asked.

"Because I knew both prostitutes. Lots of guys know Debbie, but the other one had just arrived in Kodiak. I was probably one of her few, or maybe even her only, customer on the island. If I admitted to knowing Debbie too, I thought I'd be your lead suspect."

You're right, Morgan thought, *but by lying to us, you've made yourself appear even more suspicious.*

"While we're at it," Patterson said, "You also told us you didn't know Tasha Ayers, but we know she was in your oldest son's class in high school."

Collins started to stand but then sat back down. "Ah, come on! Now you're just fishing. Do you think I know every kid in Jason's class? Sorry to tell you, but I'm not a perfect dad. I only know my kids' friends, and she was not one of Jason's friends. I did not know her."

"What about Deanna Kerr?" Patterson asked.

"Sure, I knew Deanna. I pick up the Kerrs' salmon in the summer, and I know the family. I don't know them well, and I've probably only ever said 10 words to the kids, but I know them. Deanna seemed like a nice kid. What does any of this have to do with her?"

"The medical examiner determined Deanna was murdered, and we believe her murder may be related to those of the other three women," Patterson said.

Collins shook his head. "Jack and Jody will never recover from this."

"Mr. Collins, where were you on the evening of July fourth?" Horner asked.

"The Fourth of July?" Collins shrugged. "I don't remember. On my boat, as usual, I guess."

Patterson smiled. *Gottcha.* "We have a witness who says you were at the Fourth of July set-netter picnic," Patterson said. "Deanna was also at the picnic, and it was the last place Deanna was seen alive."

Collins rubbed his face with both hands. "That's right," he said. "I forgot about the picnic. Yeah, I was there for a little while."

"What time did you leave?" Patterson asked.

"I have no idea," Collins said.

"We've been told you left around the same time Deanna Kerr left the party," Patterson said.

Morgan watched Collins carefully to see how he would respond to this statement. The guy was hard to read. He had no problem lying, but he always came up with a good explanation for his lies. As Morgan had suspected, Collins was smart, and he perfectly fit the profile of their murderer.

Collins shook his head and spread his hands wide. "Are you trying to pin her murder on me too?"

"We just want the truth, sir," Patterson said.

"I didn't see Deanna Kerr leave the party. I really don't even remember seeing her at the picnic, but I did talk to her dad. I like the family, and I would never hurt any of them, especially not the kids. I don't know what else I can tell you."

"What kind of car do you drive, Mr. Collins?" Patterson asked.

"Why? What does that have to do with anything?" Collins' face sprouted red blotches.

"Please answer the question, sir." Patterson said.

"I have two cars, not that it's any of your business. I have a dark green 2015 RAV 4 SUV and a 2010 black flatbed Ford truck."

"Mr. Collins," Morgan spoke for the first time, "you visit the various fish sites around Uyak Bay, and you know the fishermen and their families. Is there anyone you can think of who we should be talking to about Deanna's murder?"

Collins exhaled and seemed relieved to have the focus of this interrogation switch to someone other than himself. "Kevin Ladke and his brother Ken have a fish site in Zachar Bay. They're both mean drunks, but I can't imagine they would hurt a little girl. They'd be more likely to beat up her father if they felt he had wronged them in some way."

"Anyone else?" Morgan asked.

Collins thought for several seconds. Finally, he said, "Rick Carson. I've never known the guy to be violent, but he gives me the creeps, and he's friends with the Kerrs."

"In what way does he give you the creeps?" Morgan asked.

"He's strange. He stands too close, he says odd things, and I've seen him leer at kids. The crew and I call him Pervert Rick."

"Was he at the Fourth of July picnic?" Horner asked.

"I couldn't tell you," Collins said. "I really wasn't there long, and I mostly talked to other tender captains."

Morgan wished they had probable cause to hold Jerome Collins. He believed the man knew Tasha Ayers, and Collins had finally admitted to knowing the other three victims. Even Collins said he was probably one of the few people on the island who had spoken to Amy Quinn after her recent arrival on Kodiak, but they had no evidence Collins had murdered any of the women, and until they did, they couldn't arrest him.

"Mr. Collins," Patterson said. "You're free to go back to the Bering Sea, but we'd like you to return to Kodiak when the crab season closes."

"I have to bring my boat back to Kodiak," Collins said. "Hopefully by then, you'll have the real killer, and I can take a vacation someplace warm."

Patterson, Morgan, and Horner remained in the conference room after Collins left. Patterson shut the door and sat at the table with Morgan and Horner. "What do you think?" he asked.

"I think it's suspicious he lied about being at the Fourth of July party," Horner said.

Morgan nodded. "I also think it's interesting Collins acted as if he did not know Deanna Kerr's death had been ruled a homicide. If he didn't know she'd been murdered, why did he ask David Sturman to lie about his presence at the picnic?"

"Good point," Patterson said. "I guess he could have gotten the news from one of his kids, but it's hard to believe it could have gotten to him so quickly. We didn't tell the teachers about the homicide ruling until yesterday afternoon, and Collins was either on his boat or traveling to Kodiak yesterday afternoon and night."

Horner shook her head. "Never underestimate the speed of the Kodiak grapevine. I'd wager by the time you walked out of the high school yesterday, most of the town knew Deanna had been murdered. I only wish the internet here were half as fast as the gossip net."

"I still like Collins for this," Patterson said.

"He fits the profile," Morgan said, "but I'd also like to interview Rick Carson. His name keeps coming up, and he was in Uyak Bay when Deanna disappeared."

"At least we think he was," Horner said. "That fact should be easy enough to verify, though. His friends the Kerrs should know whether or not he was there."

"He'll probably tell us himself when we interview him," Morgan said. "It would be stupid of him to lie about being at a party with so many other people. Someone would remember him being there."

"At some point, we may have to interview everyone who was at the party," Horner said, "and that will be a pain in the butt because most of the fishermen and 90 percent of the crew probably live somewhere else and are only here on the island during the summer."

"Maureen," Patterson said, "I haven't had a chance to talk with Ben yet. How did your interview with Samuels go yesterday?"

"Not well," Maureen said. "He was high as a kite on something, and we could barely get him to stay awake, let alone make any sense. We can try again, though."

"I don't think interviewing Samuels is a good use of your time, at least at this point," Morgan said. "I think it's unlikely someone with a drug problem could pull off these murders without getting caught. These are well-planned crimes, and I believe they were carried out by a smart, organized, sophisticated perpetrator. From what you've told me about Samuels, he doesn't have any of those attributes."

"I agree," Patterson said. "What do you think, Maureen?"

"I've never believed he murdered Deborah Sidle. Just because he talked to her, doesn't mean he killed her. Mr. Samuels is far from an upstanding citizen, but I agree with you and I don't think he has what it takes to pull off a murder and get away with it."

"Do you want to sit in on this interview with Bobby Saunders?" Patterson asked Horner.

She shook her head. "I'll look at the tape of the interview later. I have some other cases I need to work on this afternoon."

"Do you want to go with us tomorrow to interview Rick Carson?" Patterson asked.

"I wouldn't miss his interview for the world," Horner said.

When Morgan and Patterson left the conference room, Irene told them Saunders was waiting in the interrogation room. Morgan had suggested interviewing Jerome Collins in the conference room where he was more likely to feel at ease and not as apt to call his lawyer. He thought Saunders, on the other hand, should be interviewed in the interrogation room where they could more easily intimidate him. There was a small danger that Saunders also might lawyer-up, but from all Morgan had been told about the man, he didn't think Saunders would call a lawyer unless he were backed into a corner.

Saunders sat sprawled in a hard-backed wooden chair in the small room, his head was turned up to the ceiling, eyes closed and mouth open; he was sound asleep and snoring.

Patterson slammed the door, and Saunders jumped. He sat straight, rubbed his eyes, and looked dazed. "What the...? Man, you scared me."

"I'm glad you find our chairs so comfortable, Mr. Saunders, but we didn't ask you here to sleep."

"Why do you want to talk to me? I haven't done nothin'." Saunders folded his arms across his chest and tried to look tough. He didn't succeed.

From reading his rap sheet, Morgan knew Saunders stood five-feet, six-inches tall and weighed 152 pounds. He had small hands, small feet, and even a small face. Hair sprouted from Saunders' chin in what Morgan guessed was supposed to be a goatee. His cheeks were pock marked by acne scars, and even though Morgan knew he was only 27 years old, his thin, brown hair had already receded from his forehead. He squinted his brown, beady eyes at Patterson, trying to stare him down. Morgan fought the urge to laugh at his pathetic demeanor.

Patterson flipped one of the wooden chairs backward and positioned it a few feet away from Saunders. He straddled the chair and folded his arms around the backrest. Morgan sat in the other chair and observed the interview.

"We hear you've been busy, Mr. Saunders," Patterson said.

"I ain't done nothin', "Saunders said.

"Agent Morgan here and I flew down to Uyak Bay and had a little chat with David Sturman this morning. Do you know who David Sturman is?"

"Yeah, so?"

"Mr. Sturman told us an interesting story involving you and a rape."

"No way, man." Saunders pushed his chair further back into the corner. "I never raped no one."

"That's not the story we heard."

"That girl wanted it, and then the next day she lied. The little bitch got me fired!"

"You don't much like women, do you?" Patterson said.

"Of course I do," Saunders said. "I'm not into men!"

"I've read your rap sheet," Patterson said. "Four arrests for spousal abuse and two more for beating up women at a bar. That's pretty lame, Bobby."

"I wasn't convicted on any of them," Saunders said.

"So far you've been lucky, but in my book, an innocent man doesn't get arrested six times by accident."

Saunders shrugged and glared.

"Did you know Deanna Kerr?" Patterson asked.

"Who?"

"Deanna Kerr, the girl who went missing in the boating accident last summer."

"Oh her. No, I didn't know her; why would I?"

"You worked at the same cannery that bought her family's fish."

"So? The cannery crew isn't allowed to mingle with the hoity-toity fishermen. I wouldn't know her if I saw her. Why do you care if I knew her, anyway?"

"Do you ever associate with prostitutes, Mr. Saunders?"

"What? I can't afford to throw my money away on prostitutes, and why would I need to? I have all the ladies I could ever want."

Patterson barked a laugh. "Is that so?"

"Yeah, it is."

"Did you know Deborah Sidle or Amy Quinn?"

"No, I've never heard of them."

"What about Tasha Ayers, did you know her?"

"Who? Why are you asking me all these questions? I don't know any Tanya Ayers."

"Tasha Ayers," Patterson corrected.

"I don't know her either."

"What type of vehicle do you drive?"

"A piece of crap 1995 rusted-out Toyota when it works and when I can afford the gas."

"You'd better not be lying to me, Bobby. If I find out you knew any of the women I just asked you about, we'll have another visit, and next time, I won't be so nice."

"I told you I don't know them!"

Patterson issued a heavy sigh. He walked to the door and opened it. "You're free to go," he said, "but stop hitting women. That's just wrong."

Bobby Saunders wasted no time jumping to his feet and hurrying out of the interrogation room.

When he was gone, Patterson turned to Morgan and asked, "What did you think?"

Morgan shook his head. "He's either a great actor or not the sharpest knife in the drawer. I found myself believing he had never heard the names of our victims, but considering their names have been splattered all over the newspaper, radio, and television news lately, how could he not have heard of at least one of them?"

Patterson sighed. "Yes, Bobby Saunders is probably too stupid to be our guy, and that's a shame because I'd like to get that piece of slime off the street."

"I don't think we should mark him off our list quite yet," Morgan said. "As he said, he has already managed six times to stay out of jail after being arrested for abusing women. He may be smarter than we think. He also apparently hates women, and so does our perpetrator."

"Our suspect list keeps getting longer instead of shorter," Patterson said. "Let me get Ben in here and see what he's been able to dig up on Coach Small."

Patterson left the conference room and returned a few minutes later with Trooper Johnstone. Johnstone nodded to Morgan when he entered the room.

"Maureen told us about your encounter with Samuels yesterday," Patterson said. "Agent Morgan and I think we should put him on the back burner for now."

Johnstone nodded. "That guy's not capable of making a peanut butter sandwich, let alone committing a murder without leaving trace evidence."

"What have you found about Coach Small?" Patterson asked.

"Not much of interest," Johnstone said. "He's 44 years old and has been married 19 years. No kids. Principal Daniel thinks he's great and says the kids, parents, and other teachers all like him."

"How long has he been a coach here?" Morgan asked.

"Twenty years," Johnstone said. "He's been here his entire career."

"Any arrests?" Patterson asked.

Johnstone shook his head. "Nothing. His record is clean."

Patterson looked at Morgan. "If you hadn't seen the poster in Small's locker, he wouldn't even be on our radar."

"But I did see it," Morgan said, "and to me, it was a big, red flag. I guess we'll have to go back to the school and interview him, but let's wait until after we have a chance to talk to Mr. Carson."

"I'll ask Carson to come in here tomorrow morning," Patterson said.

Morgan remained silent for several moments, deep in thought. Finally, he said, "Instead, why don't we pay Mr. Carson a surprise visit tomorrow morning. I'd like to get a look inside his home."

Patterson nodded. "We can do that. Let's drop in on him around 9:00 tomorrow morning. I'll postpone the task force meeting until the afternoon."

"Shall we drive out to Bell's Flats and talk to Tasha's brother tonight?" Morgan asked.

Patterson nodded. "I'll pick you up at your hotel at 7:00 pm."

At 5:00 pm, Johnstone offered to give Morgan a ride back to his hotel. Morgan was surprised when he stepped out into the dark; the temperature had risen at least 20 degrees.

"It's supposed to rain tonight," Johnstone said, looking at the black sky.

"Rain?" Morgan asked. "How warm is it?"

"Thirty-nine degrees, the last time I checked," Johnstone said. "It's supposed to rain and then clear off again. By tomorrow morning it will be cold, and the streets will be an ice rink."

"Interesting weather here," Morgan said.

Morgan ate a hamburger and drank a cup of coffee in the hotel dining room. He thought about the upcoming interview with Tim

Ayers. While Tasha had written in an essay that her brother had sexually abused her, even her English teacher doubted the veracity of Tasha's statement. Everyone else they'd interviewed had nothing but good things to say about Tim Ayers, and he sounded like a good son, helping out his mother financially and in other ways. Morgan hoped Tim knew more about his sister's life than everyone else they'd interviewed.

Chapter Seventeen

Wednesday, December 4th 7:00 pm

P atterson pulled up in front of the hotel a few minutes after 7:00 pm, and Morgan climbed into the SUV.

"Sorry I'm late," Patterson said, "these roads are treacherous."

"Icy?" Morgan asked.

"Yes, and getting icier by the minute."

Freezing rain pelted the windshield as the SUV crept down the road. They seemed to be the only vehicle out on this miserable night.

"Ayers lives in Bell's Flats," Patterson said, "and it's a winding highway along a sheer cliff to get there. I don't know about you, but I have no desire to fly off a cliff into the surf tonight. I plan to take it nice and slow."

"That sounds good to me," Morgan said. "I try to limit myself to one harrowing flight a day."

Patterson laughed. "Have you been to Bell's Flats before?"

I interviewed a lady who lived in Bell's Flats when I was here last time. It's about 10 miles from town, right?"

"Right, it seems like a nice community. My wife and I have looked at a couple of small homes out there, but we haven't seen anything we want yet."

"Are you expecting to be stationed on Kodiak for a long time?" Morgan asked.

"Who knows," Patterson said. "I could be transferred to Nome tomorrow. I hope not, though; I like it here. Kodiak has its share of problems, but most of the people are great."

Patterson remained quiet for the remainder of the drive, his eyes fixed on the road as the icy rain continued to fall. Morgan wanted to get this interview over with and go back to the hotel.

Tim Ayers lived in a tiny cabin at the top of a steep road.

"This should be fun," Patterson said before beginning the ascent.

The tires slid twice on the steep climb, but then gained enough traction to make it to the top of the drive. A warm glow filled the small window on the front of the cabin.

"Thank God he's home," Patterson said. "I'd hate to think that white-knuckle drive was for nothing."

Patterson's knock on the front door was answered by a tall, muscular man with shoulder-length straight, brown hair and a full beard. He looked different than he had in the photo in Tasha's bedroom. Patterson introduced himself and Morgan, and Tim Ayers opened the door wide.

"Come in," Ayers said. "This must be serious to drive out here on a night like this. It's not my mom, is it?"

"No sir," Patterson said, "nothing like that. Agent Morgan and I would like to ask you a few questions about your sister."

"Of course," Ayers said. "Come in by the stove where it's warmer."

Patterson and Morgan removed their boots and hung their raincoats on the pegs by the door. Ayers' cabin was small but tidy and comfortable. Throw rugs covered the hardwood floors, and flowery curtains framed the small windows. A tiny kitchen sat to the right of the door, but they followed Ayers through a doorway to the left into a cozy sitting room. A black wood stove sat against the far wall, and a brown, upholstered couch and two rocking chairs faced the source of heat. A floor lamp stationed by the couch provided the only light in the room, and an open spy novel hung over the arm of the couch.

Tim Ayers gestured to the two rocking chairs. "Have a seat. Can I get you anything to drink?"

Morgan and Patterson both sat and declined the offer of beverages. Ayers sat on the couch.

"What can I do for you?" Tim Ayers asked.

"We talked to your mother yesterday, and she said she had no idea who Tasha's friends were or what Tasha did with her time. We're hoping you can tell us more about your sister's personal life."

Tim sighed. "I wish I could help you, but Tasha didn't confide in me. We were close when we were little, but once she started high school, she barely talked to me."

"So you don't know who any of her friends were?" Patterson asked.

"If she had friends, it's news to me," Ayers said.

"Tim," Patterson said, "Did you know Tasha was a little more than two months pregnant when she was murdered?"

Tim nodded and sank back into the couch cushion. "My mother told me."

"Do you have any idea who the father of Tasha's baby was?"

Tim shook his head. "I never saw her with anyone."

"Your mother said Tasha was experiencing mood swings in the months before her death. Some days she was happy, and others days, she was so depressed she wouldn't speak. Did you notice her mood swings?" Morgan asked.

Tim Ayers shrugged. "Not really. She always seemed depressed to me."

"Your mother let us take this photo from Tasha's room." Patterson pulled the party photo from a file folder. He glanced at it and was about to hand it to Ayers when he stopped and studied the photo for a moment. Finally he handed it to Ayers. "Can you tell us who the other people in the photo are?"

Ayers took the photo from Patterson and smiled. "It was at a party at Buskin Lake in September," he said. "Tasha didn't usually hang out with me, but that night she asked if she could ride with me to the party." A tear escaped his right eye as he looked down at the photo. "I don't know why she wanted to go. I don't think she said two words to anyone, and she asked me to take her home after only a couple of hours. I think Samantha posted this photo on Facebook, and Tasha must have downloaded and printed it. I didn't even know she had it." He shook his head. "I guess these were her pretend friends, how sad."

143

"Can you tell me who this guy is?" Patterson pointed to one of the figures in the photo.

"Sure, that's Bobby Saunders," Tim said.

Morgan sat straight and looked over at the photo. He and Patterson had first seen the photo before they had interviewed Bobby Saunders, so neither of them had recognized Saunders in the photo at the time. When they had interviewed Saunders earlier in the day, he had stated he did not know Tasha Ayers. Yet, here they both were in the same photo standing a few feet from each other.

"Is he a friend of yours?" Patterson asked.

"Not really, why?"

"His name has come up before in our investigation," Patterson said.

"You think Saunders killed Tasha?" Ayers asked and started to stand.

"Calm down, Tim," Patterson said. "It's not like that. We'd just like to know more about Saunders. How well did Tasha know him?"

"She didn't. I mean, she knew who he was I'm sure, but they didn't have anything to do with each other. Saunders sometimes hangs out with Brian Beown, a casual friend of mine. That's Brian there in the red jacket." Ayers pointed at a tall, thin guy with dirty blonde hair. Saunders probably came to the party with Brian. Saunders is a loser, man. I don't have anything to do with him."

"Can you tell me the names of everyone else in the photo?" Patterson asked.

"Sure," Ayers said, "but I don't think it will do you any good. This was taken a year before Tasha died."

Ayers recited the names, while Patterson jotted them down in his notebook. Morgan doubted knowing the names of the party-goers would help the investigation either, but at this point, they needed any information they could find about Tasha Ayers' life. He was beginning to think the girl simply disappeared when she walked out of a room.

Once Tim had given him the names of everyone in the photo and told him what he knew about each individual, Patterson said, "There's one more thing, and this is a sensitive subject, but I need to ask you about it. Tasha wrote an English paper about her life, and in it, she indicated you had sexually abused her."

"What?" Ayers' face turned bright red, and his jaw tightened. "That's a load of—"

Patterson held up a hand to stop him. "Calm down, take it easy," he interrupted.

Ayers glared at Patterson for several seconds and then exhaled. "I have no idea why she would write such filth," Tim said. "She was probably mad at me about something and thought it would be a good way to get back at me." He sighed. "I love my mother, but she wasn't a great mom. Tasha and I practically raised ourselves, and Tasha, especially, had the childhood from hell. I don't know if any of my mother's so-called friends abused Tasha, but I wouldn't be surprised if one or more of them had. Something certainly turned her into a sullen, unapproachable creature about the time she started high school, but I did not abuse her." He clearly enunciated this last declaration, his gaze never wavering from Patterson's face.

Patterson nodded and looked at Morgan. "If you don't have anything else, I think we're done for now."

Morgan shook his head, and both he and Patterson stood and shook Tim Ayers' hand. Ayers said nothing as he opened the door and ushered them out.

Patterson edged the SUV onto the steep drive and started to descend, but about half way down the road, he lost control of the vehicle, and it fishtailed wildly from side to side and finally slid sideways down the drive, ending the skid in the middle of the road.

Patterson let out a breath. "Sorry," he said. "I didn't plan to do that."

Morgan looked at him and laughed. "I love Kodiak," he said.

They snaked their way through Bell's Flats and turned north onto the Chiniak Highway. Patterson eased into the right lane and crept toward Kodiak. "I hope we don't come across any car accidents," he said. "I really don't want to deal with one of those right now."

Icy rain continued to pelt the windshield, and Morgan remained quiet, allowing Patterson to concentrate on the road.

Finally, Patterson said, "What did you think of Tim Ayers?"

"He seemed sincere to me," Morgan said. "He may have molested his sister, but I don't believe he did. In any case, I think it's very unlikely he's our killer. Bobby Saunders, on the other hand, has taken two steps up the list of suspects."

"That little scab sat there and said, 'Tasha who?'" Patterson said. "I'll have him picked up tonight and held until tomorrow. We'll see if a night in jail improves his memory."

"Good idea," Morgan said. "It would be nice to keep an eye on him anyway. If he is our guy, we may have spooked him today."

Patterson told Morgan he would pick him up at 9:00 the following morning, so they could pay Rick Carson a surprise visit. "That is if I can even drive on these roads by morning."

Morgan headed up to his room and sat at the desk. He unfolded the case file on the desk and began reading his sketchy notes from the day's interviews. He turned on his laptop and expanded on his notes, recording not only what had been said during each interview but also his insights into the body language and demeanor of each interviewee. These notes would not be part of any formal case file; they were simply for his use. Weeks from now he wanted to be able to recall not only what each interview subject had said, but also how he or she had acted during the interview, and how these actions had made him feel. *Despite what they show on TV, police work isn't all science. A good cop listens to that little voice in the back of his head.*

Morgan worked for an hour without a break and then sat back in the chair and stretched his neck. He stared at his cell phone laying on the desk next to the computer, and without giving it a second thought, he snapped up the phone and dialed Jane's number. It rang four times before she answered.

"Hello," she said, panting hard.

"You okay? Is this a bad time?"

"Nick?"

"Yes."

"I was just exercising. Let me catch my breath."

"I'm impressed," Morgan said. "Are you at the gym?"

Jane laughed. "You do remember you're in Kodiak, right? No big gyms here. I'm at home. I have an elliptical. How was your trip here?"

"Fine. I can't say much for your weather, though."

"It will be an icy mess tomorrow; I can't wait. Are you staying at the Baranof?"

"I am."

"How's the investigation going?"

It both pleased and disturbed Morgan to realize how much he enjoyed hearing Jane's voice. He wished he was in the same room with her, but that would be a bad idea. This phone call was also a bad idea, but it was too late now to worry about it.

"I can't say much about the investigation, but we have our hands full. I'm working with Trooper Dan Patterson. Do you know him?"

"No," Jane said. "I hope you catch this monster soon, though. He has the entire town on edge."

"I still believe Deanna Kerr's murder is the key to solving these murders," Morgan said.

"Why?"

"Not only was she a low-risk victim, but she was killed in a fairly isolated setting."

"I've been wondering about Deanna," Jane said. "It seems like a long shot that she had engine problems and this murderer just happened to be in the middle of Uyak Bay to take advantage of her predicament."

"Wow," Morgan said, "how do you know so much about our investigation? Did I miss seeing you at the task force meeting?"

Jane laughed. "Better than that," she said, "I have friends who are connected."

"I guess you do," Morgan said. "No, I don't think Deanna bumped into her murderer by accident. I think the perpetrator did something to Deanna's engine at the Fourth of July picnic. He knew she would have engine problems, and he stood by until that happened, probably watching her through binoculars. He let her fight with the engine for a while until she was scared and out of ideas on how to fix it, and then he motored toward her and offered help."

"You think he was at the party then?"

"I think it's likely he was at the party, and if he was there, we should be able to narrow down our suspect list," Morgan said.

"I think Deanna was a convenient victim. I believe our perpetrator decided to attack her only after he saw her arrive alone at the party; he considered her easy, convenient prey."

"You don't think he stalked her?" Jane asked.

"No, but I'm basing that assumption mainly on the fact that she doesn't look like our other victims. I could be wrong; psychopaths don't necessarily follow a game plan."

"Do you think Deanna knew her attacker?"

"Possibly, but I think she would have accepted an offer of help from anyone who approached her. She had to be scared. The engine wouldn't start, and she was probably taking waves over the side of the boat. Even if her would-be rescuer frightened her, he'd still be a better alternative than a swamped boat."

"That poor kid must have been so scared, and then just when she thought she was being rescued, her nightmare got much worse."

"This is confidential, Jane, but I know I can trust your discretion. You're friends with Deanna's Aunt Sandy. Has she ever mentioned a man named Rick Carson to you? He's a friend of the Kerr family."

"I don't remember the name, why?"

"His name has come up a few times in our inquiries."

"Do you want me to ask Sandy about him?"

Morgan paused for several moments while he thought. Finally, he said, "Sergeant Patterson wouldn't be happy with me if he knew I was giving out confidential information, but as I said, I trust you, and since you're friends with Sandy Miles, you can talk to her in a way we can't. Ask Sandy if there's anyone close to the Kerr family who makes her uncomfortable. Can you do that in a way that doesn't make her wonder why you are asking that question?"

"I'll come up with something. You don't want me to mention this Rick Carson by name?"

"No, she would wonder how you know about him. Ask her in a way she doesn't suspect the question is coming from the police." He paused. "Are you sure you're okay with this? She is your friend, and I don't want to put you in the awkward position of deceiving her."

"I don't think that will happen. Sandy desperately wants you to find the person who killed Deanna, and I am sure she would do anything to help. I won't tell her I'm planning to report back to you, but I don't think she'd mind even if she knew I was a snitch. What is it about this guy that makes you suspicious of him?"

Morgan sighed. "I haven't even laid eyes on the man yet, but he helps coach the girls' volleyball team, and some of the girls think he's creepy and paid too much attention to Deanna. He has a commercial salmon fishing site near the Kerrs' site and is a friend of the family. We plan to talk to him tomorrow, but I'd like to have more insight into the guy."

"Do you want me to call her tonight?"

"No, that's not necessary. Ask her the next time you see her; wait until the moment seems right."

"I don't know if you can tell me this, but is he your main suspect?"

Morgan laughed. "At this point, we have more suspects than we know what to do with. I hope to shorten the list in the next few days."

"I'll let you know what I find out," Jane said.

"It's nice talking to you," Morgan said.

"You too."

"I'd like to see you, Jane."

"I'd like that too."

"I'll call when the investigation slows down."

"Take care, Nick."

Morgan disconnected, put his phone on the desk, and stared at it. He knew he probably shouldn't have called her, and he definitely shouldn't have told her inside information about the investigation and then asked for her help. As for telling her he wanted to see her, well, it was done now.

Morgan usually approached situations in his life, especially personal situations, with caution and restraint, but there was something about Jane Marcus that made him reckless. He didn't seem to be able to forget her.

Chapter Eighteen

Thursday, December 5th

Although it was still dark outside, Morgan could see the gleam of ice on the streets reflected by the street lights, and it was still raining. He didn't understand why the rain had never turned to snow but guessed the temperature must be hovering right at freezing. He was glad they had no plane trips planned for the day, but driving on these roads would not be an easy task. The troopers probably had their hands full with traffic accidents that morning. He decided to phone Patterson at 8:00 am to see if he wanted to delay their interview of Carson. Meanwhile, Morgan had time for some calls back to the East Coast.

Morgan's phone buzzed a few minutes before 8:00 am.

"Are we still on for 9:00?" Patterson asked.

"Sure," Morgan said. "I thought you might be busy dealing with cars in the ditch."

"We've had a few reports, but not as many as you might think. The roads started to get icy after most people had driven home from work last night, and I hope they are smart enough this morning to stay home. It also helped that this storm happened on a weeknight and a school night instead of the weekend."

"Good to hear," Morgan said. "I'll be waiting at the front door at 9:00 am."

Patterson arrived five minutes early, and Morgan was already at the front door. The sky had lightened a bit, but unless the clouds lifted, even mid-day today would be as dark as evening on the East Coast.

"How are the roads?" Morgan asked as he climbed into the SUV.

"Terrible. Maureen can't even get out of her garage because the garage door is frozen shut. We'll stop by and pick her up."

A few minutes later, they pulled up in front of a small, white house. Maureen Horner had apparently been watching from a window for their arrival because she hurried from the front door, the hood of her parka pulled tight over her face. When her feet hit the concrete walkway leading from the front door, she slipped and nearly fell. She caught her balance and proceeded with more caution. She opened the rear door of the SUV and slid onto the seat.

"Yuck!" she said. "This ice will make our lives hell if it doesn't melt soon."

"It's supposed to warm up this afternoon and stop raining," Patterson said.

"I heard on the radio it will be in the forties tomorrow," Maureen said. "I hope they know what they're talking about."

"Yes, but the forecast is also calling for storm-force winds tomorrow night," Patterson said.

"Wonderful," Maureen said. "Pick your poison; it's winter in Kodiak."

Patterson drove slowly, inching his way out Spruce Cape Road and finally turning into the driveway of a small, white house. The house didn't look like much from the front side, but Morgan suspected windows covered the rear wall offering a vista of Spruce Cape and the Pacific Ocean.

Patterson rang the front door bell, and he, Morgan, and Horner stood in the shelter of the porch, listening to the bells chime for several seconds. Morgan was beginning to think Carson wasn't home, but then the door flew open, revealing a man in gray sweatpants and a red sweatshirt. Rick Carson stood nearly six-feet tall. He had a full head of light-brown hair, an aquiline nose, small mouth and milky blue eyes. His features were delicate, almost feminine. A red tongue shot out of his mouth and licked his pale pink lips.

"Yes?" he said in a quiet, high voice that made Morgan think of Michael Jackson.

"Mr. Rick Carson?" Patterson asked.

"That's right."

"I'm Sergeant Patterson with the Alaska State Troopers." He gestured to Horner and Morgan. "This is Detective Horner with the Kodiak Police Department and Special Agent Morgan with the FBI."

"Oh, my." Carson blinked and took a step back. "What did I do to deserve a visit from you three?"

"May we come in?" Patterson asked.

Carson turned to look at the interior of his house and then returned his gaze to his visitors. "Sure, I guess so, but I wasn't expecting company. The place is a mess."

"I'm sure we don't mind, sir," Horner said.

Carson opened the door and Patterson, Horner, and Morgan entered a wide foyer neatly arranged with coat hooks and a bench for removing boots and shoes. From what Morgan could see of the rest of the house, it appeared immaculate, and he wondered why Carson had been so reluctant to invite them into his house.

Patterson, Horner, and Morgan removed their boots, coats, hats, and gloves and followed Carson into his great room. As Morgan had thought, the great room faced a bank of large windows, revealing a spectacular view of the cape and the stormy ocean. Morgan, Patterson, and Horner all stared at the stunning view for several seconds before taking in the rest of their surroundings.

Morgan's eyes widened when he saw the corner of the great room. It was decorated like a little girl's bedroom. Pink cushions sat on a small couch, and shelves above the couch held dolls and stuffed animals of every size. A tea set sat on the small table in front of the couch. Patterson, Morgan, and Horner all noticed the unsettling display at the same time, and they stood in the middle of the great room, staring at it.

A giggle escaped Carson's pink lips. "That's for my nieces," he said. "They like to play in here."

Morgan couldn't stop staring at the dolls, but Patterson returned his gaze to Carson. "How many nieces do you have?"

Carson's gaze darted around the room, looking everywhere except at Patterson's face. "Well, I only have one brother, and he has a girl and a boy. They live in Des Moines, but my friends' kids call me Uncle Rick, and I think of them as my nieces and nephews."

"I see," Patterson said, "and you have a lot of friends?"

"Yes I do, Sergeant." Carson pointed to a brown leather couch and three leather chairs, all facing the windows and the view. "Please sit," he said.

Patterson and Horner both sat on the couch, but Morgan stood staring at the dolls and the tea set. He was trying to record the display in his memory, and he hoped to have a chance to surreptitiously photograph it with his phone before they left Carson's home.

"It's stuffy in here, don't you think?" Carson's gaze flitted to Morgan who was still examining the dolls. "Agent Morgan, would you mind turning on the ceiling fan above you, so we can get some air circulation in here?"

Morgan slowly turned away from the dolls. He wanted Carson to know the display interested him. He hoped to make Carson uncomfortable. If the man was nervous, he might say more than he wanted to say.

"Sure," Morgan said. He walked to the center of the room and tugged on the fancy crystal fan pull. The brass blades slowly began to turn, and Morgan made his way to one of the leather chairs near the window. As he lowered himself into the chair, he asked, "Mr. Carson, do you have young girls over to your house often?"

"Only when their parents are visiting," Carson said, a frown on his face and his voice raised.

"You mentioned entertaining boys and girls, but I don't see any toys for boys," Morgan said.

"I have plenty of toys for boys," Carson said. "I have a toy train, a football, video games, and plenty of things for boys. What are you suggesting?"

"It's odd to see so many dolls and a tea set in a bachelor's home," Morgan said. "Surely you must understand that."

"What I understand," Carson said, his face red, "is you have a dirty mind. I like kids, there's no crime in that." He looked from Morgan to Patterson to Horner. "Why are you here anyway? You have no cause to come into my home and start insulting me. I've done nothing wrong."

"Mr. Carson," Patterson said. "Did you know Tasha Ayers?"

"The girl who was murdered?" Carson asked. "No, I didn't know her. Why would I?"

Patterson shrugged. "You help coach at the high school, and she was a student there."

"She wasn't on the volleyball team," Carson said. "I don't know all the kids in the high school. Why would you think I would know her?"

"Did you know Deborah Sidle or Amy Quinn?"

"No," Carson said. "Weren't they the other two women who were murdered? Why are you asking me these questions?"

"You did know Deanna Kerr, though; didn't you?" Patterson continued.

Carson held up his hands in a stopping motion. "Wait a minute," he said, "I heard Deanna was murdered. I knew her, yes, but I never would have harmed a hair on that sweet girl's head. Why would you think that?"

"Were you at the set-netter's picnic on the Fourth of July?" Patterson shot the questions, one after the next.

"Yes," Carson began to nod but then shook his head. "Wait a minute, no, I didn't go to the picnic last year; I had company."

"Who was that?"

"Who was what?" Carson yelled the question.

Morgan studied him carefully. The man was losing his cool.

"Your company," Patterson said. "Who was your company?"

"Gordon Small," Carson said. "Coach Small came out to visit for a week. He wouldn't have known most of the people at the party, so I let my two crew members go, and I stayed at the site with Gordon."

This surprising piece of news interrupted Patterson's barrage of questions. He stopped and stared at Carson for several seconds. Finally, he said, "Were you and Coach Small together all that day?"

"You can't expect me to remember that." The pause in questioning had allowed Carson to regain his equilibrium. His voice sounded calmer, his face a shade paler. "I have three boats. Sometimes Gordon took one to go fishing. As I recall, I had work to do on the net that day. While I was mending the net, Gordon probably took the skiff out to halibut fish."

"Did you stay at your place all day?" Patterson asked.

"I'm sure I did. I don't know where else I would have gone."

Patterson changed tactics. "You help Coach Small with the volleyball team, don't you?"

"That's right," Carson said.

"We talked to the girls on the volleyball squad, and they told us you paid an unusual amount of attention to Deanna."

Carson's face flushed again. "Deanna's parents and I are friends. I've known Deanna and her sister and brother since they were babies! I truly did love her like a niece, so of course I paid attention to her. She and I were close. I spent hours and days searching for her when she went missing, and I cried like a baby when the skiff was found without her in it. I cried again when I heard she had been murdered." Carson sobbed and he placed his hands over his mouth.

Morgan noted that his eyes remained dry.

Patterson leaned forward and his gaze pierced Carson. "What type of relationship did you have with Deanna?"

"I told you," Carson whined. "I loved her like a niece. I never would have hurt her."

"Did you molest that little girl, Rick?" Patterson yelled the question.

Carson let loose a keening wail. "No! I told you no." He put his head in his hands and sobbed and then looked up several seconds later, his eyes red, and his face damp. "Maybe you should talk to her father," he said. He gulped in air and tried to steady himself. "No, scratch that I didn't mean it. I shouldn't have said it."

"Why should we talk to her father?" Patterson pushed.

"Oh no," he began to sob again. "Forget what I said. Please don't tell Jack I said that."

"You did say we should talk to her father, sir, and you need to tell us what you meant by your statement."

Carson wiped the palms of his hands on his sweatpants, and his eyes darted around the room. "I shouldn't have said anything. It's just that Deanna didn't seem close to her father. In fact, I never thought she liked him much. One time last year after volleyball practice, I asked Deanna if I could give her a ride home, and she told me her mom wouldn't be home for a couple of hours, and she didn't want to go home yet because her dad was the only one at home. I don't think she wanted to be home alone with him." Carson shrugged. "I asked her if there was a problem with her dad, and she said they'd had a fight, and maybe that was all there was to it, but I got the feeling she wasn't telling me something."

"Did you ask her dad about it?" Patterson asked.

"No, I felt it was none of my business, and I never saw him do anything to Deanna. As a matter of fact, I rarely ever saw them talk to each other. Jack was probably overprotective of his teenage daughter, and Deanna resented him for it. Listen, please don't tell Jack I told you this. That poor man was devastated after Deanna went missing, and I haven't even been able to bring myself to call him after hearing Deanna was murdered. I'm sure his heart is crushed, and the last thing I want to do is bring more pain to that family."

Interesting, Morgan thought. *You don't want to bring more pain to the Kerr family, but you made sure to tell us you thought Jack Kerr might be abusing his daughter. Do you really believe that, or are you trying to draw attention away from yourself?*

Patterson and Horner had no evidence tying Rick Carson to the other murders, but the lack of evidence didn't mean he wasn't at the top of their list of suspects. They told him not to leave the island, and while they talked to him, Morgan eased his phone out of his pocket and snapped two photos of the dolls and tea set. He wanted to learn as much as he could about Rick Carson.

"Carson has my interest," Patterson said when he, Morgan, and Horner were back in the SUV.

"His house was spotless," Horner said. "He wasn't worried about us seeing a messy house, he was concerned about hiding his kiddy fantasy land. The guy has a problem."

"I would love to get a look at his computer," Morgan said.

"Unfortunately, no probable cause for a search," Patterson shook his head. "I would like to tear that house apart."

"Let's put pressure on him and see if we can't find a reason to get a judge to issue a search warrant," Morgan said.

"It will be too late by then," Horner said. "I'm certain that as we speak, Mr. Carson is destroying his computer hard drive and dumping every piece of incriminating evidence in his home."

"He has a beautiful home," Morgan said. "Do we know where he got his money? He doesn't seem to work anywhere."

"Ben has been looking into Carson's financial status," Patterson said as he steered slowly down the icy streets. "I guess he invented some sort of door for a crab pot that keeps the crab from escaping once they get inside the pot. Ben says it's only a little piece of plastic, but Carson has made millions on it. Apparently, Carson is good at investing and spends his time doing that now."

"The sky is clearing," Morgan said, peering out of the windshield

Patterson grunted. "Clear skies are both good and bad. The freezing rain should stop, but the temperature will drop so the ice won't melt."

"What do you think about Carson pointing the finger at Jack Kerr?" Horner asked.

"It was a desperate attempt to distract us," Patterson said. "When he felt himself drowning, he grabbed one of his closest friends and pulled him down with him."

"I agree with you," Morgan said, "but we should look into Jack Kerr's whereabouts during the other murders. It is a possibility, a distant one I grant you, but still, a possibility, that if Jack Kerr murdered Deborah Sidle and Deanna found out about it, he killed his daughter to keep her quiet."

"I guess we need to check Jack Kerr closer, but I can't believe he murdered these women," Patterson said. "Do you know the Kerrs, Maureen?"

"I know who they are from their real estate business," Horner said, "but I've never met them. They have good reputations, though."

"Rick Carson is a much more interesting suspect than Jack Kerr," Morgan said. "I took some photos of his doll collection, and I'll send them to an associate of mine who is an expert on child predators."

"That's not a job I would want," Horner said. "Pedophiles are the lowest form of scum."

Patterson drove to the jail, where he and Morgan parted ways with Horner. Maureen had another case she needed to deal with but promised she would be at the 2:00 pm task force meeting."

Morgan and Patterson waited in an interview room until Bobby Saunders was escorted into the room in handcuffs and an orange jumpsuit.

"You've got no reason to hold me!" he yelled as soon as he walked through the doorway. "I want out of here now."

Patterson told Saunders to sit while he and Morgan remained standing. Patterson hovered over Saunders and then bent, so his face was only a few inches away from Saunders' face. "You lied to us, Bobby."

Saunders tried to back away from Patterson, but there was nowhere to go; his chair was already backed against the wall. "What do you mean?" he said, his voice lowered, his gaze averted.

"Did you think we weren't going to find out you knew Tasha Ayers?" Patterson moved in even closer.

"I didn't really know her." Saunders shrugged.

"Bobby we have a photograph of you and Tasha at the same party. You're going to tell us you didn't know her?" Patterson barked these last few words, and Saunders cringed as if he'd been slapped.

"I didn't know her very well," he said.

"Yesterday you didn't know her at all." Patterson held his position, his voice now low and menacing. "Will we find out tomorrow you were best friends, or maybe you were lovers?"

"No," Saunders said, "it wasn't like that. I tried to talk to her a few times, but she wouldn't have anything to do with me. She thought she was too good for me, but she was just white trash."

"When did you try to talk to her?" Patterson asked.

"What? I don't know, at the party you're talking about, and I saw her a few times at Dog Bay when I was living on my buddy's boat."

"What was Tasha doing at the boat harbor?"

"How am I supposed to know that? I told you, she wouldn't talk to me."

"Did you ever see her with anyone at the boat harbor?"

Saunders stopped and thought for a few seconds. "No. She was always by herself. Once I saw her early in the morning with a duffel bag. It looked like she'd been sleeping on someone's boat."

"Did you see her near the boat where you were staying?"

"No. I saw her once in the parking lot and two or three more times near the main ramp."

"So you have no idea where she was staying?"

"For all I know, she was visiting a friend," Saunders said.

Patterson straightened and sat in the chair facing Saunders. "I'd better not find out you lied to us again, Bobby."

"No, man, I'm telling you the truth. The only reason I was at the same party as Tasha was because her brother and I have a couple of the same friends. That's it."

Patterson asked Saunders several more questions and then released him, telling him not to leave the island. Saunders assured Patterson he couldn't afford to leave Kodiak.

Patterson asked Morgan if he'd prefer to go back to trooper headquarters or his hotel.

"If no one's using it, I can work in your conference room. I need to make some calls on another case," Morgan said.

"Good," Patterson said, "I'll take you to Henry's for lunch."

Patterson and Morgan returned to trooper headquarters at 1:45 pm after a late lunch. They were walking toward the door when Ben Johnstone pulled into the lot in his red Toyota pickup. He took the turn into the lot too fast, hit a patch of ice, and the truck began fishtailing. Morgan held his breath as the pickup careened out of control toward one of the trooper SUVS. A pendant on a long chain hanging on Johnstone's rear-view mirror swung furiously back and forth as Patterson and Morgan watched helplessly. At the last moment, Johnstone got the truck under control and braked to a stop. He reached up and grabbed the pendant to stop it from swinging and then grinned sheepishly at Patterson and Morgan. He slowly pulled into a parking space and exited the truck.

"Sorry sir," Johnstone said to Patterson. "Guess I was going too fast."

"Your truck is a little light on this ice," Patterson said. "Until the road conditions improve, why don't you drive one of our SUVs? You could be called out to an accident scene at any hour of the night, and the SUVs have better traction."

"Yes sir," Johnstone said.

"A few minutes later, Patterson, Morgan, Troopers Mark Traner and Ben Johnstone, and Park Ranger Liz Kelley all sat in the conference room. "Maureen called and said she was running a few minutes late, so let's wait for a bit to start," Patterson said. "These icy roads are slowing down everything today. How are the roads in the park, Liz?"

"A nightmare," Liz said. "I haven't been able to do rounds as often as you wanted me to, but only a few people have been stupid enough to try to drive around the park in the last two days."

"No red trucks, I'm guessing," Patterson said.

"No, sir. Nothing that looked like what I saw the other day."

Maureen Horner breezed into the conference room, "Sorry I'm late," she said. "Did I miss anything?"

"Liz was just telling us that she hasn't seen the red truck again," Patterson said. "We haven't talked about anything else, yet. Do you know if Chief Feeney plans to attend our meeting?"

"No," Maureen said, "he told me he wouldn't be able to make it."

Morgan noticed a smile start to spread across Patterson's face before he quickly contained it. Morgan knew Feeney grated on Patterson's nerves, and he suspected they would all get more done without the police chief in the room waging a turf war.

Patterson began the meeting by telling the task force members about the interviews of the past few days. Both Traner and Johnstone had spent the better part of the day dealing with traffic accidents on the icy roads, so they hadn't been able to spend much time on the murder investigations. Traner was still looking through vehicle registrations but had not found a red truck matching Liz's description that belonged to anyone of interest in their investigation.

"I have a list of everyone we've interviewed in the investigation and the vehicle or vehicles each person owns," Johnstone said and passed a copy of the list to each task force member. "I don't know how this will help us, but it might come in handy."

Patterson asked Morgan to share his opinions of the investigation up to this point.

"We have more questions than answers," Morgan said. "Tasha is an enigma because we haven't found anyone who can tell us much about what she did or who her friends or even acquaintances were. We know she didn't spend much time at school. She was failing several classes, including English, her favorite class. Her English teacher told her she was getting an F, and it upset Tasha so much she stormed out of the school. The school counselor tried to help her, but he said Tasha didn't seem interested in school or her grades. Why not? What was going on in her life? Who was the father of her baby? If we can answer some of those questions, we may be able to narrow down our list of suspects."

Morgan paused and looked around the room. "Bobby Saunders told us this morning that he'd run into Tasha a few times at the Dog Bay boat harbor. I'm not sure we can believe Bobby, but if it's true, why was Tasha at the harbor? Was she staying on a boat there? I recommend we check with the harbormaster to see who had boats in the harbor in October. The answer to that question may point us in a specific direction."

"That might help," Horner said, "but Tasha could have been staying on a fishing boat with one of the boat's crewmen."

"Someone in the boat harbor must have seen her come and go from a boat," Patterson said. "We need to get down to the harbor, talk to the harbormaster and guards and then start walking the docks and interviewing anyone who is spending the winter on a boat."

Traner groaned. "That sounds like a fun job for an icy winter day."

"Great," Patterson said. "Thanks for volunteering, Mark."

"What about the father of Tasha's baby?" Morgan asked. "Does anyone have an idea who that could be?"

"I think Bobby Saunders' name should be at the top of the list," Maureen said. "I watched the tape of your interview with him, and he admitted he was staying in the boat harbor when he saw Tasha there. Sure, if he was the father, then it was pretty stupid for him to admit he saw Tasha near where he was staying, but he's not the sharpest knife in the drawer, and he has already lied once."

"What about Rick Carson?" Johnstone asked. "He sounds like a creepy guy."

"Carson is a creepy guy, but we don't yet have any proof he knew Tasha. No one has reported seeing them together."

"Jerome Collins claims he didn't know Tasha," Traner said, "but Tasha was in his son's class, and we know Collins frequents prostitutes. It's possible he was paying Tasha for sex."

"Or maybe he romanced her, and it didn't cost him anything," Horner said.

The room quieted, and Morgan looked around at the task force members. "Who else?" he asked.

"Coach Small is a possibility," Patterson said. "He claims he didn't know Tasha, but he would say that, wouldn't he?"

"Let's come back to him," Morgan said. "There is someone else we should consider. This is not someone I would put high on the list, mainly because of the two prostitutes, but we shouldn't discount Brad Wells."

"The high school kid?" Horner asked.

"Yes," Morgan said. "He knew Deanna and probably also knew Tasha, and he was at the Fourth of July party with Deanna."

"Mark, you were going to check on that," Patterson said. "Have you found anyone who can tell you when Brad Wells left that party?"

"Sir, I called Brad's parents and told them we were trying to learn as much as we could about who was at the Fourth of July party," Traner said. "I asked when their family left the party and if they all left in the same boat. They told me they stayed late and all left together around 8:00 pm."

Patterson nodded. "If that's true, we can mark Brad off our list. Agent Morgan and I will pay the Kerrs another visit. We would like to interview Jody Kerr if she's less sedated today, and we would also like to talk to Jack about his relationship with his daughter."

"I'd like to separate the two of them," Morgan said, "and find out what each one thinks about Rick Carson and Coach Small."

"We'll see if Jody is stable enough to question," Patterson said.

After the meeting had ended, Morgan walked to the white board to study the photographs of the murdered women. *What horrors did these women experience during the last minutes of their lives? Whose face had they last seen? Did their murderer surprise them, or had they known they were about to die?* He studied each photograph, searching for anything he had missed. It occurred to him that the photo of Tasha Ayers portrayed an aura of toughness as well as one of fragility. She wore Goth-style makeup, but her hair was tied with a red ribbon. Of all these women, he most would have liked to have known Tasha Ayers. *Complicated and mysterious describes what we know about Tasha so far. She was a young woman at the crossroads of her life. According to her English teacher, Linda Bragg, she possessed great potential, but according to the school counselor, Paul Mather, as well as her other teachers, her life was spinning out of control. Did the father of her baby murder her?*

Morgan stood back and studied the group of murdered women as a whole. There was something about these photos that nagged at him. He felt certain he was missing something. He left the conference room, found Patterson in his office and asked Patterson if he would e-mail him the photos of the four women. When he returned to his hotel room tonight, he would examine each photo more carefully.

"Are you up for another visit with Jack and Jody Kerr?" Patterson asked.

Morgan nodded. "Let's go."

The sky was still blue when they left trooper headquarters at 3:30 pm, but the light was already beginning to fade. A stiff wind blew out of the north, dropping the ambient temperature at least 10 degrees. Patterson unlocked the SUV and started the heater. Morgan climbed in and rubbed his hands together.

"I thought you and Maureen said it was supposed to get warmer," Morgan said.

"I thought we said that too," Patterson said. "There is a big low-pressure system headed our way, so we should start seeing clouds soon."

"I'm looking forward to clouds," Morgan said.

"Be careful what you wish for," Patterson said. "We're expecting rain with winds of 60 knots; that's nearly 70 mph."

"Do you ever have nice, warm days here in the winter?"

"This is my first winter on Kodiak," Patterson said, "but from what I hear, nice, warm winter days don't exist here. You either have nice and cold or warm and ugly and of course, there's also cold and ugly."

"Right now, I think I'll take warm and ugly."

Morgan studied the stained-glass salmon window as they waited for the Kerrs to open the door and was surprised when they were greeted by Jody Kerr. She looked better today and was dressed in a sweatshirt and jeans. Her hair still hung around her face in strands, though, and her skin gleamed a ghostly pale. Her face remained expressionless as she looked from one man to the other, and Morgan wasn't certain she knew who they were.

"Mrs. Kerr," Patterson said. "Do you remember us? I'm Sergeant Patterson with the troopers, and this is FBI Special Agent Nick Morgan."

She nodded but didn't invite them inside. "Jack isn't here; he's picking up the kids from school. He'll be back in a while."

She started to close the door, but Patterson took half a step forward, putting his foot between the door and the frame. "Ma'am, would it be alright if we speak to you for a minute?"

Jody Kerr's eyes opened wide in surprise, the first emotion other than sorrow Morgan had seen on her face. "Sure, I guess," she said.

She opened the door wider, and Morgan followed Patterson into the entryway. Jody stood in the entryway and did not seem inclined to invite her guests into her home.

"Would it be okay if we sit in there by the fire?" Patterson asked.

Jody shrugged and turned to walk toward the great room. Morgan and Patterson removed their boots and made their way to the chairs in front of the fireplace. Jody sat across from them on the couch.

"How are you doing ma'am?" Morgan asked.

Jody shrugged. "I am trying to find the strength to go on living for the sake of my kids, but it isn't easy."

Morgan could tell Jody was still sedated, but at least she seemed coherent today. She might not be coherent enough to testify in court, but he felt she was clear-headed enough to answer their questions, and they were fortunate to find her home alone without Jack Kerr there to keep a watchful eye on her.

"A few things have come up in our investigation that we need to talk to you about," Patterson said.

Jody nodded but said nothing.

"What was Deanna's relationship like with you and Jack?" Patterson asked.

Jody stared at Patterson for several seconds. "I don't understand the question," she said. "She was our daughter. We laughed and cried together. Sometimes she got in trouble, but more often, she did something wonderful, and we were proud of her. She was a good student, a good athlete, and a nice person." Tears fell from Jody's eyes. "She was a wonderful big sister, and the best daughter we could have asked for."

"How did she and Jack get along?" Patterson asked.

"I don't know," Jody said. "They had their ups and downs. Deanna was a teenager. Jack tried to protect her, and he can be strict. Sometimes they butted heads, but they usually got along fine."

"Did Deanna mind being alone with Jack?" Patterson asked.

Morgan knew Patterson needed to tread lightly here. Jody Kerr was a fragile woman, and it would be easy to upset her.

Jody's head recoiled as if she'd been struck. "What is that supposed to mean? Of course, she didn't mind being alone with her father. Why would she?"

"Yes ma'am," Patterson said. "What can you tell us about Rick Carson?"

Jody Kerr crossed her arms and hugged herself. "I don't understand what you mean. He's a friend. He has a fish site near ours, and we've known him for several years."

"What was his relationship with Deanna like?"

Jody jumped to her feet, and Morgan thought she was about to run out of the room, but instead, she paced the length of the great room back and forth several times before she said, "I knew it. I knew he had something to do with this."

"Ma'am?" Patterson said.

"What did he do to my baby?" Jody wailed.

Patterson stood and walked toward Jody. "Please sit down, ma'am. I didn't mean to upset you. We don't know that Mr. Carson did anything to Deanna. We only want to get a feeling for how he and Deanna got along together."

Jody paced for two more minutes, and then her energy seemed to drain, and she slumped back onto the couch. She dropped her head into her hands and rubbed her temples. She looked at Patterson. "I don't know what I think anymore," she said. "Rick Carson has always been a friend to us, and he loves to babysit our kids. He never misses one of their soccer matches, recitals, or plays; he's always there to cheer them on. The kids, including Deanna, adore him, and I have never seen him act inappropriate with any of them, and if I had, I wouldn't have left him alone with the kids." She stopped and seemed to be lost in thought.

"But?" Patterson prodded.

"But, I have to admit that Rick is an odd guy, and more than once I've wondered why a bachelor would take such an interest in kids, and not just my kids mind you, but kids in general. I think he's gay, but he's never said he is, and I'm not sure he's even admitted it to himself. In any case, that doesn't explain his interest in kids."

"Does he pay more attention to your girls than he does to your son?" Morgan asked.

Jody gave Morgan a surprised look as if she just now remembered he was in the room. "I never thought about it," she said, "but I think he treats all the kids the same. As I said, I've never seen him leer at the kids or touch them in inappropriate ways. He's a strange man."

"Do you have any reason to think he may have been involved in Deanna's death?" Patterson asked.

"No. I don't know. I keep running this stuff over and over in my head. At this point, I suspect everyone who was in Uyak Bay on the Fourth of July."

Her list isn't much longer than ours, Morgan thought.

At that moment, a side door opened, and a boy and girl rushed into the house, followed by Jack Kerr. Morgan knew from Deanna's file that Evelyn was her 12-year-old sister, and William was her eight-year-old brother. Both kids ran toward their mother but stopped short when they saw Patterson and Morgan.

"Sergeant, Agent," Jack Kerr said, "we weren't expecting you today."

Morgan knew by the tone of his voice Jack Kerr was not pleased to have them sitting in his great room talking to his wife, and Morgan wondered whether his concern was for his wife or for what she might say.

"Jack," Patterson stood and held out his hand. "Some things have come up in our investigation, and we wanted to run them by you and Jody."

"You kids go to your rooms and work on your homework," Jack said.

Jody stood, "I think I'll lie down," she said. "I'm tired."

"Thank you for talking to us, ma'am," Patterson said, and he, Morgan and Jack Kerr stood and watched Jody leave the room.

"I'd rather you didn't talk to Jody without me here," Jack said. "She's very fragile."

"She seems better today," Patterson said.

"We're taking it day by day," Jack said. "Some days she's okay, and other days she's a wreck."

"I know this has been a terrible time for all of you, and the sooner we catch the monster who murdered Deanna, the sooner you can begin to heal," Patterson said.

"I understand," Jack said. He sat on the couch where Jody had been sitting, and Patterson and Morgan returned to their chairs. "What can I help you with?"

"How would you describe your relationship with Deanna?" Patterson asked.

"What does that have to do with anything?" Jack asked. "I'm her dad. We had a typical father-daughter relationship."

"Did you fight a lot?"

"Look, I don't know what you're getting at here, but I don't appreciate it." Kerr did not raise his voice, but his words were measured, his anger barely concealed. "Instead of worrying about Deanna's and my relationship, why don't you spend your time searching for her killer?"

"It helps our investigation if we can get to know the victim better," Patterson said.

"I don't see how this can possibly help your investigation, but Deanna and I had a normal relationship, no different than my relationship with Evelyn or Will. Deanna was a teenager, and I may have been too overprotective at times. We clashed on occasion, but Deanna was a good girl, and I had little reason to get mad at her."

Morgan carefully studied Jack Kerr. Jack would never admit to abusing his daughter. The purpose of Patterson's questions was to see how Kerr reacted to them, but Morgan couldn't read Jack Kerr. The questions had certainly angered him, but he'd maintained his composure. He had reacted as a normal, innocent man would react, but he could also be mimicking what he knew to be acceptable normal behavior. It was difficult to tell with this man.

Patterson changed his line of questioning. "I understand Rick Carson is a friend of yours?"

"That's right," Jack said and Morgan saw his muscles relax at the change in questioning.

"What did you think about his relationship with Deanna?"

"Okay, I know where you're going here." Jack held up a hand. "I admit Rick is a little strange, and when Deanna was young, I thought he took too much interest in her. Then I realized that Rick loves kids, and I don't mean he loves them in the way you're suggesting. He enjoys being around them; he should have been a school teacher. He's a great babysitter, and all my kids love him."

"We talked to Deanna's volleyball teammates, and they think Rick is creepy and that he took too much interest in Deanna," Patterson said.

Kerr nodded. "Deanna talked to her mother and me about that. She felt bad for Rick because the other kids didn't understand him. She tried to tell her friends he's a nice guy who is just a little strange, but they thought he was odd."

"What was your advice to her?" Patterson asked.

"Jody told her to stand her ground and treat Rick the same at volleyball practice as she would anywhere else. Jody felt the other girls would come around once they saw Deanna being nice to him."

"And your feelings about him didn't change after Deanna went missing?" Patterson asked.

"Not at all," Jack said. "If anything, I felt closer than ever to Rick after we lost Deanna. He spent hours and hours searching for the boat. He pulled his nets, and all he and his crew did was search for Deanna until our boat was found. He lost quite a bit of money by not fishing during that time, but all he cared about was finding Deanna. Rick may be odd, but he'd give you the shirt off his back if you asked him for it. He's a good guy and a solid friend. The other day he even dropped off a pickup load of wood. He cut it, hauled it, stacked it, and even split some of it. He's a good guy."

Morgan wondered if Jack's praises would be less effusive if he knew Carson had thrown him under the bus by suggesting Deanna did not like to be alone with her dad.

"You don't really suspect Rick murdered Deanna, do you?" Jack asked. "That's absurd."

"At this point, sir, everyone who was in Uyak Bay on the Fourth of July is a suspect."

"Jack Kerr is not at the top of my suspect list for the guy who murdered two prostitutes and two girls," Patterson said when they were back in the SUV. He turned the heater to high. No clouds had invaded the sky yet, but the wind had increased.

"He's a hard guy to pin down," Morgan said. "On the one hand, he has been over-sedating his wife, or at least standing by doing nothing while she takes too many pills, but from what little I saw of his kids, they seem happy and well-adjusted."

"He could be sedating his wife out of love; he doesn't want her to feel the pain of their loss, but it's also clear he doesn't want her talking to us unless he's in the room," Patterson said. "I think he's just a guy who likes to control every situation, and he doesn't know how to handle Deanna's murder."

"That's very possible," Morgan said. "I was impressed he stood up for his friend, Rick Carson. Carson certainly didn't do that for him."

"No, and I like Carson more and more all the time for these murders."

"I have a question for you," Morgan said. "Does the timeline fit for Jack Kerr to leave the party, take his family home and then find Deanna and offer her help?"

"It's possible," Patterson said. "It would only take him an hour to get home from the party, so he had plenty of time. He could have told Jody he was heading out to check his fishing gear, and she wouldn't have given it another thought."

Patterson dropped Morgan at the hotel. Morgan didn't feel like eating in the hotel dining room, so he ordered fish tacos and a drink from the room-service menu. This time, Morgan paused before calling Jane, but he finally convinced himself he had a legitimate reason to talk to her. He leaned against the headboard of the bed in his hotel room and placed the call.

"Agent Morgan," Jane said when she answered, "how are you this evening?"

Morgan smiled at the sound of her voice. "Lonely, so I thought I'd bother you." He sat his scotch on the bedside table. *Get a grip. Keep this professional* he scolded himself.

"Lucky for you I'm not out taking a stroll on this lovely evening," Jane said.

Morgan laughed. "You'd get blown off the island if you tried that."

"At least it has warmed up, and the ice is melting," she said.

"I'm not sure I could survive a winter here," Morgan said. "This is extreme weather."

"Ah, but it makes spring all that much sweeter."

"And spring is when?"

"Sometime in June if we're lucky."

"You're from tougher stock than I am," he said.

"How is the investigation going?" Jane asked.

"That's actually why I'm calling. Have you spoken to Sandy Miles yet?"

"No," Jane said. "I'm getting together tomorrow night with her and some other friends, and I thought I'd talk to her then. You said you weren't in a hurry."

"That's right," Morgan said. "I'd like you to ask her about something else, and this is extremely delicate."

"What is it?"

"Try to get a general impression about how Deanna and her dad got along with each other."

"Okay," Jane paused, "is there anything particular about their relationship that interests you?"

Morgan didn't answer for several seconds. "Someone told us Deanna didn't like to be alone with her dad. I suspect the person who said this was lying and attempting to deflect suspicion away from himself, but if it is true, I'd like to know."

"It might be difficult to think of a way to ask that question, but I'll try to get a general impression of their relationship from Sandy. I know Sandy thinks Jack should be trying harder to get Jody off the tranquilizers and anti-depressants, so she might be willing to talk about him."

"Thanks, Jane; I appreciate it."

After Morgan had disconnected, he carried his scotch to the desk and sat in the chair. He opened his laptop and brought up the photos of the murder victims. Patterson had e-mailed him both the photos of the women displayed on the whiteboard in the conference room and the photos taken of them when their bodies had been discovered. He started in chronological order.

Morgan again noted the hard look on Deborah Sidle's face. *The woman is so thin she could have been anorexic. Was she a drug addict? The large, gold, hoop earrings look too big for her small face. Was she wearing those or the beautiful purple, possibly amethyst, necklace when she was murdered?* Morgan brought up the photo of Deborah Sidle's pale and bloated body after she'd been discovered in the boat harbor. She'd been found nude, and she was wearing no jewelry in this photo. She had been in the water for several hours though, so any jewelry she'd been wearing may have fallen off her.

Victim number two, Tasha Ayers, looked toward her photographer with big, blue eyes rimmed in black. Her hair was pulled back with a tie-dyed red ribbon, revealing the large, pointed, silver studs in her ears. Silver studs also decorated the black leather choker around her neck. He looked at the photo of her dead body. Tasha had also been found naked, and she wore no jewelry in the photo. *Was she wearing the earrings and necklace when she was murdered?* He made a note to call Hope Mills the following day to ask if the necklace and earrings were missing. Whether or not Tasha was wearing the necklace and earrings, Hope had mentioned a bangle Tasha wore all the time and Hope believed Tasha had been wearing the bangle the night she was killed.

Morgan also made a note to ask the Kerrs if Deanna always wore the silver and pearl chain she had around her neck in her photograph. If the killer collected jewelry from his victims as trophies, and they found Deanna's silver chain in his possession, they would have one piece of solid evidence against him for her murder. Of all the victims, Deanna's case would be the most difficult to prove because her remains had yielded so little physical evidence. Even though the state medical examiner was convinced she'd been murdered, it would be an uphill battle to prove her death hadn't been an accident. A decent defense lawyer could find any number of medical examiners who would, for a price, argue that Deanna died from falling out of the boat in a storm.

In her photo, the fourth victim, Amy Quinn, wore a gold locket on a long chain around her neck, but she had been wearing no jewelry when Liz found her body. Morgan suspected the murderer had taken the women's jewelry as trophies, and if the police were lucky, he would still have the jewelry in his possession when they arrested him. He had probably hidden it somewhere, but the hiding place would be easily accessible to him, so he could look at the jewelry often and recall the murders.

Chapter Nineteen

Friday, December 6th
7:30 am

Morgan's phone rang at 7:30 am the following morning.

"I think we found the truck," Patterson said.

"The red truck? Who does it belong to?"

"It took awhile because it's registered in Washington State, but Ben ran it down last night. A William Small in Seattle owns a 2014 burgundy Ford F-150."

"What makes you think it's our truck?" Morgan asked.

"William Small is Coach Small's brother," Patterson said. "Ben made up some story about the driver of the truck being a possible witness to a traffic accident and called William Small in Seattle to ask him if his truck had recently been in Kodiak. Mr. Small didn't miss a beat. He said his brother, Gordon, drove his truck back to Kodiak this past summer and is planning to buy the truck from William."

"That's good police work," Morgan said. "I'll congratulate Ben when I see him. How long did it take him to run it down?"

"He has been working on it in his spare time over the last several days. He said he finally came across Small's name around 7:30 pm last night."

"Should we pay Coach Small a visit at the high school?"

"I'll pick you up at 7:45 pm."

It was still pitch black when Morgan walked out of the hotel. A strong wind pelted him with rain from every angle, but he barely noticed the weather as he waited for Patterson to arrive. When he climbed into the SUV, he could see that Patterson looked as focused as he was.

Patterson pulled into the staff parking lot at the school and was looking for a place to park when Morgan said, "Stop!"

Patterson stepped on the brakes and followed Morgan's gaze. Three rows over sat a dark red Ford F-150 pickup truck. Patterson parked, and he and Morgan got out of the SUV and walked toward the truck. It matched the description Liz had given them. Both men peered in the windows of the truck at the spotless interior.

Morgan walked to the rear of the truck and looked at the license plate. "Washington license," he said. "This must be Small's truck."

Morgan and Patterson walked in the front door of the school with a group of students. The halls were full of giggling, talkative teenagers, most of whom stopped what they were doing to stare when Patterson and Morgan walked past. Patterson's trooper uniform left no doubt they were cops.

Jeannie Daniel was in the outer office chatting with a secretary. When she saw Morgan and Patterson, she straightened. "Sergeant Patterson, Agent Morgan," she shook their hands. "What can I do for you today?"

"Can we speak in private?" Patterson asked.

"Certainly," Daniel said, and Morgan and Patterson followed her into her office. She shut the door behind them.

Patterson wasted no time getting to the point. "Does the red truck in the staff parking lot belong to Gordon Small?"

"Yes," she said. "Well, that's not exactly true. Gordon's brother owns it. Gordon drove it up here from Seattle, and I think he plans to buy it from his brother."

"We need to talk to Coach Small," Morgan said.

"I'm afraid he's not here," Daniel said.

"Where is he?"

"He took a personal day," Daniel said.

"Then why is his truck here at the school?" Patterson asked.

"I should have explained," Daniel said. "My husband and I are borrowing his truck for the weekend to haul some wood. We don't have quite enough firewood to get us through the winter, and Gordon offered us the use of his truck."

"I see," Patterson said. "Does Mr. Small make a habit of loaning out his truck?"

"Sure," she said. "He is very generous with it. I know he's loaned it to a few other teachers. My husband and I are thinking about buying our own truck so it will be nice to drive his around for a few days to see how we like it."

"Ma'am," Morgan said. "We have some concerns about Mr. Small. When we went to his office to talk to him the other day, he had a poster of a swimsuit model taped to the inside of the locker door in his office. Does that sound out of character for him?"

Jeannie Daniel's eyes widened. "Oh my," she said and then said nothing for several seconds; Morgan could almost see the gears turning in her mind. "I'm sure Gordon has a good explanation for the poster," she said. "It does not sound like something he would have in his office for his personal pleasure."

"Yes ma'am," Patterson said. "Would you give us Coach Small's address so we can interview him at his home?"

"Yes I will, and it would be better if you could interview him away from the school, but I'm not sure he is there today. I think he planned to go somewhere for this weekend."

"You don't know where?" Patterson asked.

"No, I'm sorry, Sergeant. Some of the teachers might still be in the lounge. You're welcome to go in there and ask if anyone knows what Gordon's plans are."

When they entered the teacher's lounge, they found only William Dean, the Earth Science teacher, and Paul Mather, the school counselor still in the room. The two men stopped their conversation and greeted Patterson and Morgan.

"Sorry to bother you gentlemen, but we're looking for Gordon Small," Patterson said. "Principal Daniel said he took a personal day and suggested we ask in here to see if either of you know what his weekend plans are."

"Sure," Mather said. "He is going hunting. He invited me to go with him, but I'm not much of a hunter."

"Where was he going?" Patterson asked.

"Chiniak," Mather said. "He has a small cabin there."

"Do you know how long he plans to stay there?" Patterson asked.

Mather shrugged. "I'm sure he'll be back at school on Monday, so he'll probably return to town on Sunday. You could ask his wife."

Patterson and Morgan thanked the men and headed back to the parking lot. They took another look at the pickup before they got in the SUV, and Patterson snapped two photos of the truck with his phone. Patterson sighed. "I don't think we have enough for a search warrant, but I would love to get a look inside Small's truck and office before he gets back from Chiniak."

"Chiniak," Morgan said, "isn't that where Tasha Ayers' body was found?"

"Yes," Patterson said. "Ben found her when he was deer hunting there. The day after Ben discovered her body, we interviewed the handful of residents in Chiniak and asked if they had seen any strangers near town, and no one had, but if Coach Small owns a cabin there, then he isn't a stranger. No one would have thought it was odd for him to be there. I guess we'll have to go back there and re-interview everyone to find out if they can remember seeing Small in or near Chiniak before or after Tasha's remains were discovered."

Everyone was present at the task force meeting that afternoon. Patterson told the group that Johnstone had discovered Gordon Small's brother owned a red truck similar to the one for which they'd been searching.

"The good news," Patterson said, "is Gordon Small drove his brother's truck to Kodiak. The bad news is Small has a habit of loaning out his truck to others to use. Even if this is the truck we've been searching for, we'll still have a tough time putting Small in it at Abercrombie on the day after Liz found Amy Quinn's body." Patterson showed Liz the photo of the truck he'd snapped with his phone. "Does this look like your truck?"

Liz carefully studied the photo. "I think so," she said. "It was dark red like this, and this looks like the make and model."

"Coach Small is currently at his cabin in Chiniak, which is interesting, since Chiniak is where Ben found Tasha Ayers' body."

"Let's pick him up and bring him in," Feeney said.

"I think we should wait until he gets back to town, Chief," Patterson said. "He's not going anywhere, and I don't want to spook him. I want the chance to interview him without a lawyer present, and if we charge into his cabin and confront him, he'll lawyer up immediately."

"What if he kills another woman in the meantime?" Feeney asked, crossing his arms and sitting back in his chair.

He was obviously not happy about having his suggestion rebuffed, but Morgan silently applauded Patterson for not letting the over-bearing police chief push him. Patterson needed to stand his ground because he was right. Spooking Small now could blow their investigation.

Patterson looked at Johnstone. "I hate to do this to you, Ben, but would you mind heading to Chiniak to make sure Small is at his cabin?"

"Sir," Johnstone said. "If you need me to go, I will, but I have a dentist's appointment this afternoon. I lost a filling, and it's painful."

Patterson looked at Traner. "How about you, Mark?"

"Sure," Traner said. "Can I take Weston with me?"

"Absolutely," Patterson said. "Good idea."

"What about Carson?" Johnstone asked. "Should we keep investigating him?"

"You bet," Patterson said. "He and Small are tight. We may find out they're in on this together."

"I have a thought," Morgan said. He looked at Patterson. "Do you remember Jack Kerr telling us yesterday that Carson brought a load of wood to their place?"

"Yes," Patterson said. "Why?"

"Didn't Ben learn from a check of Carson's vehicles that he doesn't own a truck?"

Patterson's eyes widened. "So whose truck did Carson use to deliver the wood? Could it have been his friend Gordon's truck?"

Morgan nodded. "I think it's worth asking Jack Kerr what Carson was driving."

"Even if we can put Carson in that truck, we still have the same problem," Feeney said. "There is no way to prove he was driving it when Liz saw the truck in the park."

"True," Patterson said. "It would never stand up in court, but it might help move our investigation forward."

"I've been studying the photos of the victims," Morgan said, "and I would like to know if any of the jewelry the women were wearing in the photos was jewelry they wore all or even most of the time. Can we check on that?"

Patterson looked at Johnstone. "Ben, do you want to be in charge of that?"

"Sure," Johnstone said. "Amy Quinn's aunt told me Amy always wore the gold locket she's wearing in the photo. It had a photo of her grandmother in it, and Amy and her grandmother were close."

Morgan nodded. "I suspect our perpetrator collects trophies, and he probably keeps them hidden, but also accessible so he can look at them frequently."

"That makes sense," Horner said, "but how will knowing he collects jewelry help us catch him?"

"It probably won't," Morgan admitted, "but when we do get a search warrant, we'll have some specific items to search for, and if our suspect does have the victims' jewelry in his possession, we'll have a good case against him."

The room remained silent for several seconds, and then Patterson asked if anyone else had anything to discuss. When no one spoke up, he adjourned the meeting.

Chapter Twenty

Friday, December 6th
2:00 pm

Billie Clark couldn't stop smiling. She thought she might be in love. It all seemed too good to be true, but she was falling hard and fast. For now, Tony was her secret lover. He wanted to keep the relationship just between the two of them, and she had honored his wish. He told her if they had any chance of making it as a couple, they had to get to know each other first, without any outside influences that could tear them apart. Billie had been through a bad divorce two years earlier, and she had been lonely these past several months. She was willing to do whatever it took to make this relationship work and to have a future with this man.

Two days ago, Tony had called and asked her to spend the weekend with him on his boat. It had been freezing cold out then, and she had asked if he'd rather come to her place. He promised he'd keep her warm, and she had giggled and agreed to a weekend on his boat. If the wind calmed, he said they would cruise to Afognak Island and anchor in a secluded harbor, but if it was too windy for a cruise, he said they would cuddle on his boat in the harbor.

"Wipe that smile off your face, girl," Tara, the teller who worked next to her at the Alaska Bank, said. "I don't want to hear about young love."

Billie brushed back her long, silky, black hair with the back of her hand. "Young! Don't I wish? I turn 44 in two weeks, and I have a grown daughter. Young came and went a long time ago."

"You've been acting like a love-struck teenager lately," Tara said. "It's downright repulsive to someone like me who's been married 24 years."

"You're just jealous." Billie smiled at her.

"Ain't that the truth," Tara said. "I could wrap my naked body in Saran wrap, and my husband wouldn't notice."

The thought of all 250 lbs. of Tara wrapped in Saran wrap made Billie giggle.

"Where is your Romeo taking you tonight?"

"Not just tonight," Billie whispered. "We're spending the weekend together."

"Get out of here."

Billie's smile stretched the width of her wide, pretty face, and her blue eyes twinkled. She nodded. "Yep, the whole weekend."

"Doesn't that seem a little sudden, girl?" Tara asked.

"Maybe," Billie admitted, "but we get along so well together. We really have fun."

"I'm sure you do." Tara's big, brown eyes opened wide. "But can you trust this man not to break your heart, hon? That's the question."

"I think so," Billie said. "It just feels right to me."

"If it feels so right, why haven't you introduced him to your friends? For that matter, why don't I even know his name?"

"He wants to wait to go public until we get to know each other better," Billie said.

"Girl, I don't like the sound of that. Why is he so secretive? Does he have a wife?"

A customer walked up to Billie's window, and she turned, red-faced from Tara's comment to help the woman. Several more customers followed, and it was 20 minutes before Billie and Tara were alone again. By then Billie was so mad from stewing over what Tara had said she didn't even look at her friend but instead busied herself at her desk.

"Sorry," Tara called over to her. "I worry about you, girlfriend. I know you've been lonely, and I don't want you to get hurt. You've had to deal with too much already."

Billie slowly turned toward Tara. "I know your hearts in the right place, but be happy for me. My guy isn't married. I trust him."

Tara held up her hands in surrender. "Okay, I believe you. Have a fun weekend, and tell him if he doesn't treat you right, he'll have to answer to me."

Billie smiled. "Thanks, Tara, you're the best."

Billie could hardly wait for her shift to end. Tony had told her he'd pick her up from work, and she had a duffel packed and in the trunk of her car. At 5:00 pm when the bank closed, Billie told Tara and the other tellers goodbye and hurried out the front door into the dark, December evening. She didn't see Tony's car, but as if by magic, he appeared the moment she pulled her duffel out of her trunk. He pulled up behind her car and waited while she tossed her bag in the back seat and climbed in the front passenger seat. She would leave her car parked at the bank until Monday. No one would care.

"Hi Babe," Tony said when she climbed into the car. He didn't look at her but was busy scanning the rearview mirror. Even though it was dark out, and they were nearly invisible inside the car, she knew he wouldn't kiss her until they were alone, and there was no chance of anyone observing his display of affection.

Tony wore a blue stocking cap pulled low over his forehead and a black down jacket and blue jeans.

"Are we going straight to the boat?" Billie asked.

"Yes we are," Tony said. "I have everything ready to go." He glanced at her. "You don't need to go anywhere, do you?"

A giggle escaped Billie's lips. "No, I'm ready for our weekend to begin."

Tony looked at her but didn't smile, and for a moment Billie felt strangely uncertain about her decision to spend the weekend with this man.

Tony didn't say anything as he drove over the Near Island Bridge on his way to the Dog Bay boat harbor. Billie sensed he didn't want to talk, so she suppressed her desire to ask him about his day and tell him about hers. He parked in a space in the lot above the harbor and pulled his hood over his head before stepping out of the car. He didn't have any bags or other gear in the car, and Billie assumed he'd already put his stuff on the boat. He grabbed her bag from the back seat and hoisted it on his shoulder.

The snow and ice had melted, but a stiff wind pummeled the harbor, dropping the ambient temperature several degrees. Billie zipped her coat and cinched the hood around her face as she followed Tony down the steep ramp to the harbor. She knew his boat was tied the end of the eighth finger of the long dock. As the wind cut through her coat and battered the exposed skin of her face, she wished she had been able to talk him into spending the weekend at her place, or better yet, they could have flown up to Anchorage for a weekend getaway.

When they finally reached Tony's 36-ft. cabin cruiser, he pushed open the door, and she climbed on board. She waited shivering while he unlocked the door to the cabin, and she was happy to find the interior of the boat warm. Two bottles of wine sat on the counter in the galley.

Billie smiled and pushed any reservations about spending the weekend with Tony to the back of her mind. She shouldn't have listened to Tara. She had tried to ignore her friend's words of warning, but they had seeped into her subconscious, causing her to doubt this wonderful man and her chance of a future with him. *If Tara could only see us together, she would know Tony is serious about making this relationship work. Soon, I will be able to introduce Tony to my friends, and they will all love him for making me so happy.*

Billie slipped out of her coat, and Tony removed his coat and hat. He took both of their coats and hung them on the pegs beside the door, and he smiled at her. "I don't think we'll be able to go to Afognak in this wind," he said, "but we can have our own little boating adventure right here in the harbor."

"That sounds nice," Billie said. She felt relieved he wasn't planning to take her anywhere in this gale. She loved a nice outing on a boat in calm seas in July, but she had no desire to roll around in a stormy ocean in December. She would have endured anything to spend time with Tony, though.

"Would you like a glass of wine, my dear?" Tony asked. A bottle of white and a bottle of red had already been uncorked; two wine glasses sat in front of them. Tony drank red wine, and Billie favored Chardonnay.

"I'd love a glass," she said.

"Sit down, and I'll bring it to you along with an appetizer," Tony said.

Billie sat on the couch in the salon and looked around. As always, the boat appeared spotless. Tony liked to keep things tidy.

A few minutes later, Tony arrived with the wine and a plate of crackers and sliced cheese. He returned to the galley for his wine and then sat beside Billie on the couch. He gave her a peck on the mouth. She had expected something more passionate, but they had the entire weekend for that.

"How was your day?" Billie asked him.

"It was fine," he said, "but I really don't want to talk about work."

"Okay, what shall we talk about then?"

"How are you feeling?" he asked.

"I feel great," Billie said. "I'm looking forward to this weekend."

"So am I," Tony said.

"What's for dinner?" Billie asked.

"I haven't decided," Tony said.

"We have all night."

"That we do," Tony agreed, "and I have a fun one planned."

Billie giggled and reached for a cracker. The wine was going straight to her head. She'd been on a strict diet for the last several weeks, and today, she had only eaten a small carton of yogurt for breakfast and a granola bar for lunch. She didn't want to get drunk tonight; she put the glass of wine on the table beside the couch.

"Is the wine okay?" Tony asked.

"It's fine, but I'm drinking it too fast. I need to pace myself."

Tony smiled but said nothing.

Why is Tony so quiet tonight? He usually likes to talk about himself and ask me questions about my life. He doesn't seem nervous, but something is different. He keeps watching me strangely.

After several moments of silence, Tony returned to the galley and brought the two bottles of wine back with him. He topped off Billie's glass. "Drink up," he said, "and then maybe we can enjoy a different type of appetizer."

She smiled and took another long swallow of wine. "What do you have planned for the weekend?" she asked.

"I thought we'd watch some movies, listen to music, sleep late, and enjoy our time together."

"That sounds great," Billie said. She shook her head to try to clear the cobwebs. If she didn't slow down with the wine, she'd be asleep by 8:00 pm and miss all the fun tonight. She knew Tony would forgive her if she fell asleep, but she did not want to miss one minute of this fabulous weekend.

"Do you ever think about dying?" Tony asked.

"What?" she asked.

"That's the game I want to play tonight," Tony said.

"What?"

"The game of death."

Billie shook her head. She felt dizzy and was certain she had misunderstood him, but why was he looking at her so oddly?

"The game of death?" she asked.

"Yes," he said, "after we have a bit more wine." He poured more wine into her glass, even though it was still nearly full. "Drink up my dear. You look very pretty tonight."

He watched her as she held her wine glass in front of her. "I feel funny," she said. "I don't think I want more wine."

"You're not going to ruin our night together, are you?" Tony asked.

Billie wanted to please Tony, so she drank. He kept staring at her, so she drank more. *Why do I feel so drunk? I haven't consumed enough wine to be drunk.* She reached for cheese and a cracker and watched Tony slowly sip his wine.

"I want to tell you a story about myself," Tony said.

"Okay," Billie said, her physical and mental equilibrium so impaired she welcomed any excuse to remain silent and try to regain her composure. She concentrated on Tony's words and fought to clear her head.

"When I was 17 years old," Tony said, "I fell in love with a 23-year-old woman." A smile curled his lips. "How I loved Irene. She had sky-blue eyes, rose-pink lips, alabaster skin, and raven-black hair parted in the middle. Irene was much thinner and younger than you." He laughed. "I wrote poetry about her and heeded her every beck and call. I thought we would be together forever." He shook his head. "I was so young and stupid. One day, Irene told me she'd gotten engaged to another man and wouldn't be able to see me again." Tony's face burned red. "She dismissed me."

"I'm sorry," Billie said.

Tony sat quietly for several seconds and then chuckled. "Irene destroyed me. I cried and whined. My grades dropped, and I started drinking too much alcohol, but then, six months later, I came to my senses, and I decided no woman would ever do that to me again. Since then, I've taken charge of every relationship I've been in; whether it lasts a year or a night, I control things."

"I'd never do that to you; I'd never hurt you," Billie said. *Why is Tony telling me this story, and why does he look so angry?* "I need a drink of water," she said.

"What?" Tony seemed to pop back into the present. "Sit there," he said. "I'll get you a bottle of water." His voice sounded low and sweet, but his hard stare scared her.

Tony returned with the water, and he watched her curiously while she downed most of the bottle.

"Drink more wine," he said.

"No, my head feels funny. I don't want more wine."

He handed her the wine glass. "Drink." His voice barely rose above a whisper, but his black eyes bored into her. "I have a fun night planned for you."

"Okay," Billie said, and she took a small sip of wine. She took several deep breaths and shook her head. She was beginning to feel sick to her stomach. "I'd hate to ruin our weekend together, but I don't feel very well, maybe I should go home."

Tony smiled. "You are not going anywhere, my dear. Listen to me and drink your wine. You don't want to make me angry."

Billie forced a laugh. "You're scaring me, Tony. I feel sick; I don't want to drink more wine."

"Drink!" Tony snapped the word at her.

Tears poured from Billie's eyes. She drank and then sobbed, her sobs turning into hiccups. She fought to control her breathing and to calm herself. *What is happening here? Tony has never spoken harshly to me before now.* "What's wrong, Tony?" Billie fought to get her hiccups under control. "Did you have a bad day? Did I do something to upset you?"

Tony stared at her, his expression blank.

Billie stared back. "I haven't told anyone about us," she said, "not even my daughter."

"And now you won't need to," Tony said.

"Are you breaking up with me?" Billie asked, a fresh torrent of tears pouring from her eyes.

"Nothing like that. I would never break up with you."

Chapter Twenty-One

Friday, December 6th
6:00 pm

I really just wanted to go home and stay there. Relentless wind battered me when I left the marine center at 5:15 pm, and it was starting to rain again. Dana had texted me at 3:00 pm to tell me that due to the weather, our weekly Friday girl's night had been moved from The Rendezvous, which was several miles from town, to Henry's, a restaurant and bar in the middle of Kodiak. Dana hoped to get to Henry's at 5:30 pm, and the rest of our gang planned to arrive between then and 6:00 pm. I made a quick trip to Safeway for groceries and then headed to Henry's. Dana and Sandy sat at a large table in the bar. A mug of beer stood in front of Dana, and Sandy sipped a glass of white wine.

"Good evening, ladies," I said as I approached their table.

"Jane, you look wet," Dana said. "Is it raining hard?"

"I'm afraid so," I said. "I'd rather have snow than this stuff." I pulled off my coat, hat, and gloves and perched on a bar stool. "Who else are we expecting tonight?"

"The whole gang," Sandy said. "Cassie, Carolyn, and even Linda and Liz said they were coming."

"It's December in Kodiak," Dana said. "We all have cabin fever."

"That on top of holiday depression," Sandy added. "It's a double whammy."

The waitress stopped by the table, and I ordered a glass of Merlot.

"How is your sister handling the approaching holidays?" I asked Sandy.

"Jody?" She asked. "She isn't handling anything. She's pretending Christmas doesn't exist." She shook her head. "I wish for the sake of Evelyn and William she could move forward. I know she'll never forget Deanna, but she still has two kids who are alive and need her."

"Is she getting any better?" I asked.

"A little, she's taking fewer pills anyway, so that's a start."

"It must have been a terrible blow to hear someone murdered Deanna. I don't know how a parent deals with that sort of news," I said.

Dana nodded. "That poor kid," she said.

"I need wine!" Carolyn said as she and Cassie stripped off their coats and sat on two of the stools.

"Make mine a double martini," Cassie said.

"I guess you can tell which one of us is driving," Carolyn said.

Linda and Liz followed behind Carolyn and Cassie, and soon we were all chattering about the weather, work, and the Christmas holidays. I waited patiently to get the topic back on the Kerrs.

"I hear you're on the task force for these homicides," Dana said to Liz.

"You really do know everything that happens in this town, don't you?" Liz said.

Dana shrugged. "I have my sources."

"I can't talk about it," Liz said, "but I'm not an investigator on the case. I was only asked to sit in on the task force meetings because I found one of the bodies in the park."

"Can you at least tell us if they are getting anywhere on solving these murders?" Linda asked.

"I hope so," Liz said, "but it's complicated." She paused. "Linda, I am sorry about Tasha. I didn't realize how close you were to her."

Linda smiled sadly. "Poor Tasha," she said. "She was one of those students whose life projection I desperately wanted to alter, but I couldn't do it."

"I hear you," Sandy said. "I have a few of those too."

"Tasha had talent," Linda said, "but something happened to her over the summer. She just wasn't interested in school this year. I tried to get her excited about writing again, but nothing I did worked."

"A boy or a man happened to her," Dana said. "I heard she was pregnant."

"Really?" Cassie asked.

The teachers and Liz all nodded.

"Nearly three months," Linda said.

"Do they think the father of the baby murdered her?" Cassie looked at Liz.

Liz pretended she hadn't heard the question and instead said, "The counselor said she was flunking English as well as several other classes."

Linda nodded. "Unless she turned things around, she wouldn't have graduated with her class."

"One more uneducated, unwed mother," Carolyn said. "Just what the world needs."

"We've had the police and the FBI in our school asking questions all week," Sandy said. "I can't believe they think a teacher committed these murders. What kind of teacher kills his students? Besides, most of our teachers have been at the school for years, and I know them well. Some aren't great educators, but that doesn't mean they'd murder their students."

"I heard they were asking about Gordon Small," Linda said.

"Gordon?" Sandy said. "That's ridiculous. He's been a shop teacher and a coach for at least 20 years. What? They think he suddenly decided to start murdering prostitutes and teenage girls? I don't buy it."

Linda shook her head. "I don't believe Gordon could be involved either, but I had an interesting conversation with Gordon today. He told me the police were asking him about Rick Carson. Rick is Gordon's friend, but Gordon seemed a little freaked out by the whole thing. He asked me if I thought Rick could kill a student."

"What did you say?" I asked.

"I told Gordon I thought Rick was strange, but I didn't think he was a serial killer, and then we started talking about Tasha."

"About what?" Liz asked, her eyes focused on Linda's face.

"I said I felt guilty about Tasha, and he told me I shouldn't," Linda said. "He said everyone knew Tasha was a lost cause, but he said I tried harder than anyone else to help her. He said we can't save them all." Linda paused. "I know he meant well, but his last comment really bugged me. How can a teacher write off any kid?"

Sandy reached over and patted Linda's hand. "I'm sure he was trying to make you feel better. We've all been crazy lately. I can believe the police are taking a hard look at Rick Carson, though; that guy makes my skin crawl. Jack and Jody are friends of his, and I've been to a few get-togethers with him. He's one strange man."

"How so?" I asked. I forgot about my wine and paid careful attention to Sandy's every word. *This is better than I had hoped. Linda and Sandy have brought up Rick Carson themselves. I don't have to come up with a way to ask Sandy about him.*

"When he's at a party, he doesn't hang out with the adults but instead plays with the children. One time, I went to a party at his house, and there must have been 10 kids there. Rick has an area of his great room with dolls and race cars and other toys, and he sat there and played with the kids while his adult guests mingled. I thought it was bizarre, but I guess it's normal for him."

"Does he have kids of his own?" Carolyn asked.

"No, I don't think he's ever been married. I've never seen him with a date, male or female. He seems fixated on kids."

"Is he more interested in boys or girls or both?" Carolyn asked.

"He seems to like the little girls best," Sandy said.

"How did he act around Deanna?" I asked.

"Not normal," Sandy said. "Of all the kids, he fawned over her the most. He never missed one of her recitals, plays, concerts, or athletic events, and come on, I love supporting my nieces and nephew, but those school events can be brutal. Who attends them if they don't have to? I told Jody I didn't trust Rick around the kids, but she laughed at me and said he was harmless. They even let him babysit the kids."

"Why were the police asking about him at the school?" Carolyn asked.

"He helps coach some of the teams," Linda said. "He mainly helps Gordon with the girls' volleyball team and with boys' track. He assisted Paul Mather with girls' basketball for a while, but Paul told me he didn't feel comfortable having him around the girls."

"But Gordon thought he was okay?" Carolyn asked.

"I guess so," Linda said. "Rick is strange, but I think he's harmless."

"I don't know," Sandy said. "Think about it. He was in Uyak when Deanna disappeared, and he was probably in Kodiak when the other women were murdered. How many people can you say that about?"

"Too many, unfortunately," Liz said. "In Kodiak, everyone either owns a boat or has access to one in the summer, and that makes us a very mobile population."

We all sat and thought about Liz's statement for a while.

She's right. Morgan thinks Deanna's murder will provide the key to identifying the killer because Deanna disappeared in such a remote place, but does he realize how easy it is for an individual to get from one side of the island to the other either by boat or floatplane on a calm, summer day? Uyak Bay is several hours away from Kodiak by boat, but in calm seas, a person with a boat can make the trip and return to Kodiak within a day, possibly without anyone noticing he's left town.

"How did Deanna get along with her family?" I asked. This was a tricky subject, and I wasn't sure how to approach it. I hoped my question didn't sound odd, but Sandy answered it with ease.

"They had a good relationship. She was a teenager, so she had her moments. She got along better with Jody than she did with Jack; she and Jack sometimes butted heads because he was so overprotective of his little girl. Of course, at times, she fought with her brother and sister, but most of the time they played together and had fun." Sandy sighed. "To be honest, I used to be a bit jealous of Jody because she had this perfect family, and I can't even manage a long-term relationship with a man." Tears rolled from Sandy's eyes. "Now, I feel like crap for ever having thought that."

Dana put her arm around Sandy, and Cassie said, "Ah honey, you are a wonderful sister to Jody. You've been there for her through all of this. Stop being so hard on yourself."

As if on cue, the waitress stopped by the table, and we ordered another round of drinks and appetizers. I reminded myself I was driving and asked for a cup of coffee instead of another glass of wine. I considered pushing Sandy harder on Rick Carson and Deanna's relationship with her parents, but the subject of the conversation had clearly upset Sandy, and I didn't feel I should continue my questioning.

"I heard the troopers asked Jerome Collins to fly back from Dutch Harbor so they could question him. His sister told me he was raging mad at losing fishing time," Cassie said.

"Interesting," Dana said. "Believe it or not, I hadn't heard that news."

"You'd better fire your sources," Liz said with a smile.

"Why did the troopers want to talk to him?" Dana asked Liz.

"I can't answer that," Liz shook her head.

"He does run the tender that picks up Jack and Jody's fish," Sandy said.

"As I said earlier," Liz said, "I think nearly anyone on this island could have been in Uyak Bay over the Fourth of July. Just because Collins was in the bay does not mean he killed Deanna and the other women."

"I'll be glad when this whole thing is over," Sandy said. "I'm worried to death about all the high school girls until they catch this monster."

"I'm worried about all the women in Kodiak," Cassie said. "Two of the victims were girls, but the other two weren't. I don't go anywhere without my can of mace."

"I carry a .22," Dana said.

"You would," I laughed.

"A gun is not a bad idea," Cassie said.

"By the way, Jane," Dana said, "you're holding out on us. Your hunky FBI agent is back in town, and we haven't heard any details about him from you."

I felt my face grow hot. "I'm afraid I have nothing juicy to report," I said. "Nick has called a couple of times, but I haven't seen him. He's very busy with this case." I glanced at Liz who was studying me curiously. She was working with Morgan on this case, and I didn't want her to think I was trying to distract him when he had a job to do.

"Uh huh," Dana said.

I held up my hands. "Honestly, I haven't seen him yet."

"Ooh," Linda said. "Did you ladies catch the 'yet'?"

I received a round of whistles and toasts as they all laughed.

I called Morgan as soon as I got home and told him what Sandy had said about Carson and about Deanna's relationship with her parents.

"I hope this information helps you," I said.

"It does, Jane. Thanks for talking to Sandy. It confirms what almost everyone has said about Carson. He's a strange guy, but no one has any proof he has ever touched a child inappropriately."

"As a psychologist, do you think a pedophile would be interested in molesting and killing adult women?" I asked. "Even Deanna and Tasha weren't little girls; they were nearly grown women."

Morgan sighed. "Would I expect a pedophile to attack adult women? No, but humans are complicated, and I learned a long time ago that psychopaths do not fit into neat little categories. If Carson is our killer, who knows what's going on in his brain."

"I hope you get this guy off the streets soon."

"We're working on it," Morgan said.

Chapter Twenty-Two

Saturday, December 7th
12:00 pm

The call came when Patterson was sitting at his desk rereading the case interviews from the past few days. Irene Meadows didn't usually work Saturdays, but she was pulling overtime like everyone else was for the case. She buzzed Patterson on his intercom. "Sergeant," she said, "you'll want to take this call."

Patterson braced himself. He could tell by the tone of Irene's voice this would not be good news. "Patterson," he barked into the receiver.

"Dan, it's Maureen. We have another one."

"Where?" Patterson asked.

"The dumpster outside the Alaska Bank. One of the employees found her when he went out to dump the trash around 9:00 am this morning."

Patterson checked his watch; it was nearly noon. *Why is Horner only calling me now?*

Horner read his mind. "I apologize," she said. "For the record, I wanted to call you immediately, but Feeney was adamant that I and other KPD officers investigate the scene first. The body has not been moved, but we have conducted interviews and dusted the dumpster for prints. We also notified the victim's daughter."

"I'm on my way," Patterson said. He called Morgan at the hotel, and Morgan said he'd be downstairs waiting for him. Before he left his office, Patterson kicked his trashcan so hard Irene came running to his office to make sure he was okay.

"I'm fine," Patterson said, "but it's better I kick my trashcan than Chief Feeney."

Irene smiled. "It would be more fun to kick Feeney, though."

When Patterson and Morgan arrived at the bank, yellow crime-scene tape surrounded the green dumpster at the rear of the building. Patterson knew Horner was a capable detective with a laser-sharp mind and good insight, but she did not know every facet of this case the way he did, and she did not have the profiling background Morgan had. They should have been here with her from the start. Still, he could hardly blame her. She'd been put in a difficult position by her idiot boss, Feeney. The man was too busy peeing in every corner to mark his territory to worry about catching a murderer.

As soon as they climbed from the SUV, Maureen Horner approached them. She must have been examining the crime scene before they arrived because she was wearing blue nitrile gloves. "We haven't moved the body," she said.

Patterson nodded and remained silent, not wanting to take out his anger and frustration on Maureen. He and Morgan followed her to the dumpster and peered inside the bin. Sprawled on top of half a dozen black trash bags was the nude body of a 40-something-year-old woman with shoulder-length black hair. He estimated the woman weighed approximately 150 pounds. Her throat gaped where it had been sliced, her head nearly decapitated.

"Do you know who she is?" Patterson asked.

"Billie Clark," Horner said. "She was a teller at this bank."

"Interesting," Patterson looked at Morgan. "It's brazen to dump a body in the middle of town next to where the victim worked."

Morgan nodded. "He's getting cocky. Let's hope he made a mistake this time."

"It rained early last evening, but it cleared up by 10:00 pm, and we haven't had any precipitation since then, so maybe we'll find some forensic evidence this time," Patterson said.

"We dusted for prints, but it's a dumpster, so it's covered with prints," Horner said. "Even if the murderer was dumb enough not to wear gloves, I don't know how we'll separate his prints from the rest."

"Have you already taken photos?" Patterson asked.

Maureen nodded. "We're done with the body."

"Did you notice anything significant?" Patterson asked.

"Bite marks," Maureen said. "This body has more bite marks than the others had."

"I suggest we send her to Anchorage as soon as possible," Patterson said. "Jarod Libby did the autopsy on the other victims, so I think you should request him for this one as well."

"I've already called him," Maureen said. "We'll get the body to him this afternoon."

Morgan motioned toward the bank. "Have you interviewed her colleagues?" he asked.

"I've talked to the few who are working the short Saturday shift, but they all told me I should talk to Tara Hughes, another teller at the bank. She and Billie were close. We also need to talk to the victim's daughter. An officer went to the house to inform her that her mother had been murdered, but I haven't had a chance to interview her yet."

"Do you think your illustrious boss would mind if we accompany you for those interviews?" Patterson couldn't help himself.

"Screw him," Maureen said. "Let's go to Tara's house first. I asked the other bank employees not to call her until we have a chance to talk to her, but she'll hear the news before long, and I would like to get to her before that happens. She might tell us more about her friend if she doesn't have time to think about what she should and shouldn't say."

Patterson followed Horner's police sedan to a small house a few blocks from the center of town. Horner knocked on the door, and a few seconds later, an African-American man in his mid-forties opened the door. His eyes widened. "Good day, officers," he said. "How may I help you?"

"We need to speak with Tara Hughes," Horner said. "Is she here?"

The man looked over his shoulder and called, "Tara! You have company."

A heavyset African-American woman entered the room wiping her hands on her apron.

"Hello," she said. "What can I do for you?"

"You are Tara Hughes?" Horner asked.

"That's right."

Horner introduced herself and then introduced Morgan and Patterson. "Perhaps you'd like to sit down, ma'am. I have some bad news for you," Horner said.

Tara exchanged a worried glance with her husband and then sat on the edge of an upholstered chair in the small living room. "What is it?" she asked.

Horner sat in a chair across from Tara. "I'm sorry to tell you your friend and co-worker, Billie Clark, was found murdered this morning."

Tara's hands flew to her face, and her husband stepped closer to her and rested a comforting hand on her shoulder. "Aw, hon, I'm sorry," he said.

Tears streamed down Tara's pretty face. "Where?" she asked, her voice trembling.

"Her body was found in a dumpster behind the bank."

"No!" she said, her sobs growing louder.

Her husband pulled a handkerchief from his pocket and handed it to her. "I'll get you some water," he said and hurried from the room.

"Tara," Maureen said after Tara drank a few sips of water, "when did you last see Billie?"

"At quitting time yesterday. She was the first one of us to leave the bank. She had a hot date for the weekend and couldn't wait to get off work."

Maureen glanced at Patterson and Morgan. Patterson ached to interview Tara, but Maureen had developed a rapport with Tara, and she was doing a good job with the interview, so he stood still and remained quiet.

"Who was the date with?" Maureen asked.

"Some mystery guy," Tara said, and then the import of the question hit her, and she again covered her mouth with her hands. "I told her," she wailed.

"Told her what, ma'am?" Horner asked.

Tara wiped her nose. "Billie wouldn't tell me his name. She said he wanted to keep their relationship secret until they were sure it was going to work. He said they didn't need outside influences tearing them apart. I told her I didn't like the sound of that and asked her if he was married."

"What did she say?"

"She got mad at me, and I apologized," Tara said. "I was worried about her, though. She went through a nasty divorce a couple years ago, and she has been lonely since then. I was afraid she would jump into a relationship with anyone just so she wouldn't be alone. I worried he'd hurt her, but not like this."

"Tell me everything you can remember Billie saying about this man. Did she mention where he works or say what he looked like?"

Tara closed her eyes for several seconds. "She didn't say much except that he was handsome and considerate of her feelings. She wouldn't tell me what he looked like, and she never mentioned a job. He picked her up at the bank right after her shift ended, so he must work near there."

"Did you see her get in his car?" Horner asked.

"No, but she must have. Otherwise, he would have come into the bank looking for her, wouldn't he?" She thought for a moment. "Of course the doors would have been locked so he couldn't come inside, but I left right after she did, and her car was there, but she was gone."

"Was she planning to leave her car at the bank?"

"Yes, he wanted to pick her up at the bank so they could get their weekend started."

"Do you know what they were planning to do?" Maureen asked.

"I asked her if they were going away, and she said maybe, but it depended on the weather."

"Were they planning to fly somewhere?"

Tara shrugged. "I don't know. She wouldn't say." She sobbed. "If she had only listened to me."

Maureen handed Tara one of her cards. "Tara if you remember anything else, anything at all, no matter how insignificant it seems, about Billie's date or this mysterious man, please call me right away."

Tara looked into Maureen's eyes and nodded. "I will," she said.

"Do you think Tara is in danger?" her husband asked. "This guy has no way of knowing whether or not Billie told Tara anything about him."

Tara's eyes widened as she looked from her husband to Maureen.

Maureen glanced at Patterson. "I don't think she is in danger." Maureen looked at Tara. "But be cautious. Don't go anywhere alone, and take a few days off work. If he were worried about what you knew, he would have done something to you before you had a chance to talk to us. There would be no point in harming you to keep you quiet now."

Tara nodded, tears rolling down her cheeks. Her husband put his arms around her, and she buried her head in his chest.

"What did you think?" Horner asked Patterson and Morgan as they walked toward their vehicles.

"I don't think there's much doubt Billie's date is our guy," Patterson said, "but I don't know how knowing he's our guy will help us. Let's hope she told her daughter more than she told her friend about the man."

Beth Clark sat in the living room of her apartment, surrounded by friends. A young woman led Horner, Patterson, and Morgan into the room, and they introduced themselves to Beth and her friends. Beth's red eyes and nose suggested she had recently been crying, but her face was dry now, and she looked dazed. She sat in the middle of a couch with one woman sitting on either side of her, each holding one of Beth's hands. An older woman brought in a carafe of coffee and several cups. Three other women sat in the room looking curiously from the police to Beth.

"Ms. Clark, we are very sorry for your loss," Horner said.

Beth nodded but said nothing.

"I know this is a bad time," Horner continued, "but we need to ask you some questions about your mother."

For the first time, Beth made eye contact with Horner. "It was that man, wasn't it?"

"What man is that Beth?"

"She called him her secret beau." Beth's voice was so low Maureen moved closer and kneeled down in front of her.

"Can you tell us anything about this man?" Horner asked.

Beth Clark stared at Horner, her expression flat. "She wouldn't tell me anything about him," Beth said. "She promised she would introduce him to me soon, but she said he wanted her to wait to tell anyone about their relationship until they had time to get to know each other better." Beth shook her head. "It was stupid, and I told her it was stupid, but she refused to tell me anything about him. I actually wondered for a while if he was real. I thought maybe Mom made him up." She sat back, expressionless.

"Did your mother correspond with this man on her computer?" Horner asked.

Beth shook her head. "She doesn't have a computer or a tablet, just her smartphone. Did you find that when you found her?"

"No," Horner said. "Her purse and other belongings were not with her body, but we can check phone records. Did they call, text, e-mail?"

Beth shrugged. "I know they talked on the phone, but I have no idea how else they communicated."

"Did she tell you how she met him?" Horner asked.

"I think he came into the bank." Beth shrugged. "I don't know if she told me that or if I just assumed it, though."

"Did your mother go out and socialize much?" Horner asked.

"She was active in the Lutheran church. She liked to quilt and was part of a quilting circle at a local shop; and sure, she went out for drinks with her friends occasionally, but if you're asking me if she hung out at the bars, the answer is no."

"Were there any other men in her life?" Horner asked.

"Men she was dating? No, none I knew of, but then she wouldn't tell me anything about this man, so who knows what else she wasn't telling me."

"I understand she went through a difficult divorce a couple years ago," Horner said.

"Yes, Beth said. "She and my dad had been married 22 years when he decided he didn't want to be married anymore. He broadsided her and nearly tore her apart." A single tear trickled down Beth's face. "She was just starting to enjoy life again."

"And your dad?" Horner asked.

"He's in Seattle now. He's married to a woman half his age. He never looked back; he left Mom and me in his dust."

"I know you are very upset," Horner said, "but I want you to think carefully about anything your mother said about her 'mystery beau.' Any detail you can remember could help us find this man."

Beth put her hands over her face and rubbed her temples. She stayed in that position for several minutes while Horner, Patterson, and Morgan watched her. Finally, she looked up and shook her head. "She told me he was handsome, caring, compassionate, and a good conversationalist but nothing concrete. She never mentioned the color of his hair, skin, or eyes. She never said whether he was short or tall or thin or fat. She never even told me where he worked, and I asked her what he did for a living. I worried he was taking advantage of her. She was so desperate to meet a man and be in a relationship; I thought he might be preying on her."

He was preying on her, alright, Patterson thought, *but this predator was after more than just her money.*

Horner looked at Patterson and Morgan. "Do either of you have any questions for Beth?" she asked.

"Ms. Clark," Morgan said. "After your mother started dating this man, did any of her habits change?"

"What do you mean?" Beth asked.

"Did she start dressing differently, styling her hair in a different manner, stocking different types of food or alcohol in her home, or did she begin wearing less or more makeup?"

"I see what you mean," Beth said. "Yes, she started parting her hair in the middle. She used to part it on the side. I didn't think it looked as good parted in the middle, and I asked her about it, but she said she wanted a new look. She also started wearing more makeup, but I assumed that was because she had a new man friend."

"Anything else?" Morgan asked.

Beth sat forward on the couch, and she looked at Morgan, her pretty brown eyes focused and sharp for the first time since they had arrived at her apartment. "Yes," she said, "she started wearing blue jeans and flowy tops. She didn't dress like that for work, but that's how she started dressing when she was home or when she went out with friends. I thought she wanted to look younger, but do you think he told her to change her hair and wear those clothes?"

"To be honest, ma'am, I don't know," Morgan said. "Those changes could represent her desire to change her life, or they may reveal something about the man she was seeing. At this point in the investigation, any detail, no matter how small it seems, could be important. Can you remember if she changed her hair before or after she started seeing this man?"

Beth shook her head. "I don't know. It all happened about the same time."

"What about jewelry?" Morgan asked. "Did your mother wear any particular piece of jewelry, such as a necklace or a ring all the time?"

"Sure, she always wore her gold cross," Beth said. "She wasn't wearing it when you found her?"

"No," Morgan said, "she wasn't."

"Do you have a photo of your mother wearing her necklace that we could borrow?" Patterson asked. "We'll scan it and give you back the original."

Beth pointed to a shelf above a desk in the corner of the room. One of her friends walked over and retrieved a photo of Billie and Beth, arms around each other's waist, bright smiles lighting their faces. The friend handed the photo to Patterson, and he studied it. The photo must have been taken in the summer because both women wore short-sleeved t-shirts and were standing outdoors in front of a garden.

"It was taken at the community garden this past summer," Beth said. "You can see her necklace in it, can't you?"

Indeed, Patterson could clearly make out the small gold cross on the short gold chain that ringed Billie's throat. "Did your mother lose weight recently?" Patterson asked. Billie Clark appeared to be at least 20 pounds heavier in this photo than she was now.

Beth nodded. "She's been on a diet for a long time. I know she started her diet before she met this guy."

Patterson nodded. "We'll get this back to you later today."

"Thanks," Beth said. "The policeman who came earlier took the keys to Mom's house and asked me if they could search it. Will someone lock it and bring those keys back to me?"

"We will keep it locked," Horner said, "but we will need to hang onto the keys until we're sure we've searched it thoroughly. If we're lucky, we'll find something in the apartment with this man's name on it."

When they were back in the SUV, Patterson turned to Morgan, "Do we have a weirdo who has a thing for women with dark hair parted in the middle and dressed like a hippie?"

"He certainly does seem to like a type," Morgan said. "Except for Deanna Kerr, all the victims had dark hair parted in the center. It would be interesting to know whether Billie Clark changed her hairstyle before she met this guy, and the new hairstyle is what attracted him, or if the change in her hairstyle was his suggestion. If he's the one who wanted her to change it, then I think it's likely he is trying to mold her into someone from his past."

"Such as his mother?" Patterson asked.

"Perhaps," Morgan said, "or a past girlfriend or even a teacher. He is likely fixated on someone in his life that left him or treated him badly."

"I hope Maureen can come up with a number for this guy from Billie's phone records."

Morgan shook his head. "I hope so too, but I think this guy is too smart to make that type of mistake. I suspect he used a disposable cell phone."

Patterson called an emergency task force meeting for 3:00 pm. Horner was too busy to attend, but she called Patterson to tell him Billie's phone records had been a dead end. She'd made several calls to and received calls from a number they could not trace, and Patterson knew the phone in question was now either at the bottom of the ocean or smashed into a thousand pieces. Horner also told them that so far, they had found nothing helpful at Billie's house, but they were still searching. She promised to call if she found anything of interest.

Patterson smiled when Feeney called to tell him he was too busy to make the task force meeting. He feared he might slug the smug police chief in the nose if he saw him, and his dissenting voice added nothing to their group.

Patterson looked around the room at Traner, Johnstone, Liz Kelley, and Morgan. "Let's go over what we know," he said. "We know Billie Clark has been involved with a 'mysterious beau,' as she referred to him to her daughter, for several weeks. According to the phone records, she's been talking to someone on an untraceable phone for over a month. This man did not want her to tell anyone who he was or anything about him, and apparently, she didn't. We still hope to find some trace of him at her house, but maybe he never went to her house. Her friend and co-worker, Tara Hughes, said Billie was excited about spending the weekend with this man, and if the weather improved, they planned to leave the island. Tara assumed this meant they were planning to fly or take the ferry to the mainland, but that doesn't make sense. The weather was bad yesterday, but not so bad that it kept flights from getting into and out of Kodiak. Also, there was no ferry scheduled for yesterday and none scheduled for today or even tomorrow."

Patterson paused while he looked at his notes. "We know Billie made some lifestyle changes either right before or right after meeting this man. She started losing weight, and her daughter said she'd been losing weight for the last several months, so the weight loss may or may not have anything to do with this man. She started parting her hair in the middle, instead of on the side, and she began wearing more make-up. We also know she started wearing blue jeans and flowing tops." He shrugged. "I don't know what any of this means."

"As the only woman in the room, can I tell you what I think?" Liz asked.

"Certainly, Liz, I'd appreciate your input," Patterson said.

"I'm not sure you can read too much into her change in clothes and the extra make-up. She'd recently lost weight and probably felt better about herself than she had in some time. Maybe she believed she wanted to start a new relationship, so she wore jeans to look younger and more makeup to look attractive. I don't think her behavior is odd; I think it's normal."

"What about the change in hairstyle?" Patterson asked.

"The new hairstyle also could have been an effort to look younger," Liz said, "but I admit the hairstyle change doesn't make as much sense. I think her hair looks great in the photo taken with her daughter. I don't know why she'd suddenly want to start parting it in the center, but we all do crazy things with our hair."

"Her daughter also thought the hairstyle change was odd. Let's talk to Tara Hughes again and see if she can give us an explanation for Billie's new look."

"I don't see why any of this matters," Traner said. "It won't help us catch the murderer."

"It may help us," Morgan said. "Any clue that will get us inside this perpetrator's head gets us closer to identifying him."

"I admit, Mark," Patterson said, "I'd rather have a fingerprint or some DNA, but this guy isn't giving us much to work with, so we need to look at everything we have."

"I think he has a boat or at least has access to a boat," Johnstone said. "It was too stormy for small boat travel last night, but if it calmed down, they could have left the island. Maybe Billie's comment to Tara about going someplace if the weather improved meant they would take his boat somewhere if the wind subsided."

Patterson nodded. "Have you gotten the list of boat owners with slips in the Dog Bay Boat Harbor?"

"I have the list here," Johnstone said, "but it doesn't narrow our suspect list. "I think every teacher at the school owns a boat. Coach Small owns the *Dream Lady*, a 32-foot cabin cruiser, and Rick Carson has the *Enchanter*, a 44-foot boat. We already know Jerome Collins owns a boat. Caden Samuels has a boat, and Bobby Saunders doesn't own a boat, but he has been staying on one this winter."

"What about the Kerrs?" Patterson asked.

Johnstone nodded. "They have a small cabin cruiser, but it doesn't look like its set up for overnight use."

"What about Coach Small?" Johnstone asked. "Was he in town last night?"

"He was at his hunting cabin in Chiniak yesterday afternoon," Traner said, "but I didn't stay out there late. He could have driven to town after I left."

"I think it is time we find Mr. Small and bring him in here for questioning," Patterson said. "Take someone with you, Ben and run him down. He's probably still at his cabin in Chiniak. Go out there, ask politely if you can come in and talk to him for a minute, and while you're there, take a casual look around the place to get a feel for it. He won't be expecting us, so if we're really lucky, you'll see something to give us probable cause to get a search warrant. Don't intimidate him; we want him to cooperate with us at this point. Ask him where he was yesterday, and then tell him we would like him to return to town this afternoon and come in here to answer a few questions about our investigation. It's okay to tell him there's been another murder."

"What if he wants to get a lawyer?" Johnstone asked.

Patterson shrugged. "Then we'll know we've rattled him," he said.

Patterson looked around the table, "Is there anything else?" As if on cue, his cell phone buzzed. He looked at the display and then answered. "Patterson."

Maureen Horner said, "We have something."

Chapter Twenty-Three

Saturday, December 7th
3:50 pm

It took Patterson only 15 minutes to drive to Billie's house. The sky had once again cleared and the temperature had dropped several degrees. The heater in the SUV struggled to warm the interior, but it failed to do the job in the short time it took to drive across town.

A large picture window covered most of the front wall of Billie's house, and a small porch wrapped from the front door around the side. The white siding gleamed and looked new, and the bright red front door added color to the house. A flower basket hung by the front door, the foliage long gone.

Patterson knocked on the door, and a patrolman opened it. Patterson and Morgan stepped inside, and the patrolman left to find Horner. She returned a few minutes later holding an evidence bag in her right hand. "Does this look familiar?" she asked.

Both Patterson and Morgan studied the contents of the bag. "Amy Quinn's locket?" Morgan asked.

"That's what I think," Horner said. "We didn't notice it on the first search but caught it the second time around."

"Any other missing jewelry from our victims?" Patterson asked.

"I didn't recognize any, but I'd like you to take a look." She led Patterson and Morgan down a short hall and into a small bedroom. A flowered quilt covered a full-sized bed and neatly folded, green, fleece pajamas lay on the foot of the bed. A night table to the right of the bed held a water glass, three pill bottles, and a paperback novel with a bookmark sticking out of it. A white dresser sat across from the bed, and an open jewelry box perched in the middle of the dresser. Patterson donned a pair of nitrile gloves and began sifting through the contents of the box. Morgan stood beside him, touching nothing but scrutinizing each piece of jewelry. When Patterson finished examining each bracelet, necklace, and earring, he glanced at Morgan.

"Anything?" he asked.

Morgan shook his head. "No, but you should photograph each piece and we can show the photos to the friends and relatives of the other victims."

"Will do," Horner said.

"Have you found anything else?" Patterson asked.

"One other thing," Horner said. "We found a note in the kitchen that said, 'Ask Tony about what food to bring.'" She shrugged. "It may or may not mean anything. I just called Tara Hughes, and she said she would meet me at the station in 20 minutes to answer more questions. Would you gentlemen care to be present for the interview?"

"You bet," Patterson said. "Will your boss object?"

"I don't plan to ask him," Horner said. "I'm sure he's home watching football by now, anyway."

Tara Hughes sat in the conference room dressed in a gray sweatshirt and sweatpants. Her red eyes and smeared mascara betrayed the fact that she had been crying. Horner, Patterson, and Morgan sat at the conference table, and Horner pushed a box of Kleenex toward Tara.

"I'm sorry to bring you in here, Tara. I know this has been rough on you, but we want to find the monster that killed Billie, and I'm sure you want to help us with that."

Tara nodded. "My husband is worried I'm in danger, but I'd love to have a few minutes alone with the creep who killed Billie. He'd never hurt another woman after I took care of him."

Horner smiled. "You're a good friend," she said. "I would want you on my side."

Tears sprang from Tara's eyes. "Billie didn't deserve to be killed. I never heard her say an unkind word about anyone. She was always there for her friends, and she was a great listener." She shook her head. "I just wish she hadn't been so gullible."

"Tara," Horner said, "we found a note in Billie's kitchen that said, 'Ask Tony what food to bring.' Does the note make sense to you?"

Tara stared straight ahead, lost in thought. "We work with a guy named Tony Munrowe, but I can't think of any reason Billie would ask him about food."

"Could Tony Munrowe be Billie's mysterious man?"

Tara laughed. "No way," she said. "He's 65 years old, bald, and always in a bad mood. All the tellers try to stay out of his way. I don't ever remember seeing Billie talk to him. He's a loan officer, so we don't have to work with him."

"What about any customers named Tony?" Horner asked.

"Sure, we have a few guys named Tony who come into the bank," she said.

"Could you write down their names for us?" Horner asked. "I'd also like you to try to think of any other male customers who paid more than the usual amount of attention to Billie."

"I've already been thinking about it," Tara said. "Billie was so friendly. She always joked and chatted with the customers, and so do I. She was pretty, and a few guys paid attention to her, but I can't think of anyone special." She nodded. "I'll try harder to remember."

"Tara," Morgan said, "when we talked to Billie's daughter, she told us Billie had recently lost weight, started wearing jeans, and had changed her hairstyle. What can you tell us about these changes?"

Tara nodded. "She looked good, and I know the weight loss gave her more confidence. I even tried to lose weight with her for a while, but I couldn't do it."

"Did the weight loss have anything to do with this new guy?" Patterson asked.

"Not at first," Tara said. "She started losing weight before she met him, "but I think her relationship with him inspired her to stay on her diet."

"Did he want her to lose more weight?" Morgan asked.

"I don't think so." Tara paused. "I never got that idea from Billie. According to her, he kept telling her she was beautiful just as she was."

"What about the jeans and the hairstyle?" Morgan asked.

"That was him," Tara said. "She said he brushed her hair one night and told her he liked it parted in the middle, so she started wearing it that way. Then he bought her this beautiful pink, flowing tunic and asked her if she had jeans she could wear it with. After that, he bought her several more, similar blouses." Tara shrugged. "She looked good wearing that style. I would look like I was wearing a tent, but on Billie, a tunic made her look slimmer."

"Did Billie ever say why this guy liked tunics and jeans?" Horner asked.

"He told her it made her look relaxed and young. What woman doesn't want to look young?"

"Did this man ever give Billie jewelry?"

Tara nodded. "I forgot about the jewelry. I should have mentioned it sooner. He gave her an antique gold locket. She loved it because it was from him, but it wasn't really her style. Billie never wore much jewelry other than her gold cross."

Horner told Tara to go home and make a list of all the men named Tony who were customers at the bank. She also asked Tara to write down the names of any other customers who joked or flirted with Billie. Tara was a bit hesitant about naming bank customers without their permission, but Horner assured her the information was in no way confidential.

Chapter Twenty-Four

Sunday, December 8th
9:30 am

Morgan listened to church bells and looked out of the window of the SUV at the beautiful, blue onion dome roof of the Russian Orthodox Church. The sky had brightened to a pale blue a few shades lighter than the church dome. The cold air bit his face, but there was no wind behind it this morning. Johnstone had not been able to find Coach Small until the previous evening when Small returned to his cabin after a day of deer hunting. Small had shot a deer and wanted to process it, so Patterson told Johnstone to ask Small to drive into town the following morning.

"Keep an eye on him," Patterson said. "We know he has a boat, and we don't want him leaving the island on it."

Johnstone had spent a cold, sleepless night sitting in his SUV watching Small's cabin. Morgan imagined the trooper was barely awake, and he certainly wasn't talkative as he drove Morgan to trooper headquarters. Patterson had called a 10:00 am task force meeting. He wanted to discuss the latest developments in the cases before he, Horner, and Morgan interviewed Coach Small.

Everyone looked tired. Since finding Billie Clark's body the previous day, the investigation had ramped up to a furious pace.

"Let's start with Maureen," Patterson said once they were all seated around the table.

Even Feeney had managed to make it to this meeting.

"First of all," Maureen said, "I heard from Dr. Libby, the medical examiner, early this morning. He performed the autopsy on Billie

Clark late yesterday. He of course doesn't have all the results back, but he wanted me to know she had 23 bite marks on her breasts, abdomen and legs. He also found what he believes is condom lubricant on her."

"He's either escalating or this was personal or both," Morgan said. "Billie Clark was more than just a casual acquaintance of our killer."

"On another matter," Horner said, "Tara Hughes e-mailed me a list of 'Tonys' or 'Anthonys' who are bank customers. She also included the names of any customers who seemed excessively friendly, chatty, or flirty with Billie." She held up her hands. "I know this may seem like a lame move, and it probably won't result in any information. I have already been told it's a waste of time," she shot Feeney a look, "but her list has some interesting names on it."

Feeney gave Horner a startled look, and Morgan nearly laughed aloud. Obviously, Horner hadn't shared this information with her boss. She would probably pay for the slight in the long run, but for now, she wore a look of satisfaction.

"What do you have?" Patterson asked.

"Some interesting businessmen named Tony that we can talk about later," Horner said, "but it's Tara's other list that intrigues me the most. The third name on the list is Gordon Small."

"Interesting," Patterson said. "Did Tara tell you why she put Coach Small on the list?"

"She said he had a thing for Billie and always flirted with her. The downside to this news is he's been flirting with her for the past 10 years, but I called Tara and talked to her, and she said Gordon kicked up the flirting a notch after Billie started losing weight. Tara said she teased Billie about him, but Billie laughed it off."

"Isn't Small married?" Traner asked.

"He is," Horner said, "but since when has being married stopped a man from flirting?"

"Did Tara mention if the flirting seemed one-way?" Patterson asked. "Did Billie seem interested in Small?"

"Tara didn't think so," Horner said and shrugged. "But if Billie was trying to keep their relationship secret, maybe she seemed uninterested on purpose."

Maybe, Morgan thought, *but if this mystery man was so interested in keeping the relationship quiet, why would he flirt with Billie in front of her co-workers?*

"Anyone else of interest on Tara's list?" Patterson asked.

"Jerome Collins is on it," Horner said, "but Tara said he flirted with all the tellers."

"I asked Tara if Rick Carson conducted business at her bank, and she said he did. She said he is always polite and very quiet. She didn't know who Bobby Saunders or Caden Samuels were."

"I guess we'll have to talk to everyone on the list," Patterson said. "How many names are there?"

"Twelve," Horner said.

"We'll have one of our people go through the list," Feeney said, making it clear Billie Clark's murder was the Kodiak Police Department's case.

Morgan knew Patterson was happy to have Feeney volunteer his officers to question the men on the list. *Patterson doesn't have the manpower and doesn't want to waste time interviewing a bunch of guys named Tony who probably have nothing to do with Billie's murder. Just because Billie called her lover Tony doesn't mean it is his name. We have no evidence her killer is a regular bank customer or that she even met him at the bank. She could have met him in the checkout line at the grocery store for all we know, and it's a mistake to get too distracted by the possible bank connection. Still, it is interesting to see Coach Small's name near the top of the list of customers who had flirted with Billie. Now, we can link Small to Tara as well as to Deanna Kerr, and he did have the red pickup, which in a roundabout way links him to Amy Quinn.*

"What else do we have on Billie Clark?" Patterson asked.

"I talked to Amy Quinn's aunt," Horner said. "I e-mailed her a photo of the locket, and she said it looked like the locket Amy usually wore. She asked me if there was a photo inside, but of course, the photo had been removed, probably by our killer."

"We're getting more links between the murders," Patterson said. "Did we ever look through Tasha Ayers' jewelry?"

"I called her mother," Horner said, "and she said we're welcome to look through Tasha's jewelry box, but she didn't see anything new when she looked through the box. Of course, our murderer may have given jewelry to Tasha several months ago, so maybe her mother doesn't consider it new. She did confirm the spiky jewelry Tasha was wearing in the photo is in her jewelry box, so we know she wasn't wearing that when she was killed."

"What about the bracelet her mother said she wore?" Patterson asked. "It was something Tasha got recently, and her mother wasn't sure where it came from. Could our killer have taken it from Deborah Sidle or Deanna Kerr before he killed them and then given it to Tasha?"

Horner shrugged. "Give me the description, and I'll talk to Deborah's friends and Deanna's parents. I think I remember you saying it was a big bracelet like a cuff and that sounds more like something Deborah might have worn. From the photos I've seen of Deanna, she didn't wear much jewelry, and I don't think I've ever seen a photo of her wearing big jewelry." She shrugged again. "Still, you never know."

"Anything else on the Clark murder?" Patterson asked.

"We're still processing the fingerprints from the dumpster and from the house, but we don't have much else," Horner said. "Even the note referencing Tony could have been referring to someone other than her secret boyfriend. My gut feeling is that our guy was never in Billie's house. It would be too dangerous. One of Billie's friends or her daughter, Beth, could have dropped by at any minute and seen him there."

"I think it was incredibly risky for this guy to date Billie as long as he did before he killed her," Feeney said. "How did he know he could trust her not to tell her friends or her daughter something about her mysterious lover?"

"This perpetrator is a narcissist," Morgan said. "He thinks he can control any situation, and I'm sure he felt he had total control over Billie." Morgan paused for a minute. "Maybe he killed her when he did because he felt his control slipping. Perhaps Billie was pushing him to let her tell her daughter or her friends who he was. He was running out of excuses to stop her from talking, so he did the only thing he could to maintain control."

"He killed her." Horner finished his thought for him.

"Did anyone check Carson's whereabouts during the time frame when Billie was murdered?" Feeney asked.

"He was in town," Patterson said. "I called him and asked if he used Coach Small's truck to deliver the wood to the Kerr's house, and he said he did, but he insisted it was the first and only time he had borrowed the truck. I then asked him where he'd been the last few days, and he told me he'd never left his home except to go to the grocery store." Patterson shrugged. "Of course, I don't know if he was telling me the truth on either issue."

Morgan said, "I think this may be a good time to sum up what we know about our perpetrator."

"Go ahead, Agent Morgan," Patterson said.

"We know this guy is smart, and he doesn't leave much evidence behind either on his victims or at the crime scene. We also know he's narcissistic and feels he can control nearly every situation. He is escalating; the time frame between the murders is decreasing. He murdered Deborah Sidle in May, Deanna Kerr in July, and Tasha Ayers in October. Then he picked up his pace. Amy Quinn was murdered in late November, and already in early December, he has attacked again."

"Does that mean he's spiraling out of control?" Traner asked.

"Not necessarily," Morgan said. "Billie's murder was well planned and executed. I don't see any evidence that our perpetrator is getting sloppy. He may just be feeling invincible, and that would be a mistake on his part. On the other hand, he may be planning to wrap things up here before he leaves the island and moves his hunt to a new location."

"The last thing we want is for him to leave Kodiak," Patterson said. "We need to catch him on our watch while he's on our island."

"We've developed a few suspects," Morgan said, "but I think it's important not to get too attached to our list. With the possible exception of Deanna Kerr, we don't know where our victims met their murderer. Our victims have very little in common with each other. Did they meet their killer at a restaurant, a bar, the school, a church, the post office, or some other place? We don't know that Billie Clark's secret lover was a customer at her bank. We don't even know if the guy we're looking for was the driver of the red truck in the park. At this point, we still can't rule out anyone."

"Don't you think we've made some progress?" Horner asked.

"Every time this guy does something we learn more about him," Morgan said. "This is a small town, so how has he stayed hidden this long?"

No one answered, so Morgan continued. "I think he has been hiding in plain sight." He let his words sink in for several seconds. "Our perpetrator is an intelligent man, probably in his late twenties or his thirties. He has above-average intelligence, and he's not flashy. He's the kind of guy you wouldn't notice in a crowd. He is likely also the type of guy who is above suspicion. No one would suspect him because he's trustworthy."

"Like a priest?" Johnstone asked.

"Possibly," Morgan said. "We know Billie was involved in a church, but what about Deanna and Tasha? Deborah Sidle could also have been seeking counseling from a preacher or a priest. Amy Quinn doesn't fit as well into this scenario since she just arrived on the island, but she could have been an impulse on the part of our killer. Perhaps she was simply in the wrong place at the wrong time."

"A policeman," Horner said. "I don't like to say it, but a policeman would work with every victim. The prostitutes might not be happy about being approached by a policeman, but they wouldn't be afraid of him."

"And Deanna Kerr would welcome help with her outboard if she knew it was being offered by a Kodiak policeman or trooper," Patterson said.

"That brings up an interesting question," Feeney said. He looked Patterson square in the eye. "Were the troopers in Uyak Bay with their boat over the Fourth of July?"

Patterson didn't flinch, but Morgan knew the sergeant must have hated the question and hated Feeney for asking it. "I'll check," Patterson said, "and you should check on the whereabouts of your officers over the holiday."

Feeney replied with a tight smile and a nod.

"A teacher would also be trustworthy," Johnstone said.

Morgan nodded. "Yes, but would a teacher be recognizable to the prostitutes?"

"Good question," Horner said, "but as we've already noted, prostitutes are accustomed to doing business with men they don't know. As long as the guy didn't set off an internal alarm, there's no reason a prostitute would shy away from the guy."

"What else can you tell us about our murderer?" Patterson looked at Morgan.

"I think we can rule out our less-organized suspects," Morgan said. "Caden Samuels, in my opinion, would not be capable of pulling off these crimes without leaving evidence. I believe our perpetrator has above average means, and Bobby Saunders does not have above-average intelligence or wealth. Coach Small may not be wealthy, but he does have a boat, so he must do fairly well, and he seems intelligent to me. Rick Carson has it all. He is wealthy, smart, has a nice boat, and he knew Deanna Kerr well, but I don't see him as the Don Juan type who could sweep Billie off her feet, and it is difficult imagining him approaching prostitutes." Morgan shrugged. "I certainly would not remove him from the top of your list of suspects. It is possible there is a side to him we haven't seen yet. He comes across as meek and even effeminate, but he could be playing a part for us."

"What about Jerome Collins?" Liz asked.

"I like him as the murderer," Morgan said. "He's smart and wealthy, and we can tie him to all of our victims, but if he's in the

Bering Sea where he's supposed to be, I don't see how he could possibly be our guy, at least not for Billie's murder."

"Excellent point," Patterson said. "I'll call the cannery in Dutch Harbor and see if Collins is on his boat."

Chapter Twenty-Five

Sunday, December 8th
10:45 am

Patterson adjourned the meeting and returned to his office. He dialed the number for King Crab Cannery in Dutch Harbor and waited while the receptionist went in search of the cannery superintendent.

"Drogan," a rough voice said on the phone several minutes later.

"Mr. Drogan," Patterson said. "I'm Sergeant Patterson with the Alaska State Troopers, and I am trying to track down the whereabouts of Jerome Collins. Can you help me with that?"

"Well, I talked to him late yesterday. He was in our office. I think his boat is gone now. Hang on a second." A few minutes later Drogan was back. "The boat's gone. The dock foreman told me it left in the middle of the night. Do you need to reach him?"

Patterson thought for a moment. "How long was he tied up to your dock?"

"He was tucked in here for this last big blow we had," Drogan said. "I'd say he was here for the last three nights."

"Do you know if Mr. Collins stayed on his boat the entire time?" Patterson asked.

"That I couldn't tell you," Drogan said. "Why don't you tell me what you want to know, and maybe I can help you." He did not attempt to disguise the annoyance in his voice.

"I want to know if he left Dutch Harbor and flew back to Kodiak," Patterson said.

"I don't think so, but I guess it's possible. Can't you check with the airlines?"

"I can," Patterson said. "I just wanted to be certain he didn't run his boat back to Kodiak."

"No way," Drogan said. "Not in the storm we just had. I'll double check with the dock foreman for you, but I'm certain his boat was tied to the dock for the entire blow. Most of our boats were here."

Patterson thanked Drogan for his time, and Drogan promised to call back as soon as he talked to the dock foreman. In the meantime, Patterson assigned a trooper the task of checking whether or not Collins had purchased and used a commercial plane ticket to Kodiak.

Coach Small sat in the conference room, elbows braced on the table, chin resting on folded hands. Patterson entered the room first with Morgan and Horner right behind him.

"Mr. Small," Patterson said, "thank you for agreeing to talk to us. I'm sorry if we cut short your hunting weekend."

Small sat back in his chair and folded his arms across his chest. "I didn't see I had a choice," he said.

Patterson let the comment pass. "Trooper Johnstone informed you we had another murder," he stated.

Small nodded. "I don't see what another murder has to do with me," he said.

"Coach Small," Patterson said, "any information you can give us will help. I believe you know the latest victim."

"Who was it?" Small's eyes narrowed, and he squeezed the arms of the chair. If he was acting, he was very good at it.

"Billie Clark, one of the tellers at the Alaska Bank," Patterson said.

"Oh no," Small said, and he slumped in the chair.

Is he upset or relieved, and what do either of those emotions mean? Patterson wondered.

"How well did you know Ms. Clark?" Patterson asked.

"I didn't," Small said. "She was a teller at my bank. She handled my deposits, we joked, and I left. That's the only relationship we had."

"One of the other tellers told us you flirted with her," Patterson said.

"Oh come on, that's ridiculous; don't be telling my wife I flirted with a bank teller. It was harmless banter."

"Do you own a Ford F-150 pickup truck?" Patterson asked.

"Yes," Small paused, "why is that important?"

"I understand you sometimes let your friends use your truck?"

"Sure," Small said. "I think I loan it out more than I drive it myself." He laughed. "I had planned to drive it to the cabin this weekend, but then Jeannie Daniel, the principal at the school, asked me if she and her husband could borrow it, so I let her have the truck and drove my car to go deer hunting. Now, I'll have to drive back out there in the truck to get the deer. I guess I have to learn how to say no."

"Do you remember who borrowed your truck on November 18th and 19th?" Patterson asked.

"I'd have to think about it," Small said. "I think I may have loaned it to Rick Carson then, but I can't say for certain. Nearly everyone at the school has borrowed it, and I've loaned it to several other friends as well. Not only that," he continued, "but often one friend loans it to another. It has become the community pickup."

"Who else have you loaned it to at the school?" Patterson prodded.

Small looked at the ceiling while he thought. "Chad Johnson, Pete Shriver, Linda Bragg, Paul Mather," he rubbed his eyes. "Let's see, Tony Dylan used it one weekend, and I've loaned it to Jeannie Daniel and her husband twice. I'm sure there are more, but I'll have to think about it. I'll make a list," he offered.

Morgan and Patterson exchanged a look.

"Tony Dylan," Patterson said. "What does he teach at the school?"

"Tony teaches shop with me. His expertise is outboard motor repair. Tony is also the coach of the swim team."

"Coach Small," Morgan said. "When we first interviewed you in your office, I saw a poster of a swimsuit model hanging in your locker. Would you care to explain what it was doing there?" Patterson and

Morgan had planned this questioning barrage, changing subjects frequently, hoping to throw Small off balance.

Small didn't rise to the bait, though. Instead, he chuckled. "I was afraid you saw the poster," he said. "I assure you it was not my poster, and please don't tell my wife about the poster, either." He laughed again. "I imagine it did look odd to you. I confiscated the poster from one of the boys. I saw it in his locker in the gym, and I took it from him and made him run 50 wind sprints every day for the rest of the week. At the end of the week, I gave it back to him and told him if I ever saw it or another one like it at school again, I'd throw it away and report him to the principal."

Morgan and Patterson said nothing but waited for Small to continue.

"Look," Small said. "The kid's name is Gavin Banks. Ask him if you don't believe me. Do I need to call my lawyer? This is ridiculous; I've dedicated my life to teaching kids, and now you're suggesting I've killed two plus two prostitutes and a lovely lady from the bank!" His face turned red, and he pushed himself up from the table until he was standing and looking down at Patterson, Morgan, and Horner. "I'm leaving now," he said.

"Mr. Carson," Horner tried to be the voice of reason. "We're not accusing you of anything, but we have to ask these questions. Please bear with us. If you are innocent of these crimes, we'll be able to rule you out with your help."

Small was having none of it. He grabbed his parka from the back of the chair and stormed out of the conference room. Patterson, Morgan, and Horner watched him go.

"Either he's innocent, or he deserves an Oscar," Horner said.

"What's your take on his performance?" Patterson asked Morgan.

Morgan leaned back in his chair and tossed the pen he had been holding onto the table. "To be honest, I don't know what to make of Gordon Small. I can't read the man. He has a ready answer for everything, and maybe he's telling the truth."

"But?" Patterson asked.

"That's the problem," Morgan said. "This type of perpetrator gets excited by playing games, and manipulating the police is the ultimate game for him. If Small is our guy, then he enjoyed every minute of our interview, but Small's behavior also fits the way an innocent man might act."

"I thought psychopaths lacked emotions and empathy," Horner said. "If Small is a psychopath how would he know how an innocent man would act?"

"Most psychopaths are great at mimicry," Morgan said. "They watch others and learn. They know the right things to say and do to get what they want."

"Have we looked at this Tony Dylan yet?" Horner asked.

"Not really," Patterson said. "His name has been mentioned a time or two, but he was off our radar until now."

"I'll ask Tara Hughes if she knows him and if he is a bank customer. It would be a neat fit if he turned out to be our Tony."

"I am also intrigued by the idea that Mr. Dylan teaches outboard mechanics," Morgan said. "Someone with outboard expertise may have disabled Deanna Kerr's motor."

Horner laughed. "Agent Morgan," she said, "you are on an island where 90% of the population can take apart an outboard engine. We are all outboard repair experts."

No airline tickets from Dutch Harbor to Anchorage and from Anchorage to Kodiak for Jerome Collins were found. It was beginning to seem unlikely Collins was on the island when Billie Clark was murdered. On the one hand, Patterson was disappointed by this news because Collins had seemed like such a good suspect. On the other hand, it would be nice to mark someone off the suspect list so they felt they were making headway in the case. It seemed as if their suspect list kept getting longer instead of shorter. This reminded him of what Feeney had said at the meeting. *Had the trooper boat, The Protector, been in Uyak Bay over Fourth of July weekend?* The idea that a trooper, a man under his watch, could be the monster responsible for these crimes made him ill, but if the murderer were a policeman or a trooper, it would explain how he had gotten close to the women and girls. They would have no reason to fear a policeman. The prostitutes might want to avoid a trooper, but they wouldn't worry he might harm them.

Patterson pulled up *The Protector* schedule for the past summer. The normal crew on *The Protector* consisted of a captain, an engineer, and two wildlife protection officers. Some troopers liked to work wildlife protection, others did not, but most troopers spent some time out on the boat checking commercial and sport fishing permits and licenses as well as hunting licenses. They also served as law enforcement in the villages and for the vast wilderness that comprised most of Kodiak Island. Patterson easily logged into the schedule for *The Protector* and saw it was patrolling the west side of the Island over the Fourth of July weekend. The west side would include Uyak Bay, but whether *The Protector* was in Uyak Bay on the Fourth or in one of the other bays on the west side of the island, he didn't know. For that information, he would have to view the logs for those specific dates. The log book was handwritten and then supposedly transferred to the computer. The troopers had been slowly upgrading their computer system for the last several months, though, and they were still lagging behind on data entry. Patterson knew the troopers in charge of data entry considered the logs from *The Protector* low priority, and they had not gotten around to scanning them yet. The latest logs he could find on the computer were from May. He would have to track down the original, written logs and look at them.

He thought about how unlikely it was one of the troopers on *The Protector* could be their murderer. The usual protocol was for *The Protector* to anchor in a cove or other protected spot. The captain and engineer stayed on board while the two troopers launched a rigid hull inflatable boat with a 200 hp outboard. They then used this boat to speed around the area and check licenses and permits and talk to the permanent and temporary residents to learn if anything was happening in the area that might require trooper intervention. It was not normal for one trooper to take the inflatable out alone. In fact, it was against regulations. Patterson believed if a trooper had taken the inflatable out by himself on the Fourth of July, either the other trooper, the captain, or the engineer would have reported the transgression. Still, he needed to check the log book and if necessary interview the troopers and the captain who were on duty that Fourth of July weekend. *If I have a murderer in my ranks, I want to be the one to discover who it is. I'll resign my post if Chief Feeney or anyone else besides me discovers the monster is one of my own men.*

Patterson's thoughts were interrupted by the buzzing of his cell phone. "Patterson," he barked.

"Dan," Morgan said, "I've been reading through the case file, and an interview caught my eye. In our interview with the school counselor, Paul Mather, he mentioned several of the high school and middle school coaches went up to Anchorage for a meeting in November. Do you remember him saying that?"

"Vaguely," Patterson said. "He told us he saw Rick Carson playing with some of the kids on the ferry, and he thought his behavior seemed odd."

"That's right," Morgan said. "I checked the ferry schedule, and I think it is likely they were on the same ferry Amy Quinn took from Homer to Kodiak."

Patterson sat back in his chair. There were only two ferries a week from Homer to Kodiak, so there was a good chance Morgan was right. "Let me call Mather and double check the date with him. If they were on the ferry with Amy Quinn, I'll e-mail Mather a photo and ask him if he remembers seeing her, and if he does, we can ask him if he saw any of the coaches, particularly Small or Carson talking to her."

'Yes," Morgan said. "It would be quite a coincidence if they were all on the same boat. It would link Carson and Small to another victim."

Patterson contacted Paul Mather at his home and asked him what day he took the ferry from Homer to Kodiak.

"Hang on," Mather said, "let me get a calendar." Several minutes later he was back. "It was Sunday the 17th. I got a stateroom because I wanted to get some sleep; I had to work in the morning."

"Did you see any of the photos of Amy Quinn in the paper? She was one of our murder victims," Patterson said.

"I'm sure I did," Mather said, "but I don't remember what she looked like. Why?"

"We think she was on the ferry with you and your colleagues."

"Oh," Mather said. He paused for a moment. "Is that important?"

"Maybe or maybe not," Patterson said. "Would you mind if I e-mail the photo to you?"

"Sure," Mather said. "I'll look at it more carefully and see if I remember her. To be honest, though, I had a drink with the other coaches and then went to my stateroom; I was in my cabin for most of the rest of the trip. It was not a smooth voyage, and I just stayed in bed and rode it out."

"E-mail me a list of everyone in your group who took the ferry to Kodiak that night," Patterson said. "I'll see if anyone else remembers her."

"Sure," Mather said. "I'll call you back as soon as I look at the photo."

Mather called back 10 minutes later. He said he'd studied the photo and did not remember seeing Amy Quinn getting on the ferry in Homer, during the voyage, or disembarking in Kodiak. He told Patterson the ferry was nearly full that night, and he didn't pay much attention to anyone. Twenty minutes later, he sent Patterson an e-mail with the list of the other coaches who had been on board with him. As Patterson already knew, the list included Gordon Small and Rick Carson. What interested Patterson the most, though, was that Tony Dylan's name was also on the list.

Patterson didn't know much about Dylan except that he coached swimming at the high school and taught classes on outboard repair. Until now, he hadn't been on Patterson's radar, but after finding the note in Billie's house with the name "Tony" on it, anyone named Tony who was connected to the victims had to be considered a person of interest.

Patterson called Horner and told her about the latest development.

"I'll call Tara Hughes and ask her if Tony Dylan is a bank customer," she said. "His name wasn't on Tara's list of men who flirted or joked with Billie, but I'll see what she has to say about him."

Ten minutes later, Horner called back. "Tara says Tony is a bank customer, but she doesn't recall him flirting or spending extra time with Billie. I think he warrants a closer look, though. Do you want to go talk to him?"

"Yes," Patterson said. "Let's pay Mr. Dylan a surprise visit. Since it's Sunday, we might catch him at home."

Patterson called Morgan and told him Mather had included Tony Dylan on his list of coaches who took the ferry from Homer to Kodiak on November 17th, and Tara Hughes confirmed Dylan was a bank customer. He asked Morgan if he would like to join him and Horner on a trip to Dylan's house for an interview.

Morgan paused for a moment but then told Patterson he wanted to continue sifting through the evidence and interviews. "I feel as if I'm missing something here," he said, "and I don't want to stop until I've gone through everything."

Patterson picked up Horner at the police station. Tony Dylan lived outside the city limits of Kodiak at the end of the Monoshka Bay Road, and Patterson was relieved the ice and snow had melted from the roads. The trip would only take about 30 to 40 minutes on dry roads, but ice and snow would have stretched the journey to double or even triple that amount of time. He and Horner discussed what they wanted to ask Dylan, but they engaged in little conversation other than that. Patterson knew that like him, Horner was probably exhausted and focused only on the investigation. They both wanted to catch this guy before he killed again.

As they neared the end of the road, Horner studied the posts next to the nearly-invisible turn-offs. Patterson slowed the pace to a crawl until Horner said, "There it is. I see the name Dylan on the next post."

Patterson turned into a muddy, rutted, dirt driveway and drove a quarter of a mile before he saw a small log cabin. As soon as they pulled up in front of the cabin, two black labs charged the SUV. Patterson didn't know if it was safe to get out of the vehicle, but Horner had no qualms. She threw open the door and yelled, "Hi guys." The dogs ran to her, and she knelt down to get her face licked. "Aren't you boys great guard dogs," she said.

Just then, the front door flew open, and a man said, "Tucker, Tank, stop that; no one wants your slobber all over them."

The dogs backed away, and Horner stood. She held out her hand. "I'm Detective Maureen Horner with the Kodiak Police Department, and this is my colleague," she jerked a thumb over her shoulder, "Sergeant Patterson with the Alaska State Troopers. Are you Tony Dylan?"

"I am," the man put down the dish towel he'd been holding and shook Horner's hand and then Patterson's. "Would you care to come in for a cup of coffee?"

Dylan walked up the stairs of his front porch and held open the door for Horner and Patterson. The small, cozy cabin reminded Patterson of Tim Ayers' place in Bell's Flats. Like Tim's Cabin, Tony Dylan's was warm and tidy. After removing their boots, they followed Tony into a small kitchen. The floor was painted dark green, and the walls were a glossy white. An overhead bank of lights brightened the small room.

"Nice place," Patterson said.

"Thanks." Tony grabbed two coffee cups from a cupboard and a third from the sink.

Patterson guessed Dylan was around 40-years-old. He was tall with dark brown hair and deep, blue eyes. He had a strong jaw line and teeth that were so white Patterson knew he must bleach them. Patterson bet this teacher was popular with the high school girls.

Dylan poured the coffee and offered cream and sugar. "Please sit," he gestured to the chairs surrounding the kitchen table.

Patterson and Horner both sat at the table, and Dylan asked if they would like anything to eat.

"No thanks," Horner said. "We need to ask you a few questions."

"Sure," Tony Dylan said. He sat at the table and looked expectantly from Horner to Patterson. "What can I help you with?"

"Mr. Dylan," Horner began. "Do you own a boat?"

"Yes," Dylan said, and now he looked concerned. "Did something happen to it?"

"No sir," Horner said, "not as far as we know. Is it at the boat harbor?"

He nodded. "It's in Dog Bay," he said.

"Something else," Horner said, "we understand you went to a coaches' meeting in November and came back to Kodiak on the ferry on November 17th. Is that right?"

Dylan frowned and turned his head to one side. "That sounds about right. Why, what does that have to do with my boat?"

Patterson pushed the photo of Amy Quinn in front of Dylan. "Do you remember seeing this woman on the ferry?"

Dylan picked up the photo and studied it for several seconds. "No," he said. "To tell you the truth, though, I don't remember much about that trip. I drank several beers with some of the guys and then crashed in the solarium."

"Who did you drink with?" Patterson asked.

"Let me think." He paused. "Gale Brown and Buck Lowe, they're both middle school coaches, and Gordon Small, Jim Beekly, and Paul Mather. They're high school coaches. Paul and Buck turned in early, and Gordon, Gale, Jim and I had a few more drinks. I don't usually drink that much, and when I crawled into my bag, I had no trouble sleeping. I woke up just as we were pulling into Kodiak."

"How well did you know Tasha Ayers and Deanna Kerr?" Patterson asked.

Dylan tapped the table several times and then looked from Patterson to Horner. "I don't like these questions," he said. "Before I answer anything else, you need to tell me why you're asking me these things. Am I in some sort of trouble? Do I need to call an attorney?"

"Sir, you are welcome to call an attorney," Horner said. "As I'm sure you know, several women have been murdered on the island in the last several months, and we are questioning everyone we can find who had ties to those women. We are particularly interested in individuals who knew two or more of the victims, so that includes most high school teachers. We need your help in solving these crimes."

"I'd like to help you catch this guy," Dylan said, "but I don't think I know anything that will help you."

"Did you know Deanna Kerr and Tasha Ayers?" Patterson repeated his question.

"I knew Tasha only by sight," Dylan said. "Her brother was on the swim team for two years, and I talked to him a few times about his family life. I know those kids had it rough, and Tim worried about his little sister. I never spoke to Tasha, though."

"And Deanna?" Patterson prodded.

"Deanna took Beginning Outboard Repair from me," Dylan said. "She was a good student, a fast learner."

"Outboard repair?" Morgan asked.

"Sure," Dylan said. "Lots of girls take my classes. We are a fishing community, after all. I think Deanna's dad insisted she take outboard repair. He didn't want her working as a crewman until she understood something about the engine she'd be operating. Unfortunately," he shook his head, "the things she learned in my class probably didn't help her much if her outboard quit before she disappeared."

"Why is that?" Horner asked.

"I'm sure she had a four-stroke outboard, and those aren't easy to repair on the fly. They're not like the old engines where you could swap out spark plugs in a few minutes and solve the problem. Four strokes are nice until they quit in the middle of the ocean, and then you have a big problem on your hands."

"With your expertise, I'm sure you would know how to disable a four stroke outboard," Horner said.

"Of course," Dylan said, "but so would a lot of other people in Kodiak. Fishermen depend on their outboards."

"Did you know Billie Clark?" Horner asked.

Dylan blinked at the rapid change of subject. "Billie from the bank?"

"Yes sir," Horner said.

"Sure, I know Billie. Why, did something happen to her?"

"She was murdered," Horner said. "Her body was found Friday night. You hadn't heard?"

"No," Dylan said. "That's terrible news. She seemed like such a nice lady. I didn't know her outside the bank, but she always had a smile on her face."

"You never dated Billie?" Horner asked

"No," Dylan said. "Did someone tell you I did?"

"Did you know Deborah Sidle?" Patterson asked.

Dylan thought for a minute. "The woman found in the boat harbor a few months ago?"

Patterson nodded.

"No, I didn't know her." His voice was strong, and he looked Patterson squarely in the eyes. His steely gaze betrayed the fact that he was growing weary of these questions.

Patterson sipped his coffee. "Are you married, Mr. Dylan?"

"No, I'm not," Dylan said.

"Have you ever been married?" Patterson asked.

"Once, 10 years ago for about five minutes," Dylan said.

"Are you dating anyone?" Patterson asked.

"No one in particular. Why is that any business of yours?"

Patterson shrugged. "Do you have any thoughts about who could be murdering these women?"

"No," Dylan said. "Why would I?"

Horner stood. "Thank you for your time, Mr. Dylan. We appreciate you talking to us."

"Sure," he said and stood at the same time as Patterson rose. Patterson held out a hand, and Dylan paused before shaking it.

"By the way," Patterson said. "Have you ever borrowed Gordon Small's red pickup?"

"No," Dylan said, "I don't believe so."

Tony Dylan stood on his front porch and watched Patterson and Horner climb into the SUV. He was still standing there when they drove out of sight.

"What did you think?" Patterson asked.

"I don't believe for one second Tony Dylan hadn't heard Billie Clark was murdered. The entire town knows what happened to her. I can't begin to tell you how many times I've been stopped on the street and asked what we know about the murder and what we are doing to apprehend the killer. There is no way the news has not reached his ears."

"That struck me as odd too," Patterson said. "Do you know how long Dylan has been a teacher and coach at the school?"

"No, but I plan to find out tomorrow. At this moment, Tony Dylan is near the top of my list as a suspect in the murder of Billie Clark."

Patterson looked at her out of the corner of his eye. "Because his name is Tony?"

Horner smiled at him. "That's all I've got, and he's too damn handsome to be innocent."

Chapter Twenty-Six

Sunday, December 8th
5:30 pm

Mark Traner and Ben Johnstone left trooper headquarters at the same time.

"I plan to kick back tonight and watch a movie about something other than murder and dead bodies," Traner said.

Johnstone remained silent, looking down at his feet as they walked toward their vehicles.

"What's up?" Traner asked. "You look lost in thought."

Johnstone stopped walking and glanced at his colleague. "I have to do something. We aren't getting anywhere with this case. We seem to be chasing our tails."

"I hear you," Traner said, "it's frustrating, but what can we do?"

"I want to start over." Johnstone said. "I think our guy had Billie Clark on a boat. I'm heading over to walk the docks at the boat harbor and check out every boat related to anyone mentioned in our case files. I think we missed someone."

"Are you nuts?" Traner asked. "It's dark."

"The boat harbor has lights," Johnstone said. "I also might drive out past where Tony Dylan lives. We need to take a harder look at him."

"Do you want me to go with you?" Traner asked.

Johnstone shook his head. "No, you go home. I'm sure you're right, it's a fool's errand, but I have to do something. I'll tell you tomorrow if I find anything of interest."

Traner nodded. "Be careful; don't do anything stupid. These roads are slick."

Chapter Twenty-Seven

Sunday, December 8th
7:00 pm

Morgan sipped his scotch while he stared again at the photos of the victims. He had added the photo of Billie Clark to his array, bringing the total number of murdered women to five. *What am I missing?* Except for Deanna Kerr, the victims all had dark, straight, center-parted hair, but other than that, their features varied. They had different eye colors, different facial features, and different body types. Deborah Sidle had been nearly anorexic, while Billie Clark could be described as plump, despite her weight loss. He zoomed in on the jewelry of each victim. They knew what had happened to Amy's locket; the killer had given it to Billie as a gift. Deanna's delicate silver and pearl necklace had not been found, but it could have fallen from around her neck during all those months her body was in the ocean. They knew that when Tasha was killed, she had not been wearing the spiked, dog-collar jewelry she wore in the photograph because her mother had found it in Tasha's jewelry box. But her mother also believed she had been wearing a copper bangle, and it was not found with her body. Morgan noted again the disparity between the spiky jewelry and the red ribbon that tied back Tasha's ponytail. He suspected Tasha had been a sweet kid trying to act tough. If only she'd had more time to forge her identity. He was zooming in on the photo of Billie Clark to get a better look at the gold cross around her neck when his phone buzzed.

"Morgan," he said without looking at the display.

"Hey, just thought I'd call to see how you're doing," a female voice said.

Morgan leaned back in the desk chair, suddenly realizing how stiff his neck muscles felt. He massaged his neck with his left hand and said, "Jane, it's nice to hear your voice tonight. It has been a tough couple of days."

"I heard about Billie Clark," she said. "I've been thinking about you. It must be very upsetting to have another victim."

"Yes," Morgan said. "We wanted to catch this monster before he killed again. This guy is smart; he doesn't make many mistakes."

"You'd think in a town this size, someone would know something."

"If he keeps hunting on Kodiak Island, we will catch him eventually," Morgan said. "My biggest worry is he'll leave the island and find a new hunting ground."

"Have you narrowed down the suspect pool?"

Morgan laughed. "We've ruled out a few early suspects, but we've added more. I know I'm missing something. I've spent the day looking over the case notes and staring at photos of the victims. I can't help but think we already have the answer here somewhere."

"You'll figure it out," Jane said.

"Did you know Billie?"

"I knew her from the bank, but that's it. I talked to my friend Dana, and she, of course, knew her better than I did, but Dana knows everyone."

"Tell me what Dana said about her. Did she mention if Billie was dating anyone?"

"I don't know how reliable this is; it's really just gossip, but Dana said there was a mysterious new man in Billie's life. She said Billie seemed very happy."

"Did Dana know anything about this man?" Morgan asked.

"Nothing, and that's unusual for Dana. She usually knows everything that's going on in Kodiak."

"Billie managed to keep her new boyfriend a secret from everyone," Morgan said.

"You think he's the murderer, don't you?"

"Yes, I do."

"I'll let you know if I hear anything," Jane promised. "I know you're busy, but I wanted to see how you were doing."

"Thanks for calling," Morgan said. "You brightened my day."

Morgan disconnected and returned his attention to his computer screen. He took a closer look at Billie Clark's gold cross. There was nothing flashy about the necklace, and he knew even if they found such a necklace in the possession of their suspected killer, a common necklace like this would not make good evidence at trial. A defense lawyer could easily argue there was nothing distinctive about the necklace and no way to prove it had belonged to Billie. Morgan enlarged the photo of Deanna Kerr and studied the delicate pearl and silver chain that encircled her neck. He had thought before when he'd examined the photo that the pearls were white, but now he noticed they had a pink hue to them. The necklace could have been lost in the ocean, but if they did find it in the possession of a suspect, he felt it was unique enough to serve as critical evidence in a trial.

Next, he looked at the photo of Deborah Sidle. For a few moments, he studied her hardened face, the straight line of her mouth and the wrinkles around her eyes. The fine lines around her mouth suggested she had been a smoker at least at some time in her life. Her cheeks looked sunken, and her skin had a gray cast to it. *Was she sick when this photo was taken?* Morgan zoomed in on the long necklace around Deborah's neck. He looked closer at the purple stone. He wasn't sure whether the pendant was amethyst or deep purple glass cut like a crystal. They didn't know if Deborah was wearing this necklace when she was murdered, but if she was and they found it in her killer's possession, this necklace was also unique enough to make good evidence at trial.

He sighed and sat back. *Why am I worrying about a trial? We have to catch the killer before he can be tried, and there are still too many questions left unanswered. We have mostly focused on teachers and coaches, but could the murderer be someone else these victims trusted and had no reason to fear? The prostitutes might allow any man to get close, but Deanna, Tasha, and Billie must have trusted their murderer to let down their guard. It's possible the murderer is a preacher or even a cop, or perhaps it is someone who has been posing as a preacher or a cop.*

Morgan did not want to believe the murderer was a Kodiak city policeman or a trooper, but those possibilities had to be considered. He rubbed the back of his neck and began looking through the case files again, this time paying special attention to who was on duty when the bodies were found and what each policeman or trooper had contributed to the investigations.

Nothing in the files for Deborah Sidle or Deanna Kerr raised a red flag, and he was just beginning to reread Tasha Ayers' file when his phone rang again.

"I'm feeling sick to my stomach," Dan Patterson said.

"What happened?" Morgan asked.

"That comment Feeney made at the meeting today about the killer possibly being one of my guys really irritated me, but I knew I had to open my mind to the possibility."

"I'm just now studying the files from that angle," Morgan said. "What do you know?"

"Johnstone found Tasha's body. At the time, I thought it was a lucky break because he knew how to preserve the scene. As it turned out, though, it was raining so hard any possible evidence was washed away."

"It was probably chance that he found the body," Morgan said

"It occurred to me, though," Patterson said, "Ben drives a red Toyota pickup. That's not exactly the truck Liz said she saw, but it's close."

"I remember seeing his red truck," Morgan said.

"That's not all," Patterson said. "In July, Johnstone was assigned to *The Protector*, the trooper boat that provides enforcement for all of the island beyond the road system."

"Yes?" Morgan asked. He didn't understand where Patterson was headed with this.

"According to the log book, *The Protector* was in Uyak Bay over the Fourth of July," Patterson said. "Ben was on the boat in Uyak Bay when Deanna Kerr went missing."

Morgan pushed his chair away from the desk and again massaged his neck. "I see."

"I haven't spoken to the captain, the engineer, or the other trooper who was on board the boat with Johnstone, and I can't imagine a scenario where Johnstone would have taken the rigid hull inflatable out on his own since that's against regulations, but it was a holiday so he might have convinced the other guys he wanted to go fishing, or he wanted to run to the cannery for supplies."

"Do you think the other trooper would remember if Johnstone took the boat on his own?"

"I think so," Patterson said. "His name is Craig Martin, and he's out of the office today, investigating a robbery in Karluk. I'll talk to him as soon as he gets back tomorrow, but I wanted to ask you how you think we should proceed in light of this information."

Morgan remained silent for several moments while he thought, and then he said, "I wouldn't do anything until you have a chance to talk to Martin. If Martin remembers Johnstone leaving the boat on his own, then I think we need to get Johnstone in a room and hit him hard with questions. If Martin is fairly certain Johnstone didn't leave the boat, though, I think we can have a more civil conversation with Ben."

"But he's on the task force," Patterson said.

"Keep him at his desk, at least for tomorrow, until we talk to Martin," Morgan said.

"I've known Ben since I came to Kodiak," Patterson said. "I can't imagine he could do this."

"We don't know that he did, Dan, but we can't ignore the connection until we know more."

"Right," Patterson paused for several seconds and then said, "what I can't get out of my mind is that Ben was in the meeting when Feeney asked where the trooper boat was when Deanna Kerr disappeared. If Ben was innocent, why didn't he speak up and say he was on the boat and the boat was in Uyak Bay over the Fourth of July?"

"It's possible he didn't want to give Feeney any meaningless ammunition. If Feeney learned Ben was in Uyak over the Fourth of July, he might have demanded Ben be removed from the task force,"

Morgan said. "I don't think anyone on the task force is very fond of the police chief."

"Yeah, maybe," Patterson said.

"How did it go with Tony Dylan?" Morgan asked.

"He claims he knew Billie but not well. He did have Deanna as a student in one of his outboard repair classes, though."

"That's interesting," Morgan said. "What about Tasha?"

"No, but her brother was on his swim team."

"Did he claim to know Deborah or Amy?" Morgan asked.

"He said he didn't know either of them."

"Did you believe him?"

Patterson sighed. "I don't know. At this point, I don't believe anyone."

Morgan disconnected and continued to read through the case files for another two hours. *Could Ben Johnstone be our murderer?* Morgan hoped not, but he knew monsters sometimes carried badges.

Chapter Twenty-Eight

Monday, December 9th
5:00 am

Morgan awoke at 5:00 am; he was wide awake and wired. He turned on the desk lamp and opened his laptop. He opened the file containing the photos of the victims and clicked on the photo of Tasha Ayers. He zoomed in on the red hair ribbon that held her thick, black hair in a ponytail. *That's it.* He had been so focused on the jewelry he hadn't given the hair ribbon much thought, but he had seen this ribbon or one just like it on the desk in Coach Small's office. It wasn't solid red but was tie-dyed red and white. *Wasn't the ribbon in Small's office also tie-dyed?* He looked at his watch. He'd wait until 7:00 am to call Patterson, and then they could go together to confront Small at the school.

Morgan showered and shaved and went downstairs for the complimentary breakfast and coffee. Time seemed to crawl by, and as soon as his watch hit 7:00 am, he dialed Patterson's personal cell.

"What did the ribbon on Small's desk look like?" Morgan asked.

"What?" Patterson sounded wide awake, but Morgan's question obviously took him by surprise.

"The ribbon on Coach Small's desk, do you remember it?" Morgan asked.

"The ribbon," Patterson repeated. "Let's see. It was red, wasn't it?"

"What else?" Morgan asked.

"I think there was some white in it," Patterson said.

"Exactly," Morgan said. "Now look at the ribbon in Tasha's hair in the photo."

"Hang on," Patterson said. "Let me get my computer." The phone remained quiet for several minutes, and then Patterson said, "Holy cow, that's it."

"I don't know how distinctive this type of hair ribbon is, but I think Tasha's ribbon is like the ribbon we saw on Small's desk," Morgan said.

"I think we should pay Small a little visit this morning."

"I'm ready when you are."

"I'll pick you up in half an hour."

Patterson and Morgan arrived at the school at 7:45 am. They again parked in the faculty lot and briskly walked through the front doors. The halls were not yet full of students, but the few who lingered near their lockers stared as Patterson and Morgan hurried down the hall. Patterson knocked on Coach Small's office door.

Small pulled open the door and blew out a breath through clenched teeth. "Sergeant Patterson and Agent Morgan," he said. "Now what?"

Patterson wasted no time with small talk. "Where is the red ribbon you had on your desk when we first questioned you?" he asked.

"What?" Small asked. "What ribbon?"

"Don't play stupid with us," Patterson said. "You had a red ribbon on your desk."

Small shrugged. "It was probably something I picked up off the floor in the girl's locker room."

"We have a photo of Tasha Ayers wearing that same ribbon in her hair," Patterson said.

Small laughed. "Seriously? Do you think there's only one red hair ribbon in this school?"

"This one was tie-dyed," Morgan said.

"Yes," Small said, "so what? Tie-dyed ribbons are apparently popular with the girls right now. Walk through the halls, and you'll see at least a dozen of them. They aren't unique, gentlemen."

"What happened to the ribbon that was on your desk?" Patterson asked.

Small shook his head. "I don't know. I put things like that in the lost and found basket in the girls' locker room." He stood. "Come on, let's see if it's still there."

Morgan and Patterson followed Small to the locker room and waited while he knocked on the door. After a few seconds, he opened the door and turned on the lights. He led them to a small, blue basket mounted on the wall. He pulled out three socks, a belt, and a pair of sunglasses but no hair ribbons. He shrugged. "I guess someone took it. If I find something on the floor in the locker room, I put it in the lost and found basket. I certainly have no use for a girl's hair ribbon." He patted his balding head. "Why are you so interested in this ribbon?"

Patterson didn't answer him but asked instead if they could return to Small's office. Once they were again seated, Patterson brought up the photo of Amy Quinn on his computer. "You took the ferry from Homer to Kodiak on November 17th." It was a statement, not a question.

Small stared at him for several moments. Finally, he said, "I guess that's right."

Patterson turned the computer toward Small so he could see the photo of Amy Quinn on the monitor. "Do you remember this woman on the ferry?"

Small studied the photo. "I can't say I do," he said, "but that trip was over three weeks ago. How could you expect me to remember someone on a crowded ferry?" He paused. "She's one of the dead women, isn't she? I saw her photo in the paper."

"That's right," Patterson said. "What do you remember about the ferry trip?"

Small blew out a breath. "I remember having too many beers with the guys and then throwing up as we pitched and rolled on our way to Kodiak."

"Did you sleep in the solarium?" Patterson asked.

"No, I had a stateroom. I always get a stateroom if I can. I don't like sleeping with a bunch of people."

"Did you share the stateroom with anyone?"

"No, I was alone and sick most of the night."

"Do you remember driving your red truck after you got home that weekend?"

Small laughed. "Honestly? It was three weeks ago. I'm getting sick and tired of being harassed by you."

"This is very important, sir."

"Let me think," Small said. He tapped his fingers on the desk while he stared at the ceiling. "I remember," he said. "Rick had my truck. He had it for nearly two weeks hauling firewood. I told him to park it at the school when he was done with it, and he left it at the school sometime the next week. Why are you so interested in my truck?"

Patterson stood abruptly. "Thank you, sir," he said.

"Look," Small said. "The next time you want to talk to me, contact my lawyer." He handed Patterson a business card with his lawyer's name and phone number on it. "I'm getting tired of you bothering me at work."

Morgan stood and followed Patterson out of Small's office and out of the building.

Patterson slammed the door of his SUV and barked into his cell phone. "Get Carson down to headquarters now!" He looked at Morgan. "I am getting damn sick and tired of this case going in circles. Who loans a nice truck to half the town?" He shook his head. "I thought we had Small with the hair ribbon, but he seems to be able to talk himself out of every corner."

Morgan knew how much Patterson wanted someone other than one of his troopers to be guilty of these crimes. "I still think the hair ribbon is suspicious," Morgan said. "Do you think you could find a judge who would sign a search warrant for Small's house, office, and truck?"

Patterson shook his head. "Not with what we have. We might be able to get a warrant for the truck, but what good will it do? We can't even figure out who was driving it, and I'll wager Carson will claim he loaned it to someone else."

Patterson was right. Forty minutes later, they faced Rick Carson in the conference room of the trooper headquarters, the photos of the slain women displayed in full view.

"I did borrow Gordon's truck," Carson said, "but Tony called me not long after we got home from Homer and asked if he could use it the next day. I was done with it, so I told him I'd bring the truck to him, he could give me a ride home, and when he was done using the truck, I told him to leave it at the high school. That's where Gordon told me to park it."

"You loaned out Mr. Small's truck without his permission?" Patterson asked.

"Yes," Carson said. "I knew he wouldn't care if Tony used it."

"By Tony, I assume you mean Tony Dylan?"

"Yes."

"You and Tony and Gordon are all friends?"

"Sure," Carson said. "We're all coaches. We play poker a couple times a month, and sometimes we watch football together with a few of the other teachers."

"Would it surprise you if I told you Tony Dylan claimed he'd never borrowed Gordon's truck?"

Carson shrugged. "He did borrow it, but maybe he forgot. I don't know why he'd tell you that."

"Rick," Morgan said, "one of the other coaches told us he thought it was strange that you hung out with a group of kids on the ferry."

Carson's face turned red. "Who said that? It's not true! Who would tell you something like that?"

"Are you sure you're not lying when you say you loaned the truck to Tony Dylan?" Morgan asked.

"Why would I lie about loaning Tony the truck?" Carson's face deepened to a darker shade.

"Maybe you don't want us to know you were driving the truck on Monday, November 18th," Morgan said.

"That's ridiculous," Carson snapped.

"Did you sleep in the solarium on the ferry or did you get a stateroom?" Morgan asked.

"I had my own stateroom," Carson said. "I wasn't feeling very well, and I went to bed soon after we boarded."

Morgan stood and walked around the table. He tapped the photo of Amy Quinn. "Did you see this woman on the ferry?"

"Her?" Carson stammered. "Was she on the ferry with us?"

"Do you know her?" Morgan asked.

"Of course not," Carson said, "but I read the paper. I know she's one of the murder victims."

"But you never talked to her?" Morgan asked.

"Never."

Morgan looked at Patterson and could tell his colleague was deep in thought.

"Mr. Carson," Patterson said. "Would you stay here for a few minutes while Agent Morgan and I confer?"

"Do I need to call my attorney?" Carson asked.

"That's up to you," Patterson said, "but you're not under arrest at this time."

Morgan followed Patterson back to his office and sat in the chair in front of Patterson's desk.

Without saying a word to Morgan, Patterson opened a file, located a phone number and dialed. He was silent for several moments, and then he said, "Tony Dylan? This is Sergeant Patterson with the Alaska State Troopers." There was a pause, and then he said, "That's right, I have a follow-up question from our discussion with you yesterday. You told us you never borrowed Gordon Small's truck. Is that correct?"

Patterson listened for several seconds and then said, "Uh-huh, I see, you forgot." He rolled his eyes at Morgan. "You parked it at the school? What did you do with the keys?" He listened awhile longer. "Okay, Mr. Dylan. I'll let you know if we have more questions."

Patterson slammed down the phone and sighed. "He says he borrowed the truck late Monday afternoon, but he only used it for about an hour to pick up a new freezer and drive it to his home. He says his freezer went out while he was up in Anchorage, so he had to buy another one and get it installed as quickly as possible before he lost all his frozen game meat."

"What did he do with the truck when he was done with it?" Morgan asked.

"He took it to the school and parked it in the faculty lot, just as Rick Carson asked him to do," Patterson said. "A friend gave him a ride back to his place."

"And the keys?"

Patterson pushed a pen across his desk. "He stuffed them under a tool box in the bed of the truck. He said that's where Rick told him to leave them."

"Wonderful," Morgan said. "So anyone could have found those keys and driven the truck through the park that night."

"I'm guessing it's a common place for Mr. Small to hide his keys, so anyone who knew the hiding place could have borrowed the truck," Patterson said.

"Let's ask Carson if Small often hid the keys there, and then, Dan, I think you need to show Liz a photo of Ben's red Toyota and ask her if the Toyota could have been the truck she saw. It is possible the truck Liz saw in the park was not Gordon Small's truck."

"I know," Patterson said. "We seem to be chasing our tails with this line of questioning. It's time to take a step back."

Morgan volunteered to return to the conference room and ask Carson about the keys for Small's truck, while Patterson called Liz Kelley.

Carson confirmed he had told Dylan to leave Small's truck at the school and to place the keys under the toolbox. "The toolbox sits on a raised board, and there's a hollow space between the board and the truck bed," Carson said. "Anyone who uses the truck leaves the keys there."

Patterson and Morgan had agreed they didn't have cause to hold Carson at this time, so Morgan told him he could go home and thanked him for his time. Once Carson left the conference room, Morgan again walked to the board and studied the photos of the women. The hair ribbon seemed like too big a coincidence to him, and he planned to suggest to Patterson that they dig deeper into Small's background. *Small fits the profile for the most part, and he is clever.* Morgan did not expect this perpetrator to be married and Small was, and the fact Small had lived in this community for 20 years also bothered Morgan. *Why would he suddenly start killing now? Has there been some sort of stressor? Has something changed in his life to cause him to start killing?* Morgan sighed. *Or is Small an innocent teacher and coach who has nothing to do with these murders?*

Morgan heard footsteps behind him and turned to see Patterson close the door to the conference room. "I e-mailed Liz a photo of Ben's truck. She doesn't think it's the truck she saw, but she can't be certain."

Morgan told Patterson that Carson had confirmed everyone who used Small's truck knew to leave the keys under the toolbox.

Patterson laughed and shook his head. "Craig Martin is back in the building. I asked him to meet me in my office. I'll let you know what he has to say about Johnstone and the Fourth of July."

Morgan looked again at the photos of the women. His eyes were drawn to the necklace around Deborah Sidle's neck. He now believed it was a purple crystal of some sort. He thought it looked familiar, but he probably only thought that because he'd looked at it so many times.

Chapter Twenty-Nine

Monday, December 9th
11:35 am

"Have a seat, Craig," Patterson said.

"Yes sir," Martin slid into the chair and sat ramrod straight. Patterson knew the young trooper must think he had been called to the boss' office to be reprimanded for some reason.

"You were on *The Protector* on the Fourth of July?"

"Yes, sir."

"According to the log, you were in Uyak Bay," Patterson said.

"Yes sir, we were in Uyak Bay when that girl went missing. We helped search for her for the next week."

"Ben Johnstone was on the boat with you?" Patterson asked.

"That's right, and Charlie Christen was the captain, and Boyd Blair was the engineer," Martin said.

"I want to keep this conversation between us," Patterson said.

"Yes, sir."

"You won't get in trouble if you did something against regulations, but I need you to tell me the truth; it is very important. Do you understand?"

"Yes, sir."

"Did Ben take the inflatable by himself at any time on the Fourth?"

Martin didn't answer for several moments. Finally, he said, "Sir, I don't want to get Ben in trouble."

"I'm not worried about a breach of regulations," Patterson said. "We have a much bigger problem here, and I need you, to be honest."

"Yes sir," Martin said, but he said nothing for several seconds. Then he hesitantly said, "Sir, Ben did take the inflatable by himself."

"Why?" Patterson asked.

"He did me a favor. It was a holiday, but we were scheduled to check several fish sites for proper permits. We both went out in the morning. We came back to the boat for lunch, and Ben told me to knock off the rest of the day, and he'd check the other sites on his own."

"Do you remember how long he was away from *The Protector*?

Martin relaxed a little. "I'd say two or three hours, but it could have been longer."

"When he returned, was there anything unusual about him?"

Martin stared at his feet while he thought. "No sir, nothing I can remember."

"Did he check all the sites he was supposed to check?"

"He couldn't check them all, sir, because most of the gill-net fishermen were at a party. He did check some seiners, though."

"Is there anything else you can remember about that day?" Patterson asked.

"Later that night we got the call about the missing girl, and we started searching for her."

"Did Ben have anything to say about the missing girl?"

"Nothing I can remember, sir. Do you mind if I ask why?"

"That will be all, Craig. Thanks for your time."

Craig nodded, stood, and left the office. Patterson called Irene on the intercom. "Irene, would you send Ben to my office right away."

"Sir, I haven't seen Ben today," Irene said.

"Did he call in sick?" Patterson asked.

"I didn't talk to him," Irene said.

"Call him and see where he is," Patterson said.

Irene knocked on Patterson's office door a few minutes later. "Ben's not answering his phone, sir. I'm worried; this isn't like him."

Patterson opened his top desk drawer and pulled out a roll of Tums. He popped two in his mouth. "Does he have one of the trooper vehicles?"

"Yes sir," Irene said. "His truck is here."

Patterson had a bad feeling.

"Sir, it was very icy last night. I'm afraid he might have been in an accident."

"Did he radio or call in at all last evening?" Patterson asked.

"I left at 5:00 pm," Irene said. "Jaden was here last night, but I checked the call log, and there was nothing from Ben."

"Doesn't Ben have a girlfriend?" Patterson asked.

"Yes, but Susan is down in Wisconsin visiting her family," Irene said.

"Someone must know where he is. Work your sources, Irene."

"Yes sir," Irene said and backed out of Patterson's office.

Patterson checked his watch. *It's only noon; maybe Ben has a doctor's appointment this morning, but why isn't he answering his phone?*

Morgan knocked on Patterson's open office door. Patterson had been deep in thought but now looked up at Morgan.

"Mark said he'd run me back to the hotel," Morgan said. "I want to go over everything again. I know I'm missing something."

"Ben is missing," Patterson said.

Morgan shut the door and took a seat in the chair by Patterson's desk. "Since when?" he asked.

"We haven't heard from him since sometime last evening. His truck is still parked here, and he's not answering his phone. I need to put out an APB on his vehicle."

Morgan nodded. "Feeney will love that."

"Nick, he has a Trooper SUV. He could be out there hunting a woman in an official vehicle. What woman wouldn't trust a trooper?"

"Is there anything I can do?" Morgan asked.

"No, have Mark talk to me before he takes you back to the hotel. I want him to go out and look for Johnstone."

Chapter Thirty

Monday, December 9th
12:15 pm

Traner was quiet on the drive to the Baranov Inn.

"Do you have any thoughts where Ben might have gone last night?" Morgan asked.

"He said he wanted to walk the docks to get a closer look at some of our suspects' boats. He also talked about driving out past Tony Dylan's house to see where he lived. I know he wants to break this case. Since he was the one who found Tasha's body, he feels like this is personal."

Morgan nodded. "Are you planning to drive out to Monashka Bay toward Dylan's house?"

Traner nodded. "It was icy last night. I nearly slid off the road, and I'm afraid that's what happened to Ben."

"How well do you know Ben?" Morgan asked.

"I've known him for five years," Traner said. "We don't hang out much outside of work, but we talk quite a bit at the office."

"And you trust him?" Morgan asked.

"Sure, why?" Traner asked. "That's the same thing the sergeant asked me."

"You know it's possible our murderer is an authority figure, someone most people would trust," Morgan said.

"I was at the meeting," Traner said. "I heard the comment about the killer possibly being a cop, but I don't believe it." Traner stepped on the brakes and pulled to the side of the road. "You're not suggesting Ben is the murderer, are you?"

"There's no evidence to directly tie him to the murders, but he was the one who found Tasha Ayers, and he was on *The Protector* in Uyak Bay when Deanna Kerr went missing."

"No way," Traner said. "I don't believe Ben is involved in this."

"Probably not," Morgan said, "but be cautious and watchful."

Traner pulled back onto the road. "Sure," he said.

Morgan tried to sit at the desk in his hotel room, but he couldn't do it. He stood and paced, but he felt as if the small room was closing in on him. He changed into sweat pants and a sweatshirt, grabbed his key and ran downstairs to the fitness center. He was happy to see he had the room to himself. He stepped on the treadmill and ran for 20 minutes. Next, he did 30 minutes on the elliptical followed by another 20 on a rowing machine. His muscles ached from the torture, but his mind finally began to relax. He stopped rowing and looked up at the ceiling where several, short, gold, blue, and purple streamers hung. He let his mind wander as he stared at the streamers. He felt an idea forming but couldn't seem to grasp it. He jogged up the stairs to his room and stood under a hot shower for several minutes.

After Morgan dried off and changed into a sweater and blue jeans, he brewed a pot of coffee and sat at the desk with the steaming cup in front of him. He turned on his computer and once again looked at the photos of the victims. From Deborah's angry stare to Deanna's sweet smile to Billie's hopeful laugh, these photos evoked a range of emotions. He thought it was incredibly sad that none of these women or girls had any idea when they posed for these photos how little time they had left on this earth or how violently they would leave it. Morgan again examined Deborah's necklace for several minutes. Finally, he reached for his phone and dialed Patterson.

"This is Patterson."

In those three words, Morgan imagined he could hear fatigue, anger, and perhaps fear.

"Nick Morgan here, Dan. Have you heard from Ben yet?"

"Nothing," Patterson said. "I have all my guys out looking for him, but if I don't hear something soon, I'll have to involve the Kodiak Police Department."

"I hope it doesn't come to that," Morgan said. "I hate to bother you with this, but something has been nagging at me."

"Go ahead," Patterson said.

"The necklace Deborah Sidle is wearing in the photo looks familiar to me. Am I imagining things or have we seen that necklace somewhere?"

"Hang on, let me bring up the photo on my computer," Patterson said. "What is it, some sort of stone?"

"I think it's a crystal," Morgan said.

"I guess so," Patterson said. He said nothing for several moments and then murmured, "Oh, no."

"What is it?" Morgan asked.

"Johnstone's truck," Patterson said. "He had some sort of crystal hanging from his rearview mirror. I didn't get a close look at it, but it was big like this one."

"The truck is still there, isn't it?" Morgan asked.

"I'm headed out to the lot now," Patterson said.

Morgan waited for several minutes, and finally, Patterson said, "The truck is locked, but there's nothing hanging on the mirror now. Do you think it was the necklace?"

"I don't know," Morgan said. "I guess I did notice something hanging from Ben's mirror, but I didn't pay much attention to it."

"I can't just sit around," Patterson said. "I'm heading out to look for him."

"Keep me posted," Morgan said.

Chapter Thirty-One

Monday, December 9th
4:00 pm

S andy Miles stepped into the English classroom. "Are you going to the gym with me this afternoon?" she asked Linda Bragg.

"Sure," Linda looked at her watch. "I have to meet with a student and do a couple of other things, so I'll meet you there around 5:00 pm. Is that okay?"

"It will work," Sandy said. "That'll give me time to run to the grocery store first."

Linda had trouble concentrating during her meeting with Chelsea Phillips. Chelsea was a bright student, but English was not her best subject. Still, she worked hard at it, and Linda wanted to do everything she could to help Chelsea become a better writer. This afternoon, though, Linda's mind wasn't on English.

"Mrs. Bragg, did you hear me?" Chelsea asked.

"Sorry, Chelsea," Linda said. "I think this draft is much better than your last draft. Why don't you go over it five more times and try to tighten it on every pass? Bring it to me in two days, and I'll take another look at it."

"Okay," Chelsea said, "thanks."

Linda watched Chelsea leave the room, and then she stood, smoothed the front of her skirt, and without giving herself time to think about her plan, she marched out of her office and down the hall. His door stood partially open, and Linda paused for a moment while she watched him. His attention was focused on something he held in his hand, but from where she stood, she couldn't see what it was. She took a deep breath and marched into his room without knocking on the door. She closed the door behind her.

He looked up, surprised. "Linda, how are you?"

"We need to talk. Something has been bothering me," she said.

"What is it?"

Linda's eyes dropped to the object he held in his hands. Her hand flew to her mouth, and she stepped back. "That's hers!" The words tumbled from her mouth before she had time to think.

He glanced down at the copper, cuff bracelet he held in his hands. He dropped the object, looking surprised as if unsure where it had come from. Slowly, his eyes rose to Linda's, and he smiled. "I can explain," he said. He stood and walked around his desk.

Linda backed toward the closed door. Her legs felt rubbery. "You're a monster," she said.

"Linda, come on, you know better than that." He smoothly grasped a large, brass trophy from a shelf and continued to walk slowly toward Linda.

Linda's eyes locked on the trophy. She stood still a moment and then turned and sprinted the last few steps toward the door. She fumbled for the door knob and opened her mouth to scream. A searing pain split her skull, and then she felt nothing.

Chapter Thirty-Two

Monday, December 9th
6:00 pm

T he temperature had dropped back into the twenties, and an icy glaze covered the road. Patterson drove slowly down the highway on his way to Johnstone's cabin in Chiniak. Johnstone wasn't at his home in Kodiak, and Traner had called to report he wasn't on his boat in the harbor. The only other place Patterson could think to check was his cabin in Chiniak. Meanwhile, the other troopers were driving the roads around town. It was possible Johnstone had been in a car wreck, and his car had slid off the road, but it was nearly dark, so there was little chance they would see a vehicle in the ditch or on the side of a cliff tonight.

Patterson's cell phone buzzed. He eased his foot off the gas pedal and pulled to the side of the road.

"Mark found the SUV," Irene said into his ear. Patterson had told her to call on the phone, not the radio if she had any news.

"Where?"

"In the parking lot at St. Paul Harbor."

"The boat harbor in the middle of town?" Patterson asked. "What's it doing there? Isn't Ben's boat in a stall at Dog Bay?"

"Yes sir, it is, and Mark thought Ben was headed to Dog Bay last night."

"Did Mark tell you anything else?"

"He said Ben's SUV is parked behind a big truck and isn't visible until you drive through the lot."

"Tell Mark not to touch anything," Patterson said. "I hate to say it, but the SUV could be evidence. I'm on my way, but it will take me the better part of an hour to get there. Tell Mark to stay with the SUV and keep a low profile. We don't want to attract attention."

"Shall I call the other troopers back to headquarters?" Irene asked.

"Yes, but don't give them any details, especially over the radio. I don't want anyone speculating on what happened until I get a look at the SUV," Patterson said.

Patterson considered calling Morgan with the news about Ben's SUV, but he decided he wanted to look at the vehicle before he called in another law enforcement agency. He had come to like and respect Morgan, and he respected and trusted Horner too, but he didn't want either one of them asking questions about one of his men until he had a better understanding of what was going on here.

Chapter Thirty-Three

Monday, December 9th
6:30 pm

W hen the phone rang at 6:30 pm, I found myself hoping it was Morgan. I glanced at the display and fought back a rush of disappointment. "Hi, Sandy."

"Hi Jane, you haven't heard from Linda, have you?"

"Linda Bragg?"

"Yes."

"No," I said. "I haven't talked to her since Friday. Why?"

"She was supposed to meet me at the gym at 5:00 pm, but she never showed up. I called her husband, and he said she wasn't at home. He assumed she was with me."

"Did you try calling her?" I asked.

"It goes straight to voice mail."

"That's strange."

"I drove back to the school, but her car is gone from the lot."

I suddenly felt chilled. I paced the kitchen and living room of my small home. "Is her husband worried?" I asked.

"I don't know," Sandy said. "I didn't want to alarm him too much, so I just made it sound as if we got our signals crossed. I told him she might be at a meeting."

"But you're sure she isn't?"

"She told me she had to meet with a student and do a couple of things but said she'd meet me at the gym by 5:00."

"I think we should call the police," I said.

Sandy paused for several seconds. "Could you call your FBI friend? You know how it is; the police won't take us seriously until she's been missing for 24 hours, but maybe you could persuade Agent Morgan to start looking for her sooner than that."

"I'll call him," I said, "but you need to call Linda's husband and tell him you're worried about her."

"I know," Sandy said. "I'll call him now."

"And Sandy," I said, "go home and lock your door. This town is dangerous."

The phone rang twice, and then Morgan answered.

"Nick, it's Jane."

"Nice to hear your voice," he said.

"This isn't a social call," I said. "I think we have a problem." I could feel my heart beating fast. I didn't want to believe Linda had been taken by the murderer, but I feared the worst.

"What's going on?" Morgan asked.

"My friend Linda Bragg was supposed to meet Sandy Miles at the gym at 5:00 pm this afternoon, but she never showed. Her husband hasn't heard from her, and her car is gone from the high school parking lot."

"Take it easy," Morgan said. "There's probably a logical explanation, and Linda will show up at any moment. Maybe she got a phone call from someone asking to meet with her, and she forgot to call Sandy."

His words were calm but I could tell that he didn't believe what he was saying. "Can you convince the police to start looking for her now?" I asked.

"As soon as we disconnect, I'll call Detective Horner with the Kodiak Police Department and ask her to initiate a search," Morgan said.

"Will you let me know if you find her?" I asked.

"Yes. We're all a little jumpy with everything that's been going on, but I'm sure Linda is fine, Jane."

I thanked Morgan and disconnected. I certainly hoped he was right. Linda had a husband and two little boys who needed her. She had to be okay.

Chapter Thirty-Four

Monday, December 9th
7:00 pm

Linda's head throbbed, and she was freezing. He'd thrown a blanket over her before he left, but she wore no coat or sweater, and there was no heat in the boat. It had all happened so fast. She'd regained consciousness on the floor of his office, and several minutes passed before she remembered where she was and why she was there.

He had murdered Tasha and the others too, probably. She still couldn't believe it, but there was no other explanation. He'd had Tasha's bracelet. He was a monster, and now he had her. She knew he planned to kill her, and she didn't even understand why she was still alive.

He had locked the door to his office, tied her up, and taped her mouth. Then he turned off the lights in the room and sat there with her for an hour, saying nothing the entire time. Finally, he forced her at knifepoint to go back to her room and get her car keys. He held the knife to her ribs while they walked out of the building toward her car. Her hands were still tied, but he'd removed the tape from her mouth, and despite the knife, she would have screamed if she'd seen another person, but there was no one at the school after 6:00 pm on a cold, December night.

He had driven her car across the Near Island Bridge to the boat harbor, and from there, he'd forced her down the boat ramp, across the floating dock and to the very end of one of the long fingers, the biting wind slapping her face and cutting through her thin, cotton blouse. He'd held her in front of him while he'd unlocked the padlock on the door of his small boat. He'd pushed her into the cabin and onto a padded seat. He'd then tied her to the seat and placed another strip of duct tape over her mouth. He'd searched the pockets of her skirt until he found her cell phone. He'd removed the battery, dropped the phone on the floor and stomped on it. Then, without saying a word, he'd turned out the light and walked out the door. She could hear the padlock snap shut, and his footsteps walk away.

She had no idea how long he'd be gone, and she couldn't think of a way to free herself. *Is my husband looking for me yet? Did Sandy report me missing? How long will the police wait before they begin searching for me, and will it be too late by then?*

She tried to fight back the tears and panic, but she lost the battle and sobbed.

Chapter Thirty-Five

Monday, December 9th
6:40 pm

Morgan called Horner's cell phone. She answered after one ring.

"Maureen, it's Nick Morgan. Jane Marcus, a friend of mine here in town, just called me to report Linda Bragg is missing."

"The school teacher?" Horner asked.

"Yes, she was supposed to meet Sandy Miles at the gym at 5:00 pm and never showed. Her husband hasn't seen her."

"So she's only been gone a couple of hours?" Horner asked.

"I know, under normal circumstances, it would be too soon to be concerned, but these aren't normal circumstances, and Linda Bragg and Sandy Miles are already connected to this case and to the school. I don't like the coincidence. I think we should take this seriously until she turns up."

"Yes, of course, you're right. I'll get the ball rolling, and we'll start searching for her."

"Thanks, Maureen. Would you give me a call if you learn anything?"

"Will do," Maureen said.

Nick called Jane back to let her know the police were beginning their search. "Do you have any thoughts where they should look?" he asked.

"No," Jane said. "Sandy said there are no school events going on tonight. I can't imagine where she'd go on a cold, Monday night."

Chapter Thirty-Six

Monday, December 9th
6:55 pm

Patterson pulled into the small parking lot at the St. Paul Boat Harbor. He had little trouble locating the two trooper SUVs sitting side by side. The lights were off on both vehicles, but exhaust streamed from the SUV on the right. He pulled up beside it, and Traner stepped out of the vehicle as soon as he saw Patterson.

"Have you looked inside?" Patterson asked.

"No, sir. It was locked when I got here. I called Irene, and she had Sid run the spare keys over to me, but she told him not to stay, and she told me not to open the SUV until you got here."

Patterson nodded. He'd have to thank Irene for following his instructions and handling the situation perfectly. He held out his hand for the spare set of keys. "Let's see what we have here then. Put on your gloves. Until we know better, we're treating this as a crime scene."

"Yes sir," Traner said.

Patterson shined his flashlight through the windows but saw nothing unusual. He inserted the key into the driver-side door. He didn't know what he expected to find. He had been trying not to speculate on why Ben had parked his SUV at St. Paul Harbor or where he had gone from there. His boat slip was in the other boat harbor, and according to Traner, the boat was still in its stall, and there was no sign Ben had been on it recently. *He probably parked his SUV at St. Paul Harbor and then called a taxi to take him to the airport. By now he could be in Mexico.* Patterson pulled open the door and used the flashlight to look in the interior. It was spotless.

"Ben's a clean freak," Traner said. "The only time I ever made him mad was when I dropped potato chips in his vehicle and forgot to clean them up." He laughed. "He actually yelled at me."

Patterson pressed the button to unlock the doors and told Traner to get in the other side and search the glove compartment. Meanwhile, Patterson looked behind the visor, checked the compartment between the seats, and felt under the front seat.

"Nothing in here but the owner's manual and the registration," Traner said.

"I don't have anything either," Patterson said. "Let's check the back seats."

After a few minutes, both men backed out of the vehicle.

"Nothing," Traner said.

"Let's look in the back," Patterson said.

Patterson doubted they would find anything of interest in the back of the SUV. Like the rest of the vehicle, he expected it to be spotless and empty. The sight that greeted him when he looked down into the recessed space caused him to jump back. For a moment, he felt as if he was going to vomit or faint. He spun around and gulped several breaths of cold, fresh air.

"Oh God," Traner yelled. He ran toward the edge of the lot, and Patterson heard him retch.

Patterson stood with his back to the SUV for several moments while he calmed his breathing and tried to think. Slowly, he turned back to the vehicle and studied the horrific scene. Like a pile of laundry, someone had stuffed Ben Johnstone's body into the rear of the SUV. Congealed blood pooled around his limp form. Most grizzly of all, though, his decapitated head sat atop his feet, eyes open wide as if in surprise. His tongue protruded from his mouth. *What happened? Did Johnstone get too close to the murderer and try to confront him by himself, or did he unwittingly stumble on something and see more than he should have?*

Patterson heard sobs and turned to see Traner standing beside him. "Where did you say he was going the last time you talked to him?" Patterson asked.

"Back to the boat harbor. He wanted to take a look at every boat that belonged to anyone related to this case," Traner said.

263

"Why?" Patterson asked.

"He thought we'd missed something. He said we either dismissed a suspect too quickly or had overlooked one altogether. I asked him if he wanted me to go with him, but he told me to go home and said he could do it by himself." Another sob escaped Traner's lips. "I should have been with him."

"Don't do that," Patterson said. "There's no reason to blame yourself. I'm sure Ben didn't think a visit to the boat harbor would place him in danger, and maybe it didn't. For all we know, he was murdered later in the night."

Patterson shut the back of the SUV. "I'll call Detective Horner; this is KPD's jurisdiction, not ours."

"But sir," Traner protested.

"I know Horner will invite our help and assistance, but to be honest, Mark, we are too close to Ben to be objective. It is a good idea to hand the investigation into Ben's death to someone else."

Traner dropped his head. "Yes, sir."

"We'll still keep looking for the guy who murdered the five women, and I have no doubt he is the same monster who killed Ben."

Chapter Thirty-Seven

Monday, December 9th
7:15 pm

M aureen Horner had just pulled into the driveway of Linda Bragg's house when her cell rang. The conversation with Sergeant Patterson lasted less than a minute. Horner backed out of the driveway too fast and lost traction on the ice, nearly shooting across the road and into the ditch. Once she gained control of the vehicle, she sped forward, fishtailing down the road. *Ben Johnstone's dead and stuffed into the back of his Trooper SUV! Who would do that? What happened? Did he ask the wrong question, or maybe the right question, and get himself killed?*

Horner called the dispatcher and told him to call in the crime scene techs and have them meet her at the boat harbor. A murdered police officer was a big thing. They couldn't make any mistakes on this one. She dialed Feeney. At first, the police chief did not sound happy being disturbed at home, but when she told him about Johnstone, his tone changed.

"I'm on my way," Feeney said. "I'll meet you at the harbor."

Horner groaned after she disconnected. She knew she'd had no choice but to call Feeney. He'd have had her head if she'd neglected to call him immediately, but she didn't want him in her way. The man had no detective skills whatsoever, and she would have to babysit him to make sure he didn't screw up the crime scene.

She parked by Patterson's SUV and climbed out of the car. Patterson pushed open the door of his SUV and joined her. Through the open door, she could see Traner sitting in the passenger seat, staring straight ahead.

She and Patterson shook hands. "I don't know what to say," Horner said. "I'm so sorry. Ben was young and bright. This is terrible."

Patterson nodded. "I didn't tell you everything on the phone, Maureen," he said. "Prepare yourself for what you're about to see. Ben was decapitated, and there's a lot of blood."

Horner took a step back from Patterson. "Oh my God," she said." She calmed her breathing and pulled latex gloves onto her hands. She nodded her head once. "Okay, let's see it."

Horner didn't flinch at the sight of Ben's body. She reined in her emotions, determined to remain cool, detached, and efficient. She could do nothing now to help Ben, but she would do everything she could to catch the animal that did this to him. She would let the crime scene techs examine Ben's remains and the SUV. Right now, she had questions to ask.

"When did you last see Ben?" she asked Patterson.

"Sometime yesterday at headquarters." Patterson shrugged. "I really can't remember. Mark," he pointed a thumb over his shoulder toward where Traner sat in the SUV, "said he talked to him at the end of their shift. Ben said he wanted to go to the Dog Bay boat harbor and take a look at every boat that belonged to anyone involved in this case."

Maureen glanced at Patterson's SUV. "I'd better talk to him then." Maureen climbed in behind the steering wheel of Patterson's SUV. She laid a hand on Mark's arm. He didn't even turn to look at her but continued to stare straight ahead.

"I'm very sorry for your loss," Horner said.

Traner swallowed hard and nodded once. In the glow of the halogen lights that lit the harbor parking lot, his skin appeared ghostly white. "I need to ask you a few questions is that okay?"

Traner nodded again but said nothing.

"Sergeant Patterson told me the last time you saw Ben yesterday afternoon, he was planning to drive to Dog Bay to check out some boats. Is that right?"

Another nod.

"Whose boats did he want to look at?"

Traner swallowed again, and his voice cracked as he started to speak. He cleared his throat and tried again. "He had a list of everyone involved in any way with this case: teachers, coaches, relatives, bank customers, and anyone else whose name had come up in the investigation, and for those who had boats, he'd marked their stall numbers and planned to check them out."

"What did he hope to find?" Horner asked.

Traner shrugged. "I don't know. It seemed like a long shot to me, and I don't think he thought it would do much good. He was just feeling frustrated with the case, and it was something he could do. He must have stumbled onto something."

"As I recall," Horner said, "Tasha was seen on the dock at Dog Bay, so why do you think his SUV is parked here at St. Paul Boat Harbor?"

Traner shook his head. "I don't know. I assume some of the boats he wanted to look at are here," he said. "Just because a boat is in a slip at this harbor now doesn't mean it wasn't at Dog Bay in October."

Horner nodded. "That's true," she said. "Was there anyone high on Ben's list of suspects? I know we're supposed to keep an open mind, but we all have our suspicions."

"That's just it," Traner said. "Ben thought we'd hit a wall. He thought we'd overlooked someone, and he wanted to start over, re-examine the case file, and consider everyone we've talked to as a possible suspect."

Through the closed car door, Horner heard Feeney's voice, and she hoped he wouldn't vomit all over Ben's body when Patterson showed it to him. "Mark," she said, "if you think of anything at all that might help us find Ben's killer, please call me right away, okay?"

Mark nodded, and for the first time, he turned and looked her in the eye. "We will catch this guy," he said.

When Horner got out of the SUV, she was relieved to see the crime scene techs arriving. She hoped they would be able to move the SUV as soon as possible. Even in sleepy Kodiak on a cold, December night, a congregation of cops in the boat harbor parking lot would eventually draw attention.

Horner found Feeney leaning against the back of Traner's SUV, and she breathed a sigh of relief that he hadn't leaned against Johnstone's vehicle before the techs could dust it for fingerprints. Feeney looked pasty white, his dark eyes sunken. For once, he didn't have much to say, and Horner knew Patterson had already shown him the body, severed head and all.

"Sir," Horner said to Feeney. "We have this handled. Once the techs get a few photos and check around the SUV for any evidence, I'll have them move the vehicle to our garage where it can be examined out of the public eye. We'll get Trooper Johnstone's body up to Anchorage as soon as possible for an autopsy."

"You're on top of this, then?" Feeney's voice sounded squeaky, and Horner fought back an inappropriate urge to laugh.

"Yes sir," she said. "I'll call you as soon as we know anything."

"Do that." Feeney stood straight, wobbled, and then marched toward his car.

Horner's phone buzzed. She looked at the display, "Damn."

"Agent Morgan," she said into the phone.

"Detective Horner, have you found out anything about Linda Bragg?"

"I'm afraid I got interrupted," she said. She looked at Patterson who was watching her curiously. She took the phone away from her mouth. "It's Morgan," she said. "Do you mind if I tell him?"

Patterson shook his head.

"We had an incident," Horner said. "Ben Johnstone has been murdered. Sergeant Patterson found his body in the back of his SUV."

Morgan said nothing for several moments. Finally, he asked, "Was his throat cut?"

"Our boy did it one better this time," Horner said. "He decapitated him."

"Where?" Morgan's voice was tight.

"We're at St Paul Harbor."

"The boat harbor across from my hotel?"

"That's right," Horner said.

"Do you mind if I come over and take a look at the body?"

"Of course not, but we'll be moving him soon."

"I'll be right there," Morgan said.

"Walk carefully," Horner said. "It's icy out here."

Chapter Thirty-Eight

Monday, December 9th
7:50 pm

Horner was right about the ice. Morgan nearly fell several times as he crossed the street and hurried toward the boat harbor. The sky had cleared, unveiling a panorama of stars crisscrossed by pale, dancing lights that Morgan assumed were a display of the aurora borealis. Unfortunately, he was in no mood to stop and enjoy the view.

When he crossed to the harbor parking lot, he caught a glimpse of Feeney's pale face peering through the windshield of his car as he pulled out of the lot. Morgan walked up to Horner and Patterson who stood talking behind one of the three Trooper SUVs parked next to each other. Crime-scene techs swarmed the rear of one of the SUVs, and Morgan knew that was where Ben's body must have been found.

Morgan cupped a hand over Patterson's shoulder. "I'm so sorry, Dan," he said. "Ben was a great, young guy with a bright future."

Patterson nodded and looked down at the ground. "And I thought he could be involved in this," he said, shaking his head.

"Considering every possibility and keeping an open mind makes you a good detective, Dan. Don't second guess yourself. You did all you could," Morgan said.

"That's what I told him," Horner said. "Have you heard anything else about Linda Bragg? Has she been found yet?"

Morgan shook his head. "Nothing," he said. "With everything that has happened, I'm concerned."

"I agree," Patterson said. "Maureen told me Linda is missing."

"I called Detective Wells," Horner said. "She's on her way to the Bragg house to interview Linda's husband. "She'll follow any leads she can. She's young, but she's bright."

Morgan nodded, but he wasn't happy about the situation. He understood Horner had her hands full with the investigation into Ben's murder, but bringing in another detective who was unfamiliar with these murder cases would only waste valuable time searching for Linda. *Ben Johnstone is dead, but Linda Bragg might still be alive, and if we can find her, we could save her.*

Morgan looked at Johnstone's body and severed head. He had no doubt the guy they were after had murdered Johnstone. *What did Ben stumble on? Perhaps Ben is the only investigator in this case who understood where the clues were pointing them.*

"Mark thinks Ben was at Dog Bay yesterday evening checking out boats that belonged to anyone involved in this investigation," Patterson said. "If he went to Dog Bay, I don't know why his SUV is parked here."

"Maybe the killer drove it here," Morgan said. "Was Ben checking on boats owned by the suspects at the top of our list, or was he checking on boats owned by everyone we've talked to?"

"I got the impression from Mark that Ben was less concerned with the main suspects and more interested in everyone else we've interviewed or anyone else related to the victims."

"Interesting," Morgan said. "Maybe he was onto something. We'll have to take a fresh look at things in the morning. I also think we should send someone to Dog Bay to find out if anyone there saw Ben walking the docks or better yet, saw him talking to someone."

"I've already got a crew doing that," Maureen said. "I'll let you know what we find, and I'll keep you posted on Linda Bragg."

Morgan knew Maureen had just dismissed him. Patterson said he needed to return to headquarters and contact Ben's family in Wisconsin. He offered to give Morgan a ride back to his hotel.

Once back in his room, Morgan called Jane. "I hope I'm not calling too late," he said.

"It's only 10:00 pm," Jane said. "I'll never sleep tonight anyway. Is there any news about Linda?"

"No," Morgan said. "There's supposed to be a detective at her house now. Something else happened that interfered with the police searching for her."

"What?" Jane asked.

Morgan told Jane about finding Johnstone's body, but he left out the part about his head being decapitated.

"You think this is the same guy who murdered Deanna and the other women?" Jane asked.

"Yes," Morgan said. "I think Johnstone either stumbled upon the murderer or he figured out who the guy was and confronted him on his own. I wish he would have shared his thoughts with the task force, but keeping a young cop from going rogue can be a problem. He's either too afraid of looking foolish, so he doesn't say what he's thinking, or he decides he wants to be a hero and tries to solve the case on his own. The whole point of a task force is to work together."

"Do you think he was killed at St Paul Harbor where his body was found?" Jane asked.

"No," Morgan said. "That harbor is well-lit and in the middle of town. Even in December on a dark night, I can't see our murderer killing someone where there's a chance he would be seen. Up until now, this guy has been extremely cautious and smart. Murdering someone in the middle of town would be a reckless move. I think it's much more likely he murdered Ben somewhere else and drove him there."

"Is there blood in the SUV?" Jane asked.

"Only in the trunk," Morgan said, "and a lot of it there. I think Ben was put in the back of the SUV before he was murdered. That's the crime scene."

"How did the murderer get him into the back of the SUV?" Jane asked.

"He may have forced Ben into the back with his knife or with a gun, but I can't imagine Ben not fighting in that situation. I think it's more likely Ben turned his back, and the perpetrator hit him over the head with something and then manhandled him into the rear of the vehicle. We'll know more when we get the results from the autopsy."

"I'm so sorry," Jane said. "You knew Ben and worked with him."

"I didn't know him well, but he was a young guy with a bright future. I feel bad for his colleagues," Morgan said.

"And now this animal has Linda."

"I think it's very possible he has her," Morgan admitted.

"Why?" Jane asked. "Do you think the killer is someone from the high school?"

"Yes," Morgan said. "Linda has light-colored hair and is married. She doesn't match the other victims this guy has stalked. I think just like Ben, Linda confronted him with something, and he had to shut her up."

"Do you think she's dead?" Jane asked.

"I hope not," Morgan said, "but you should be prepared for the worst."

Chapter Thirty-Nine

Monday, December 9th
8:30 pm

He sat in his darkened living room trying to think and fighting to calm his nerves. He couldn't afford to lose control, but things were happening too fast. First, the cop had stopped at his boat to talk to him and started asking too many questions. The cop had noticed blood on one of the couch cushions in the salon, and when he couldn't think fast enough to offer an explanation for the blood, the cop grew suspicious and started firing questions at him. When the cop asked him to come down to trooper headquarters, he'd agreed; what else could he do? That's when he knew he had to kill the trooper. He followed him up to the parking lot, and when they got to the SUV, he hit the trooper over the head with a heavy flashlight. Luckily, the lot had been empty at the time. He'd stuffed the trooper in the back of his SUV and cut his throat. No, he did more than that; he'd cut off the cop's head. He knew he'd gotten carried away, but he was angry at the young cop for making him kill him. That's the kind of crap that could get him caught.

He had driven the trooper's SUV to the other boat harbor and then hiked back to his truck at Dog Bay. He'd expected the trooper to be found by the morning and was surprised when he drove past the boat harbor and the SUV was still parked there in plain sight.

He had just decided to lay low for a while when that bitch, Linda Bragg, came into his office and saw the bracelet. He hadn't wanted to take her to his boat, but he didn't know what else to do with her. He'd planned to take her out to sea tonight and dump her body, but when he'd gotten back to Dog Bay the place was swarming with cops. Obviously, they'd found the trooper's body, and somehow they knew the trooper had been over at Dog Bay just before he went missing.

Soon, the cops would start checking all the boats. He had to get back there and somehow slip out of the harbor without drawing attention to himself. He doubted the police would perform a thorough search of the harbor before daylight, so he planned to drive over there around 4:00 am or 5:00 am and slide out of the harbor while it was still dark.

He stood and paced. *Am I losing control?* He had to remain calm. A vision of Tasha swam through his head. He had liked her, and she had worshiped him. *All women are the same, though. They can never leave well enough alone. When Tasha told me she was pregnant, I told her to get an abortion, but she wouldn't do it. She had stupid dreams that we would be a happy family together. She ruined it, so I killed her. Billie was also okay until she started getting whiny about telling her daughter and friends about me. Relationships are no good. From now on, I'll stick with prostitutes.*

Chapter Forty

Tuesday, December 10th
11:20 pm

Linda opened her eyes. How long had she been asleep? It was still pitch dark, but dark didn't mean much this time of year. Why hadn't he come back yet? She believed he would kill her when he returned, but she felt so cold, she couldn't stop shivering. She wanted to end this, whatever happened. Sitting here thinking about how she would never see her husband and sons again was torture, and she had given up on trying to free herself. He had built an effective prison on this boat, and she could not break out of it.

Why didn't I realize it was him sooner, and why didn't I say something to the police?

She heard footsteps on the concrete walkway and thought he was back, but the footsteps stopped, and then she heard them walking back the other way. It must be one of the guards who patrolled the harbor. If only she could make some sort of noise to attract his attention. She tried to scream through the duct tape covering her mouth, but the only sound that escaped was a muffled sob.

Chapter Forty-One

Tuesday, December 10th
3:20 am

Morgan fell asleep for a few hours but woke with a jolt at 3:20 am. He knew he would never get back to sleep, so he rolled out of bed, pulled on his sweats and headed downstairs to the gym. As he lay on his back, lifting weights, he stared at the sparkly streamers dangling from the ceiling. When he finished lifting weights, he climbed onto the treadmill and soon after he began jogging, it hit him. He knew where he'd seen Deborah Sidle's necklace, or at least he knew where he'd seen the purple crystal from her necklace.

When he first remembered where he'd seen the crystal, he'd had no doubt he was right, but after standing in a hot shower for several minutes, his certainty began to wane. It was still only 4:30 am in the morning, and he hated to wake Patterson at this hour, but with Linda Bragg missing, he couldn't afford to waste time. He might be wrong, but if he was right, they needed to move now.

Patterson answered on the first ring. He sounded wide awake.

Morgan skipped the apology and got right to the purpose of his call. "Rick Carson's house," he said.

"Yes?" Patterson said.

"Remember the ceiling fan pull in the great room near his little doll collection?" Morgan asked. "He asked me to turn on the fan when we were in his house."

"Not really," Patterson said, "why?"

"I can't be certain, but I think the purple crystal from Deborah Sidle's necklace, the one she's wearing in the photo, was attached to the chain I pulled to start the ceiling fan."

Patterson paused for several minutes. "I didn't really notice the fan pull, are you sure?"

Morgan exhaled. "I'm not sure, but it would be the sort of thing a psychopath would do: have his trophy out in the open and then ask the FBI profiler to touch the trophy to turn on the fan. That's the behavior of the narcissistic perpetrator who killed these women."

"Well, I've got no other leads, so we might as well wake up Carson and get a look at his fan. Maybe we'll get very lucky and find Linda Bragg at the same time."

Morgan opened the door and jumped in Patterson's SUV even before it rolled to a stop. Patterson eased onto Rezanof, and Morgan groaned. Patterson's wipers were moving as fast as they could, but they couldn't keep up with the barrage of snow pelting the windshield. There was no forward or side visibility in the heavy snow, and several inches of the white stuff had piled up on the roads in the last few hours, making it nearly impossible to even tell where the road was.

Patterson drove slowly, shoulders hunched, eyes staring into the white-out in front of him. "This is ridiculous," he said.

Morgan willed the vehicle to move faster, but he kept quiet. It would be reckless for Patterson to drive any faster on these roads in these conditions. Luckily, they seemed to be the only people foolish enough to be out on the roads at this hour in this weather.

Morgan thought about what they would do when they reached Carson's house. What if Carson refused to let them enter his house? They could possibly push past him and later claim they had reason to believe he was holding Linda Bragg captive in his home. He wasn't sure if there was enough evidence to support that claim in a court of law, but the truth was that Linda Bragg was missing, and he believed he had seen Deborah Sidle's necklace in Carson's house. He didn't think either he or Patterson would worry about lawyers and judges if Carson tried to keep them out of his house. If they waited to wake a judge and get a search warrant before they entered his house, Carson would have plenty of time to murder Linda, if she was still alive, and dispose of her body.

Patterson edged to the side of the road in front of Carson's house. "Are you ready?" he asked.

Morgan was out of the SUV before Patterson finished the question. Patterson jogged after Morgan over the slippery sidewalk to Carson's front door.

Morgan pushed the doorbell twice, and the men waited. When no one came to the door, Morgan pushed the bell again and pounded on the door. Next, he yelled Carson's name and pushed the bell several times in a row. They could hear the bell ring, so they knew it worked.

Patterson backed down the walk and looked up at the house. Both he and Morgan yelled Carson's name while Patterson studied the house.

Finally, Patterson returned to the porch and shook his head. "No lights," he said. "I don't think he's here."

Morgan held his hands wide. "Where would he be in this weather?"

"Maybe on his boat," Patterson said.

Morgan stared at Patterson for a moment and then said, "You're right. He's on his boat with Linda, and he's probably getting ready to murder her if he hasn't already done it."

"I know from Ben's research that Carson keeps his boat at Dog Bay. Let's go."

Both men hurried back to the SUV. While Patterson navigated the snow-covered roads, Morgan called Maureen Horner. She was awake, alert, and already at the police station. "I'll have someone work on a search warrant for Carson's home," she said, "and I'll meet you at the harbor. Do you know his slip number?"

"No," Morgan said.

"I have the guard's cell number," Horner said. "I'll get the slip number from him."

Chapter Forty-Two

Tuesday, December 10th
4:15 am

At 4:15 am, he decided it was time to go. He could park down the road and approach the harbor on foot. If he saw cops, he'd turn around, but if he didn't, he'd head to his boat.

Happy to have a plan, he dashed through the snow to his car. He turned the key and let the car warm up for several minutes before backing out of the driveway. He breathed evenly and kept his pace well below the speed limit. Several inches of snow had accumulated on the streets. He saw few other tire tracks until he reached the Near Island Bridge, and even there, not many cars had passed over the bridge since the snow started. He drove slowly, watching for any signs of danger. He was happy the heavy snow obscured the visibility. Even if someone saw his vehicle, they wouldn't be able to see much more than his headlights.

Once he'd crossed the bridge, he followed the gravel road toward the boat harbor. He saw no sign of flashing lights, and he noticed the snow on this road appeared undisturbed. No one had driven to or from the boat harbor since the snow started. *That doesn't mean police officers haven't stayed at the harbor all night to watch.* He drove slowly into the parking lot above the harbor, turned off the car lights and the engine and studied the darkness for several minutes. As far as the police were concerned, he had every right to drive down to the harbor and walk to his boat. They had no reason to stop him.

Chapter Forty-Three

Tuesday, December 10th
4:53 am

The footsteps awoke her, and this time, she heard him step onto the boat. He was back. It would all be over soon.

She heard the key in the padlock, and then the door opened slowly. He stepped inside, and she heard the bolt on the inside of the door snap shut. She needed to use the bathroom, and she knew her only chance of escape would be if he untied her to use the bathroom. *Maybe if I can find a weapon or hit him with something then I can rush out of the boat and scream for help.*

She moaned as loudly as she could through her duct tape. At first, he didn't seem to hear her. He didn't even look at her as he walked past her and up the three steps to the wheelhouse. She heard one of the engines cough several times and slowly turn over. A minute later, the second engine roared to life. He fooled with the electronics for several minutes and then descended back to the salon. She made as much noise as she could, and his head snapped toward her. The menacing look on his face silenced her.

"Shut up, bitch," he said. "You've caused me enough trouble." In the blink of an eye, he backhanded her across her face.

She lost consciousness for a few moments, and when she awoke, she felt blood running from her nose down over the duct tape on her mouth. The blood dripped in a steady stream onto her wool coat. Her eyes watered, and the searing pain from her nose made thinking nearly impossible. She knew he'd broken her nose, but what did that matter? Soon he would kill her. *Why didn't he kill me before now?*

Maybe because he wants to dump me at sea and avoid making a mess on his boat. She shivered at the thought of being thrown alive into the icy waters of the North Pacific. She couldn't imagine a worse death. *Where has he gone? Has he left again? The engines are still running; he must be here.*

He reentered the galley and hurried up to the wheelhouse. She felt the boat move and understood he must have been untying the lines from the dock. They were leaving the harbor.

Chapter Forty-Four

Tuesday, December 10th
5:15 am

They didn't need to know where Carson's boat slip was, Patterson spotted the small cabin cruiser's lights as it slid toward the harbor entrance. On a cold, December morning, it was the only pleasure boat on the move. Patterson quickly placed two calls. He phoned his office to get the combination to the lock on *The Protector*. He had never operated the boat before, but he didn't have time to wake up one of their usual boat captains and get him down to the harbor. He'd spent a week on the boat not long after he'd arrived for duty in Kodiak, and he felt confident he could operate it as long as the engines cooperated. He wondered how long it had been since anyone had been down to the harbor to start it; he hoped the batteries weren't dead.

The second call Patterson made was to the Coast Guard to request assistance in pursuing Carson's boat. The Coast Guard agreed to assist in the chase, but it would take an hour or more before they'd be ready.

"That does me a hell of a lot of good," he muttered after disconnecting.

"What's that?" Morgan asked.

"It's all up to us," Patterson said. "Are you ready for a boat ride?"

"Sure," Morgan said. "A boat ride in the dark in a blizzard. Who wouldn't want to do that?"

Patterson came to a sliding stop in the harbor parking lot. He was just about to say they didn't have time to wait for Horner when he saw the lights of her car heading down the road to the parking lot.

"Carson's on the move," Patterson said. "We'll have to chase him."

"By boat?" Maureen's voice rose an octave.

Patterson opened the rear of the SUV and grabbed a rifle. "He's on the water; we don't have any other options."

"It won't be easy in this weather. Did you call the Coast Guard?"

"Yes, they'll be an hour behind us."

"Wonderful," Horner said. She grabbed a rifle from her vehicle, and the three of them trotted down the ramp toward *The Protector*.

Patterson punched in the combination to the door lock, and he, Horner, and Morgan climbed into the wheelhouse. He said a silent prayer and turned the key on the starboard engine. It clicked. He tried again and was answered by another click. He heard Horner groan. He turned the key on the port engine and held his breath. The port engine coughed and sputtered. "Come on," he murmured. He turned the key again and this time was rewarded with a longer cough. He tried a third time, and finally, the engine caught and roared to life.

"Thank God," Patterson said. "Let's give it a minute. The other engine should start once the battery gets a little charge from the port engine." Patterson tried the starboard engine again, but it still wouldn't turn over. He flipped on the running lights and the large spotlight on the bow. "Let's go before he gets too far ahead of us," Patterson said. "Will you two untie the lines?"

Morgan and Horner hurried from the wheelhouse and untied the lines holding the boat in the slip. They jumped back on board, and Patterson expertly pulled from the stall and navigated out of the harbor. He knew right away that they had a problem. The spotlight illuminated nothing except the heavy snow blowing at it from every direction.

"Turn it off," Horner said. "I think we'll be able to see better without it."

Patterson flipped the switch to extinguish the light. The visibility was only marginally better. He turned on the radar. "This should help," he said.

"If we have to guess which way he went," Horner said, "I would choose the channel toward Spruce Cape."

"Won't Spruce Cape be miserable in this wind?" Patterson asked.

"I can't think of a good spot in this wind," Horner said, "but if he can make it around Spruce Cape, he'll be able to hide in Ouzinke Narrows."

"You know this island better than I do," Patterson said. "I'll take your word for it."

"Do you think he's trying to flee the island in his boat?" Morgan asked. "He'll never be able to do that in this weather, will he?"

"No," Horner said, "but he may be able to hide from us until the weather improves and then he can sneak across to the mainland."

"He may not even realize we're after him," Patterson said. "He's just looking for a spot to dump Linda's body. His plan may be to return to the boat harbor once he does that."

"If that's what he's doing," Horner said, "I have no idea which way he'll go." She paused. "Still, the quickest way to get away from civilization would be toward Spruce Cape."

Patterson tried the starboard engine again, and this time it roared to life. He ignored the "No Wake" signs as he sped along the channel. Snow obscured the homes and business that lined the entrance into Kodiak. He caught a glimpse of Petro Marine, the halogen lights illuminating the fuel dock appeared as fuzzy circles through the thick snow. While Patterson fought to see where he was headed, Horner and Morgan concentrated on the radar screen.

"Do you see anything?" Patterson asked.

"I can't tell what I'm looking at," Morgan said.

"I'm not used to looking at radar," Horner said. "It's tough to determine how big these objects are." She pointed at a bright blip on the screen. "That could be a buoy or a freighter for all I know."

Patterson slowly pulled back the throttle. "Maybe if we sit still for a minute, we'll be able to tell if any of these blips are moving."

"Sitting still" was a relative term as they bucked and rolled in the waves and swell. All three cops stared at the small radar screen.

"There!" Patterson and Horner said in unison, and Horner pointed at a neon dot rapidly moving away from them. Patterson pushed the throttle forward until they bounced from one wave crest to the next. Morgan and Horner grabbed handholds and braced themselves as they closed the distance between themselves and the small green blob on the radar.

Chapter Forty-Five

Tuesday, December 10th
5:35 am

He couldn't believe his good luck. He had gotten out of the boat harbor unchallenged. *Maybe I'll be able to dump the body and sneak back into town without anyone suspecting me. No one will ever find Linda Bragg's body, and just as with the other women, they'll never be able to prove I murdered her. I've outsmarted the cops up to this point so why should that end now? I know I didn't leave any evidence when I murdered the cop, and why would anyone suspect I am involved in the disappearance of Linda Bragg?*

If that damn, nosy Linda hadn't caught me looking at Tasha's bracelet, I would be in bed right now instead of rolling around in the ocean in a blizzard. Why did she walk into my office in the first place? She didn't knock and she'd seemed mad. She'd seen Tasha's bracelet before she had a chance to say why she was there, and we haven't had an opportunity to chat since then.

He stared at his radar to get his bearings. He saw buoy four but no sign of boat traffic. He'd better pay attention. He didn't want to run into the side of the ferry or a Coast Guard cutter. The waves continued to build as he rounded Spruce Cape. These seas were too big for a boat the size of his, but once he got around the corner and into Ouzinke Narrows, conditions should improve. Then he'd have a chance to dispose of his cargo and monitor radio traffic to determine whether or not it was safe for him to return to port.

The nose of his boat plunged into the crest of a large wave, and for a few seconds, all he saw was water. He gripped the wheel and pulled back on the throttle as his heart thudded.

Chapter Forty-Six

Tuesday, December 10th
5:40 am

L inda prayed as the boat sped over the waves. She couldn't see out the window, but she could tell they were in a storm. The sea was rough, and the boat pitched and rolled. She fought back fear and nausea. What little hope she'd had of escape or rescue had evaporated. *I'll die tonight, I know that. Why did I approach him when he was alone? I didn't believe he was dangerous; I just didn't understand how he knew what grade Tasha was getting in my literature class. It was none of his business. I should have been the only one besides Tasha who knew what her grade was in my class, and I had hoped Tasha would get her act together in time to improve her grade before the end of the semester. I'd only told Tasha she was failing to try to shock her and convince her to put more time into her studies.* Linda felt tears pour down her cheeks. Her ploy had backfired, though. *I failed Tasha. My strict words sent Tasha tumbling even further into the abyss, and for that, I will never forgive myself.* When Tasha had run out of her room, Linda had felt so guilty she hadn't told anyone, not even her husband, about their confrontation. *So how could he know how Tasha was doing in her class unless he was guessing, or unless he had talked to Tasha after she'd left the school that day?* Linda knew now that he had seen Tasha after she'd left the school, and he'd killed her that night.

The boat bounced and rolled. Outside the window, she heard the wind howl and the surf pound. Suddenly, she felt the boat slam into something and heard him yell. She felt herself smile. *Maybe we will both die tonight.*

Chapter Forty-Seven

Tuesday, December 10th
6:10 am

"**I** can't believe he's out here in that boat in this crap," Patterson said. "How long did Ben tell us Carson's boat is?"

"Forty-four feet," Horner said. "How big is this boat?"

Morgan glanced at Horner. Her eyes were big, and she was holding onto a safety rail so tightly her knuckles were white.

"This is 56 feet long," Patterson said. "It's built for big seas, but I wish we had someone with a little more sea time at the helm."

"You're doing fine," Morgan said. He had no idea how this situation would unfold. They had no game plan, and overtaking a boat in heavy seas would not be easy. *I am getting too old for this.*

Horner pointed at the radar. "He's slowed down," she said. "The conditions must be getting worse out there."

"Hang on folks," Patterson said, "this is our chance to catch up with him."

Horner gave Patterson a sidelong glance and tightened her grip on the rail. Morgan watched her and followed suit. As a lifelong resident of Kodiak, he knew Horner had more boat experience than either he or Patterson and while he would have felt better if she was at the helm rather than Patterson, he didn't think this was a good time to discuss a change of captain. Patterson had shown no hesitation so far, and he seemed to know what he was doing.

Morgan expected the seas to gradually build in height and force; he was wrong. In less than five minutes they went from four-foot seas to 10-foot seas, and Patterson pulled back on the throttle to keep from burying the boat in the waves.

Maureen studied the radar. "He's still making headway," she said, "but I don't know how he's managing these seas in a boat that size. It can't be fun."

Morgan agreed; *The Protector* was 12 feet longer than Carson's boat, and they certainly weren't having fun in these waves. "This might be a good time to ask you where the survival suits on this boat are located," he said to Patterson.

"In a closet by the stern cabin door." Patterson's voice sounded tense as his eyes darted from the radar to the GPS to the windshield which provided a view of heavy snow and an angry, black sea.

Morgan glanced at the time on the GPS. It was 6:15 am, so that meant what, nearly three more hours until light?

"We'll never be able to approach Carson's boat in these conditions," Horner said. "We'll have to wait until he's in calmer water."

"Do you think it will be much calmer in Ouzinke Narrows?" Patterson asked.

"Yes," Horner said. "There will be some swell, but it should be fairly calm; it's well protected in there."

"What's our plan?" Morgan asked at the precise moment they took a large wave over the bow. He wasn't holding on tight enough, and his head slammed against the bulkhead, dazing him.

"Are you okay?" Horner asked.

Morgan didn't reply as he danced on the edge of consciousness. Horner reached back to touch him when they slammed into another wave, and they both hit the wall this time.

"Hang on!" Patterson yelled, and Morgan could see him fighting to maintain his grip on the wheel.

"You're bleeding," Horner said to Morgan.

"I'm okay," Morgan said. He wrapped his arms around the safety rails and held on as tight as he could.

No one attempted conversation for the next 30 minutes, and expletives were the only sounds uttered by any of them as they pounded through the heavy seas. On the radar, the smaller boat in front of them inched ahead at a snail's pace. Morgan could not imagine what they were experiencing in these seas on that boat.

Chapter Forty-Eight

Tuesday, December 10th
6:20 am

He had cinched Linda's legs and arms tightly to the bench, but she could still roll from side to side, and without the use of her limbs, she had no way to brace herself. Her head and torso rolled back and forth as they pounded through the heavy seas. If by some miracle she survived tonight, she'd have whiplash and a messed-up spine. She had managed not to throw up so far, but she didn't know how much longer she could fight her nausea. If she vomited with this duct tape on her mouth, she knew she'd probably choke to death. She thought about her boys and their sweet faces, and she tried to breathe evenly through her nose.

Where is he heading? He can't stop or even turn around in conditions this bad. She didn't know how he was managing to keep the boat under control in these seas. She had worked on fishing boats when she was younger, and she could tell from the pitch and roll of the boat they were in a storm far worse than anything she had ever experienced on the ocean. He must be heading toward calmer water. While she welcomed less turbulence, she knew once he found a sheltered spot, he would kill her and dump her body overboard, or he wouldn't bother killing her before he dumped her body. She shuddered. *Please God, let him kill me first; I don't want to drown.*

Chapter Forty-Nine

Tuesday, December 10th
6:43 am

"It must be calming down." Horner pointed to the radar. "His boat is traveling faster."

"Good," Morgan said. "Now, I think we need to talk about a plan." He still clutched the safety rails with all his strength, but his fear lessened with the promise of calmer water.

"I'll get as close as we can," Patterson said. "We have rifles."

"I think that plan is too dangerous," Horner said. "We could hit Linda, or we could kill Carson and then what? The boat would run into a rock or the shore."

"Do you have a better idea?" Patterson barked out the words.

Morgan wondered if Patterson was beginning to crack under the pressure of running the boat through treacherous seas in zero visibility while pursuing a dangerous killer. Morgan's own stress level had hit the stratosphere a half an hour ago, and he was just a passenger on this adventure.

Horner, on the other hand, sounded calm and composed. "If you can get close enough to Carson's boat, I'll jump onto it," she said.

Both Patterson and Morgan stared at her.

"Are you crazy?" Patterson asked.

"Probably," Horner smiled, "but I think it's our only choice. I'll jump and then you guys pull alongside and keep his attention with your rifles. If you have to shoot him, at least I'll be there to pilot the boat."

"I'll jump onto the boat too," Morgan said and then caught himself. *What am I thinking? But I can't let Horner go alone.*

Horner stared at Morgan for a moment and then asked Patterson, "Can you pull alongside and point the rifle at Carson?"

"I can," he said. "The toughest part will be getting close enough to his boat, so you two can jump."

"If he doesn't already know we're following him," Morgan said, "you may be able to pull right up behind him before he detects us."

"He won't hear the engine over the howling wind, and he'll never see us in this snow," Horner said. "He won't know we're there until we jump on his boat."

"What about his radar?" Patterson asked.

"He must see us on his radar," Horner said, "but he has no reason to think we're following him. He probably thinks this is a fishing boat that got caught in the storm and is heading for calmer water. I think we can sneak up on him before he figures out we're after him."

"I wish we had back-up," Patterson said.

"Wouldn't that be nice," Morgan said.

"The deck is icy," Patterson said. "Everything is icy. You'll have to climb over the bow railing and then leap onto his slippery deck. Are you sure you can do this?" He looked from Horner to Morgan.

"I can do it," Horner said, her voice strong and steady.

Morgan was not at all sure he could leap from one icy boat to the other, and he knew his doubt would be obvious if he attempted to speak. He nodded his head instead.

"Okay," Patterson said. "He has increased his speed, but we're still gaining on him. I think we can catch him."

Half an hour later, the radar indicated they were only a mile behind the other boat. Morgan thought the sky looked lighter, but the blizzard outside the window obscured all visibility. The wind had calmed significantly in this sheltered passage, and while they wanted the wind to cloak the sound of the boat's engines, they would never manage to jump from one boat to the other in 10-foot seas. Morgan estimated the wave height had decreased to one-foot, and it seemed to be calming with each passing minute.

"We won't see the boat until we're nearly on top of it," Patterson said. "Do you want to get up there and get ready?"

Horner looked at Morgan. "Let's go," she said.

"Do you want to take rifles or just your handguns?" Patterson asked.

"I don't think I can manage a rifle," Horner said. "This will be tricky enough with the use of both hands. I have my gun in my holster, and it should be enough."

Morgan nodded and ran his hand over his coat pocket to make certain his gun was still there. Adrenaline surged through his body. Leaping off a boat in the North Pacific was not something he did every day, and it was not something he had ever wanted to do. His normal job involved sitting behind a desk, with a smattering of field work that usually involved advising local police forces. He had worked both as a profiler and in the anti-terrorism unit, and he'd had his share of excitement, but he did not think of himself as James Bond. Leaping off icy boats had never been part of his job description. *Is Horner as nervous as I am? She's definitely tougher than I am.*

A sheet of solid ice covered the deck. Each time they'd taken a wave over the bow, the ice had grown in thickness. Patterson slowed while Morgan and Horner navigated the ice to the bow of the boat. A double railing framed the bow. The top rail sat four feet above the deck, and the bottom rail was two feet above the deck. Morgan watched Horner while she carefully straddled the top rail. She then eased her other leg over the rail until she was perched atop it. She gripped the rail tightly with both gloved hands and looked back at him. He must have looked terrified because she laughed when she saw his expression. He shrugged and crawled up on the rail beside her. He leaned back so that if anything jarred him from his perch, he would fall onto the deck and not into the water.

Horner and Morgan held their position on the railing for 10 minutes while Patterson edged the boat forward. Morgan feared his gloves had frozen to the railing, but he didn't dare try to lift his hands from the railing, or he knew he would fall.

They couldn't have been more than 50 feet from the stern of the lead boat when they finally saw it, and even though Patterson had the aid of radar to help him judge the proximity of the other boat, he must have also been startled when it popped into view because he decelerated rapidly and almost knocked Morgan and Horner into the water. Morgan's legs felt numb from sitting on the cold railing so long, and he didn't know if he would be able to make them work. He saw Horner shake her legs and knew she must have the same problem.

Morgan's heart slammed in his chest, and despite the freezing temperature, sweat trickled down his back. *If I jump too soon, I'll be smashed between two boats, but if I wait too long, Patterson might ram the other boat, and the end result will be the same.* He decided to trust Patterson and to stay on *The Protector* until it nearly touched the other boat. Then, and only then, he would jump. *Will Carson see them approaching on his radar and speed up? The sooner they board his boat, the better; surprise is our biggest ally.*

Time dragged as Patterson closed the distance. Only a small chop marred the water surface. Conditions would not get better than this. They were 20 feet from the back deck of the other boat. The bow of *The Protector* was a few feet higher than the back deck of the other boat so they would have gravity on their side. If Patterson could get close enough, they might actually be able to do this. Of course, their problems didn't end if they landed safely on the deck of the other boat. Jumping on the lead boat was only stage one of their assault, and if Carson knew they were there, he might greet them with a round of rifle fire. *One problem at a time.*

Morgan focused on the lead boat. It seemed smaller than 44 feet. He could clearly read the name: *The Counselor. Was that the name Ben had given them for Carson's boat?* He blinked the snow out of his eyes. *No time to worry about boat names right now.*

They closed to within 15 feet and then 10. Morgan concentrated on nothing but the deck of the boat in front of him. He didn't think he could hear any sound over the thudding of his heart, but when they were five feet from the other boat, he heard Horner say, "Now."

To his surprise, he obeyed her command, and in a matter of seconds, they both hit the deck of the other boat hard, slid, and sprawled on their stomachs.

Chapter Fifty

Tuesday, December 10th
7:48 am

The seas had calmed. They were no longer rolling and bucking through the waves. Her nausea abated, for which she was thankful, but she feared they were nearing the spot where he planned to kill her. She said a prayer and then summoned an image of her husband and two little boys. *No matter how he kills me, I plan to leave this world thinking about the love I have for my family, not about the maniac who is killing me.* She hoped her death would be fast, and she hoped that somehow her body would be found so her family would not always have to wonder what had happened to her. Maybe she would end up in a pile of kelp like Deanna Kerr. *I wish I could tell my family goodbye, but I know they know I love them.*

She thought she heard a noise behind them. *Is it another engine?* No, it must be the wind. She heard it again and tried to lift her head so she could hear better. *It is definitely an engine; isn't it?* She glanced up to the wheelhouse and her captor. His back was to her as he stared straight ahead. *He must not have heard the other engine.*

Suddenly, she heard two large thuds on the rear deck.

"What the hell?" he said and turned to look behind them.

Chapter Fifty-One

Tuesday, December 10th
7:50 am

Morgan and Horner instinctively stayed low, below the level of the cabin windows. They each half rolled and half slid to opposite sides of the cabin. They crouched and looked at each other. As soon as they leaped from the bow of *The Protector*, Morgan heard Patterson quickly back off the stern of *The Counselor* and then pull alongside the smaller boat. Horner gave Patterson a few seconds to get into position and then motioned to Morgan that she would try the rear cabin door. Morgan nodded, and he too edged toward the door. They heard a rifle blast and knew Patterson had fired the planned shot over the bow. The rifle blast was their cue to enter the cabin.

Horner easily slid open the cabin door, and she and Morgan, guns drawn, eased inside the boat. They saw a small galley to the left, and after a few more steps, they glimpsed the form of Linda Bragg tied to the couch in the salon. She stared at them, eyes open wide.

Horner put her finger to her mouth and nodded to Linda. Linda used her eyes to signal her captor's location. At that moment, the boat made a sharp left-hand turn and rammed into something solid. The impact knocked both Horner and Morgan off their feet. *Had this maniac rammed The Protector?* Morgan and Horner had just gotten to their feet when the boat turned hard to starboard. This time they managed to hold on, but they each remained crouched.

A moment later, a loud barrage of automatic weapon fire filled the small cabin of the boat. He was firing at Patterson. They had to take him out now.

Morgan looked at Horner, and she nodded. They kept low as they rushed toward the stairs. Morgan looked up and expected to see Carson at the wheel of the boat, but the captain had dark hair, not light brown. The man frantically steered the boat back to port. Morgan grabbed the railing and placed a foot on the bottom step. The boat again rammed into the side of *The Protector*, and Morgan flew off the stairs, striking his head hard on the wooden floor.

Morgan lay on the floor stunned as he watched Horner rush past him, her weapon drawn. *Where is my gun? I must have dropped it when I fell.* He shook his head and frantically looked around him for the weapon.

"Drop it!" Horner yelled.

From his vantage point on the floor, Morgan could see the man had pointed his rifle toward *The Protector*. When he heard Horner's command, he swung the gun in her direction and fired a short burst. Horner apparently saw what he was doing, and she dodged to the side at the same moment she fired her handgun. Her shot missed its target, but she took a direct hit to her right shoulder, and the impact sent her tumbling down the stairs.

Morgan jumped to his feet and raced up the stairs toward the man. He kept his center of gravity low and hit the man in the legs. The man tried to aim his rifle at Morgan, but when Morgan hit him, he lost his balance, and the gun fell from his hands. He grappled for the gun, but Morgan sat on him. He turned his head toward Morgan, and Morgan jerked away from him in surprise.

Morgan had stared evil in the face many times over the years in his work with the FBI, but the dead eyes of Paul Mather caught him by surprise. *How have I not seen the evil in this man before now?*

Mather took advantage of Morgan's momentary lapse in concentration. He pushed Morgan off him and again started to go for his weapon. *The Counselor* sped out of control. Mather had been turning hard to port toward *The Protector* when Horner charged him, and the boat continued to turn in a circle at high speed. Mather could not retain his balance in the spinning boat, and the rifle skidded further away from his reach. Morgan lunged toward him, grabbed

Mather's coat and pulled as hard as he could. The action sent both men tumbling down the stairs to the main cabin.

Mather grabbed Morgan by the throat. They both struggled to their feet while Morgan tried to force the other man's hands away from his neck. As Mather's grip tightened, Morgan began to lose consciousness in the spinning cabin.

"No," Horner yelled, and as Mather turned to look at her, he loosened his grip on Morgan. Morgan broke free and backed toward the galley. Mather roared and lunged for Morgan. Morgan backed against the counter in the galley and felt behind him for anything he could use as a weapon.

Mather pounced on Morgan like a wild animal, and he again grabbed Morgan by the neck and began strangling him. The boat spun in circles while Morgan's vision again began to fade. He gave up trying to push Mather away and again reached behind him for the counter top. He felt along its smooth surface until his hand closed around a metal object. He knew immediately what it was. A corkscrew wouldn't be a weapon he would choose, but for now, it would have to do. Morgan fought to remain conscious as he gripped the corkscrew in his right hand. Then, with all the strength he could muster, he jammed the corkscrew into Mather's neck.

Mather screamed and jumped back. He lost his balance and fell. Morgan turned to survey the countertop more carefully. He saw the cheeseboard and the knife. He grabbed the knife just as Mather was getting to his feet. Morgan didn't hesitate. He pounced, burying the knife into Mather's stomach. Mather looked surprised. He tried to grab at Morgan, and then he tried to grab the knife. Morgan pulled the knife from Mather's stomach and stabbed the monster again.

"Okay," Mather murmured, and then blood bubbled from his mouth.

Morgan sat back and stared at Mather for a moment but then scrambled to his feet and raced to the wheelhouse. Straightening out the wheel was no problem, but it took him a few seconds to locate what must be the throttle and clutch. The levers weren't marked, so he didn't know which one was the throttle. Was it like a car with the throttle on the right and the clutch on the left? He gently eased back on the right lever, and the boat slowed. He let out a breath and pulled back the throttle all the way. He then reached for the other lever and shifted the clutch into neutral. He called Patterson on the VHF radio.

"It's over," he said. "Horner took a bullet to the shoulder; we'll need a Coast Guard chopper for her and Linda."

Chapter Fifty-Two

Tuesday, December 10th
5:30 pm

Horner was lucky. Only one bullet had hit her, and it had pierced her through the shoulder. She was in obvious pain, her face pale, but she complained little. When Morgan knelt beside her to examine her wound, she smiled at him and said, "Good job. You slew the monster."

Morgan smiled back at her. "Thanks to you," he said. "I would never have had the courage to jump on this boat without you there."

"What?" she said. "I thought you FBI guys did things like that every day."

He laughed. "A paper cut is usually the most dangerous thing that happens to me on the job."

Linda Bragg had a broken nose and had suffered minor head trauma. While her conditions were not life-threatening, Patterson convinced the Coast Guard she also needed to be airlifted to the hospital. Morgan was impressed that the Coast Guard helicopter pilots had been able to navigate and find *The Protector* in the driving snow.

After the Coast Guard evacuated Horner and Linda Bragg from *The Counselor*, Patterson and Morgan waited for weather conditions to improve before towing *The Counselor* back to Kodiak. They left Mather's body in place, the crime scene sealed for others to investigate.

Patterson called trooper headquarters and the Kodiak Police from *The Protector*. He reported the events of the day and asked the police to seal and search Mather's home and his office at the school.

He also asked the police to detain and question Rick Carson. If the purple crystal Morgan had seen at Carson's house had once been on Deborah Sidle's necklace, why did Carson have it now? Were he and Mather working together to abduct and kill women? Patterson asked Mark Traner to get Mather's past employment records from Principal Daniel and to call the police department in the town where he had last worked to see if there had been any unsolved murders in the area while Mather lived there.

Patterson and Morgan finally made it back to Kodiak at 5:30 pm that evening. Traner, two other troopers, and Chief Feeney were standing on the dock to meet *The Protector* when they pulled into port. They untied *The Counselor* and moved it to a vacant stall. They encircled the boat with yellow, crime scene tape and called the technicians to let them know their crime scene had arrived.

Morgan stared at the starlit sky as he stepped off the boat. He couldn't believe they'd been fighting a blizzard a few hours earlier. Not a breath of wind marred the surface of the ocean now, and no clouds veiled the bright jumble of constellations. The temperature had fallen several degrees.

"How are Maureen and Linda doing?" Patterson asked.

"Linda was treated and released. She's resting at home with her family now," Feeney said. "Maureen is out of surgery. She'll spend a night or two in the hospital and then have to endure desk duty until her shoulder heals. Other than that, she'll be fine. She's tough."

"That she is," Patterson said. "She was a hero today."

Morgan nodded. "That is one brave police detective you have, Chief."

Feeney nodded. "Let's head back to the station, gentlemen, and we'll fill you in on what we've learned today."

For once, Morgan agreed with the man.

They sat around the conference table with bags of hamburgers and fries and tall cups of steaming coffee. Morgan hadn't realized how famished he was, and once he'd finished eating, all he could think about was climbing into a warm bed.

Feeney told Patterson and Morgan he'd had teams searching Mather's home and office all day. They'd found nothing of interest in his home, but in his office, hanging from the ceiling of the conversation pit with the butterflies and other baubles, they'd found five necklaces dangling in plain view. One was Billie Clark's gold cross, but the other four had yet to be identified.

Morgan knew Mather must have felt thrilled anytime someone sat in that conversation pit and stared up at the hanging necklaces. Like the awards on the walls and shelves in his office, these necklaces were his trophies on display.

"We also found a copper bracelet on the desk in Mather's office," Feeney said. "It matches Hope Mills' description of the bracelet Tasha always wore."

Morgan nodded. "We won't need this evidence for trial, but at least it will let the families know we killed the monster who murdered their loved ones." He looked at Traner. "I'm interested in the four other necklaces," he said. "Did you find out where Mather worked before he came to Kodiak?"

"Coltfield, Oregon," Traner said. "It's a mid-sized town in southern Oregon." He looked down at his notebook. "He worked at the high school in Coltfield for four years before taking the job in Kodiak two years ago. The school principal had nothing but praise for Mather and said they were sorry to lose him when he moved to Kodiak, but I also talked to a Detective Franklin at the Coltfield police department, and he said five women, ages 18 to 42 had gone missing in the years when Mather worked as a counselor at the school. The murders stopped when Mather moved to Kodiak."

"Did the police detective suspect Mather's involvement in the murders?" Patterson asked.

"Not at all," Traner said. "Detective Franklin said they had no credible suspects and weren't even convinced the women had been killed by the same person."

"Did you send him a photo of the necklaces you found?" Patterson asked.

"Not yet, sir. I wanted to talk to you first."

Patterson nodded. "I'll give Detective Franklin a call tomorrow."

"What about Carson?" Morgan asked. "What did he say about the purple crystal?"

"According to Mr. Carson," Feeney said, "Paul Mather gave him the purple crystal fan pull for a host gift at a party Carson threw a few weeks ago."

"Did he know why you were asking about it?" Patterson asked.

Feeney looked annoyed. "This isn't my first day on the job, Sergeant. I went to Carson's house, pointed at the purple crystal on the fan pull and said, 'Tell me where you got that.' I took Carson by surprise. I don't believe he knew Mather had taken it off a dead woman."

"Okay," Patterson rubbed his head. "What else? Were you able to interview Linda Bragg?"

"We talked to her briefly, sir," Traner said. "She told us she went to Mather's office to confront him about telling the police Tasha was flunking her class. She had told no one except Tasha that she might be forced to give the girl an F. When Linda heard Mather told us English Literature was one of the classes Tasha was failing, she wondered how Mather knew. After she gave Tasha the news, Tasha rushed out of the school and sped away in her car. Since Tasha was killed later that night, Linda realized the only way Mather could have known Tasha was failing English was if he talked to Tasha after she left the school."

"How did Mather respond when she confronted him?" Patterson asked.

"She never had the chance," Traner said. "She walked into Mather's office and saw him sitting at his desk staring at Tasha's bracelet. She tried to run out of the room, but Mather hit her over the head with a trophy. She was pretty shaken up. That's about all I got out of her."

"Yes," Patterson said. "I'm sure she thought she would be his next victim."

"What did the name Tony have to do with Mather?" Morgan asked. "Was the note in Billie's kitchen unrelated to our case?"

"I wondered the same thing," Feeney said. "Mather's middle name is Anthony, so maybe that's why Billie called him Tony, but no one else I've talked to called him Tony. Tara told me Paul Mather was not a bank customer, so I asked Billie's daughter, Beth, if she knew

Paul Mather, and she said he sometimes attended their church, but she didn't remember her mother ever talking to him. Beth did admit, though, that she doesn't make it to church very often. The pastor of the church said Billie and Mather seemed to be casual friends, but both Beth and the pastor called Mather Paul, not Tony."

"Mather probably asked Billie to call him Tony to hide his identity from anyone who knew he and Billie were friends at church," Morgan said. "It was another way for him to control Billie and control the situation."

"Was Mather in Uyak Bay when Deanna disappeared?" Patterson asked.

"I asked Mr. Carson if he knew where Mather spent the Fourth of July," Feeney said. "He told me Mather ran his boat to the south end of the island this past summer to visit friends. He stopped by Carson's fish site in mid-June and told Carson he'd stop again on his way back to town in early July, but Carson said he didn't see Mather the rest of the summer."

"He was probably too busy abducting and murdering Deanna Kerr to pay Carson a social call," Patterson said.

"Could he have tampered with Deanna's outboard while she was at the party without anyone seeing him?" Morgan asked.

"I think so," Feeney said. "There would have been a great deal of activity at the party, and no one would have been paying attention to the boats."

"Or Mather simply saw Deanna have outboard problems and rushed toward her to take advantage of the situation," Patterson said. "Deanna knew him; she might have been surprised to see him in Uyak Bay, but she readily would have accepted his help."

"We'll never know exactly what happened," Morgan said.

Patterson rubbed his eyes and let out a long sigh. "And on that sad note, I'm heading to bed, gentlemen." He dropped Morgan at the hotel and headed home to his wife and his bed.

Morgan checked his messages as soon as he got to his room and felt what little energy he had left drain from him when he listened to the message from his supervisor at Quantico. He reclined on his bed and called Jane.

"Is it true?" she asked. "Did you catch him?"

"We did," Morgan said. "It was a long day, but that's one monster who won't hurt anyone ever again."

"Who was it?"

"The high school counselor, Paul Mather."

Her voice went up an octave. "The counselor killed his own students?"

"Sick, isn't it?" Morgan said. He paused for a minute. "I would say I'd tell you all about it if you'd join me for dinner tomorrow, but unfortunately, I've been called back to Quantico immediately."

"You can't even spend a day or two here?" she asked.

"Afraid not. They want me on the plane tomorrow. We've been following a string of murders in Florida, and there has just been another one. I'm sure I'll be in Florida in a few days."

"No rest for the wicked, I guess. Are you too tired to come over to my place for a drink tonight?"

"Now?" He suddenly felt wide awake again. "It's late; are you sure?"

"I'm not letting you out of town without seeing you," she said. "Do you have a car?"

"No, but I can get a taxi."

"How about I pick you up in 30 minutes?"

Wednesday, April 22nd

S andy called me at 7:00 pm. I'd just poured myself a glass of wine and turned on music, trying to unwind from a stressful day at work. It had been one of those days when everything had gone wrong, from telling a student his Master's thesis wasn't good enough to poor results for the test kit for Paralytic Shellfish Poisoning I had been working to develop the last two years. I feared the State of Alaska would cut the funding for my Paralytic Shellfish Poisoning study soon, and if that happened, I didn't know if I would still have a job. *Will I be able to come up with another research project?*

I grabbed my cell and checked the display. I tried to disguise my disappointment when I saw it was Sandy and not Nick Morgan on the other end of the phone. A call from him would have improved my assessment of the day.

"Don't sound so disappointed," Sandy said. "I'm sorry I'm not tall, dark, handsome, and male."

"I'm thrilled it's you," I said with a laugh. "I hope your day was better than mine."

"Uh oh," Sandy said, "maybe this isn't the best time to call and ask you for a favor. I was hoping to catch you in a good mood."

"Now you have to ask me; I'm curious."

"It's my sister, Jody," she said. "She doesn't think she can bear to return to their fish site this summer and see Deanna's things still there. I told her I'd fly out to the site and clean it out for her."

"Oh," I said, still not sure where I fit into this plan.

"I remember you telling me once after Deanna disappeared that you'd help me in any way you could."

My big mouth always gets me into trouble. "Of course," I said. "What do you need, Sandy?"

"Would you be up for flying out to the site with me on Saturday? Jack and Jody are planning a trip out there in mid-May, and this is the only weekend I have free before then."

"Sure," I said as my brain scrambled for an excuse to get me out of the trip.

"I know you don't love to fly, but the forecast is great for this weekend, and we won't even spend the night. We'll fly out to Larsen Bay on the morning flight, and one of Jack's friends will run us by boat over to their site. He'll pick us up in time to get us back to Larsen Bay for the evening flight returning to town. You should bring your toothbrush and anything else you need, though, in case we get stuck."

"Sure," I said. "That sounds fine."

I slumped into the couch after I hung up the phone, and I told myself I should do this deed to help my friend. She probably needed me there for moral support as much as anything else. I knew it would not be easy to box up the clothes and other possessions that had belonged to her murdered niece. I'd go with her and help her get through the day.

The next morning when Doctor Leslie Sinclair called me, I believed in Karma. Without a waiver in my voice or a moment of hesitation, I told Leslie that unfortunately, I could not be part of a whale necropsy team on Saturday because I had promised to help a friend. Leslie sounded disappointed I would not be part of her team to examine the dead humpback whale beached on the east side of Kodiak Island, but she understood my promise to help my friend with her grim task, and she wished me well, promising she would send the relevant tissue samples from the whale to my lab on Monday morning.

I met Sandy at the airport on Saturday morning. She arrived with a pile of unassembled boxes, and a bag containing packaging tape and marking pens.

"Are you ready for this?" she asked.

I smiled. "No, but I'm glad I can help."

"I really appreciate this, Jane."

"Hey," I said. "It got me out of a whale necropsy."

The flight to Larsen Bay took 25 minutes. Not a cloud marred the azure sky, and the surface of the ocean looked like glass, reflecting the snow-capped peaks of the mountains. I sat back, relaxed, and watched out the window, marveling at huge waterfalls and jagged rivers that cut through deep canyons and emptied into the fjord-like bays. The vegetation was still brown. Spring would not begin for another month on Kodiak Island, but a gorgeous day like this reminded all islanders that winter was loosening its grip, and soon we would remember why we loved this place we called home. Kodiak is nicknamed the Emerald Isle, and while that nickname didn't fit the brown landscape below the plane today, in a few weeks, the green jungle-like growth would leave no one questioning the moniker.

We bounced once as the wheels touched down on the gravel strip of the Larsen Bay runway. We climbed from the plane with the other four passengers and waited patiently for the pilot to unload Sandy's boxes from the cargo compartment. I carried a small backpack with a change of underwear and some toiletries just in case we ended up spending the night on this side of the island. I wore a warm coat, gloves, a wool hat, and rubber XTRATUF knee boots. The ambient temperature hovered in the mid-forties, but Sandy had reminded me to dress warmly because after we landed in Larsen Bay, we'd embark on an hour-long, chilly skiff ride.

A young Alutiiq man walked up to us and took the boxes from Sandy. "You must be Jody's sister," he said. He held out his hand. "I'm Fred Telnikof."

Sandy smiled. "Hi Fred," she said. "I'm Sandy, and this is Jane."

Fred pointed with his head. "My truck is over there."

We followed Fred to his blue Chevy pickup. He tossed the boxes in the back, and Sandy and I dropped our packs on top of the boxes and climbed in the cab of the truck. Fifteen minutes later, our gear had been transferred to an aluminum skiff, and we climbed over the sides of the boat and found seats.

We couldn't have picked a better day for a boat ride. Sandy had warned me that Cape Kuliuk where Jack and Jody had their cabin was a wind-swept point at the mouth of Uyak Bay. "Expect a rough boat ride," she'd said. "I can count on one hand the number of days a year it's calm out there. Prepare to have your spine rearranged." Today, though, not a breath of wind tickled the ocean, and as we sped out of Larsen Bay, we saw there wasn't even a swell.

I cinched my hood around my face and stared out at the placid ocean. To our left, 40 miles away, the mountains of the Alaska Peninsula towered above Shelikof Straight, their massive peaks covered in snow and ash. Sandy and I laughed as we zipped past a sleeping sea otter. He was sleeping so deeply he didn't hear us until we were nearly past him, and then he raised his head, threw his front legs in the air, and opened his eyes wide in surprise. I inhaled a deep breath of cool salt air and felt the tension from the past week at work evaporate. A day away from town was just what I needed.

"Whales!" Fred yelled over the roar of the engine as he pointed to our left, and as if on cue, seven or eight whales exhaled, sending spouts of water high into the air. Twenty minutes later, Fred pointed in front of us as a humpback waved his tail fluke in the air before diving. Fifteen minutes later, Sandy screamed, and I sucked in a breath as the water in front of us exploded, and a 35-ton humpback whale leaped into the air and splashed back onto his side, covering us with a spray of water.

"Whoa!" Fred yelled. "Not so close buddy. Are you trying to jump into the boat?"

My heart thudded with adrenaline. Sandy and I looked at each other, and I imagined my eyes were as huge as hers. I silently thanked the whale for not landing on our boat, and I reflected for a moment that instead of spending my day poking and prodding a dead whale, I'd enjoyed the experience of a lifetime, having a live whale splash me with water, and from the quick look I got of this whale, he appeared healthy to me.

Fred idled up to the beach in front of a long, green cabin. The cabin sat in a cove which would partially protect it from the raging wind and strong surges of a winter storm. Fred helped us out of the skiff and reminded us he'd be back to pick us up at 3:00 pm. We waved to him as he backed away from the beach.

"I bet it's amazing out here in January when it's blowing 70 knots," I told Sandy once we were alone on the beach.

She nodded. "I've been here in the summer when it was only blowing 40, and that was gnarly enough for me."

"I see no trees or bushes have managed to survive this environment."

"No," she said. "This is a tough place even in the summer. Jody has tried several times to talk Jack into selling and finding a more-protected fish site, but he won't do it."

"Why? Is the fishing that good out here?"

She shrugged. "They do pretty well some years, but they have bad years too like everyone else, so I don't know."

"How has Deanna's murder affected Jack and Jody's relationship?" I asked as we walked up to the cabin.

"Jody hasn't confided in me," Sandy said. "We used to talk, but since Deanna's death, she's been buttoned up tight. If I had to guess, though, I'd say their marriage is strained. From what I've seen, she doesn't talk to Jack either."

"But she's doing better?"

"Oh yes," Sandy said. She's slowly improving. I think she's off the pills. She never smiles anymore, but she doesn't act drugged all the time."

"It must be hard for the kids," I said as we reached the top of the steep beach. A small gear shed sat behind the berm of the beach, and 50 yards behind that a dark green cabin sprawled, protected on both sides and the back by steep hills and partially protected in the front by the beach berm. The cabin sat high enough on pilings to give the occupants a view of the beach and the ocean.

"It is very hard for the kids," Sandy said. "Evelyn's grades have dropped, and William has been in trouble in school several times this year. Evelyn had a straight A average until now, but she barely has a C average this year." Sandy's voice cracked, and when I looked at her, I saw tears on her cheeks.

"I'm so sorry, Sandy. This has to be incredibly tough for you, and to have to come out here and go through Deanna's things must be excruciating."

"Thanks for coming with me, Jane," she said.

I smiled. "It's the least I could do.

Sandy dug a key out of the front pocket of her pack and opened the cabin door. The cabin was larger than I'd first thought. We entered a closed porch where foul weather gear, jackets, and caps hung on pegs, and rubber boots sat on the floor, neatly arranged against the walls. A long window provided illumination for the small room. We removed our boots; Sandy opened another door, and we walked into a small sitting area.

"Wow, it's cold in here," Sandy said. "I don't really want to mess with a fire. Do you mind if we just wear our coats while we do this?"

"That's fine," I said, "but will you know what belonged to Deanna and what belonged to the other kids or even Jody? Deanna was nearly grown, so she and her mother were probably close to the same size."

"I'm sure we won't get everything," Sandy said, "but the kids all have separate rooms, and Jody told me she put most of Deanna's things in Deanna's room before the end of the summer. I'll look through the rest of the cabin, but let's start with Deanna's room."

I followed Jody through the cabin, glancing into the rooms as we passed. The first bedroom obviously belonged to Jack and Jody. A blue and pink quilt covered the queen-sized bed, and a large multi-colored rag rug decorated the blue wood floor. Sandy told me the next room belonged to William, but I would have guessed that from the model floatplane hanging from the ceiling, and the poster of Spiderman splattered on the back wall.

Painted flowers decorated the walls of the room we walked past next, and Sandy smiled and said. "Evelyn is our little artist."

The door to the room at the end of the hall was closed, and Sandy gripped the handle and took a deep breath before she pushed into the room. This room had white-washed walls decorated artfully with arrangements of dried seaweed, shells, dried grasses, and pressed flowers. A vase of dried flowers sat atop a small chest of drawers.

"Deanna had a flair for art too," I said.

"This one was destined to be an interior decorator," Sandy said and smiled sadly. "She had quite a talent." She shook her head.

"I can't let myself get emotional. If you start taping up boxes, I'll begin cleaning out the closet and chest of drawers."

We worked in silence for the next 45 minutes. Every time I looked at Sandy, I saw tears trailing down her face, but she kept at it, folding jeans and sweatshirts and stuffing socks and underwear into boxes.

Finally, she said, "I need a break. Everything else in here goes, Jane, including the bedding. I'll look through the rest of the cabin and see what else I can identify as Deanna's. If I'm not sure, I'll put it in a box and leave it here."

Sandy left the room, and I continued to pack the rest of the clothes from the closet. I found a box of Barbie dolls in the back of the closet and wondered if they might be something Evelyn would like but then decided to pack them in the box. *Any reminder of her sister will probably be too difficult for her to deal with at this point.* I found binoculars, an old iPod, and a camera. I decided I should ask Sandy before putting these items in a box, and I set them on the dresser.

Once the closet was empty, I turned my attention to Deanna's bed. I stripped the blanket and sheets, folded them, and stuffed them into a box. I took the pillow slips but left the pillows. A stuffed bear with one eye had fallen off the far side of the bed. I nearly started crying when I saw it and quickly stuffed it into a box so I wouldn't have to look at it.

A nightstand with a drawer stood at the right side at the head of the bed. I sat on the bed and opened the drawer. It held pens, pencils, a drawing pad with blank pages and several paperback books. I looked at the books and smiled. *Deanna was into dreamy vampires.*

One of the books slipped from my hands and lodged between the nightstand and the wall, and I had to get down on my hands and knees to retrieve it. I grasped the book and started to stand when I noticed a loose board on the wall behind the nightstand. I dropped the book on the bed and probed the loose board. It pulled easily from the wall.

Certain I was about to reach into a nest of spiders, I dug my headlamp from my pack and inspected the open space in the wall. I saw no spiders in the thin recess, but I did see a leather bound book.

I extracted it and opened the front cover. Deanna's journal began on January 1st of the previous year, the last year of Deanna's life. *She must have hidden the journal to keep it out of the snooping hands of her little sister and brother.*

I felt a pressure build in my head as I read Deanna's first entry about her hopes and dreams for the following year. *At this moment, she had only six months left to live.* The reality struck me hard and made me angry. *What a waste of a beautiful life.*

I thumbed through the journal, reading various girlish entries about Brad, a boy she had a crush on, and Julie, her best friend. I felt guilty reading Deanna's private thoughts, but I reminded myself Deanna no longer needed to keep secrets. Many of her entries were accompanied by drawings and doodles. I smiled at drawings of a fish with big, red lips and an eagle wearing eyeglasses.

Most of the entries were written in loopy, cursive handwriting, but an entry on June 4th, only a month before her death, caught my eye. The words slashed across the page in black ink with no loopy letters or hearts dotting the eyes. This entry looked angry.

He came again last night. I thought it was over, but he said he wanted to play our game. He hadn't come to my room in over a year, but here he was again. He expected me to do what he wanted, but I'm 17 years old! I told him NO! I told him to leave my room and never come back, and he left. Why didn't I do that years ago? I HATE HIM!!!

My mouth went dry. *Is this what I think it is? Was Deanna sexually abused? Was the man in her bedroom her father, or someone else?* I turned the page, but her next entry dated June 8th did not mention the man in her room. I hurriedly skimmed the next several entries. I heard Sandy slam the outer door of the cabin and rushed to get through the rest of the journal before she returned. *I don't know what I have here, but if Deanna was abused by her father or someone else, I'd have to tell Sandy. Deanna's younger sister, Evelyn, and even her little brother, Jack, could be in danger.*

There were no more references to abuse until the last entry in the journal written on July 4th.

He went in her room last night. I heard his footsteps in the hall and braced myself, but then I heard him open and close Evelyn's door. I tried to convince myself it wasn't him, or if it was, he only wanted to talk to her. I didn't hear anything for a while, but then I heard Evelyn cry, and a few minutes later he left her room. That did it for me. I can take care of myself, but Evelyn is still a baby. I will not let him hurt her. I knew it wouldn't help to tell Mom, so this morning I cornered him when he went out to work on the gear. I told him if he ever touched Evelyn again I would report him to the police or at least to one of my teachers at school. Aunt Sandy would know what to do, and if not her, Ms. Bragg or Mr. Mather could help me. I told him I'd had enough, and I planned to report him as soon as I went back to school in the fall. He said he'd kill me if I told anyone. My own father said he'd kill me!

I read and reread the entry, not even aware I was sobbing until Sandy looked in the room.

"What's wrong?" she asked.

I held the journal out to her and looked into her eyes. "I'm so sorry," I said. "I don't think Paul Mather murdered Deanna, and the nightmare for your family is far from over. It's just beginning."

Afterword

Kodiak Island lies 250 miles southwest of Anchorage, Alaska. The island is 3,588 square miles, and much of it is part of the Kodiak National Wildlife Refuge. There are no roads on the refuge, and the only way to access the island beyond the road system is by floatplane or boat. Most of the 13,500 residents of the island live near the town of Kodiak, but even there, less than 100 miles of road lead away from the town. The small town of Chiniak sits at the end of the Chiniak, highway, 42 miles from Kodiak.

Beautiful, rugged, inhospitable, and dangerous all describe Kodiak Island, and as I've portrayed in this novel, the weather can be and often is troublesome, especially in the winter. Kodiak has one of the largest brown bear populations in the world, and the island is home to red foxes, Sitka black-tailed deer, mountain goats, river otters, sea otters, harbor seals, Stellar sea lions, many species of whales, and an abundant array of birds, including bald eagles.

In this novel, I have attempted to portray Kodiak as honestly as possible. Kodiak is a small town, especially in the winter, when many of the salmon fishermen from the lower 48 have returned to their homes. The people of Kodiak are warm and friendly, and when something horrible happens, such as the fictional crimes in this book, we bond together and share whatever news we have.

Except for the Baranof Inn, most of the places I've mentioned in this book do exist. Henry's Great Alaskan Restaurant is real and sits in the middle of Kodiak near St. Paul Boat Harbor. The Rendezvous is a small restaurant/bar located on the Chiniak Highway a few miles past the airport heading away from town. If you ever make it to Kodiak, and I hope you do, you must visit the Rendezvous. Not only does it have the best food on the island (you can't miss Toni's famous clam chowder!), but the Rendezvous is also a place to experience an authentic Kodiak crowd. The restaurant is often packed with commercial fishermen, pilots, guides, and coast guardsmen and their families.

None of the airlines or pilots mentioned in this book exist. Don't worry, Evan only lives in my imagination. The descriptions of the harrowing plane flight and Deanna's traumatic experience in her skiff were easy for me to write because I've had first-hand experience with both situations.

All characters in this book are imaginary and not based on anyone I know, and any mistakes in this manuscript are mine.

Thanks to my husband, Mike, for understanding when my writing consumes me. His support and advice on my manuscript were invaluable. Thanks to all my friends who have cheered me on in my writing endeavors. Without your encouragement, I would have given up my writing dream long ago. Thank you, Tom from WriteByNight for your expert editorial advice on my novel, and thank you, Joanne, for your editorial advice.

Finally, I thank Evan and Lois Swensen at Publication Consultants. Evan is so much more than a publisher. His encouragement, advice, and guidance have been central to my success.

If you would like to read more about me and my books, please visit my website at http://robinbarefield.com, and while you are there, sign up for my free, monthly newsletter about true crime stories from Alaska. I also invite you to visit https://authormasterminds. com/robinbarefield where you can read excerpts from my novels and find bargains on my books and many of the other books on the site.